Heiress Gone
Wild

By Laura Lee Guhrke

LAURA LEE GUHRKE

Heiress Gone Wild

AVONBOOKS

An Imprint of HarperCollinsPublishers

First Avon Books mass market printing: October 2019

First Avon Books hardcover printing: September 2019

Print Edition ISBN: 978-0-06-295261-5
Digital Edition ISBN: 978-0-06-285372-1

FIRST EDITION

19 20 21 22 23   LSC   10 9 8 7 6 5 4 3 2 1

For my editor, Erika Tsang, who always goes the extra mile to help me make my books as good as they can be. Thank you.

Heiress Gone
Wild

Chapter 1

A prestigious girls' finishing school in White Plains, New York, was the last place on earth Jonathan Deverill would ever have expected to find himself.

Granted, he'd been living on the American continent for nigh on ten years, but most of that time had been spent on the Western frontier, among people who had little to do with genteel society.

The office of Forsyte Academy's headmistress was a plain room of distempered gray walls and Shaker furnishings, and though it was far less ostentatious than the upper middle-class British household in which he'd been raised, the watercolors on the walls and the milk-glass vases filled with purple lilacs told him he was in the room of a lady. Given the man he'd become and the life he'd been living, this was the sort of room he seldom had cause to visit.

"So, Mr. Deverill," Mrs. Forsyte's brisk voice broke into his observations, "you have arrived at last."

Her tone implied that by not arriving sooner, he had somehow failed to live up to expectations. Ah, well. It wouldn't be the first time.

"My apologies for the delay, ma'am," he said politely.

With her steel-gray hair and firm mouth, the headmistress was an indomitable-looking woman, but she inclined her head in gracious acceptance of his apology. "I assume you wish to see Miss McGann at once?"

"I do, yes."

Despite her rebuke about his less-than-prompt arrival, she seemed in no hurry to comply with his reason for coming. Setting aside the card he'd given her, she sat down behind her desk and gestured for him to take the chair opposite. "I have broken the news to her of her father's death. It was no surprise to me, of course, for I have known about his illness ever since he went into that sanitorium in Colorado eighteen months ago, but Mr. McGann insisted that his daughter not be informed. An understandable position, I suppose. Consumption is a terrible disease."

"Yes." A curt reply, but he did not want to talk about or even think about those final days in Denver, when he'd stood by helpless and watched his best friend die.

"And you are now Miss McGann's legal guardian." She looked him over, a disapproving frown drawing her brows together. "You're younger than I expected."

It was clear she thought him unable to look after a child, and who could blame her? He and Billy McGann had spent their time and made their money in the rough-and-tumble of America's mining trade. Of all the people he could think of to look after a little girl, he seemed the most inappropriate choice possible.

"You must understand, Mr. Deverill, that I have, in a sense, fulfilled the role you now intend to take on. Her father tasked me with that responsibility when he placed the girl here."

"Of course."

The headmistress's shrewd blue eyes narrowed, making him appreciate why she and her school had such an excellent reputation. Those eyes, he'd guess, didn't miss much. "I have done my best to ensure that she is safeguarded from rogues, rapscallions, and confidence men."

Despite the tragic circumstances that had brought him here, Jonathan's mouth twitched a little. "I understand."

"Mr. McGann was a very rich man, and news of his death has now appeared in the newspapers. How can I trust you are who you say you are? Anyone can print a card."

"Quite so." He reached into the breast pocket of his jacket and pulled out the sheaf of papers that had been among Billy's things, an exact facsimile of the will his friend had drafted eighteen months ago with the New York legal firm of Jessop, Gainsborough, and Smythe. "Would this satisfy you?"

Mrs. Forsyte took the document from his outstretched hand and proceeded to read every word. "This verifies who you are and confirms what Mr. Jessop told me," she said as she handed the will back to him, "but I confess, I'm no less astonished."

She was not the only one. Until a month ago, Jonathan hadn't even known his friend and partner of seven years had a daughter, much less that the other man's will put him in charge of the child. "No more astonished than I, madam," he said with feeling.

"Forgive me for being blunt, but a young, unmarried man in this role seems most unsuitable. And," she added before he could heartily concur with her opinion, "I would not have thought the girl in need of a *guardian* to take charge of her. Not at this point."

Her emphasis on the word indicated that she might fear Billy had thought Forsyte Academy hadn't been taking proper care of his daughter and that Jonathan was here to remove her. He hastened to reassure the headmistress.

"I've no doubt that Mr. McGann had full faith in you and your school, as do I. Indeed," he said as he refolded the will and returned it to his jacket pocket, "my visit today is little more than a formality—"

"A formality?" she cut in, her gray eyebrows lifting in surprise.

"I am on my way to London for a brief visit with my sisters, then I am traveling on to Johannesburg. Mr. McGann had business interests in South Africa that I must see to. I expect to be there for some time."

"I see." She fell silent, considering this information. "You do not intend to take the girl with you, I trust?"

He shook his head. "I am a stranger to her. Uprooting her, removing her from the only home she has ever known on the strength of one meeting would be traumatic, even cruel. And what would I do with her? She cannot accompany me to the mining towns of South Africa."

"Certainly not," the headmistress agreed, her voice prim.

"Therefore, I think it would be best for her to remain here for the time being. If that is acceptable?"

The question seemed to amuse Mrs. Forsyte, for her stiff, pursed lips relaxed into a hint of a smile. "I fear it might not be acceptable to Miss McGann. Be that as it may," she went on before he could point out that her pupil, being a child, didn't have much say in the matter, "your duty to her is more than a mere formality, Mr. Deverill."

"I only meant that my purpose today is to meet her and assure myself that she is settled and happy. For the present, I cannot see that much else is required of me."

"No? By the terms of the will, she has inherited a considerable fortune, a fortune you are to oversee." He could have pointed out that his own monetary worth was equal to that of his late partner, and he had little reason and no desire to embezzle the child's inheritance, but he suspected such assurances wouldn't impress Mrs. Forsyte.

"As you have read," he said instead, "the money is in trust. No one can touch the capital, not even me. And though I am to manage her investments as I did her father's, there is little I can do without Mr. Jessop's approval, for he is also a trustee. Miss McGann's fortune will continue to be protected."

"I wasn't thinking of the money itself, but of its effect upon her."

"I'm not sure I understand what you mean."

Mrs. Forsyte leaned forward, folding her hands atop her desk. "I have been a headmistress for many years, Mr. Deverill. Some of the girls who come here are accustomed to money and what it means because they are raised with it. Others are not so aware. Miss McGann is in the latter category. She is not what I would call naïve; nonetheless, her father wished her shielded as much as possible from the temptations and evils of this world, and I have attempted to accommodate his wishes to the best of my ability. She's known for some time that she is set to be a very rich woman one day, but her life here has not, I fear, prepared her for the reality of being an heiress."

"As her guardian, I'm not sure I'm prepared for that reality either, madam. But I shall do my best."

"You will have the assistance of your sisters, I presume?"

Jonathan didn't see how his sisters came into it at this juncture, nor was he sure how great a role they would eventually play, but he saw no point in saying so. "You know of my sisters?"

"Mr. Jessop has informed me. Your eldest sister is a duchess, I believe, and your second sister a viscountess?"

"Yes, and I assure you that I will be discussing the girl's future with both my sisters while I am in England. Now, may I see her?"

Seeming satisfied at last, she stood up, bringing him to his feet as well. "If you will wait here," she said as she circled her desk and started for the door, "I will send Miss McGann to you."

She departed, leaving him alone, and Jonathan walked to the window. It was a fine May morning, and as he stared out over the manicured grounds, watching girls in pinafores strolling with their teachers, he could understand why Billy had selected this place to house and care for his daughter. Given its secluded location, high stone walls, and no-nonsense headmistress, it was as much like a convent as it was a school, and a far more appropriate situation for a motherless young girl than anything her father could have provided for her.

What Jonathan could not understand was why Billy had chosen him to be the girl's guardian.

In their seven years as friends and partners, they'd done plenty of drinking, gambling, skirt-chasing, and hard, hard living. Neither of them had ever expressed the desire to settle down.

Billy, obviously, had tried domestic life and failed at it. For his own part, Jonathan had abandoned any notions of settling down the day he'd left England, and during the past decade, the three years he'd spent mining silver was the longest he'd stayed in one place.

On the other hand, the two men had trusted each other like brothers. They'd had no choice, really. When a pair of men stumbled on the biggest deposit of silver ore since the Comstock Lode, protecting it from claim jumpers and ruthless mining conglomerates had required mutual and absolute trust.

Then, too, there was the money to be considered. They'd pulled millions of dollars of silver ore out of that mine in Idaho, and since Billy had no money sense, Jonathan had been the one to invest their profits. He'd done a pretty fair job of it, so the decision to put him in charge of the girl's trust fund made sense, he supposed.

And Jonathan knew his background and upbringing had played a significant part. Billy had said as much, expressing the hope his daughter could one day benefit from Jonathan's connections in British society. But how valuable were those connections? He'd been away ten years, for heaven's sake. And it wasn't as if he ever intended to live in that world again.

He stared down at the girls and their teachers below, and he could only be grateful he didn't have to take charge of the child straightaway. She'd be in school here for several more years, giving him plenty of time to plan, make arrangements—

"Mr. Deverill?"

Jonathan turned from the window, but instead of the pigtailed school-girl he'd expected to find, he saw a woman of about twenty standing in the doorway, a woman of such remarkable beauty that he sucked in a startled breath.

Her skin had the luminescent quality of pearls, but its texture looked as soft as silk. Her hair, piled in a mass of curls atop her head, was a bright, glorious red that flamed like fire in the sunlit room. Her eyes were large and dark and surrounded by thick brown lashes, and her generous mouth was wide, lush, and rose-pink. In the ascetic severity of the headmistress's office, she seemed vibrantly alive.

The severe black coat and skirt she wore were in keeping with her surroundings, though they did her beauty little justice, and when he spied the monogram on her lapel, he realized she must be a teacher here.

She had no pupil in tow, however, and when he looked past her, he saw no child peeking shyly at him from behind her skirts or waiting in the corridor beyond.

"Mr. Deverill?"

Her voice returned his gaze to her face and his attention to the matter at hand. "I am Jonathan Deverill," he answered, frowning in puzzlement. "But I think there has been some mistake. I have come to see Miss Marjorie McGann."

"So you have," she agreed, laughing. "And here I am."

He blinked, taken aback. Her words could have only one meaning, and yet, they made no sense. But as he noted again the rich red of her hair and the deep brown of her eyes, her resemblance to Billy suddenly hit him like a punch in the gut.

On his deathbed, Billy had told Jonathan of Marjorie's existence for the first time, begging his partner to protect and look after his little girl. But as Jonathan's gaze traveled down over the generous curves of her figure, he appreciated in chagrin that Marjorie McGann was not, in any way, shape, or form, a little girl.

"Hell," he muttered, his genteel, ladylike surroundings forgotten, his tongue lapsing into the crude language of the Western mining towns and saloons he'd left behind. "God damn and holy hell."

Chapter 2

$\mathcal{H}$e wasn't at all what she'd imagined. With little information to go on, Marjorie had toyed over the years with two images of her father's British partner—one a silver-haired gentleman in tweeds and brogues, with pale eyes, a horsey face, and a weak chin, the other a burly mountain man with grizzled hair and a graying beard who'd cast aside all traces of his heritage, wore flannel shirts and Levi's pants, and cursed like the miner he'd become.

This man was neither of those. Or perhaps, he was a bit of both?

He did curse like a miner, as his oaths of a moment ago had made clear, though his British accent made the words seem more elegant than profane to Marjorie's American ears. He was a big man, quite tall, with wide shoulders and a powerful chest suited to a man of the mountains, but he was lean rather than burly, with a tapering torso, narrow hips, and long legs. He wore neither flannel and denim nor tweeds and brogues, but instead an impeccably-cut, rather worn suit of charcoal-gray wool. His hair was neither fair nor dark, but halfway between, like tobacco—thick, short strands of dark brown shot with gold, and without a touch of gray.

Her gaze moved to his face, a younger one than she'd expected, but not the least bit horsey. Instead, his countenance was surprisingly handsome, with chiseled planes, an aquiline nose, tanned skin, and tawny hazel eyes. Clean-shaven, his face displayed a strong, stubborn jaw and a chin that was anything but weak.

That, she reflected, studying him, might be a problem.

"You're Billy's daughter? You are?"

Marjorie blinked, startled by the disbelief in his voice. "Yes, of course. What?" she added as he gave a laugh, for she didn't see what he found amusing.

"You're not—" He broke off and shook his head, rubbing four fingers over his forehead as if confounded. "You're not quite what I was expecting."

"I could say the same," she countered with feeling.

"I'm sure," he said, lifting his head, any trace of humor vanishing. "Since I'm the last person your father ought to have chosen to take care of you."

Until she'd met him, Marjorie would have disagreed, for the fact that her guardian came from British society fit remarkably well with her own plans. But now that she'd met Mr. Deverill in the flesh, she wondered if he might be right.

Having a guardian at all was bad enough, but she'd hoped hers would at least be easy to manage. Sadly, as her gaze roamed Mr. Deverill's strong, lean face and came to rest again on the hard line of his jaw, she feared this man would prove as manageable as a recalcitrant mule.

"I didn't realize girls your age were allowed to remain in finishing school," he said, bringing Marjorie out of these ruminations.

"I'm not a girl," she corrected with asperity as she came into the room. "I'm a woman."

"Yes," he agreed, his voice grim, his blunt brown lashes lowering as he glanced down. "So you are. Unfortunately, no one bothered to tell me that."

"Oh, I see," she murmured, enlightened. "You were expecting braids and pinafores?"

"Something like that. Why are you still in school? Don't young ladies have to graduate at some point?"

"I did, nearly three years ago. I have been a teacher here since then."

"A practical course to choose."

"Very practical," she agreed, the admission bitter on her tongue.

"Though hardly a choice, since I had nowhere else to go. My father, you see, did not want me with him."

"I doubt it was a matter of what he wanted, but of what was necessary. The life your father led wasn't appropriate for a young girl."

In his infrequent letters, her father had given her that same excuse, and for over a decade, she'd believed it, sure that once she was grown up, things would be different. He'd want her with him then, she'd thought. They would be together again, like a real family.

Upon her graduation, however, her inquiry about joining him had been met with the same tired excuse couched in a new form. No longer was the life he led not appropriate for a young girl—no, it became inappropriate for a young *woman*, and with that new qualification, Marjorie had finally realized the brutal truth. Her father did not want her, and he never would, and all his talk of being together someday had been nothing but a pacifying lie.

All her illusions about a life with her parent had come crashing down, and she'd realized she would have to make a life for herself without him.

She had accepted Mrs. Forsyte's suggestion to stay on at the school as a teacher, but it hadn't been long before letters from Marjorie's school friends had provided her with a new, much more exciting alternative, one that could give her the home and family she craved and did not involve asking anything of her wayward parent except a dowry.

Like herself, many Forsyte graduates were the daughters of New Money millionaires. Shut out of New York society and desperate for a place to belong, some of them had gone to England upon graduation, in search of titled husbands and a new life. Inspired by their example, thrilled by their descriptions of British society, Marjorie had decided on a new destiny for herself, never dreaming that her father's death and his British partner would provide her with the perfect means to achieve it.

"Perhaps you're right," she murmured. "But what happens now? Before sending me to you," she rushed on, "Mrs. Forsyte informed me you are going to London?" When he nodded, she felt a surge of relief. "Perfect. Just what I was hoping."

His mouth tipped at one corner in a sardonic curve. "Terribly eager to get rid of your new guardian, I see. Well, I can't say I blame you."

"Get rid of you?" she echoed, bewildered. "Hardly, since I'm coming with you."

He stared at her as if she was crazy. "That's not possible."

"But . . ." She paused, suddenly uneasy. "I don't understand. When Mr. Jessop said you were coming, I thought it was to take me with you to London."

He sighed. "It's clear we've both been laboring under some misapprehensions. I am only in London for a brief visit with my sisters, then I must go to South Africa."

"South Africa?" Marjorie couldn't believe what she was hearing.

"Your trust fund has a great deal of money in South African investments, and there's talk of war breaking out between the British and the Boers before the end of the year. If that happens, those investments could become worthless. I must investigate the situation and decide what to do with those investments before that happens."

Marjorie refused to have a perfect plan spoiled by international squabbles. England was just the place for girls like her, girls who had heaps of money but no position or place. And she knew he had sisters with aristocratic connections. Mrs. Forsyte had told her so. Surely, they could be prevailed upon to help her enter British society. The fact that her guardian himself would be on another continent was, to her mind, the icing on the cake.

"Well, if you want to go to Africa while I'm in London," she said, giving him her most charming smile, "I won't object."

"As I said, it's not possible for you to accompany me. You must remain here for the time being."

"Here?" She sobered at once. "You're joking. You must be."

"I'm afraid not. An unmarried man and a young, unmarried woman cannot travel alone together, and since my ship sails tonight, I've no time to find a suitable chaperone for you. Speaking of time—"

He broke off, pulled his watch out of his waistcoat pocket, and flipped it open. "I must go, if I'm to catch my train."

"You're leaving?" This could not be happening. "Already?"

"I must," he answered, his relief at the fact painfully obvious as he tucked his watch back in his pocket. "I have to meet with Mr. Jessop about your estate before my ship sails. I've brought your father's belongings to you. He didn't have much in the way of personal effects, but—"

"I don't want his things." She could hear the sharp edge to her voice as she spoke, and so could he, for he frowned a little. Whether he was puzzled by her response or disapproving of it, she didn't care. "I've no use for them."

"Very well, but I will leave them here, in case you change your mind."

She wouldn't, but she was too preoccupied with the real problem to argue about trivialities. She'd never considered that his purpose in coming could be anything other than to take her away from here, and she was at a loss for what to do next.

"I will write, of course," he went on as she considered her options, "but if there's anything you need while I'm away, contact Mr. Jessop. And don't worry. We will make proper arrangements for you when I return. It's been delightful meeting you, Miss McGann."

"Wait," she cried as he bowed and stepped around her to depart. "You can't just leave me here."

"I'm afraid I must. But it's only temporary," he added over his shoulder as he paused by the coat tree to retrieve his hat. "This afternoon, Mr. Jessop and I will discuss what's to be done for the best, and I will inform you of the details of our discussions in my first letter."

"But I already know what's best for me," she replied, starting toward him as he donned his hat and turned to face her. "Just because you arrived here thinking I was a child, it isn't necessary for you to treat me like one."

"Forgive me," he said somberly, then immediately spoiled his apology by qualifying it. "But I didn't even know of your existence until a month ago, and from what your father told me at that point, I assumed you were a schoolgirl. The fact that you are instead a woman grown makes things much more complicated. Different arrangements will now have to be made for you, and that will take time."

Marjorie didn't have much experience dealing with the opposite sex, but she had enough experience with the evasions of children to recognize when a grown man was doing it. "How lovely to know I'm so important that you could spare me half an hour on your way from one side of the globe to the other. Since you intend to just leave me here, I wonder that you bothered to come at all. You could have shipped my father's things and sent me a letter. Wouldn't that have sufficed?"

"It certainly would have been more convenient," he said dryly, ignoring her sarcasm. "But that would not have been commensurate with my responsibilities."

"That's rich," she muttered. "You, talking of responsibilities as you walk away from them."

Her words seemed to hit a nerve, for he stiffened. "It can't be helped. As I said, I thought you were a child still in school. My reason for coming was simply to meet you, make the acquaintance of the headmistress, and reassure myself that you are well situated for the time being."

"But I'm not."

"No? Are you neglected here? Abused? Mistreated?"

Marjorie stared at him helplessly, a sick knot forming in her stomach as she realized there was no answer he'd accept. A guardian wouldn't consider that she lived like a cloistered nun any sort of mistreatment. Quite the opposite.

Think, Marjorie, she ordered herself. *Think how to make him change his mind and take you with him.*

"It isn't a matter of mistreatment," she said at last. "Mrs. Forsyte has always been very kind. But I'm twenty years old. It's time I left here and made a life of my own, don't you think?"

"Absolutely. As I said, I will discuss the situation with Mr. Jessop, and while I am away, I will consider his advice and decide what's to be done with you."

Marjorie took a deep breath, trying to set aside her disappointment and face what might be an unavoidable delay. "And how long will you be gone?"

"Eight months, perhaps. It's hard to say with things in South Africa so unstable—"

"Eight months?" Marjorie interrupted, too appalled by that estimate to be polite. "Eight *months*?"

"I wish I could be more definite, but I can't, not until I've assessed the situation. I will return as quickly as possible, I promise you."

To her mind, eight months was anything but a quick return, and given that she'd be spending that time in the staid environs where she'd already spent two-thirds of her life, it seemed an eternity. She'd made the best of things here, and she enjoyed teaching, but it wasn't what she wanted for her life.

She wanted to do what her school friends had done. She wanted to make her come-out, go to balls and parties, and meet young men. She wanted romance, courtship, marriage to a man who loved her, and children of her own. She wanted a home, a family, and a place to belong. She wanted . . . damn it all, she wanted to be *wanted*.

Desperate, she tried again. "Why can't I just go with you to London now? I could make my debut, enjoy the season—oh, why not?" she burst out in frustration as he shook his head.

"Miss McGann, I appreciate that you want the amusements of good society, and you shall have them, I promise. But such things must wait."

"But the London season is starting now. It's the perfect time to make my come-out, find a husband. I might be like some of my friends," she added, sidetracked for a moment by all the delicious romantic possibilities ahead, "and marry a man with a title and estates—"

His groan cut her off. "What is it about titles that you Americans find so alluring? They're meaningless drivel."

"But they're not. A titled husband gives a girl like me a position, something I could never have here in New York, no matter how much money my father left me."

"Even so, it's far too soon to be discussing such things. You're in mourning, hardly the time to be enjoying the London season. The mourning period is an interlude of seclusion and grief."

Marjorie could have told him she'd had plenty of seclusion already. She also could have said she had no intention of spending any time grieving for a man who'd left her over thirteen years ago and who she hadn't seen since, a man who had never spared much consideration for her anyway. But because her new guardian was already impatient to be gone, she restrained herself. The crucial thing was that he not leave her behind.

"I can mourn just as well in London as I can here," she said, trying to sound reasonable and dutiful. "I could stay with your sisters. Surely a duchess and a viscountess would be appropriate chaperones."

"Chaperoning a girl, even one in mourning, is a serious responsibility. My sisters must be given the chance to decide freely if they want to take it on, especially for a girl they've never met, an American girl who knows nothing of British life, an heiress wealthy enough to fall prey to fortune hunters. I have not seen my sisters for ten years, Miss McGann, and I have no intention of greeting them after all that time by imposing the burden of your care upon them without first obtaining their consent and willing cooperation."

She was a burden. Of course she was. Her father's neglect had told her that long ago, and yet, it stung to hear it said aloud. Marjorie looked away, blinking hard, frustration dissolving into despair. "Nothing's changed," she said. "I'm still stuck in limbo, watching life pass by while I sit here growing old."

"There's no need to be melodramatic. Eight months isn't all that long, and the time will pass more quickly for you here at Forsyte Academy, where you have a vocation. And it's not as if you won't have plenty of time to enjoy life. You're only twenty."

"I'm nearly twenty-one. A year from now I'll be on the verge of spinsterhood."

For some reason, that made him smile. "You'll have no trouble finding a husband when the time comes. Especially one with a title," he added, his smile taking on a cynical curve. "Believe me, the peers of England will find your fat American dowry just as desirable next season as they would this one."

Marjorie had no intention of marrying a man who wanted her just for her money. She wanted love, too, and she saw no reason why she couldn't have both, but her new guardian spoke again before she could clarify that vital point.

"Naturally, an heiress such as yourself requires a proper position, and your mourning period gives us the time to create one for you. If Mr. Jessop and I decide a London season is appropriate, and provided my sisters are willing to launch you, I will arrange for you to make your debut next year. We can discuss these plans in detail when I come back for you."

When I come back . . .

Those words harkened to her from the past, the exact same words her father had spoken to her when she was seven years old, the last words he'd ever said to her in person.

When I come back . . .

He never had. And now, he never would.

Pain flared up inside Marjorie, pain and anger, emotions so hot and so fierce that she had to fold her arms tight across her ribs to hold them in check.

She would not cry, she vowed, not for a man who in thirteen years had barely spared her a thought. And she would not be abandoned again, clinging to hopes of a someday that never came.

"I'm sure you're disappointed," he said in the wake of her silence, the gentleness of his voice like salt in her wounds. "And, believe it or not, I know how it feels when all one's dreams seem to have been snatched away. But I won't let that happen to you. We will see you properly settled, but you must be patient while I determine the best way to make that happen."

Marjorie wasn't about to let any man, even her guardian, decide what was best for her, especially when said man didn't seem the least bit inclined to solicit her opinions on the subject. Still, she could see that his mind was made up and arguing would be pointless, so she heaved a sigh of feigned resignation as she set her brains to work on a new plan. "I suppose you're right. You'd better go, for you don't want to miss that train."

"Is there anything you need before I depart? Do you have pin money?"

"An allowance? Mr. Jessop sends me ten dollars a month."

"Is that all?"

She didn't tell him it was more than enough. She hadn't spent even a fraction of her allowance in the years she'd been here, for what was there to spend it on? "I'm afraid so."

"I'll arrange a larger allowance for you when I meet with Mr. Jessop. You'll begin receiving it straightaway."

Marjorie gazed at him with every appearance of gratitude. "Thank you."

"Not at all. It's the least I can do."

"You will write?" she asked, clasping her hands together, trying to look the part of the forbearing little woman.

"Every month. And if you need to reach me, contact Mr. Jessop. He will know how to find me."

"You sail tonight, you said? Safe travels, Mr. Deverill," she added when he nodded. "I hope you're on one of the White Star ships? I've heard they are very fine."

"It's a Cunard ship, actually. The *Neptune*, I believe. Now, I really must be off."

She held out her hand, expecting him to shake it, but to her surprise, he bowed over it instead, lifting it to his lips, and despite that she found her new guardian both uncooperative and obtuse, she also felt an unmistakable thrill when his lips brushed her knuckles.

A kiss on the hand might be a trivial thing to most young ladies, but it was the first remotely romantic thing that had ever happened to her, and it underscored all the reasons why she wasn't about to wait any longer for her life to begin.

"Farewell, Miss McGann," he said as he let go of her hand. "We shall meet again soon."

With that, he turned away, stepped into the corridor, and started toward the stairs.

"We certainly will, Mr. Deverill," she murmured softly, leaning through the doorway, her gaze narrowing on his broad back as he walked away. "And far sooner than you think."

Chapter 3

"You can understand my shock."

"Yes, indeed." Arthur Jessop handed Jonathan a tumbler of whiskey and sank down on the opposite end of the leather sofa in his office with his own glass. "It was very wrong of Mr. McGann to appoint you guardian without telling you all the details. We did advise him to do so. I thought he had."

"He didn't," Jonathan answered, turning to face the other man. "Billy never even mentioned having a daughter until his dying moments, and from what he said then, I assumed she was a child. To discover she's a grown woman—"

He broke off, an image of his new ward's shapely figure and stunning face flashing across his mind, and he took a hefty swallow of whiskey. "As I said, it was a shock."

"And her age changes your perception of your responsibilities, does it?"

Jonathan cast him an unhappy look. "Doesn't it?"

"I suppose it does. And you feel it's more than you can take on?"

God, yes.

He didn't say those words aloud, however. Tempting as it was to dump this entire mess in the lap of the girl's other trustee, loyalty and obligation to his late friend restrained him. He'd made Billy a promise, and there was no question of breaking it. "Billy McGann was like a brother to me," he said instead. "And I will do whatever I can for his daughter. But . . ."

"But . . . ?" Mr. Jessop prompted when Jonathan paused.

"I cannot help questioning how suited I am for this. A child in school is one thing. A woman coming of age is something else. Even Mrs. Forsyte expressed doubts about the arrangement."

"Yes, yes," Jessop said, a reply Jonathan found terribly frustrating. Didn't the fellow have any useful advice?

"She wanted to come to London," he said, rather relishing the way the lawyer stiffened. "With me, now, tonight."

"That would be most precipitate. Not to mention improper. She's in mourning."

"She doesn't seem to care about that. She wants to do the season and find a husband," Jonathan went on mercilessly, sensing the other man's disapproval. "One with a *title*, if possible."

"You shall have to look into any suitors with great care, particularly the titled gentlemen she would meet during a London season. I don't wish to offend you, Mr. Deverill, but I've found that most of these British lords who marry our American heiresses have mercenary motives."

"Oh, I'm not offended, and I agree. I have no illusions about the aristocracy, believe me."

The lawyer relaxed. "I'm relieved to hear you say that, though I'm a bit surprised. I understood that your late mother was the daughter of a viscount?"

"She was. She married beneath her, and her family disowned her for it." As he spoke, he made no attempt to hide his disdain for Britain's snobbish upper classes. "Our family was in newspapers—upstarts, unworthy of notice, particularly after my father's mismanagement bankrupted the company. Society's view of us only began to change six years ago."

"Due to your silver mine, or your eldest sister's marriage?"

"Both, I'm sure. Nothing like millions in the bank and a duke in the family to elevate one's social position. My second sister also married into the *ton*."

"And your sisters like that life, do they?"

"From their letters, it seems they do, though I'll never understand why. Still, if they're happy, that's all that matters. They deserve some happiness. Our father, God rest his miserable soul, was a difficult man. And I," he added with cheer, "seem to have been equally difficult, at least in his opinion. When I was eighteen, he tossed me out, disinherited me, and told me to make my own way."

"And you did."

Jonathan shook his head. "Billy was the one who found the mine. I merely helped him work it."

"You don't give yourself enough credit. Mr. McGann, though an excellent mining engineer, had no head for business. He was wise to let you handle the money. The investments you made provided both of you with a far greater fortune than the mine alone would have done."

"I enjoy the challenge of making money, I confess."

"And spending it?"

"That's far less interesting."

Jessop chuckled. "Spoken like a true entrepreneur. So, you've no desire to become a man of leisure, buy an estate, marry a lady, and become local squire to some English village?"

"God, no. I'm not a settling-down sort of chap. I was once . . ." He paused for another gulp of whiskey. "Not anymore."

His mind flashed back to his youth, and the approving voice of his grandfather, who'd turned a handful of newspapers into a vast publishing empire.

You'll take over Deverill Publishing one day, expand our fortunes. You'll be the one to carry on my dream.

It had been Jonathan's dream, too, until his grandfather's death had changed everything.

This company's mine now, his father's voice echoed through his head, taunting him even from the grave. *If I want your advice on how to run things, boy, I'll ask you for it.*

With an effort, he forced his mind out of the past. "No, Mr. Jessop, even without Billy alongside, I fear I'm destined to wander. The proverbial rolling stone."

Jessop smiled. "That's the image every bachelor has of himself. Until Cupid's arrow hits him."

Jonathan thought of his own experience there, of the girl who'd loved him madly when he was the grandson of a wealthy newspaper hawker, whose love had died the instant his father had disinherited him. He thought of his parents—his mother cast out by her family and friends because of her love for a middle-class rakehell, and his father, whose inherent weaknesses had become so obvious in the wake of her death. No, any illusions Jonathan may have had—about love, marriage, or anything else—were long gone.

"No worries," he assured the lawyer, tapping his chest with his palm. "I've got armor plating."

He noted the other man's knowing smile in some amusement, but before the married Mr. Jessop could say something about how all men are broken to the yoke in the end, Jonathan changed the subject, for they didn't have much time. "About Billy's investments," he said, gesturing to the documents on the table beside them, "I have concerns about the South African ones. This business with the Boers is getting sticky."

"Yes, you're wise to investigate now, before things get worse. Those investments are still lucrative, but if things become unstable, the value of the shares will plummet rapidly."

"I'll cable you as soon as possible what needs to be done. And there are some mining conglomerates forming in East Africa that I'd like to investigate. What is your opinion regarding Billy's other invest-ments?"

"As I said, you've done well with them. I think they will continue to provide a good return. Have you made any plans for the girl?"

"My plan," Jonathan countered dryly, "was that she would remain in school for about half a dozen more years."

"And now?"

"She'll have to stay where she is until I can return from Africa to fetch her. By then, I'll have made new arrangements for her. She'll be all right at Forsyte Academy in the meantime, I trust? Looked after, chaperoned, all that?"

"Oh, yes. Mrs. Forsyte is an excellent woman and most capable chaperone. How does the girl feel about remaining behind? I imagine she was disappointed at not being able to accompany you to London?"

"She was, but I explained that it's the only thing to do."

"And she took it well?"

"Well enough." As he spoke, Jonathan felt a sudden uneasiness— doubt or guilt, he couldn't be sure. "It can't be very amusing for her there. Look in on her often while I'm away, see how she's getting on. Bring her down to the city to stay, take her to dinner, or the opera once she's in half-mourning."

"My wife and I have done such things in the past. We would be happy to continue."

"And double her pin money. Those things may take the sting out of waiting until I return."

"But what will you do with her then?"

He considered. "She has no family at all?"

"Her mother is from South Africa and has some relations there— very distant ones, I'm afraid. Her father was an orphan, so she has no connections here."

"Which means the Knickerbockers won't accept her, all her millions notwithstanding. Given that, the girl herself may have already deter-mined the best plan for her future."

"Possibly. But would Mr. McGann approve?"

"I know he would," Jonathan said with a sigh. "Shortly before his death, when he told me he'd made me guardian to the girl, he admitted part of the reason was my connections. The girl will need ladies to chaperone her, and I know he hoped my sisters could do that."

He didn't add that he wasn't sure his sisters would agree, not after he'd let them down six years ago. "I have no right to commit my sisters to this until I've discussed it with them. But an heiress worth millions can't be shut away from good society forever, and marriage to a peer would give her a position."

"True, but there are risks. Her money remains in trust only until she marries, or she turns thirty, whichever comes first. Word of her father's death and rumors of her enormous inheritance have already made the New York papers. We must do our best to protect the girl from fortune hunters."

"Of course." Jonathan met the lawyer's shrewd gaze with a hard one of his own. "But I trust your firm is capable of drafting an ironclad marriage settlement, should the need arise?"

Mr. Jessop smiled. "We can tie up the money tight as a drum."

Satisfied, Jonathan glanced at the clock on the wall and set aside his glass. "If that's all, I shall be on my way."

"Before you go, there is one more thing we need to decide. What are we to do with her jewels?"

Jonathan paused, frowning in puzzlement. "The Rose of Shoshone, you mean? I thought her father had Charles Tiffany cut and set it. Isn't it in the Tiffany vault?"

"Oh, yes," the lawyer hastened to assure him. "There's a substantial quantity of uncut stones in the vault as well. Being a mining engineer, Mr. McGann acquired many gemstones over the years."

"Yes, I know. Silver made him wealthy, but gemstones were his passion. That's why he went to South Africa—Idaho, too, for that matter. But to address your question, why do we need to do anything with the stones?"

"Your plan is to remain in Africa for the next eight months?"

"About that, yes. What of it?"

"The girl is supposed to receive the jewels when she turns twenty-one, and her birthday is August thirteenth. At that point, the gems cease to be part of the trust, and we are obligated to hand them over to her."

Jonathan considered. "Does she know about the gems?" he asked after a moment. "Does anyone?"

"Not to my knowledge. But once the will passes through probate, its exact terms will become public knowledge, and the existence of a necklace containing a flawless, thirty-two carat pink sapphire is the sort of sensational news the papers will jump on."

"Can't we leave the jewels where they are until I return?"

The lawyer frowned, seeming affronted. "As executor, I have a legal obligation to fulfill the will's exact terms. And even if the law did not require it, my ethics would."

Jonathan was tempted to offer a witticism about the mention of lawyers and ethics in the same sentence, but he doubted Mr. Jessop would appreciate the joke. "Still, why would she want them? Mourning doesn't allow her to wear jewels until April."

"Not publicly, no, but do you think she'll be content to leave a priceless necklace of pink sapphires and white diamonds in a vault untouched and unworn until next April?"

"Probably not," he conceded with a sigh. "She'll want it close by, I suppose, so she can try it on and show it off to her friends."

"Exactly. We can protect her inheritance far more easily than we can her jewels. They are insured, of course, but it would be a shame if they were stolen."

"I take it," Jonathan said, studying the lawyer's urbane countenance, "you have a suggestion to make?"

"Her jewels remain part of the trust until August thirteenth, and we can safeguard them however we wish. If they were moved to London now, perhaps placed in your brother-in-law's ducal vault . . ."

He paused again, and Jonathan gave an unamused laugh. "So, in addition to deciding how to manage the life of a beautiful young heiress, I now have to cart a half a million dollars' worth of her jewels across the Atlantic on a moment's notice?"

"You could have a Pinkerton man do it for you."

He could, but he'd never been the trusting sort, and since he and Billy had held off dozens of claim jumpers and the henchmen of four mining conglomerates to maintain control of their mine, he doubted any Pinkerton man could safeguard the girl's jewels any better than he could himself.

"Tiffany's will allow me to remove the jewels if I present the trust documents and my power of attorney, I assume?" he asked.

"Of course."

Satisfied, Jonathan gathered the documents from the table and stood up, bringing the other man to his feet as well. "Well, if I'm going to Tiffany's before my ship sails, I really must be on my way."

"You'll cable me the moment the gems are safely stored in London? And you'll confirm whatever arrangements you'll be making for the girl?"

"I will. And I shall see you this winter when I return for her." He held out his hand. "Until then, I leave Miss McGann in your safe-keeping."

"Mrs. Forsyte and I will continue to keep close watch over her, as we have always done," the lawyer assured him as they shook hands.

"It isn't just the British fortune hunters we need to worry about," Jonathan reminded as they walked together toward the door of Mr. Jessop's office.

"Mrs. Forsyte is perfectly capable of dealing with anything of *that* kind. Men won't get anywhere near her. And I doubt the unsavory ones will want to, given that I shall make sure her guardian's determination to have an ironclad prenuptial agreement is made known to the press immediately." Mr. Jessop smiled. "I assure you, no scoundrel will scrape up an acquaintance and elope with her to Niagara while you are away."

THE *NEPTUNE* WAS a new steamship, the very best the Cunard line could offer, with every amenity a man of wealth could expect. His stateroom was a parlor suite with windows giving onto the promenade, crisp, clean sheets, and a mattress and pillows of the softest down. But the best thing about it was the private bath, and as Jonathan eased back in the tub filled with steaming water, he couldn't help a groan of appreciation. A hot bath was a luxury that his life the past ten years had given him little opportunity to enjoy.

He did it now, though, savoring the piping hot water and castile soap provided by Cunard. After rinsing off, he stood up and started to reach for one of the thick Turkish towels that hung from hooks in the wall, but then he changed his mind.

Miss McGann's jewels were safely stowed in the *Neptune*'s vault, and the coming week stretched before him with nothing more crucial to do than explore the ship, shoot clay pigeons off the stern, read books, and sip vintage port in the smoking room. Right now, he was in a luxurious bathtub and the water was still hot. Why waste it?

He once again sank back down. His muscles, tense from days aboard crowded train cars, slowly relaxed, his eyes closed, and his mind drifted into oblivion.

Something roused him, and he woke with a jump, reflexively reaching for his Colt, realizing only after his hand emerged from the water that he didn't need it. He wasn't in a frigid mountain stream where some claim jumper might take a potshot at him, or in a chipped iron tub above a saloon where some drunken miner might fire a bullet through the ceiling. He was in a luxurious bathroom on a steamship bound for home.

Home.

It seemed an alien concept to him now, for when he'd left England a decade ago, he'd also left behind the shattered pieces of his dreams, his heart, and his future. Since then, the closest thing he'd had to a home was one of the two shacks he and Billy had built in northern Idaho's Silver Valley, crude affairs of pine timber and tar paper that had sheltered them while they'd pulled silver ore out of their mine at a frantic pace.

The shacks were gone now, sold along with most of their shares in the mine when Billy had developed that cough two and a half years ago, a hacking, phlegm-laced cough that just wouldn't go away. His suspicions awakened, Jonathan had wanted his friend to see a doctor, but Billy had shrugged off that suggestion, not confirming Jonathan's fears about his illness until nearly a year later, when he'd started coughing up blood.

At that point, Jonathan had dragged his friend to one of Colorado's famous sanitoriums for treatment, but there was little the doctors could do. Consumption was always fatal.

Jonathan leaned forward in the bathtub, plunking his elbows on his bent knees and resting his head in his hands, the pain of Billy's death squeezing his chest like a vise.

He closed his eyes, but strangely, it wasn't an image of his friend, emaciated and dying, that came into his mind. Instead, he saw the girl, with her flaming hair and dark eyes. A month ago, promising to take care of Billy's daughter had seemed an easy promise to make. Only now, after discovering she was a full-grown woman with a stunning face and the body of a goddess, was he able to truly appreciate the enormity of his responsibility.

A knock sounded on the door of his stateroom, interrupting his contemplations. It was the same sound, he realized, that had woken him a few moments ago. He heard the turn of a key and the opening of a door, and then a cheerful voice calling his name.

"Tea, Mr. Deverill," a young man called through the open doorways of his suite. "As you ordered. And I've laid out the sandwiches and cakes."

Jonathan jerked upright. "Thank you," he called back. "Tip's there," he added, remembering the change he'd tossed on the table earlier when he'd emptied his pockets.

"Thank you, *sir*." The waiter's grateful voice told him the amount of change must have been generous. There was another rattle of tea things, the sound of the change being scraped off the table, and then the waiter's voice came again. "Can I do anything more for you, Mr. Deverill?"

"No." He rose, stepped out of the bath, and pulled a towel from the hook nearby. "I'll ring if I need anything."

"Yes, sir. Thank you again."

Jonathan heard the outer door close and the key turn as he dried off. Tossing aside the towel, he walked to the washstand, opened his shaving kit, and turned on the hot water tap.

He'd already lathered his brush by the time he remembered the tea. Deciding he'd better drink it before it got cold, he set down his shaving brush and turned off the tap, then donned his dressing robe and left the bath.

Tying the sash of his robe, he pushed the door wide with his shoulder, but at the sight that met his eyes, he came to an immediate halt in the doorway. "What the devil?" he muttered.

Sitting on the petit point sofa of his stateroom, eating crumpets and drinking tea, her bright hair gleaming in the light of the lamp beside her, was Marjorie McGann.

Chapter 4

*H*ad Jonathan possessed any doubts that making him the guardian of his best friend's daughter was an awful idea, the fact that Miss Mc-Gann was sitting in his stateroom aboard a ship crossing the Atlantic instead of securely tucked away at Forsyte Academy would have shredded them.

"What are you doing here?" he demanded. Glancing past her toward the windows that opened onto the promenade deck, he was relieved to see that at least she hadn't drawn back the curtains. But then, he remembered they were far out of New York Harbor, with no way to take her back, and his relief vanished again. "I left you in White Plains."

"Fortunately for me, I know how to ride a bicycle, purchase a train ticket, and hail a taxi. And since you provided me with the name of the ship on which you had booked passage . . ." She paused to pop the last bite of crumpet into her mouth and reach for a sandwich, then she leaned back against the sofa and smiled, looking far too pleased with herself. "Here I am."

"How did you get into my room?"

"I came in with the waiter." She gave him an apologetic look as she ate a bite of sandwich. "I fear he thinks we're both terribly depraved."

"Good God," he muttered, rubbing his hands over his face as he worked to make sense of the situation. "Does Mrs. Forsyte know you've gone?"

"I imagine she does by now. I left her a note, explaining that I'd departed with you."

"And what am I supposed to do with you, in heaven's name?"

"What you should have done in the first place." She took another bite of sandwich as if she didn't have a care in the world. "Be my guardian, as my father wanted."

"That's what I thought I was doing," he countered, his shock giving way to frustration. "I ensured that you were properly looked after, as any guardian would."

Her sound of disdain told him what she thought of that. "You and I have very different notions of what a guardian's duties entail, Mr. Deverill. Mine, as I already told you, includes taking me to London, giving me a season, and helping me find a husband."

"And as I told you, you can't have a season—not yet. It would be quite inappropriate so soon after your father's death. As for the rest, I may be your guardian, but I'm damned if I'll be your matchmaker."

"Fine." She ate the last bite of her sandwich and brushed the crumbs from her fingers onto the tray before she spoke again. "I'll find my future husband without your help."

"It shouldn't be difficult," he shot back. "You'll probably be saddled with half a dozen candidates before we even disembark. The moment word gets out that the daughter of the late silver baron William McGann is on board, you'll have any number of good-looking scoundrels with no money and bad intentions interested in you."

As he spoke, he appreciated that watching over her was a duty he could now not postpone. And given the girl's smashing looks and immense fortune, he feared it would prove a more hazardous task than protecting a mine had ever been. "When these men discover you haven't a proper chaperone, they'll be chasing you all around the ship."

"Do you think so?" She smiled, the beautiful innocent. "How delightful."

All sorts of ghastly possibilities began flashing through his mind, and it took him a moment to answer. "Hardly that," he said at last, "since you could find yourself compromised by a shipboard romance and forced into marriage. Do you want to be stuck for life with a fortune hunter?"

She shrugged as if that was a thing of little consequence. "Any man marrying an heiress like me would expect a substantial dowry. And I can't condemn my future husband for wanting to spend my fortune when that's exactly what I'm going to do with it."

"I see." He folded his arms, feeling grimmer than ever. "And just what do you think you'll be spending it on?"

"Oh, the usual things," she answered with a vague wave of her hand as she leaned forward to survey the viands on the tea tray. "Clothes, furs, jewels, carriages, motorcars, redecorating the country house—"

"You don't own a country house."

"Not yet. But I will." She took an éclair from the tray and sat back again, tilting her head to one side, still smiling. "I think I'll buy a yacht as well. And maybe some racehorses. That would be exciting. And I'll have parties, too—lots and lots of parties. Fabulous, extravagant parties that'll make the New York Knickerbocker set pea green with envy." She sighed dreamily and took a bite of éclair.

"You intend to waste your father's fortune on frivolities like that?"

"Why shouldn't I?" she countered, not seeming to notice the testy note of his voice. "What else am I supposed to do with it? Watch it sit in the bank while I grow old? What fun is that? Besides, I'd have to be a pretty profligate spender to go through it all. I seem to have oodles of money—that is, if those are any indication."

She nodded to the writing desk against the wall where he'd put the financial reports he'd reviewed with Mr. Jessop. He'd placed them in a neat pile, intending to give them another perusal tomorrow, but now they were spread carelessly across the polished rosewood desktop.

"What's the Rose of Shoshone?" she asked, regaining his full attention.

"I'll ask the questions, thank you."

"You're so testy. Maybe you should have an éclair. Chocolate," she added, holding up the bit of pastry in her fingers, "can always be counted upon to elevate one's spirits."

Jonathan was in no mood to be elevated. "First, you leave the safety of Mrs. Forsyte's and sneak aboard this ship, then you burst into my room without leave and read my private correspondence? My God, for someone who's lived such a sheltered life, you're a brazen little baggage, I'll give you that."

"What I read wasn't private," she objected, not seeming the least bit put out by his description of her. "My father's will, an accounting of the money he left to me, and reports on the investments made on my behalf are documents I have every right to read, particularly since my own guardian didn't bother to inform me of the terms of my inheritance before he took off."

"There wasn't time. I had a train to catch. And—"

"Oh, please," she interrupted before he could point out that Mr. Jessop would have been able to explain the terms of the will and the extent of her property. "Don't try to justify yourself. What you did was run away."

"That's absurd." He shifted his weight, feeling the sudden, inconvenient prick of his conscience.

"And," she added before he could fashion some sort of reply, "I didn't 'sneak' anywhere. I'm no stowaway. I bought my passage, like anyone else. Not a grand parlor suite like this, of course. With my savings, an inside cabin was all I could afford. Still, it is in first class." She ate the last bite of her éclair and picked up the teapot. "Would you care for tea?"

"I don't need any bloody tea!"

She set aside the pot and looked at him again. "Hmm," she said, frowning thoughtfully, "I think you're right. You look as if what you need is a good, stiff drink. And," she added, glancing over him, "perhaps some clothes."

Jonathan followed her gaze, realizing in horror as he looked down that he was wearing nothing but a knee-length dressing robe. In front of his new ward. Billy's *daughter.* "Christ almighty."

He strode over to where she sat, bent down, and grabbed her by the elbows, his only thought to get her out of his stateroom, but the moment he hauled her to her feet, he realized his mistake, for the move brought her body right up against his, and as her full breasts brushed his chest, he was forcibly reminded that his ward was well past pinafores. And that under his robe, he was naked. And that he hadn't had a woman in a long, long time.

Desperate, he stepped back to put some much-needed distance between them, but he did not let her go. Instead, he turned, gripping her hard by the elbow. "You have to get out of here," he said as he propelled her across the sitting room of his suite. "Now."

"But I haven't finished my tea."

Ignoring that bit of nonsense, Jonathan halted by the door and, still keeping a firm grip on her, he reached for the handle. "Yes, you have."

"You really want me to leave?"

"Yes," he said firmly as he yanked the door open. After sticking his head out to verify that no one was in sight, he shoved her across the threshold and into the corridor.

"Are you sure?" She turned around, flattening her palm against the door as he moved to close it. "You want me going about the ship un-chaperoned, with so many fortune hunters and scoundrels with bad intentions on board?"

With an oath, Jonathan hauled her back inside and shut the door. Letting her go, he took a long step backward as he strove to regain his equilibrium and think—not an easy thing to do when he was barely clothed and the skin of his chest still burned from the light, inconsequential brush of her breast and his promises to take care of Billy's little girl were ringing in his ears.

"Sit down," he ordered and turned away, walking toward his bedroom. "Don't go anywhere, and don't touch anything. And if you value your life, stay away from my private papers."

Slamming the door of his bedroom behind him, he leaned back against it with a groan and wondered what he was going to do with her now. What did a man do with a beautiful, disobedient, fully grown, and damned inconvenient ward?

Hurling himself over the side of the ship came to mind, making him appreciate just what serious trouble he was in. If he was already contemplating drastic measures like that after half a day in charge of her life, what state was he going to be in a week from now when they docked at Southampton?

Jonathan didn't even want to think about it.

THE BEDROOM DOOR had scarcely closed behind him before Marjorie was laughing, and she had to bury her face in a sofa cushion to keep him from hearing it.

Oh, his shock when he'd seen her sitting here had been priceless. And when she'd rattled on about not caring if she married a fortune hunter and how she intended to spend her inheritance, he'd looked so appalled, she still didn't know how she'd managed to keep a straight face. And when she'd pointed out he was only partially dressed . . . oh, heavens.

That memory sent Marjorie into another fit of laughter, and she buried her face harder into the sofa cushion, her shoulders shaking. She'd thought having a guardian would be tedious, but she was beginning to think she'd been wrong. Just now, she found having a guardian vastly entertaining.

She shouldn't, she supposed, take such delight in teasing him, but he deserved it after the way he'd abandoned her, and she was enjoying her revenge so much that it was several moments more before Marjorie was able to contain her amusement at his expense.

At last, however, her sides aching, she sat up with a deep sigh, brushed back the stray tendrils of hair from her forehead, and returned her attention to the tea tray.

He must think her a fool, she thought, shaking her head as she selected a cucumber sandwich from the tray. Racehorses, indeed. She did mean to enjoy herself, but she wasn't about to be so silly with her money as that. Of course, fortune hunters would be swarming around her like flies—she'd already figured that out for herself, thank you. And despite her guardian's fears, she had no intention of allowing herself to be compromised and forced into marriage with a man who was only out for her money.

Still, she supposed she couldn't blame Mr. Deverill for being concerned, since he didn't know she'd already taken precautions of her own. It would be best, she thought, meditatively munching her sandwich, if she explained that and allayed his fears as soon as possible. Otherwise, the poor man might have apoplexy.

That decision had barely crossed her mind before the bedroom door opened and the object of her thoughts—properly dressed this time—reentered the sitting room.

She studied him as he crossed to the tea tray. He seemed over the initial surprise of finding her on board, but the expression on his face confirmed her initial impression of him, and Marjorie was glad she'd waited until the *Neptune* was safely out to sea before she'd come in search of him.

Fortified by the reminder that he couldn't send her back, Marjorie spoke first. "So, what happens now?"

He poured milk into his cup, added tea, dropped in two lumps of sugar, and stirred the contents before he replied. "For you?" he said at last. "Nothing."

"I don't know what you mean."

"When we're finished here, you will return to your cabin, where you will remain for the duration of the voyage."

Any lingering vestiges of Marjorie's earlier amusement vanished. "You must be joking."

He smiled at her, but there was an edge to it that showed he wasn't joking at all. "I will arrange for your meals to be delivered to you. And I'll send some books along as well. That way, you'll have something to occupy your mind besides attempting to get the better of me."

"But this is my first sea voyage. I've never traveled anywhere in my life until now. You can't—"

"Had you exercised some degree of patience and remained where you were until I could make proper arrangements for you, your first sea voyage would have proven much more enjoyable."

"It would also have been delayed by at least eight more months!"

His wide shoulders lifted then fell in an uncaring shrug. "Nonetheless, when you disobey your guardian, there are consequences."

"So, I am to be confined to my room like a misbehaving child, am I?" she countered. "Shall I have to go to bed without any supper, too?"

"By following me, you have put yourself in a precarious position. I may be your guardian, but I am not a relation, and because I am a man, I am limited in my ability to watch over you."

"I'm on a ship full of people. What do you imagine could happen to endanger me?"

"It isn't just your physical safety that I am thinking of. I am also very concerned with protecting your reputation, even if you are not."

The implication that she didn't care about her reputation caused Marjorie's temper to flare, but she tamped it down with an effort, knowing her wisest course was simply to set him straight. "If you're concerned one of those dastardly fortune hunters shall attempt to compromise me aboard ship, you needn't be. I have already arranged—"

"Gentlemen are not the only danger. If you are seen going about alone, the curiosity of the ladies will be aroused. It won't take long for them to learn your identity, and if you are seen dining by yourself or strolling unaccompanied on the promenade deck, you will at once be deemed a fast little piece."

"Yes, but I won't be alone. I—"

"Yes, you will, because as I explained earlier today, I cannot escort you. We are both unmarried, and if we are seen traveling together with no chaperone, people will think the worst of it."

Marjorie tried once again to explain. "Yes, but you see—"

"Every British matron seeks to find out all she can about her traveling companions to be sure she is not among the wrong sort of people. We won't be halfway to Southampton before we are judged and condemned."

With that, Marjorie gave up any attempts to explain that—not being an idiot—she'd already foreseen and taken precautions against all these dangers. "And as I said, your wishes would have put my new life much too far into the future."

"And you think following me to London is going to change that? The next eleven months aren't going to be any different for you merely because you moved across the pond."

She frowned, her frustration supplanted by bafflement and dread. "What do you mean?"

"You're in mourning, Miss McGann. In England or America, at least six months of seclusion is expected."

"I've been in seclusion most of my life. I have no intention of continuing that way any longer."

"Don't you think you're exaggerating a bit?"

"Am I? I watched all my friends leave Forsyte Academy and go on with their lives while I remained behind. They have done the London season, danced with dukes, and dined with princes. Many of them have fallen in love, married, and made exciting lives for themselves. I, meanwhile, have gone nowhere and done nothing. I'm an heiress, too, but for all the good it's done me, I might as well be poor. Why do you think I saved every penny I could of my allowance and my teacher's salary? Even before my father died, I'd intended to escape. I was about to begin making my own arrangements so that when I turned twenty-one, I could leave Forsyte Academy."

"And go where?"

Marjorie met his confounded stare with a hard one of her own. "Well, not to my father, since I didn't even know where he was."

He looked away, a clear sign her words made him uncomfortable, but she was in no frame of mind to care about that right now. "When the two of you left Idaho, no one would tell me where you'd gone. Mrs. Forsyte said she didn't know, and Mr. Jessop refused to say, suggesting I send any letters through him. My father, he said, was moving about and difficult to reach—a lie a child could see through."

"It wasn't a lie—at least," he amended when she gave him a skeptical look, "not until he went into the sanitorium."

"Another thing no one saw fit to tell me." Her voice rose a fraction—the aggravation of having been kept continually in the dark by those who thought they were protecting her. "So, I made my own plans to join my friends in England. Most of them are married now, and I knew one of them would agree to chaperone me there."

"And what did you intend to do for money?"

"I was gambling on the fact that even my scapegrace of a father wouldn't allow me to be destitute in another country. Once the deed was done, he'd have to have Mr. Jessop give me a bigger allowance and a dowry. But then, he died. I didn't even know he was sick—" She broke off, startled at the failing of her own voice, frustrated by the lump that rose in her throat.

"My father is gone," she managed after a moment, shoving down any stupid sentiments about her useless parent. "I now have the chance for a life of my own choosing. Did you really think I'd be willing to wait?"

"What I thought was that you would have the sense to stay put until I had things arranged for you."

"In other words, you thought I'd do what I'm told and let you—a perfect stranger—decide what's best for me?"

"As your father relied upon me to do. I will not break my word because you have an unaccountable desire to defy me, propriety, and common sense."

Marjorie could have told him she hadn't even begun to be defiant yet, but she refrained. "So, keeping me hidden away is how you intend to bring me to heel? What shall you do when we reach London? Lock me in an attic?"

"I hope you won't make it necessary."

Marjorie stared at him, appalled. "All the way until August? You wouldn't dare."

"I should advise you not to test me on what I would and would not dare, Miss McGann. And I'm not sure what you think August has to do with anything."

She frowned. "Because that's when I turn twenty-one."

"Just so," he agreed, nodding. "What of it?"

"A woman comes of age at twenty-one."

"Legally, yes. But per your father's will, the bulk of your money is held in trust for you until you turn thirty."

"Thirty?" Marjorie stared at him in horror. "But I'll be an old maid by then!"

"Until you turn thirty," he said, giving her a smile she could only describe as infuriatingly smug, "I decide how much income you receive. You seem surprised." He nodded to the documents on his desk. "I take it you didn't read far enough to get to that part?"

Marjorie rallied, sticking her chin up. "You intend to use my own money to control me, is that it?"

"I will use whatever works." He tilted his head, looking at her speculatively. "How much fun do you think you'll be able to have in London on ten dollars a month?"

"With a fortune in the bank, you'd really restrict me to the same allowance I've had since I was seven?"

"You're in mourning, so even if I gave you a larger allowance, there's not much you could spend it on. And whatever the amount, it will not be enough for yachts and racehorses."

Marjorie cursed her own mischievous sense of humor. "Will it at least be enough for decent clothes?" She gestured to her black suit coat with the Forsyte Academy insignia on its lapel. "I can't very well keep wearing my teacher's uniforms everywhere, and they are almost the only clothes I have."

"I see your point," he said, much to her relief. "When we reach London, I shall ask my sisters to take you to Jay's."

"Is that a modiste?" she asked, her spirits lifting a bit.

"Yes, indeed. They make clothes for mourning."

"Oh, no." She might have to allow this man some control over her life and make some compromises with him, but going about in black bombazine and crape was not a compromise she was willing to make. "I will not go into mourning."

"You must. It's customary after the death of a parent."

In his voice, Marjorie heard the hard resolve of an iron will. But what her guardian didn't seem to have realized yet was that her will was equally strong. "I will not go into mourning," she said again, "and I fail to see why I should."

"Because your father is dead, Miss McGann," he said, his face twisting with pain. "A fact you seem quite happy to forget. And you seem to display a pleasure-seeking disregard for his demise that is as astonishing as it is unseemly. Your lack of grief and gratitude do you little credit."

That accusation sparked Marjorie's temper like nothing else ever could. "Gratitude? Grief?" she echoed with blazing scorn. "Are those the emotions I'm supposed to be feeling?"

"I would think so, yes."

"Then you understand nothing about it. The last time I saw my father, I was seven years old, and my mother had just died. She wasn't in the ground a week before he took me to Forsyte Academy and shoved me into the arms of Mrs. Forsyte—a woman I'd never met in my life before. He kissed me good-bye, told me to be a good little girl, and then . . . he left me there."

Mr. Deverill pressed his lips together. "He probably felt that was for the best," he said after a moment. "Given his profession, he knew he'd be gone a great deal. And many widowers—"

"He promised he'd come back for me," she cut in, sparing them both the lame excuses society allowed widowers to use so that they could abandon their children, "but he never did."

"I'm sure he intended to do so."

"Yes." She folded her arms. "Just as you intended when you left me this morning."

She heard his sharp intake of breath, but it was several moments before he spoke.

"Miss McGann," he said at last, "it's clear you think I attempted to abandon you, but such was not the case. As for your father, I know he left you so that he could continue to provide for you. And he succeeded in amassing you a fortune—at great personal cost, I might add. Because of his sacrifice, you will be able to live in luxury for the rest of your life."

"I'd rather have had a father. One who visited on occasion, or who could at least manage a letter more often than once or twice a year."

"Billy never was much for letter-writing, I admit, but I doubt his decision not to visit was one of neglect, though it might seem that way. He probably didn't want you to see him ill."

"And now I shall never see him at all!" Her throat closed up, her eyes began to sting, and she realized in horror that she might actually cry over her wretched excuse for a father, and she turned her face away before Mr. Deverill could see. "He could have told me, sent for me. I'd have come."

He moved to stand in front of her. "Consumption is brutal in its final stages," he said, the compassion in his voice making her angrier, fueling her pain like paraffin on flames. "It's not something any loved one ought to see, believe me."

He was trying to console her, she knew, but she didn't want to be consoled. "And what about all the years before that?" She looked up, her eyes meeting his. "My father had plenty of chances to visit me, but he never did. Not once."

"I'm sure he thought of you a great deal."

Even he seemed to realize how inadequate those words sounded, for the moment they were out of his mouth, he grimaced.

"Are you sure?" she asked, forcing a laugh. "I can't think why, since he failed to tell you, his best friend, of my very existence until he was about to die."

He didn't reply, but then, what could he say?

"I don't remember much about my father, Mr. Deverill, for even before he went West, he was gone a lot. But I do remember my mother. It's a vague remembrance, of course, but there are things about her that stand out—how she would always beg my father not to go away again, and the awful look on her face as we'd watch him pack his kit and walk out the door. I remember the hushed sound of her sobs at night as she cried herself to sleep."

He started to reply, but she didn't want to hear it. "You talk of the sacrifices my father made on my behalf," she said, "but the truth is that for him, there was no sacrifice. He was doing just as he pleased and living just the life he wanted. Letter after letter I wrote, asking—begging—him to come back or to let me join him, but all I got were excuses."

Her hands were shaking, she noticed, and pride impelled her to clench them into fists so her guardian wouldn't see. "In the few replies he bothered to write, he always said the same things. That he'd send for me, that there'd be plenty of time for us to be together when I grew up. 'Soon,' he'd always say. 'Soon we'll see each other again—'"

Her voice broke, and she had to pause for a deep breath before she could go on. "In your judgement of my behavior," she said after a moment, "have you ever considered what my life has been like? Mrs.

Forsyte is a kind woman, but she's not and never could be a mother to me. My father was my only family, and despite all his promises, it was clear he did not want me. Do you have any idea how it feels to live year after year on promises?"

"I do, yes. Believe that or not."

"Can you also understand what it did to me when I finally realized all my father's promises were lies? That when he died, I knew 'soon' was never, ever, going to come?"

"Yes, I can." His voice was low, his reply a simple acknowledgement that made her feel worse.

Her throat tightened again, threatening to choke her, and she continued quickly, while she still could. "Forgive me, Mr. Deverill, if my father's death gives me little cause for grief and his way of protecting me fails to inspire my gratitude. I realize that for you, his passing was a wrenching loss and that pain over his death is what *you* feel, but for my part, I feel as if I've been let out of prison. And now that I'm free, I have no intention of going back behind bars. I'm not going into mourning, for I will not play the hypocrite and pretend to grieve for a man I hardly knew, a man who never gave a damn about being any sort of real father to me."

"Even if society judges you unfavorably for your choice?"

"Even then. I am going to laugh and dance and enjoy myself and wear whatever colors I please. I'm going to do the season, meet young men, fall in love, and get married. And when I do, you can bet the man I choose will be a better husband and father than Billy McGann ever dreamed of being. I intend to have a real home and a real family and a life worth living, and I don't give a damn if any of that breaks rules of propriety, offends society, or inconveniences you."

With that, she turned and walked out, slamming the door of her new guardian's stateroom behind her, taking enormous satisfaction in the very loud bang.

Chapter 5

Jonathan scowled at the closed door, fully aware that as a guardian, he wasn't acquitting himself very well. But really, he thought in baffled exasperation, could any other man put in this situation have done better?

Even as he asked himself that question, he knew that wasn't the point. Responsibility for her welfare, her reputation, and her future was in his hands now, and if anything happened to tarnish her—which given her speech of a few moments ago, was quite likely—he would be to blame. Despite all her brave talk, she was an innocent young woman, and he was a man of the world. He knew far better than she how easily her good name could be blackened by even the most trivial incident, and the girl herself seemed to possess no sense of self-preservation. Nor any sense of sorrow.

You talk of the sacrifices my father made on my behalf, but the truth is that for him, there was no sacrifice.

He'd always known Billy was no saint, but her condemnations of his late friend had nonetheless been hard to hear. And though she may have ignored his wishes and defied his plans, her fiery speech was forcing him to admit she had cause to resent her parent.

I feel as if I've been let out of prison. And now that I'm free, I have no intention of going back behind bars.

But even as her defiant words went through his mind, he felt sure she didn't truly appreciate the consequences of that defiance. She couldn't toss the restrictions of society back at the very people who imposed them and expect those people to accept her anyway. They would not, and he knew it. It was his job to see that she complied with the rules.

Once they got to London, he'd hurl himself on the mercy of his sisters, and hopefully, they'd agree to watch over the girl while he went to Africa, but until then, he was on his own in managing her. The surest way to avoid gossip, criticism, and unwanted attention was for her to stay in her cabin, but he couldn't see how to guarantee she did. Ordering her would probably be as effective as leaving her behind had been. Locking her in her cabin wouldn't do, and he doubted it would work anyway. If he locked her in, she'd find a way to pick the lock.

No, employing persuasion and reason, not authority and force, was his best option. Once her temper cooled, he could surely make her see that following the rules was the way to gain her what she wanted. And it wouldn't hurt if he reminded her of all the wonderful things she had to look forward to next spring if she behaved with decorum now.

If such a strategy was to work, he'd have to mend their fences. An apology on his part was required, as well as his reassurance that she would not be abandoned, as she felt her father had done to her.

Glad he had a specific course of action, Jonathan shaved, dressed for dinner, and left his room. He went in search of the purser, where a short explanation of his position as guardian, along with a pair of silver dollars, gained him Miss McGann's cabin number.

A few minutes later, he knocked on her door, hoping like hell she was inside and not off gallivanting around the ship. To his relief, the bolt slid back almost at once and the door opened.

His relief, however, was short-lived. She had changed out of her walking suit into a velvet evening frock, and though it was black, there was nothing else about it that resembled mourning attire. The tiny cap sleeves and low neckline revealed far too much of her creamy skin. Even worse, the garment was tightly fitted, flaring out from her body only at her knees, and the way it hugged the hourglass curves of her figure was something no guardian could ever approve.

The sight of her in such a gown served to increase both his apprehensions and his resolve, but since beginning their conversation by laying down the law about what she could wear would get him nowhere, he didn't even raise an eyebrow. Instead, he bowed.

"Miss McGann," he said as he straightened. "Might I have a few moments of your time?"

"Are you sure you should be here?" Leaning past him, she peered up and down the deserted corridor. "What if you're seen skulking about outside my room? Heavens, what would people say?"

"Don't be impudent. It's the height of bad manners to give a man cheek when he's come to make amends."

"Oh, is that why you're here? To apologize?"

Take your medicine, old chap. "I am."

"All right, then." She fell silent, waiting, making it clear that he was expected to give chapter and verse right here in the doorway.

Jonathan, however, had no intention of doing so. As she'd pointed out, the longer he lingered out here, the more likely it was someone would see him. "May I come in?"

"Into my cabin?" Her eyes opened ingenuously wide. "Why, Mr. Deverill, what an improper sugg—"

"Enough," he cut in, giving an uneasy glance up and down the corridor. "If you want to hear my apology and have the satisfaction of crowing over it, you'd best let me in."

She gave way, closing the door behind him. She then sat down at one of the two chairs at the minuscule table, gesturing for him to take the opposite chair, and it did not escape his notice that her tight-fitting gown forced her to perch on the very edge of her seat.

"After our discussion this afternoon," he said as he took the offered chair, "I appreciate that I may not have handled our situation as well as I could have done."

She didn't seem satisfied by that, but he persevered. "I can only reiterate that learning you were a woman, not the child I'd been expecting, was a shock. And I knew at once that your age would require an entirely different set of circumstances than I was prepared to meet. Then, the discovery of you aboard ship, in my room, a place you had no business to be—"

"You don't make apologies often, do you?" she cut in.

He blinked at the abrupt question. "No," he answered, "I suppose I don't."

"Obviously not, since you're terrible at it."

"I don't often find it necessary," he shot back before recalling that he'd come here in a conciliatory spirit. Exhaling a sigh, he started over. "Miss McGann—"

A knock on the door of her cabin interrupted before he could go any further.

"Ah." Marjorie rose. "That'll be the baroness, I expect, coming back to fetch me."

"Who?" he asked, too surprised by her declaration to bother with proper grammar.

"Baroness Vasiliev," she answered over her shoulder as she turned away and stepped across the tiny stateroom. "My chaperone and companion."

"Chaperone?" he echoed in bafflement as he stood up. "Companion? What are you talking about?"

"Baroness Vasiliev," she said again, as if repeating the woman's title was expected to enlighten him. "I'm so looking forward to presenting you to her."

Jonathan watched as Marjorie opened the door to a middle-aged woman of Junoesque proportions and suspiciously black hair. Dressed for dinner in a red brocade gown that was obviously new and swathed in diamonds he suspected were paste, this so-called baroness looked far more like an actress playing a part than a real aristocrat, at least in Jonathan's opinion.

"Marjorie, darling," she greeted the girl with exaggerated familiarity, flinging the end of her fluffy, feather-trimmed evening stole back over one shoulder. "How marvelous you look," she said, her voice laced with heaviness of an overdone Russian accent. "The dress fits you well."

Too well, Jonathan wanted to say, but somehow, he managed to suppress his opinion.

"I do hope you are ready to go down," the woman continued, "for I must have a drink. I'm parched."

"I'm not ready just yet, I'm afraid," the girl answered and opened the door wide. "But please, do come in, Baroness."

The woman noticed him as Marjorie moved aside and she entered the cabin. Frowning, she lifted the jeweled opera glasses that hung about her neck, plunked them onto her nose, and gave him the once-over in a way so theatrically perfect that he almost wanted to laugh.

"Baroness, may I introduce my guardian, Mr. Jonathan Deverill?" Marjorie presented him to the woman with a flourish. "Mr. Deverill, the Baroness Vasiliev."

He responded to this introduction by bowing his head a fraction. "Madam."

If he thought his refusal to address her by her title would be regarded as a set-down, he was mistaken. At once, the opera glasses dropped to nestle in the crevice of her bosom, and her disapproving face relaxed into smiles, making her look even more like the blowsy actress he suspected her of being.

"It is so good of you to trust me with the responsibility for your young ward, Mr. Deverill, and I assure you that I take my duty as her chaperone most seriously. That is why I must ask you to leave her apartments at once."

This pretense of concern was a bit much, and it took all the effort Jonathan had not to roll his eyes. "Your vigilance does you credit," he said instead, striving to keep a straight face. "But I'm afraid I have some matters of business to discuss with Miss McGann."

"My dear man . . ." She paused, flinging out her hands in an extravagant gesture. "I cannot permit it. Here, in her own cabin? No. This is not done."

He glanced past the self-proclaimed baroness to where Marjorie was standing by the door, and his expression must have been grim indeed, for she looked away at once. But he did not miss the smile that tilted one corner of her mouth, and he feared that instead of being intimidated, she was having a jolly good laugh at his expense.

"What sort of chaperone would I be," the older woman said, bringing his attention back to her, "if I allowed any man, even her own guardian, a private meeting? No, I must be able to assure the duchess when we meet again that the girl has been looked after."

Diverted for a moment, he frowned. "The duchess? Do you mean my sister, the Duchess of Torquil?"

"But of course! When Marjorie was first introduced to me—"

"Introduced by whom?"

The woman laughed again, not seeming bothered by that incisive question. "We rather introduced ourselves, did we not, Marjorie?"

"Am I to understand," Jonathan said before his ward could answer, "that you have met my sister, Irene?"

"Oh, yes! We met in Paris about four years ago. She was on her wedding journey with the duke. Dear Torquil. What a splendid man, and so handsome."

"How odd that you should have met my sister four years ago during her honeymoon," Jonathan said pleasantly, "since her wedding was six years ago."

The woman didn't even blink. "As much as that? Ach, the time, it passes so fast." Waving a hand vaguely in the air, she added, "As I was saying, the duchess will have no cause to fault my chaperonage. I—"

"Nonetheless," he cut her off, his patience with this charade beginning to wear thin, "my desire to speak privately with my ward is not the least untoward. You see, Miss McGann and I need to discuss certain financial matters." He paused, meeting the woman's blue eyes with a meaningful glance. "Specifically, those relating to my management of her money."

Whoever she was, the woman at least had enough sense to appreciate that though Miss McGann had hired her, he was the one who'd be signing the checks.

"Of course," she said, accepting the situation with a dignified bow of the head. Turning away, she walked to the door, opening it as Marjorie moved aside, but she paused on the threshold to give him and his ward a warning glance. "I shall wait for you in the corridor, Marjorie."

"With an ear to the keyhole, no doubt," Jonathan muttered as the door swung shut behind her.

"Something any good chaperone would do in this situation," Marjorie replied.

"No," he corrected at once. "A truly good chaperone would never countenance a young woman in her charge wearing a dress like that."

He gestured to her ensemble, causing Marjorie to glance down at herself. "What's wrong with my gown?" she asked, smoothing the velvet over her hips—an unnecessary move, since the blasted garment fitted her like a second skin. "The baroness told me it's the latest fashion from Paris. And it fits, though the last hour's been a scramble, since we had to call for a maid and have the sides taken in a bit."

"You took them in a bit too much, I'd say."

The acidity of his voice penetrated, and Marjorie looked up. "What have I done now?" she asked with a sigh. "I'm wearing black. I'm trying to compromise. I thought you'd be pleased."

Jonathan was acutely aware that if this were any other woman, not his ward, not the daughter of his best friend, he would have been very pleased indeed. "Just who is this woman?"

"I told you. Baroness Vasiliev. She's Russian." Ignoring his sound of skepticism, she went on, "She lost her entire family to an influenza outbreak years ago, including her young son. Very sad."

"Tragic. What part of Russia?"

"The . . . Ukraine, I think. Or is it Georgia? Oh, well, it doesn't matter, since she lives in Paris most of the year nowadays."

"Paris? I'd have guessed London." He folded his arms. "Somewhere near Drury Lane, for choice."

She tilted her head a bit to one side, studying him. "You seem upset, and I can't think why. I needed a chaperone, so I found myself one."

This situation was deteriorating from absurdity to farce. "You cannot go out and find your own chaperone. Things aren't done that way."

"Isn't it rather pointless to tell me I can't do what I've already done? She is a baroness, so you can't say she's not acceptable. And it's not as if I can't afford the expense."

An expense he'd have to approve, but Jonathan didn't bother pointing that out. Instead, he raised an eyebrow. "A baroness needs to be paid to be a chaperone?"

"I offered. She lost all her money. Bad investments. You know how it is with the aristocracy." She shook her head sorrowfully. "No money sense."

"Aristocracy? What—that woman?" Jonathan made a sound of disbelief, but Marjorie didn't seem to hear it.

"Land rents don't bring in anything for them nowadays, not with this awful agricultural depression going on in Europe."

"You seem quite knowledgeable about global economics."

"Well, it's pretty common knowledge that the aristocracy is going broke. Why do you think so many British lords want to marry rich American girls like me? And the baroness explained that when her husband and son died, the land went to the next heir, some distant cousin who refused to give his poor relation an income. The woman is practically destitute."

"And she poured out her tale of woe to you, a perfect stranger? How convenient she found such a sympathetic—and wealthy—listener."

"I don't see why you're grousing about this," she said, sounding decidedly nettled. "You wanted me to have a chaperone."

"What I wanted was for you to stay in White Plains until I could make proper arrangements for you."

"There's nothing improper about my arrangements!"

"Given all the dashing about on bicycles and trains and ships that you've been doing today, just how and when did you find the time to hire this woman?"

"We met in the ladies' reading room just after I came aboard. We struck up a rapport, talked for about an hour, and came to an agreement that suits us both. We are going to have the purser move us into adjoining cabins tomorrow. It would be better, of course, if we could be installed in a suite . . ."

She paused, looking at him hopefully.

"No," he said, quashing that plan at once. "And no adjoining rooms either. Give a woman you just met access to your cabin? Not a chance."

"What do you think she's going to do? Steal my jewelry?"

He could only thank God the Rose of Shoshone was in the ship's vault. "A likely possibility, I should say."

"No, it's not, since I don't own any jewelry except a cameo brooch and a garnet ring of my mother's—hardly worth robbery. And it makes sense for us to share rooms, since she's my chaperone."

He shuddered. "God forbid."

"You can't say she's inappropriate for the task. She's a baroness."

"If that woman's a baroness, I'm a prince of the realm. Her bloodlines aside, no woman who uses hair dye could possibly be an appropriate chaperone for you, or any girl."

Marjorie gave him a look of pity. "You have been away from civilization a long time, haven't you? Many older women dye their hair nowadays. It's quite the fashionable thing to do. Why, I believe Oscar Wilde even mentioned something about that in one of his plays."

"Oscar Wilde also went to prison," he pointed out. "I'm hardly reassured."

"Oh, for heaven's sake!" she cried. "It's not as if I picked a perfect stranger off the street. She knows your sister and brother-in-law."

"Indeed? Did she mention that connection before or after she learned you were William McGann's daughter, and that I, his business partner and your guardian, am the brother of a duchess?"

"I didn't say anything about you," she answered with dignity. "Or about my father."

"Then it's clear you didn't have to. It's likely that she already knew all about you." Jonathan decided this was the perfect time to offer a lesson on just how hazardous a place the world could be for an innocent, unaccompanied woman. "I'm sure she reads the New York papers, as I'd wager all the talented confidence swindlers who work the liners do."

"You seem to know a great deal about confidence swindlers," she said acidly. "I wonder how."

"My guess is that she saw you sitting alone in the ladies' reading room, inquired of a member of the ship's company who you were, and the moment she heard your name, she recognized it from the papers. Seizing her opportunity, she approached you, made some friendly comment, and you, like a lamb, invited her to sit with you?"

Marjorie shifted her weight, not meeting his gaze, and Jonathan knew he was on the right track. "She discovered you were unchaperoned, no doubt, and pretended to be appalled by the fact. She then poured out her tale of woe—her unfortunate circumstances and her money troubles and how hard life is for the impoverished nobility in our modern, uncivilized age."

She jerked her chin, confirming the accuracy of his reconstruction of the afternoon's events. "Now you're just being absurd," she muttered.

"My point is, what do you really know about this woman?"

When she didn't answer, he pressed his advantage. "After an hour's acquaintance, there's nothing you could know except what she's told you. She says she knows my sister, but we have no idea if that's true. You must understand that many people will try to become intimate with you because of who you are, and that not all of them have good intentions."

"I already realize that."

"You may realize it, but you can't possibly understand it. Not yet. You don't have enough experience to see all the ways in which people can take advantage of you, and how to guard yourself from them. My job is to see that you are introduced to the wider world gradually, by the proper people at the proper time."

"If you believe the baroness has nefarious intentions, you could have interviewed her yourself," Marjorie pointed out as she picked up a white silk rose ornament from the table and clipped it into her hair. "But, no," she added, slipping on a pair of long white evening gloves, "you decided to play the indignant, overprotective guardian and shove her out into the hallway."

"I didn't shove the woman anywhere. And I have no intention of being anything but protective where you are concerned."

His reply seemed to slide off her back like water off a duck. "If you're so concerned about her background, I suppose you can pump her for information during dinner."

"Dinner? We are to dine with this woman?"

"We're all sitting at the captain's table. I've already accepted the invitation."

Jonathan studied her face, appreciating that with a chaperone to accompany her, an evening gown to wear that made her look like a Parisian fashion plate, and an invitation to the captain's table in the offing, his plan to persuade her to stay in her room was now about as likely as flying pigs. "How did we merit an invitation to sit with the captain?" he demanded, and his eyes narrowed as he watched her tug guiltily at one ear. "What did you do?"

"Nothing," she insisted, but when he continued to look at her in disbelief, she capitulated. "Now that you mention it, I did happen to run across the purser a short while ago."

"What an astonishing coincidence."

"Wasn't it?" she agreed, ignoring the sarcasm. "He was happy to tell me all about the amusements available for ladies on board—quoits, piquet, shuffleboard, and such. He even offered to give me a tour of the ship and show me all the hidden, secret places where the passengers aren't allowed to go."

"I'll just bet he did," Jonathan muttered.

Marjorie gave a dreamy sigh, her gloved palm pressed to her bosom. "Sailors are wonderful, aren't they? So nice to women."

He felt a lurch of fear. "Marjorie," he began.

"But," she went on as she reached for a white velvet wrap from the bed and slung it around her shoulders, "he became even nicer when he found out a duchess was my guardian's sister. Why, he was tripping over himself after that to assure me anything on board was at my disposal."

"You told the purser about my sister?"

"I did happen to mention her." Marjorie looked at him, her eyes wide. "Just in passing."

Staring into his ward's deceptively innocent brown eyes, Jonathan realized he might have been laboring under a misapprehension. He had taken it for granted that the so-called baroness had tricked Marjorie into becoming acquaintances, but now, listening to how his ward had manipulated the purser, he began to wonder if perhaps Baroness Vasiliev had been the true victim in the ladies' reading room a few hours ago. "And it was after you dropped my sister's title into your conversation with the purser, I suppose, that an invitation to the captain's table appeared at your door?"

"It did." She gave him a bright, beaming smile. "Wasn't that nice? The invitation includes you, by the way, and I accepted on your behalf. The baroness will be joining us, too, of course."

"How did the captain know the baroness was your chaperone?"

"Oh, but he didn't," she informed him with triumph. "She had already been invited to sit with him. So, you see? Your concerns are groundless. If she's good enough to merit an invitation to the captain's table, I think she's good enough to chaperone me. And speaking of dinner," she went on before he could respond, glancing at the clock on her wall and picking up a beaded black evening bag from the table, "they are serving cordials at half past seven and dinner is at eight. We'd best go down."

"I suppose we must, since you've already accepted the invitation," he gave in with a sigh as he followed her to the door, consoling himself with the thought that a shady, faux baroness was better than no chaperone at all. "But I still can't believe you used my sister's position to curry favor aboard ship."

"You know . . ." She paused to frown at him over one shoulder. "Given that you were my father's best friend, I'd have thought you an adventurous, carefree sort of man."

"I used to be," Jonathan countered with a pointed stare. "Then I met you."

"You're more like a parson, so old-fashioned and stuffy." Shaking her head, she turned away to open the door into the corridor. "Such a shame."

Jonathan scowled at her description, for it made him sound as if he had a foot in the grave. "I am not stuffy," he corrected. "I simply have a much better appreciation of the proprieties than you seem to possess."

Even as he spoke, Jonathan realized in dismay that stuffy was just how he sounded. Stuffy, snobbish, and dry as a stick. That, he appreciated, studying Marjorie's shapely, velvet-sheathed hips as he followed her out the door, was what being guardian to a madcap ginger with a body like a goddess did to a fellow.

Chapter 6

As a student and as a teacher, Marjorie had hovered on the periphery of Knickerbocker New York, given teasing glimpses of high society but never allowed to be part of it. Now, however, she was no longer just an observer, and as she sipped champagne with the other first-class passengers waiting to go in to dinner, she felt more strongly than ever that this world was where she belonged.

"Ach, there is Lady Stansbury," the baroness murmured beside her, interrupting Marjorie's thoughts. "She is a cow, that one."

Marjorie turned her head to where a gray-haired woman in a severe, high-necked gown of matte black stood about a dozen feet away. Though elderly and frail, leaning on a jeweled cane, she nonetheless gave the impression of an indomitable will.

"What makes you say that?" Marjorie asked, returning her attention to her companion. "Do you know her?"

The baroness downed her champagne, set her glass on the tray of a footman standing nearby, and picked up another before answering. "I have friends—Russian nobility like myself—who wish to raise funds for émigrés fleeing the Volga famine. Many had already starved to death. Many who do not die come to England, but they have no money, no food, nowhere to live, so my friends decide to have the charity ball to raise funds. One sells rich patrons the *billets* . . . tickets . . . ach, what is the word I think of?"

"Vouchers," Marjorie supplied, aware of the procedures involved in giving a charity ball.

"*Da*," the older woman said, nodding. "Vouchers, yes. My friends lease the public ballroom, make the guest list, begin to sell the vouchers . . . all is superb, but—"

The baroness broke off, glancing past Marjorie to glare at the Englishwoman. "But then she comes to ruin all our good work. This ball was to be on the same night as hers, and she could not allow that, no. So, she spreads vicious lies about my friends, saying that they intended to keep the money and not help the poor émigrés."

"Because her ball was on the same night? What an odious thing to do."

"It was for her granddaughter to make the debut. But some of my friends are intimates of Alexandra, Queen Victoria's own granddaughter, and favorites at the Russian court. All the most important British lords and ladies, they want to go to the Russian ball, and will not be so interested in this Lady Stansbury's, so she spreads the rumors and makes the sabotage, and we must cancel."

"How cutthroat."

"That's the *ton* for you," a low, deep voice murmured by her ear, and when she turned, she found her guardian beside her. "They're a ruthless lot. If you wish to live among them, you must prepare yourself for that."

She opened her mouth to reply, but the baroness spoke before she could. "Some acquaintances of mine have just come in. The Contessa de la Rosa and her son. There, at the pillar by the staircase. He is handsome, the count, do you not think?"

Marjorie followed the baroness's glance to where a debonair man with a perfectly groomed mustache and well-cut evening clothes was standing by the door, greeting the captain of the ship, an elegant, silver-haired lady in midnight blue beside him.

"Very handsome," she agreed, noting the count's tall form and dark good looks with appreciation.

"He is also most charming," the baroness replied. "Perhaps you would care to meet him?"

Happy to meet anyone, Marjorie nodded. "I'd be delighted."

"Then I go to make the inquiries. I will see if he and his mama consent to the introduction."

"As if there's any doubt," Jonathan commented dryly as they watched the baroness toddle off across the room, the feathery end of her stole trailing behind her. "And this so-called count is probably panting to meet an heiress. Once he sets—"

"Oh, I see." Marjorie faced him, her delightful mood dampened a bit. "It's not that a man might wish to meet *me*, that he might see me across the room and find me attractive. No, it's that I'm an heiress, and any heiress will do?"

"Once he sets his eyes on you, my sweet," Jonathan resumed, ignoring her acerbic reply, "he'll think he's found nirvana. And though I know you are inclined to always believe the worst of me," he continued as she stared at him, astonished by the compliment, "you might wait for me to finish my sentences before you draw conclusions about what I mean."

"Oh." Marjorie grimaced, appreciating that she was far too prickly where he was concerned. "Sorry."

"Apology accepted. But as we both know, most members of the aristocracy are broke. It is not unreasonable to question their motives."

The disdain in his voice was palpable. "You hate them," she murmured in surprise. "Why?"

"I don't hate them." He swirled his champagne and took a swallow. "I simply have little use for their way of life. Lilies of the field, most of them."

Marjorie frowned, confused. "But you come from British society, don't you?"

"My mother came from society," he corrected. "My father did not. He was the son of a newspaper publisher—very lowbrow and middle-class."

"But what about your sisters? They married into the *ton*."

"And they seem happy there, but I have no desire to join them in that sphere."

"Why not?"

"I'd find it deadly dull. You see, I spent my first three years in America working across the continent. By the time I met your father in Idaho, I had been an oyster shucker, a fishing boat captain, a cattle wrangler, a journalist, the secretary to a railway magnate, and the manager of a gambling hall. For a while, I was even a bounty hunter. Good thing, too, for it proved to be good practice."

"Practice?" she echoed, struck by the word. "For what?"

"Owning a mine. When your father and I staked our claim, we soon discovered that we'd have to fight off claim jumpers and mining magnates constantly in order to keep it."

"I can see I shall have to take back what I said about you being stuffy," she murmured. "It sounds as if you really are an adventurous sort after all. You must like a challenge."

"Like it? No." He paused, giving her a grin—a pirate's grin, white teeth in a suntanned face. "I love it."

"I suppose British country life would seem a bit slow-paced after the things you've done."

"I've done more during my ten years in America than the average British gentleman does in a lifetime," he told her. "The farthest my fellow countryman usually journeys is to Scotland or Paris, but I've traveled across plains so vast, Scotland's a tiny speck by comparison. I've crossed mountain ranges so beautiful, so awe-inspiring, the sight of them takes your breath away and makes your chest hurt."

Even though the life he'd lived wasn't the sort of life she wanted, as Marjorie studied his face, she couldn't help feeling a faint, answering thrill. "The only place I've ever seen that might be described as remarkable in any way is Niagara Falls."

As she spoke, her thrill faded away, replaced by a strange and pensive melancholy. "I've never been anywhere," she murmured. "Nor done anything, really."

"Until now."

"True," she agreed, brightening at the reminder. "I am on my way to a whole different world."

"I hope you enjoy that world more than I."

"So . . ." She paused, nodding to their opulent surroundings. "None of this is enjoyable to you?"

"I wouldn't quite say that." Something changed in his face as he looked at her, and when his lashes lowered, his tawny gaze sliding down, a wave of inexplicable heat washed over Marjorie—through her midsection, along her limbs, and into her face—a sensation so unfamiliar and unexpected that she couldn't seem to move, or even breathe.

"To look at beautiful women," he said gravely, his gaze lifting again to her face, "is always a pleasure."

He thought she was beautiful. Suddenly, her wits felt thick as tar, her heart was pounding in her chest, and her body seemed to be tingling everywhere.

She'd never felt like this before, but then, no man had ever really looked at her before, not this way. The only unmarried men she'd ever had occasion to meet were the widowed fathers who'd come to Forsyte Academy on Visiting Days, and those men were rare as hen's teeth. They were also far too occupied with the state of their daughters' education to take notice of her as anything more than a schoolteacher. This was the first time, she realized, that any man had looked at her as if she was a *woman*.

The sensation was both dizzying and scary, rather as if she were a baby bird perched on a limb, longing to leap into space and fly, but also aware she could crash to the ground.

"To eat good food," he went on, "to drink fine champagne, sleep on luxurious sheets, engage in erudite conversation—I enjoy all of that, believe me. But after a time, I grow weary of the petty small-mindedness, the gossip, the snobbery, the triviality, and the excruciatingly slow pace, and I long to be off to the wilds again. I don't mind stepping into a world of high society once in a while, but I have no desire to live in it permanently."

With that, any romantic excitement Marjorie felt fizzled and died. Everything he'd just told her confirmed what she'd already suspected. Forever inclined to wander, able to leave behind those who cared for him without regret, he sounded just like her father, and that made him the last man in the world any girl with sense ought to have romantic notions about.

Marjorie knew that when she settled down, it would be with a man who'd stick, a man who wanted to build a home and make a life, not one who was always looking to the next horizon.

"No wonder you and my father were such good friends," she remarked. "He didn't seem to fancy staying in one place any more than you do. Frankly, I'm amazed you two worked that mine as long as you did. But then," she added thoughtfully, "it's not as if I knew him well enough to understand his motives for anything."

"Is there . . ." He paused to give her a searching look. "Is there anything about him that you want to know? What he was like, or—"

"No." Aware of the uncompromising quality of her voice, she added, "I don't really want to talk about him, or even think about him. I'm sure you think that's awful."

"Actually, I don't." He expelled a sigh. "You were quite right in what you said earlier."

"I was?" Marjorie was amazed that he'd admit she was right about anything.

"It was unfair of me to judge you so harshly for not grieving a man you didn't know, even if he was your father."

She felt a glimmer of hope. "So, I don't have to go into mourning after all?"

"You're persistent, I'll give you that," he commented ruefully. "Sorry, but I intend to see that you do whatever propriety requires."

She groaned and gave up. "So, if you're such a restless man, why did you stay? At the mine, I mean?"

"Well, when you tap into an enormous vein of silver worth millions of dollars, it's deuced hard to walk away."

"So the two of you stayed just because of the money?"

He considered, taking a sip of champagne before he replied. "I can't speak for your father. But for myself, let's just say I had things to prove."

"What things?"

"I started out with nothing. I didn't want to end up with nothing."

"A newspaper business doesn't sound like nothing to me. Weren't you the only son?"

"That didn't cut ice with my father. He and I never got on. When I was eighteen, he cut off my allowance and disinherited me."

"How awful. What did you do?"

He gave a shout of unexpected laughter. "You do have a poor opinion of me, don't you? Assuming straightaway I did something to deserve being disinherited."

"That wasn't what I meant! I was asking what you did in response."

"Well, with no money but the sixteen pounds in my bank account, it wasn't as if I had many options. I left and came to America."

"You left, just like that? At eighteen, broke and alone?"

His smile faded, a hard glint coming into his eyes, but when he spoke his voice was light. "Well, I did ask my fiancée to come with me, but somehow, she couldn't see marrying a man who no longer had prospects or an income and going off with him to another country. Love is one thing. Material comforts, as she pointed out to me at the time, are something else."

"I'm sorry."

"Don't be. It was a long time ago. And honestly, I'm not sure we'd have been happy together. We'd probably have moved into some tiny, low-rent flat in Brooklyn, and I'd have spent the past ten years pegging away at some office job in Manhattan, a life we'd have both despised. She's quite comfortably situated now, I heard, married to a wealthy banker and living in a luxurious house in Grosvenor Square."

She began to see why her teasing talk about furs, motor cars, and lavish parties had flicked him on the raw. "Is her husband wealthier than you?" she asked.

"I doubt it."

She grinned. "How gratifying."

That made him laugh. "You are a wicked girl, Marjorie."

"I'm not," she protested. "Don't misunderstand. I have a lot of sympathy for her position. A woman needs to know that her children will have a home and be taken care of properly, and a tiny apartment in

Brooklyn wouldn't be very nice for them. But I see your side of it, too. She didn't trust you to take care of her, and that, on top of what your father did, must have been a painful betrayal. And you said you had things to prove, so it must have been quite satisfying to know that you ended up richer than the man she did marry."

"Perhaps," he admitted, "but she wasn't the main one I wanted to prove things to. That would be my father. And though I enjoy making money for the challenge of it, material considerations don't really matter much to me. I came to realize that once I struck it rich."

"What does matter to you, then?" she asked, curious. "What do you want from life?"

"That," he said slowly, "is an interesting question. Ten years ago, I was sure I knew the answer, but . . ."

"But?" she prompted when he paused.

He looked down, staring into his glass, watching the bubbles rise, silent so long, she thought he wasn't going to reply.

"Do you remember our conversation this morning?" he asked at last, looking up. "When I told you I know how it feels to have all one's dreams snatched away?"

"Yes."

"My grandfather was a shrewd man of business. He inherited two newspapers from his father and proceeded to build Deverill Publishing into an empire. In its heyday, we had twelve dailies, five weeklies, and several magazines."

She could hear a new note come into his voice as he spoke, a note of pride. "So, running the family business was your dream?"

"More than that, I believed it was my destiny. My grandfather seemed to believe it, too. He often said I was just like him—that I had ink in my veins instead of blood, and that he knew I would be able to carry on what he had built, expand Deverill Publishing even more and take it into the next century. Unfortunately, he never got around to putting his faith in me in writing."

"Meaning?"

"He never made a will."

"What? But why not?"

"The attorneys said he kept procrastinating. It's quite common, they said. Anyway, when he died, everything went to my father, who proved to be a dismally bad steward of my supposed destiny. By the time I was eighteen, the company was sailing very near the wind. I tried to avert the disaster, but my father wasn't about to listen to advice from his adolescent son. We had a flaming row—not our first, by the way—and he told me that since I thought myself a better man of business than he, I ought to have the chance to prove it."

"That's why he disinherited you and left you destitute? Because you tried to help him?"

"Well, in all fairness, I also called him an incompetent idiot and told him he was unworthy of the Deverill name. It was stupid, but then, my father and I had always been like matches and gunpowder, even when I was a boy. Whenever we were in the same room, there were bound to be explosions."

"Couldn't you have mended your quarrel? Apologized?"

"For what? Being right? Hell, no." He grinned, but in his hazel eyes, she could see a glittering defiance, something she suspected his father had seen often. "You said yourself I'm not good at apologies."

"Or compromises," she replied, giving him a pointed look.

He gave her a wry one in return. "That's rich, coming from you. But," he added before she could reply, "in all seriousness, I don't think any attempts to compromise with my father would have made any difference. He was a weak, vain, and selfish man, and after my mother died, he began to crack. Later, when my grandfather died, when he found he'd inherited everything, it went to his head, and because he didn't have my mother's steadying influence, he fell completely apart. Only my sisters could reason with him, and even they couldn't save him from his own incompetence. After I left, he eventually bankrupted the company. I sent money when I could, but there wasn't much else I could do."

"Your sisters couldn't smooth things over?"

"They tried, but my father wasn't having any. In fact, for the first couple years I was gone, my sisters didn't even know where I was.

Unbeknownst to them or me, our father was suppressing our letters. He was a spiteful cove."

"What happened to the company? Did it go under?"

"Irene, my eldest sister, managed to save it. She salvaged one of the newspapers by inventing an advice column called *Dear Lady True-love*. The thing became wildly popular, enabling Deverill Publishing to stave off the creditors, and she ran that paper for several years. She left my father's name on the masthead and pretended to consult him to soothe his pride, but she's the one who kept it afloat and made it a success."

She smiled. "It sounds like you're not the only one in your family with ink in your veins."

"Oh, no, both my sisters have proved themselves to be just as much chips off Grandfather's block as I was." He glanced past her. "Here's your baroness coming back, and since she's looking like a cat who's fallen into the cream, I think it's safe to say that the count and his mother do indeed want to meet you. As if there was any doubt."

She made a face at him. "Their willingness to meet me doesn't validate your opinion of the count's intentions."

"Maybe not, but I've no doubt the man's a bounder. He's got an oily, predatory look about him. As your guardian, I intend to make it clear that if he's angling for anything beyond an introduction, he's doomed to disappointment."

Marjorie made a sound of protest at such high-handedness. "I have no say in this?"

He gave a laugh that answered her question even before he spoke. "No."

"But how do you know anything about the man's character?" she asked. "Have you met him before?"

"Never in my life, but he makes my boot itch."

Marjorie frowned, bewildered. "What's your boot got to do with it?"

"Whenever I glance his way, I experience an instinctive, almost ir-resistible urge to kick him straight out the door and over the side."

"Since it would likely ruin everyone's evening, I'd ask that you refrain," she murmured, pasting a smile on her face and turning toward the baroness as she halted in front of them.

"My dear," the older woman said, slipping between her and Jonathan to take her arm, "the *contessa* does wish to meet you, so I come to bring you to her. With your permission, Mr. Deverill?"

"How kind of you to consider my wishes, madam."

Baroness Vasiliev didn't seem to notice the sarcasm. "The count is from Spain," she told Marjorie as she began leading her across the room. "But his English is excellent and his manners impeccable. You will find him most agreeable, I am sure."

Behind her, Marjorie thought she heard Jonathan give a snort of derision, but with the voices eddying all around them, she couldn't be certain. Either way, unlike her guardian, she was prepared to be open-minded. "Being a count," she said to the baroness, "he has estates, I suppose?"

"Oh, yes. Vast estates."

"Where?" she asked when the baroness did not elaborate.

"Oh, somewhere in the middle, I think. Cádiz, would it be?"

Marjorie knew Cádiz was nowhere near the middle of Spain, but she didn't point that out, for the baroness was clearly guessing, and besides, they were coming within earshot of the count and his mother.

"Contessa," the baroness greeted as she and Marjorie halted in front of the other woman. "May I present my friend, Miss McGann? Marjorie, the Dowager Contessa de la Rosa."

Thanks to the rigorous training of Forsyte Academy, Marjorie was able to offer a perfect curtsy, though because of the tightness of her gown, it wasn't very deep. "My lady."

"Miss McGann." The countess gestured to the man beside her. "This is my son, the Count de la Rosa. Étienne, Miss Marjorie McGann."

The count stepped forward. "I am delighted to meet you, Miss McGann," he said in a deep, languorous voice that seemed to bring with it all the warmth of his homeland.

He bent over her hand, and when his lips brushed her glove, Marjorie felt for the second time in her life the thrill that came from such masculine attentions, and when he straightened, that thrill grew stronger at the appreciation she saw in his black eyes.

Jonathan must have seen it, too, for he stepped forward as if to come between them, but Marjorie could have told him that playing the overprotective guardian was pointless.

This is what I've longed for, she thought, basking in the count's admiration like a plant in a sunlit window. *I will never go back to living in seclusion.*

Chapter 7

Jonathan had lived on the American frontier for a long time, a place where a woman's romantic interest—the kind that wasn't paid for, anyway—was hard to come by. Nonetheless, he'd been the recipient of such interest often enough to recognize it when he saw it. And he saw it now, on Marjorie's face as she looked at the Count de la Rosa.

He stared at the innocent beauty he'd sworn to look after, and as she bestowed a dazzling smile on the other man, Jonathan's hackles rose and warning prickled along his spine. When her cheeks flushed pink and her gloved hand lifted to touch the side of her neck in a fluttering, feminine gesture, he knew damn well what it meant, though he could not for the life of him understand how the count could inspire her attraction.

He glanced at the count, baffled that any girl with sense would be attracted to this blackguard. De la Rosa was staring at Marjorie, his full-lipped, too-red mouth curved in an answering smile that told Jonathan at once what the fellow was thinking.

His own lip curled in instinctive response, and from his throat came a sound that he'd never made in his life before, a low, deep, almost primal snarl.

Unfortunately, Marjorie and her pestilential admirer didn't seem to hear it, though he wasn't sure if that was because of the noise of the crowd eddying around them or because they were too fascinated with each other to notice anything else. Either way, he knew this little tête-à-tête had to be cut off before it could blossom into a romance.

The baroness introduced Jonathan, forcing de la Rosa's attention away from Marjorie, at least for the moment. After bowing to the *contessa*, Jonathan turned toward her son, his body tensing, and as they faced each other, he felt rather as if they were duelists en garde.

"Comte," he said, inclining his head a fraction, the briefest acknowledgement civility allowed, his gaze locked with the other man's. "Delighted."

His voice made it clear he was anything but, and much to his satisfaction, the count's dark gaze faltered and slid away. Just then, the notes of a bugle sounded, indicating that dinner was about to be served, thereby saving them both from any pretense of civil conversation.

"Ah, dinner," Jonathan said, injecting a joviality into his voice he didn't feel in the least. "We'd best go in. A pleasure to meet you both." He gave another slight bow, then turned to the woman beside him. "Marjorie?"

He offered his arm, and she took it, though the wry look she gave him made it clear she was aware of the undercurrent of tension, a tension Jonathan soon learned was not destined to be relieved by the evening meal, at least not as far as he was concerned.

As they took their places at the long center table reserved for the captain and his guests, he discovered, much to his chagrin, that Marjorie was seated beside the count, the baroness on her other side, while his own seat was across the table and several places farther down, making it impossible for him to hear their conversation or intervene in it should the need arise. And if all that wasn't bad enough, he could see the count's smarmy face every time he looked up from his plate.

The man was a jackal, ready to pounce on Marjorie the moment Jonathan's back was turned. It would be well within his character to attempt to get her alone, to tempt her to secret assignations, perhaps even to compromise her. There would soon be other jackals circling as well, and his ward seemed to have no inclination whatsoever to keep any of them at bay. Making things worse, his ability to watch over her was limited, and the baroness could not be relied upon to assist him.

Really, he thought in aggravation, if Marjorie was going to hire herself a chaperone, couldn't she have at least hired a competent and trustworthy one?

But that sort of chaperone, he supposed grimly, might get in her way.

I am going to laugh and dance and enjoy myself . . . and I don't give a damn if any of that breaks rules of propriety, offends society, or inconveniences you.

As her words of earlier came back to him, he looked past the baroness, scanning the remaining faces along that side of the table in a desperate search for help, but it was a useless effort, for of course he recognized no one. He needed allies aboard ship, but where was he going to find any?

"Mr. Deverill? Jonathan Deverill?"

He turned at the sound of his name. Standing by his chair was the elderly countess Marjorie and the baroness had been discussing earlier, and he rose to his feet at once.

"I am Lady Stansbury," she said as she waved him back down and settled herself into the seat beside him. "It isn't quite the thing to introduce oneself, I know, but . . ." She paused, gesturing to her place card. "It seems we are to be dinner companions this evening, so I hope you won't mind."

"Not at all, Countess," he answered, rather glad of the distraction.

"I'm more familiar with your family than you might realize. I know the duchess, your sister, quite well. We're neighbors." She smiled in the face of his surprise. "Chalton, the Earl of Stansbury's estate, is not far from Ravenwood, the Duke of Torquil's ducal seat."

"Indeed?" Jonathan studied the countess, noting her firm mouth and imperious eyes, and he realized the solution to his problem might very well be sitting right here beside him.

THE COUNT, MARJORIE was delighted to discover, was every bit as charming as the baroness had claimed. He made a point of signaling for the waiter whenever her wineglass was empty, even blotting wine from her fingertips with his own napkin when several drops of the claret being poured spilled over her hand.

Having been cut off from any sort of male company for most of her existence, Marjorie couldn't help being both flattered and thrilled by the count's assiduous attentions, especially since he proved a most entertaining dinner companion.

One mention of his family vineyards in Spain, which were not near Cádiz at all but Córdoba, and she was captivated. As he told stories of his Continental lifestyle, so different and so much more exciting than her own life had been, she couldn't help hanging on every word.

Of course, it didn't hurt that he was such a treat to look at. Jonathan thought the man a "bounder," and though she wasn't certain just what that British term meant, it was clear her guardian hadn't intended it to be a compliment. But regardless of what Jonathan thought of it, Marjorie was as happy as the next girl to bask in the attentions of a man with flashing dark eyes, a dazzling smile, and impeccable manners.

Sadly, such delights never lasted as long as one might wish. The dessert course had just been cleared away when the men began rising to depart for the smoking room, and Marjorie found her guardian at her elbow, hovering like a black cloud about to dump rain on a picnic. Even worse, he had company.

"Miss McGann," he said, gesturing to the gray-haired English-woman by his side as Marjorie and her companions stood up. "The Countess of Stansbury has expressed the desire to make your acquaintance."

"Lady Stansbury," she murmured, glancing at Jonathan as she offered a curtsy. "You two know each other?"

"We didn't, but then we found ourselves seated side by side at dinner," the countess explained, "and discovered we have acquaintances in common. The Duke and Duchess of Torquil are my neighbors in Hampshire. I also know Mr. Deverill's other sister, Lady Galbraith, and their grandmother, too. So, Mr. Deverill and I were able to have a most pleasant chat over dinner. Baroness," she added coolly, giving the woman beside Marjorie a brief nod before turning to the count. "De la Rosa," she greeted him, her manner growing even colder. "I thought you were still on the Riviera."

He bowed. "I had a fancy to see New York, Lady Stansbury. Now, I go to London."

"Indeed? How lovely." With that polite, dismissive remark, she returned her attention to Marjorie. "Miss McGann, please allow me to offer you my sympathies on the death of your father."

Without warning, a lump formed in Marjorie's throat, a reaction she didn't understand at all, and she forced herself to say something. "Thank you, Lady Stansbury."

"I was devastated to learn of your situation."

"My situation?"

"Why, yes. Losing your only relation, going into mourning . . ." She paused, one gray eyebrow lifting in well-bred censure as she glanced over Marjorie's gown. "This must be such a difficult time for you. Not, I fear, a good time to be without help and guidance."

The one difficulty with her situation as far as she could see was her interfering guardian, but Marjorie didn't say so. "Thank you, ma'am," she murmured, "but I'm managing well enough."

"Of course you are. But Miss McGann, let me reassure you that you are not alone in this awful time."

"That is true," Baroness Vasiliev put in. "Dear Marjorie has me to look out for her."

"Yes," Lady Stansbury drawled, managing to insert a wealth of skepticism into the word. "Quite so. But Mr. Deverill has asked for my assistance as well."

Marjorie stiffened in alarm. "He has?"

"Yes, indeed. I have many friends aboard, and we shall see to it that you are chaperoned at all times." She beamed complacently at Marjorie. "By the time our voyage is over, we shall be the best of friends, I'm sure."

Oh, that impossible man.

"How nice," she said, forcing a happy note into her voice even as she turned to give Jonathan a scathing glance over her shoulder.

It was wasted on him, however, for he wasn't looking at her. He was looking at Lady Stansbury, but there was a tiny smile curving the edges of his mouth that told her he knew quite well how she felt at this moment.

"Forgive me, ladies," he said with a bow, "but with Marjorie in your capable hands, I shall adjourn with the other gentlemen to the smoking room for a glass of port. Count? Shall you join me?"

De la Rosa shook his head. "No, thank you. I do not care for port. I prefer to remain with the ladies."

"Of course you do," Jonathan murmured, and it struck Marjorie with force just how accomplished the British were at making the most innocuous words sound like an insult.

A provoking smile still hovering on his lips, Jonathan bowed and turned away to join the other men filing up the grand staircase to head for the smoking room.

Marjorie watched him go through narrowed eyes, hoping he could feel the daggerlike stare she was giving his back, but somehow, she doubted it. Daggers couldn't penetrate granite rock.

ALL IN ALL, Jonathan was satisfied with his arrangements. Lady Stansbury had been sympathetic over his partner's death, appalled that the girl had no one but Baroness Vasiliev to chaperone her until they reached London, and happy to tell him just how inappropriate the other woman was as chaperone for an impressionable young woman.

"Charity ball, my eye," the countess had said with a disdainful sniff. "She and her friends intended to pocket most of that money for themselves, Mr. Deverill, don't tell me otherwise."

Jonathan, who'd already formed a similar theory about the incident the baroness had related, had possessed no desire to contradict her. Instead, he'd expressed the proper amount of astonishment at the countess's information, concluded with sad resignation that the baroness's connection to his sister the duchess must have been exaggerated, and expressed his abject shame at having been deceived.

Lady Stansbury had forgiven him for his lapse as a guardian. As a mere man, he'd been told, he couldn't be expected to watch over a young lady, especially not one who'd been subjected to American notions of good society. Their dinner together had concluded quite satisfactorily, and now, with Marjorie in the care of the right sort of chaperone and a glass of excellent vintage port at his elbow, Jonathan began to feel his worries were at bay.

That thought had barely floated across his mind before a flash of scarlet caught his eye, and Jonathan looked up to find Baroness Vasiliev passing the open doorway of the smoking room, her steps hurried as she walked along the promenade deck.

Jonathan frowned as she passed out of his line of vision. It didn't matter to him that she was neglecting her duty, since he knew Lady Stansbury was sticking to Marjorie like glue, but he was curious. Where was the baroness going?

As if in answer to his unspoken question, the Count de la Rosa walked by, his steps every bit as quick and furtive as the baroness's had been.

Jonathan's brows rose as de la Rosa passed the doorway and vanished from view. The baroness and the count engaged in a romantic rendezvous? Or perhaps, he thought, staring at the open doorway, something far more devious was in the wind, something that might involve his ward.

I'm such a suspicious devil, he thought as he downed the last of his port and stood up. "Pardon me, gentlemen," he murmured to the other men at the table, "but I feel the need for some air."

Bowing, he left the smoking room and slipped out to follow the count. De la Rosa was nowhere in sight, but Jonathan turned in the direction the other man had been heading, glancing into the various rooms that opened onto the promenade as he walked. He spied neither the count nor the baroness in the billiard room, the reading room, or the observation saloon, but when he rounded the bow, familiar voices came to his ear, and he paused, straining to listen.

The voices were low, coming from behind the stairway leading to the deck above, but though he could not hear what they were saying, he could discern that the voices did in fact belong to the people he was looking for.

Certain something devious was afoot, he had no compunction about eavesdropping on the pair, and he eased closer, moving softly so as not to be detected.

"I've introduced you to an heiress, just as you asked," the baroness was saying as Jonathan paused again. "I even got you placed beside her at dinner."

"An amazing accomplishment, Katya. I wonder how you managed it?"

"I sneaked into the dining room earlier when no one was there and rearranged the place cards," the baroness answered and laughed. "Did you notice how I put that guardian of hers far, far down the table?"

"You are a woman in a thousand."

"Flattery is all very well," she murmured, "but it is not what you promised me."

"Indeed."

There was a brief silence, during which money no doubt changed hands, then the baroness said, "I hope you made the most of your opportunity?"

"These things always take time to arrange," de la Rosa answered. "But yes, I believe the young lady is amenable to my company."

Those words and the complacency in the man's voice as he said them made Jonathan want to grind his teeth, but he refrained. Instead, he leaned closer.

"If your intent is to win the girl's hand in marriage, you've got a long way to go," she replied. "She may be innocent, but she is not a fool."

"My dear Katya," de la Rosa said, sounding amused, "you do not have to tell me how to deal with women."

"Perhaps not, but in any case, she is not your greatest problem," the baroness said, her voice suddenly sharp. "It is her guardian and Lady Stansbury about whom you should worry."

"Bah." The count made a dismissive sound. "They can't watch her every minute. I can easily persuade the girl to slip free if I choose."

Not while I breathe air, Jonathan vowed.

"You are far too arrogant," the baroness complained. "The girl is more intelligent than you give her credit for. As for her guardian, you underestimate him at your peril."

Jonathan decided he'd heard enough and stepped around the staircase. "Indeed, he does, baroness," he said, smiling with satisfaction as he watched the other man's eyes widen in alarm. "Indeed, he does."

Chapter 8

The nefarious pair stared at him for several seconds, clearly nonplussed. The Count de la Rosa recovered first.

"I believe eavesdropping on conversations is not considered comme il faut," he said. "Even among the English."

"Bad form, I agree," Jonathan said with an air of cheer he didn't feel in the least. "On the other hand, I've never been a man to be hampered by the niceties of etiquette."

"That," the count said coldly, "does not surprise me."

"No?" Jonathan smiled. "Then we are both tediously predictable, it seems."

The man had the gall to seem bewildered. "I do not take your meaning."

"Comte de la Rosa, your dishonorable intentions toward my ward are clear as glass."

"I?" de la Rosa gasped, pressing a hand to his breast, staring at Jonathan as if astonished. "Have dishonorable intentions toward a young lady? You misjudge me, sir."

"Do I?"

The count assumed a pretense of haughty dignity. "I am willing to send my seconds to you, Monsieur Deverill, if that is what you desire."

Jonathan laughed. "My dear count, there's no need for such theatrics. Duels are quite passé nowadays. But I'm sure your tales of such exploits impress the ladies at dinner parties."

"I am in earnest, sir."

"I doubt it. But either way," he went on before the other man could argue, "you aren't worth the trouble of a duel. I must confess, however, that the idea of giving you a sound thrashing tempts me enormously." He moved closer, grinning as the other man took a step back. "If I see you anywhere near Miss McGann again, I'll do it, too, by God. Now go, before I forget I'm a gentleman."

"The English are savages," the count complained, but when Jonathan took another step toward him, he seemed to decide retreat was in order. "Baroness, I fear I must leave you."

The count gave her a hasty bow, whirled around, and fled, almost running in his haste to be away. Laughing, Jonathan watched him go, but when he returned his attention to the baroness, his amusement faded, for she was attempting to follow the count's example by escaping in the opposite direction.

"One more step," he called, "and I will inform the purser of the liberties you take with his table arrangements."

She stopped, heaved a sigh, and turned around. "You're mad," she said with an air of aristocratic dignity that was almost convincing. "I have no idea what you are raving about."

"Spare me protestations of innocence, madam." He reached into the breast pocket of his evening jacket and pulled out his notecase. "They are futile and unnecessary."

She stared as he opened the case and pulled out a handful of notes. "How much did the count offer you for tonight's little escapade?" he asked as he began counting dollars.

"I—I—" She broke off any stuttering attempts at denial when he paused and looked up. "One thousand dollars."

He lifted a brow at the sum, rather impressed by the count's thoroughness. "I suppose anything worth doing is worth doing well," he murmured as he resumed counting. "And how much has he offered for you to arrange an assignation between him and my ward that would be witnessed by others?"

The baroness made a sound of outrage, causing Jonathan to pause.

"Really, baroness," he said in amusement, "I thought I'd made it clear there's no need for pretenses between us now."

"I make no pretense. Allow a man to compromise a young lady to ruin her? Never would I do such a thing. Never!"

"Your scruples prohibit it, do they?"

"I would not do what you say. Rearrange a few place settings? Yes, why not? Encourage the girl to consider his suit? Yes, perhaps. But open her to scandal and shame? No, I would not ever do that."

She was so vehement that Jonathan couldn't help being impressed. "You're a better actress than I gave you credit for. But let's not argue. Believe me, it's better for you to place your bets on me than on de la Rosa. More lucrative, too."

He folded the wad of notes he'd counted and held them out. "Here is five hundred dollars. See me tomorrow, and I shall pay you a thousand more. You will also have an additional thousand when we reach London, if you do as I say. Betray me," he added, pulling his hand back when she stretched out hers to take the money, "and not only will you not be paid the remainder, I will hound you, and ruin you, and drive you out of any position you may have somehow managed to carve for yourself in good society. Is that clear?"

"Yes." She pulled the money from his fingers. "What is it you want me to do, Englishman?"

LADY STANSBURY, SADLY, was a much less entertaining conversationalist than Baroness Vasiliev. The Count de la Rosa seemed to share Marjorie's opinion of the Englishwoman, for after the baroness had excused herself with a discreet murmur in Marjorie's ear about needing to visit the ladies' withdrawing room, the count had managed to tolerate just a few minutes of Lady Stansbury's conversation about the breeding of terriers for ratting before remembering a promise to join his friends in the cardroom. Wistfully, Marjorie had watched him escape, trying to take some consolation in the long, lingering glance of admiration and regret the count had given her over his shoulder as he left.

In the wake of his departure, several of Lady Stansbury's elderly friends joined Marjorie and the countess, and the subject of terriers was abandoned. That brought Marjorie no relief, however, for the conversation somehow became centered on the moral laxness of young people nowadays.

This discussion was accompanied by several glances at the low neckline of Marjorie's evening gown, making her feel terribly self-conscious, and it was a struggle not to squirm under their disapproving scrutiny. She also began to feel the effects of her three glasses of wine, and when the conversation turned to what constituted a proper herbaceous border—whatever that was—she almost fell asleep in her chair. When the baroness finally returned, Marjorie's relief was so great, she wanted to hug the Russian woman in gratitude.

Hoping to spare herself any more discussion of alstroemerias and verbascums, she stood up. Expressing the wish for a bit of fresh air, she suggested to the baroness that they take a stroll on the promenade deck before bed, but the other woman shook her head in refusal.

"Forgive me," she said and reached for her evening bag, "but I do not feel well and must return to my cabin. Lady Stansbury, would you be so kind as to escort Marjorie to her stateroom when you retire?"

She turned away without another word, and Marjorie frowned in bewildered concern. "Whatever is the matter, I wonder?"

"Probably ate something that didn't agree," the countess commented.

Marjorie wasn't quite satisfied by that explanation, nor did she have any intention of being stuck here with Lady Stansbury on her own. "Perhaps," she murmured. "But if you will forgive me, ladies, I think I should go with the baroness and make sure she's all right. After that, I shall retire to my own cabin for the night."

"If you're going after the baroness, you'd better hurry," the countess advised, glancing past Marjorie's shoulder.

Turning her head, Marjorie was surprised to find the baroness already starting up the grand staircase. She rose, slung her wrap around her shoulders, and reached for her bag, then mumbled a quick farewell, dipped a curtsy, and followed as quickly as she could.

Ascending a staircase in a tight-fitting gown, however, wasn't easy, and by the time Marjorie reached the top of the stairs, the baroness had already turned down the corridor that led to the first-class staterooms. Marjorie quickened her steps, but she was only halfway to the corridor before she heard a voice calling her name, and when she turned her head, she saw Jonathan coming through the doors that led out onto the promenade.

"Hullo," he greeted as he joined her. "What are you doing up here? I thought you'd be with the other ladies in the dining room."

"I was, but the baroness seems to have taken ill, and I want to be sure it isn't anything serious."

They turned into the corridor together just in time to see Baroness Vasiliev stepping into her room.

"Baroness?" Marjorie called, causing the other woman to pause in the doorway. "Are you all right?"

"I shall be," she answered, giving them an abstracted smile. "I'm sure I soon shall be."

"We all hope so, of course," Jonathan murmured.

"Is it a headache?" Marjorie asked. "If so, a poultice of ice and salt applied to the head works wonders. Shall I call a ship's maid to make you one?"

"No, no." Baroness Vasiliev shook her head. "That is very sweet of you, but all I need is sleep."

"Then we shan't keep you," Jonathan said politely. "Good night."

With a nod of farewell, the baroness went inside her cabin.

"Well, that was awfully sudden," Marjorie commented as the door closed behind the other woman. "I do hope she'll be all right."

"She's probably just tired. What about you?" he asked before she could reply.

"I think I'll go to bed as well."

"You don't wish to rejoin the other ladies?" he asked, falling in step beside her as she started down the corridor to her own room.

"Did you think I would?" she asked, giving him a wry look. "If you are going to set watchdogs upon me, you might at least make them interesting company."

A smile twitched his lips. "I don't know what you mean."

"Yes, you do."

"Well, yes, perhaps, I do," he conceded as they paused before her door and she opened her evening bag to retrieve her passkey. "And since we're on the topic of the company you keep, there's something I need to tell you."

He sounded so grave that Marjorie paused in unlocking the door and looked at him. "Something about the baroness?"

"Yes, indirectly, but I'm actually referring to that scoundrel, de la Rosa."

"Him again?" She groaned and resumed unlocking her door. "Just because he 'makes your boot itch,' as you put it, that doesn't prove he's a scoundrel."

"No, but what I witnessed earlier this evening does."

With an air of long suffering, she returned her key to her bag and snapped it shut. "What did you see him do?" she asked. "Drink too much wine with dinner? Lose too much money at the card table?"

"He paid the baroness for an introduction to you, and for her to arrange the seating so that you would be beside him."

"He did?" Marjorie laughed. "How clever of him. And what a compliment to me."

He blinked as if disconcerted, making it clear her reaction wasn't quite the one he'd been expecting. "You think what he did was a compliment?"

"Of course! From the sound of it, he went to a great deal of trouble. Any girl would find that flattering."

"His intentions are more nefarious than gaining your company for dinner."

"You don't know that. In fact, how do you even know that he did this at all? Or that the baroness was involved?"

"After dinner, I saw her go by the smoking room, and then I saw the count coming hard on her heels. I was curious, so I followed them. I overheard them talking—"

"So, we can add eavesdropping on other people's conversations to the list of things I can expect from you?"

"If that's what it takes to keep you from bad company, then yes. The count is on the hunt for an heiress, just as I suspected, and he's been paying the baroness to assist him with introductions. Neither of them can be trusted, but the count is the real danger. His intention is to win your hand by any means, however dishonorable."

"That may be clear to you, but it isn't to me. Wrangling for an introduction and having a few seats rearranged seems rather flimsy evidence to condemn a man's entire character."

"A true gentleman doesn't need to pay for such things."

"I don't doubt that a true lady would be offended by such conduct, but since no man has ever had any intentions about me, dishonorable or otherwise, I just can't work up the proper amount of ladylike outrage to condemn him for it. I appreciate the warning, but I shall reserve judgement for now."

"Just don't ever allow yourself to be alone with him."

"I don't intend to," she said with dignity. Shoving open her door, she stepped inside her cabin and turned to face him again. "That's why I hired myself a chaperone in the first place."

"One who now seems ill and unable to fulfill her duties."

"I'm sure the baroness will be fine tomorrow," she cut in before he could suggest any more nonsense about her staying in her room. "Good night."

With that, she shut the door between them, and she could only hope the baroness's illness was temporary, because staying in her room for the next six days was just not an option she was willing to consider.

The following morning, however, Marjorie's hopes for the baroness's quick recovery were futile, a fact she learned from a most unlikely source.

"Seasick?" Through the doorway of her cabin, Marjorie stared at Lady Stansbury in dismay. "The baroness is seasick?"

"I'm afraid so." The countess shook her head sadly. "If she'd eaten a few digestive biscuits when she first came aboard, she'd be right as rain, but now it's too late. She'll just have to lie abed until it passes."

"How awful. Will she be ill for long, do you think?"

"Who can say? Some people find their sea legs in a day or two, while others spend the whole voyage in bed. At present, the poor woman's quite indisposed."

"I see. Well, um . . . thank you, my lady," Marjorie murmured, uncertain what else to say. "It was thoughtful of you to inform me of the situation."

Most people would have taken those words as an end to the conversation, but the countess was oblivious to such subtleties.

Instead of departing, she smiled and leaned through the doorway to pat Marjorie's arm. "You mustn't worry, my dear. Your guardian and I have discussed the situation and made all the arrangements."

"What arrangements?"

"With the baroness ill, Mr. Deverill has asked me to step in."

A feeling of dismay began settling in Marjorie's stomach. "You are to be my chaperone until the baroness recovers?"

"Yes, indeed. Won't that be lovely?"

"Lovely" wasn't how Marjorie would have put it. "How kind you are," she said instead, forcing a smile. "But—"

"I'm happy to do it. Having raised four daughters of my own, I know just how crucial it is for a girl to have strict guidance and strong support at all times. Now," she added before Marjorie could ponder just how strict the said guidance was likely to be, "I've already spoken with ship's housekeeping, and they will have your things moved into my suite by luncheon."

Marjorie cursed herself for ever opening her door. "Oh, that's not necessary. I am very comfortable here in my own cabin."

Lady Stansbury laughed, dismissing any possibility that she could remain here. "You can't stay in a cabin by yourself, my dear. It's unthinkable. What the baroness was about to allow such an arrangement, I can't imagine."

Marjorie murmured something vague about a mistake in the reservations and how the purser was to arrange for her and the baroness to move into adjoining cabins today.

"Ah, well, that explains things, I suppose," Lady Stansbury said dubiously. "In any case, with the baroness ill, it's been decided you'll stay with me for the rest of the voyage."

Marjorie didn't have to ask whose decision that had been.

"Now," the countess continued, "I understand you've brought no maid with you? That's all right," she added as Marjorie shook her head. "My maid can easily attend you."

"I shouldn't wish to be any trouble," Marjorie began, feeling a bit desperate.

"Nonsense. How much trouble could you be? You're in mourning, so you won't be needing to change your ensemble multiple times a day. In fact, I don't see that you'll be going about the ship very much at all. I hope you brought your needlework?"

Marjorie, who hated needlework, shook her head.

"Ah, well, my friends and I have plenty to keep you occupied. No idle hands in our set," she said with a laugh. "We've formed a little circle for the voyage. Embroidery, knitting, a bit of gossip, that sort of thing. We're far too old for shuffleboard and such things. And since you shan't be doing any of those things either, it's perfect for you to join us. And you can make yourself useful in so many ways—fetching things, you know, and reading aloud, threading needles, and winding wool."

"How lovely."

The countess missed the lack of enthusiasm in her voice. "In grief, it's so important, I think, for one to keep busy." She smiled, giving Marjorie's arm another pat. "So, you see? You won't be an inconvenience to anyone."

When it came to Lady Stansbury, that might be true, but Marjorie knew that when it came to her guardian, she intended to be a great inconvenience indeed.

WITH MARJORIE IN the hands of Lady Stansbury and her friends, and with the baroness consigned to her cabin for the remainder of the voyage, Jonathan was finally able to enjoy a bit of peace and quiet.

He ate a leisurely breakfast, then put himself in the hands of the ship's barber for a shave and a proper haircut, pleasures of civilized life he hadn't had much opportunity to enjoy during the past decade. He then sought out the purser, inquired about a tour of the ship, and— probably due to Marjorie's mention the night before of his sister the duchess—he was immediately offered one by the purser himself.

The next few hours passed in the blink of an eye, for Jonathan found the intricate workings of an ocean liner absolutely fascinating. As a result, he missed the first seating for luncheon, and he did not see Marjorie and her slew of elderly chaperones at the second, but when he took a stroll late that afternoon, he spied her holed up in a sheltered corner of the promenade deck, suitably dressed in her black suit and an unadorned black blouse buttoned up to her chin. Around her hands, she was holding a skein of wool so that her chaperone could wind the yarn into a ball.

"Ladies," he said, doffing his hat and giving her a smile as he went by. Marjorie gave one in return, but he wasn't the least bit fooled by it, for he could feel her gaze boring into his back as he walked on.

He did feel rather sorry for her, surrounded as she was by women at least four decades older than she, but he couldn't afford to soften, even a little. If he did, she'd take full advantage of it.

With a couple hours until dinner, he decided it was an ideal time to get some work done, and he returned to his stateroom. He was soon immersed in financial statements and stock reports, but it wasn't long before a knock on his door interrupted. "Come in," he called, thinking only a member of ship's staff would be knocking on his door at this time of day.

He found he was mistaken, however, for it was Marjorie who walked in, already dressed for dinner in the baroness's scandalous black velvet gown. "We need to talk. Right now."

Jonathan fell back in his chair with a sigh. So much for peace and quiet.

Chapter 9

*P*utting his ward in Lady Stansbury's hands had enabled Jonathan to enjoy a serene, relaxed afternoon, but one look at Marjorie's face told him that blissful interlude had just come to an end.

"Tell me," he said as he tossed aside his pen, stood up, and turned toward her, "is invading my rooms going to become a habit with you?"

"You did say, 'Come in,'" she pointed out as she closed the door behind her.

"So I did," he conceded, consoling himself for the fact that Marjorie was in his cabin with the reminder that this time around, he was at least fully dressed. "What have you done with Lady Stansbury?"

"I tossed her overboard."

A picture of that scenario came into his mind, and he almost smiled. He checked it just in time, giving her a skeptical look instead.

"It will happen," she said, noting his expression, "if this intolerable situation is allowed to continue."

From what he knew of Marjorie thus far, he could not be *completely* sure her threat was tongue-in-cheek. "Tossing certain people overboard," he said, giving her a meaningful glance, "is a temptation I'm coming to know rather well."

"Oh, you poor man," she said as she turned away and began to pace. "You're so put upon, having to deal with me. But you have no idea what I've been dealing with."

"Unless I miss my guess, you're about to tell me. On the assumption that you did not toss her over the side, where is Lady Stansbury?"

"She and her friends are still having tea and enjoying a healthy dose of scandalmongering along with it. You should hear the way they gossip about people—the odious conclusions they draw and the rumors they spread, and all of it without a shred of evidence that I can see. Horrid cats."

"Gossip is a favorite pastime of the typical British matron, so you'd best get used to it, if you want to be in British society. And if they're having tea, then why aren't you with them? You certainly shouldn't be here," he felt compelled to add, though as he studied her in that dress, he was uncertain if that reminder was for her, or for him. "Where does the countess think you are?"

She stopped pacing. "Oh," she groaned, swaying on her feet, pressing one hand to her forehead while she reached out with the other to grasp the back of the wingback chair beside her. "I've such a headache," she mumbled. "I must go lie down."

Alarmed, he started toward her, then realized he'd just been made for a mug and stopped again.

"Were you this accomplished a liar at Forsyte Academy?" he asked as she abandoned the pretense of a headache and resumed pacing. "Or has the baroness been giving you acting lessons?"

"She's in no condition to do that, or much else, either. She's seasick, as you already know."

"Yes, I did hear something about that," he acknowledged, trying not to laugh. "Poor woman."

Despite his best efforts to sound nonchalant, some of his amused satisfaction must have shown on his face, for when she glanced his way, she stopped again, her eyes narrowing in suspicion. "What did you do?" she demanded. "Pay the waiter to put an emetic in her dinner last night?"

Caught, he made the best of it and smiled. "I didn't pay the waiter to do anything."

She understood his clarification at once. "You paid the baroness to pretend seasickness? You did," she added as his smile widened. "Of all the devious, highhanded—"

She broke off with a sound of exasperation and continued to pace. "I should have known you'd do something like that. And how like you to stick me with Lady Stansbury instead."

"It's not my fault you chose a chaperone who could be bought. And the baroness, being a practical woman as well as stone broke, appreciated that I would be a more lucrative source of income than you. As for Lady Stansbury, she is a much more appropriate chaperone than Baroness Vasiliev. And," he added as she made a sound of derision, "you'd be wise to stay in her good graces. She lives very near my sister, and if you end up staying with Irene, you'll see a great deal of the woman in the future."

"Lucky me," Marjorie muttered, turning at the wall to go back across the cabin. "She's a dragon."

"She is, isn't she?" he agreed with immense satisfaction, knowing de la Rosa wouldn't dare come anywhere near Marjorie if Lady Stansbury was in the vicinity.

"She's moved me into her suite, you know—lock, stock, and barrel. She unpacked all my things without even asking me, and went through all my clothes, piece by piece. She even went through my unmentionables!"

Involuntarily, Jonathan's gaze lowered, skimming over Marjorie's figure in immediate speculation.

"Do you have any idea how embarrassing it is for me to have a woman I don't even know studying my undergarments and clicking her tongue with disapproval over even the tiniest bit of lace or ribbon?"

How much lace? he wondered, watching the sway of her hips as she moved back and forth in front of him in her tight-fitting gown. *How many ribbons?*

"She said all the falderals—as she called them—will have to be removed. What does it matter if there's lace on my petticoats?" Marjorie demanded, her voice rising a notch as Jonathan's mind began sinking into the gutter. "No one's going to see them anyway. It's so ridiculous."

It seemed that way to him as well, but then, he was a man, and though he did possess some useful knowledge of women's underwear, he didn't know what mourning underwear was supposed to look like. Before he could offer an appropriate reply, however, Marjorie was off again.

"And then, she bundled up all the clothes that she'd decided were unsuitable and packed them into a trunk, declaring I'm no longer allowed to wear them."

"Even the underclothes?" he couldn't resist asking.

She gave him a scathing look as she passed him, clearly unamused. "Those she gave to her maid—all the ones I'm not wearing right this minute, anyway. She ordered the woman to remove anything that might be considered ornamental from every pair of drawers, every petticoat, every chemise, and every corset I own."

"That," he murmured with a most unguardianlike regret, "is a shame."

"And then do you know what she did? She ordered the purser to have the trunk with all my *unsuitable* clothes put in the hold. Oh, she was so superior, so arrogant, is it any wonder I want to pitch her overboard?"

With those words, Jonathan was forced to pull his mind away from the rather dangerous direction it had been heading and address the problem at hand. "Cheer up," he said, deciding an attempt at consolation was his best bet. "At least she didn't pack up your evening gown and put that in the hold."

"Oh, she tried." Marjorie gave him a triumphant smile as she passed. "But I explained that this gown belonged to Baroness Vasiliev. She immediately returned it, which I knew she would, and after I pleaded a headache, I went to the baroness and got it back."

"Of course you did," he murmured with a sigh.

"I don't even know this Lady Stansbury. Who is she to tell me what I can and can't wear? Who is she to tell her maid to alter my underclothes?"

"She is a woman of great influence, and when the time comes, she could prove a valuable connection for you. And having raised four daughters, she is fully aware of how to be a chaperone. For the time being, at least, I should advise you to trust her judgement."

"Do you, indeed?" Marjorie stopped and turned to face him. "I'm also under orders to stay in my room from the end of teatime onward, did you know that? I am not even to come down to dinner in the dining room."

"I can see," he said, glancing over her figure, "that's a dictum you don't intend to obey."

"Why should I? It's absurd. She says I can only dine in our suite. Anything I own that's even remotely pretty, I can't wear. I can't play shuffleboard, or cards, or games of any sort. I can read—but no novels. Provided, of course, she and her friends don't need me for other things. Because her maid's busy ruining all my undergarments, I'm expected to act as stand-in, threading needles, winding wool, and fetching and carrying without so much as a please or a thank-you. When did I become Lady Stansbury's second maid, second seam-stress, and general dogsbody?"

"Such tasks are probably meant to provide you with acceptable ways to occupy yourself during the voyage, not because she thinks you are a maid."

"Forgive me if I'm not willing to give the countess the benefit of the doubt on that score."

He tried again. "Marjorie, I realize that Lady Stansbury may seem overly strict, and she may not have approached taking over as your chaperone in the most tactful way. And I grant you, she and her friends are bound to be rather dull company, but—"

"Dull?" she interrupted with a groan. "Dull isn't the word! I know you think I'm difficult, and maybe a bit willful. But," she went on before he could concur with that assessment, "I hope to heaven I'm not dull."

"No," he conceded, and this time he just couldn't stop a smile. "I don't think I shall ever be able to say that about you, Marjorie."

"If that woman and her friends had anything interesting to discuss, I might be willing to sit and wind wool and embroider tea cloths with them, but all they seem able to talk about are gardens, dog breeding, and the latest scandals."

"Of which I do not want you to be one."

"I realize that, but—" She stopped, lifting her arms in utter frustration and letting them fall. "There has to be some middle ground here."

"Sadly, no. Even the most trivial thing can hurt your reputation, and I am not about to let that happen. A week of strict supervision won't kill you."

She set her jaw in a mutinous line. "If anyone's dead by the time we reach Southampton, it's going to be Lady Stansbury, not me."

He studied her face, realizing that if she was pushed too hard, she might rebel outright. What he needed was an incentive, something that would show her all that she could look forward to later on if she behaved with proper decorum now. "Wait here," he said on impulse and turned to pull his jacket from the back of his chair.

"Where are you going?"

He slid into his jacket and walked to the door. "Lock the door behind me, and for God's sake, don't let anyone in. I'll be right back."

He left the cabin, returning about ten minutes later.

"I want to show you something," he said as he relocked the door of his stateroom behind him and pocketed his key. "Come with me."

He walked into his bedroom, beckoning her to follow. "Sit here," he said, pulling out the chair in front of his dressing table as she came through the doorway.

"You're always talking about proprieties," she murmured, perching on the edge of the offered chair. "Being in your bedroom seems terribly improper to me."

It was an absolute scandal, but there was no point in underlining the fact by saying so. "It'll be our secret. And this won't take long. Close your eyes."

"Oh, very well." With the indulgent air of a schoolteacher humoring a pupil, she gave a sigh and complied. "I can't imagine what this is about."

"You'll see." He paused behind her chair, stretched out his arm, and tilted the mirror on his dressing table down so that when she opened her eyes, she'd have a full view of her reflection. Then he pulled the rectangular box of robin's egg blue from his breast pocket, set it on the table, and opened it.

"No peeking," he told her as he removed the necklace from its velvet background and lifted it over her head, then he paused, dangling it just under her chin without allowing it to touch her. "Keep your eyes closed."

"They're closed, they're closed," she muttered, wriggling on the seat. "But you might hurry a bit."

He ought to, he knew, but as Jonathan looked at her reflection, her dark lashes like tiny fans against her cheeks, her hair piled high and gleaming like fire, he felt compelled to take his time.

"Remember I told you that when you finished your mourning period, you'd have a season?" he asked.

"Yes. A year from now."

She sounded so aggrieved that he couldn't help smiling. "I know that seems like a long time away," he murmured, leaning down until his face was beside hers, until a loose tendril of her hair tickled his cheek and the lavender scent of her skin was in his nostrils. "But patience is a virtue, Marjorie."

She gave a derisive sniff, but she didn't open her eyes. "Having exercised patience throughout most of my life—something which is very much against my natural temperament, by the way—I find it overrated."

"Well, I'm about to prove you wrong about that." Still looking at her reflection, he turned his head a bit, inhaling lavender fragrance, savoring the warmer, deeper scent beneath.

"Believe it or not," he murmured, his breath stirring the loose lock of her hair as he spoke, "some things are worth waiting for. Things like this." He pulled his hands back slightly, bringing the necklace into the proper position around her throat, letting the jewels fall against her skin as he looked in the mirror and said, "Open your eyes."

She did, and immediately inhaled a sharp gasp. Her eyes, almost black in the dim light of his bedroom, went wide as she stared at her reflection. Her lips, the same soft pink as the sapphires, parted in pure astonishment.

She wasn't the only one astonished. To Jonathan, jewels meant little—colored stones and bits of metal strung and soldered together, that was all—mere baubles when they were sitting in a velvet-lined box. But around Marjorie's throat, displayed to perfection against the backdrop of her creamy skin, jewels became something else, something that made his throat go dry.

The necklace, a collar of marquise diamonds interspaced with cushion-cut rose-pink sapphires fitted perfectly around her long, slender neck. Along the bottom of the collar, larger pear-shaped diamonds dangled, dancing and sparkling in the light, grazing her collarbone. Below the hollow between her clavicles and above the cleft of her breasts, surrounded by the leaflike points of more marquise diamonds, sat the Rose of Shoshone in all its dazzling pink glory.

"Oh," she breathed, a soft huff of air between her parted lips. "What is it, a ruby?"

"Pink sapphire—which is the same thing, really, though lighter in color. Remember you asked me yesterday what the Rose of Shoshone was?" He nodded to her reflection in the mirror. "Now you know."

"Good heavens. This is mine?"

"When you turn twenty-one, yes. Do you like it?"

"It's . . ." She paused, laughing a little as if descriptions were beyond her. She lifted one hand to her bosom, her fingertips grazing the Rose's polished surface. "But where did it come from?"

"Your father found it, and all the other jewels in the necklace, long before I knew him. The diamonds he acquired in South Africa, the sapphires in Idaho. As to the latter, he was panning for gold on the Payette River—"

Jonathan broke off, his voice failing, for he saw something in her face that he hadn't seen before, something in her dark eyes, parted lips, and quickened breathing, something that as a man, he instantly recognized—a dawning awareness of herself as a woman and the power that came with it.

His body responded at once, arousal flaring up within him like a match set alight, and he knew he was in serious trouble.

This was his best friend's daughter, Billy's little girl, who he'd sworn to safeguard and protect, and yet, right now, he felt as protective of her as a wolf did a lamb.

He told himself to withdraw, but then, she laughed, a low, throaty sound of feminine exultation that pinned him in place and shredded any thought of withdrawal. Instead of diminishing, the desire within him deepened and spread, and he could only stare at her, riveted, as heat spread through his body. Suddenly, a deathbed promise to his best friend seemed like nothing at all, and he realized what he'd just done had been a huge, god-awful, disastrous mistake.

He'd intended to give her a reason to do things his way. A rather selfish thing to do, he appreciated now, engineered as much for his own convenience as for her well-being, and like most selfish actions, it was coming back to punish him. In spades.

Pull back, he told himself, but he was powerless to make his body obey his will. His senses were aware of every aspect of this moment—the warmed metal of the necklace clasp in his fingers, the loosened wisps of hair at her nape tickling the backs of his hands, the lavender and woman scent of her in his nostrils. He was aware of the glittering jewel nestled above her breasts, the softness of her skin beneath his wrists, and his own rock-hard arousal hidden by the back of the chair.

Reflected in the mirror, he could see the bed, located a scant six feet behind them. Six feet, he thought, all the distance that existed between a girl's innocence and her ruin. He stared at the bed, anarchy inside him as he fought man's eternal battle, the battle between desire and honor.

He tore his gaze from the bed, knowing he had to stop this sort of dangerous thinking before it could take hold, but when he looked at her again, radiant and beautiful, with glittering jewels around her throat and a glimmer of Eve's knowledge in her eyes, he couldn't resist postponing for just a few more exquisite seconds what he knew he had to do.

She wasn't laughing now. Perhaps the sense of power he'd awakened in her gave her an inkling of what he felt, because she wasn't staring at the jewels any longer, but at him, her eyes wide, her lips parted, her cheeks flushed.

Billy's daughter, looking at him in a whole new way, and yet, still too innocent to know what she could unleash with those soft brown eyes and those kissable pink lips and that smashing body. But he knew, and as he thought of it, the heat inside him grew stronger and hotter, deepening into raw lust.

He was a dog.

Sucking in his breath, he pulled the necklace from around her throat. "You will be making your debut in the spring," he said, his voice harsh to his own ears as he strove to regain his equilibrium. "You'll have all the delights of a London season, complete with a coming-out ball, at which you will be able to wear this." He paused, holding up the glittering jewels in his fingers. "But that won't be possible if you become an object of shame or ridicule."

In the mirror, he watched as everything he'd awakened faded from her expression then vanished as if it had never been.

"I see." She rose to her feet, sliding from behind the chair and turning to face him. "You showed me that necklace so that I would comply with your wishes, is that it?" she asked, a cool, metallic quality in her voice he'd never heard before. "You dangled it in front of me, as if it's a toy and I'm a child?"

"That wasn't my intent—"

"'Be good, little girl, and someday, you'll have nice things.' Was that the understanding I'm supposed to get from this little lesson?"

He stirred, appreciating that there was a kernel of truth in her assessment. Worse, in her cool voice, there was anger and unmistakable hurt, but though it cut him to the quick, he knew she'd be hurt a hell of a lot more if he did not do his duty as her guardian.

"My intent was not to manipulate or cajole you, but merely to make you see what's at stake. If you want to move in society, you must play by society's rules. It's that simple."

She didn't move. Her expression, so devilishly beguiling a few moments ago, was now pale, polished, and as hard as alabaster, but he shoved aside any regrets.

"For your debut, I can arrange the most lavish ball London has ever seen," he said, "with the best food and the finest champagne.

You can order a gown from the most famous dressmaker in Paris, and my sister can send invitations to the finest families in Britain, but if you have done anything to earn society's disapproval, all those arrangements for your debut will be for naught, because no one will come."

She stirred, the hardness in her face softening to uncertainty. She looked away, biting her lip.

Hoping she was beginning to understand and accept the realities of the life she'd chosen, he continued, "I know it's hard, having to wait when you've already been waiting for so long, but there is no way around it, Marjorie. You must observe a mourning period, be scrupulous in your conduct and judicious in your choice of companions. It's vital that you trust the judgement of those who know more about British society and its pitfalls than you do."

He'd feared showing her the necklace might have been a mistake, but when she gave a sigh, her shoulders sagging a little, her face taking on a resigned expression, he knew his gambit had succeeded.

"It's only until we reach London," he said. "Once there, I am hopeful my sisters can be prevailed upon, and I'm sure you'll find them much more agreeable chaperones than Lady Stansbury."

"If your sisters are unwilling to chaperone me, I have several married friends who would."

"Either way, the point is that there will be many wonderful experiences for you to enjoy, if you exercise a little patience now and trust me . . ."

He paused, grimacing a little, appreciating that when they were standing in his bedroom and raw masculine need was still thrumming through his body, asking for her trust was the height of hypocrisy. But the stakes for her were high, and if a bit of hypocrisy on his part was required, so be it.

"On the other hand," he said as he opened the box and laid the necklace inside, "if you prefer to taint the future you want for a little momentary excitement, that's your choice."

There was a long silence, and as was often the case with Marjorie, he had no idea what she was going to do, but at last, she nodded.

"All right," she said. "We'll do this your way. I don't want . . ." She paused, then whispered, "I don't want to be tainted."

Jonathan was relieved by her answer, but he also felt a curious sense of disappointment. Somehow, a compliant, obedient Marjorie seemed terribly dull.

Frustrated by his own inexplicable ambivalence where she was concerned and by the desire still seething within him, he put the lid on the box and shoved the box into his jacket pocket. "Good. Now, I shall go put this back in the ship's vault, and I ask you to return to your room and take off that dress . . ." His voice failed, and he had to pause a moment before going on.

"If you can find something more suitable for a woman in mourning to wear," he managed at last, "I will tell Lady Stansbury you are free to dine with everyone else. In all other respects, however, I ask that for the next six days, you do what she advises and try to remember all that you have to look forward to."

Desperately needing to escape, he walked past her, but by the time he reached the door, he was impelled to say one more thing.

"Marjorie?" His body in chaos, he paused and forced himself to look at her, with her splendid body and her stunning face and a bed just a few feet away from them both. "I know you're not a child. I am fully alive to the fact, believe me."

He left his stateroom, working to regain his control and put his priorities back in order, and by the time he reached the ship's vault, he felt he had succeeded. Nonetheless, once he'd seen the Rose of Shoshone safely locked away, Jonathan headed straight to the bar. He badly needed a drink.

Chapter 10

Marjorie had never had ice water thrown in her face in the literal sense, but metaphorically, thanks to Jonathan, she knew just how it felt.

One moment, she'd had glittering jewels around her neck and Jonathan's heated gaze on her, and she was no longer a school-teacher from White Plains, New York, or an heiress on her way to a new life. No, she'd transformed into something else entirely—a seductress, a temptress, a siren of lore like those who lured sailors from the sea. With her heart racing and fire raging in her blood and Jonathan looking at her in the mirror, she'd felt beautiful and wild and powerful, and all she'd wanted was to pull him down with her into some dark, sensuous underworld. It had been the most extraordinary moment of her life.

But then, he'd broken the spell and hauled her back into reality with just a few simple words.

That won't be possible if you become an object of shame or ridicule.

Had he tossed ice water in her face, he couldn't have spoiled the moment more effectively. In only a few seconds, she'd gone from beautiful siren to naughty child, and she'd felt like an utter fool.

Making things worse, during the five days that followed, she was virtually ignored, giving her cause to wonder if those magic moments in his cabin had even happened. Though he stopped by the countess's little sewing circle every afternoon, he only lingered long enough for a polite inquiry about her health before moving on, and her invitations to join them for tea had been met with polite refusal. He hadn't appeared in the main dining room even once for lunch or dinner, and her only other sight of him had been an occasional glimpse into the billiard room or smoking room as she walked the promenade with Lady Stansbury.

How could a man do that? How could he make her feel as if she was queen of the earth, turn her upside down and inside out, and then act as if she was of no consequence whatsoever? It was the most aggravating, baffling thing she'd ever experienced.

Marjorie looked up from the tea cloth in her hands, desperate for something to distract her from the tedious task of embroidering forget-me-nots, but every sight that met her eyes only served to increase her aggravation.

To her left, a group of young ladies were playing shuffleboard, and to her right, several groups of four were gathered at tables, playing bridge. Either activity, so she had been told, was unseemly for a woman in mourning.

Men and women strolled past her, enjoying the crisp, cool air through the open windows of the promenade, the ocean beyond them stretching into the distance. Staring out over the endless blue expanse, she couldn't help thinking again of sirens and sailors and those extraordinary moments in Jonathan's cabin, even though she no longer felt anything like a seductive figure of Greek mythology. More like a cursed princess in a fairy tale, she decided with a snort.

"Really, dear," Lady Stansbury's well-bred drawl broke into her thoughts and forced her attention back to the tea cloth in her hands. "If one must make an indelicate noise, it is always best to muffle it with a handkerchief."

Marjorie paused again, pasted on a smile—the same smile she'd always employed when talking to the mothers of difficult pupils—and turned toward the older woman.

"Quite right, ma'am," she said, trying not to clench her jaw. "I do beg your pardon."

Lady Stansbury inclined her head and returned her attention to the basket in her lap. "Heavens, I bought all those lovely new embroidery threads when I was in New York. What has Bates done with them?"

"Are you certain they aren't there, Abigail?" asked the countess's friend, Mrs. Anstruthur, pausing in her needlepoint to peer shortsightedly into her friend's sewing basket. "Give it a good stir and look again."

"Ooh, there's Lady Mary Pomeroy walking with her father," murmured Mrs. Fulton-Smythe, her dentures clacking along with her knitting needles. "They must be on their way home at last."

"Twenty-three," said Mrs. Anstruthur with a meaningful cough. "And still not married. Poor thing."

"One could hardly expect otherwise," Lady Stansbury put in. "After the scandal."

Here we go again, Marjorie thought and returned her attention determinedly to her task, thanking heaven they were to dock at Southampton tomorrow. *One more day*, she reminded as she pulled blue embroidery floss through the tea cloth with her needle. *Just twenty-four more hours, and I'll never have to sew another thing or listen to these scandalmongers.*

"Sir Henry was beside himself," said Lady Osgoode. "He took her to stay with her grandparents in New York right after, but something like that can't be hushed up just by leaving town."

Not when gossiping cats insist on talking about it all the time, thought Marjorie.

"Still," said Lady Anstruthur, "it's been three years. You'd think they'd have found someone to marry her by now. Even an American would have been better than no one."

Exercising considerable willpower, Marjorie pressed her tongue hard against her teeth and kept stitching.

"Even Americans have some standards, I suppose," Mrs. Fulton-Smythe put in. "A clerk in her father's law offices—what was the girl thinking? Sir Henry put a stop to it, naturally, but I'm afraid it was too late by then. Now, she's damaged goods."

Goaded beyond bearing, Marjorie paused and looked up. "But if they wanted to marry, and her father stopped it, isn't he the one to blame for the resulting scandal?"

Five faces turned in her direction, and there was a long silence as five pairs of eyes stared at her. Clearly, this particular point of view was a new one to the ladies present.

"I'm afraid it's not that simple, dear," Lady Stansbury said and patted her arm. "And one can't blame Sir Henry. After all, the young man was a *clerk*."

As if that explained everything, she resumed rummaging in her basket while Marjorie's bourgeois American mind tried to make sense of the idea that the ruination of all a young woman's marriage prospects was less undesirable than marriage to a clerk.

"I cannot understand what Bates has done with those threads." Lady Stansbury gave a sigh as if sorely put upon. "And I can't even ask her, for she's gone to speak with the chef about his dinner preparations. Though why she must do that *again*, I cannot understand. Six times she's tried to explain how to make a proper boiled pudding, and the chef still can't seem to manage it."

There was a chorus of sympathy from all the other ladies of the sewing circle, save one. It was Marjorie's opinion that an experienced *chef de cuisine* might be a teeny bit resentful of being told how to cook, particularly by a lady's maid, but it wouldn't do to say so. No, she needed to be scrupulous in her conduct and trust the judgement of those who knew more about British society than she did.

As she repeated Jonathan's words from five days ago, Marjorie could only hope his sisters had a less rigid view of the world than Lady Stansbury and her friends. If not, her life in British society was going to be far less exciting than she'd imagined.

"No, they are simply not here," Lady Stansbury declared at last. "She must have put them in my other sewing basket."

Appreciating the chance to get away, Marjorie was on her feet in an instant. "Shall I go and fetch them?"

Lady Stansbury nodded agreement, and Marjorie tossed down her embroidery hoop and was off like a shot.

"Don't run, dear," the countess called after her as she raced along the promenade deck. "And bring my other shawl. The mohair one, not the silk. It's in the—"

The location of the shawl was lost in the wind as Marjorie vanished around the stern of the ship, making her reprieve all the better. A search for the shawl would mean several extra minutes of freedom.

When she entered the suite, she found the other sewing basket almost at once, reposing on the floor of the sitting room beside Lady Stansbury's chair. The mohair shawl, however, proved elusive. She looked through every trunk, suitcase, and drawer she could find, to no avail. Deciding at last that she'd milked her precious freedom as long as possible, she picked up the basket and started out of the suite, but she'd barely opened the door into the corridor before realizing she hadn't looked in the trunk under the countess's bed, and as she stepped over the threshold, she glanced over her shoulder, wondering if she ought to go back.

She had no time to decide, however. Still moving forward, still looking behind her, she ran straight into someone passing along the corridor.

"Oh!" she cried as the force of the impact sent her stumbling backward through the doorway. A strong pair of hands gripped her wrists to keep her from falling as the door of the suite banged against the wall behind her and the basket dropped from her fingers, spilling its contents at her feet.

"I beg your pardon," the man cried, his hands still clasping her wrists. "How clumsy of me."

She looked up into the handsome face of the Count de la Rosa. "Why, hullo!" she said in agreeable surprise.

"Miss McGann," he greeted as he let go of her and bowed. "What a pleasure it is to see you again. You have come to no harm because of our collision?"

"None at all," she hastened to assure him. "This is quite a coincidence."

"A delightful one for me. Though perhaps not for you." He paused, making a face as he glanced down at the carpet between them. "I seem to have disarranged your belongings. Let me rectify that."

Remembering Jonathan's words of caution about de la Rosa, she voiced a protest, but when the count overrode it with a wave of his hand, then knelt on the floor and turned the basket upright to begin retrieving the scattered sewing supplies, she relented, for she just couldn't see any harm in allowing him to assist her.

"I didn't know your rooms were along this corridor," she said, sinking to her knees on the other side of the open doorway to help him gather spools of thread and packets of needles.

"They are not. I was exploring the ship, and I took a wrong turn. Although," he added, lifting his head to look at her, smiling a little beneath his mustache, "it is not so very wrong, I think, if the result is your company."

She laughed, pleased. Here, at least, was someone who seemed glad to see her. With Jonathan treating her as if she had leprosy, de la Rosa's obvious delight at encountering her was like a balm to her wounded feminine pride.

He glanced past her shoulder to the stateroom beyond. "Is this where you stay?" he asked, leaning forward a little on his knees to peer past her into the sitting room beyond. "I did not realize the parlor suites were so large."

"You don't have a suite?"

"Alas, no. I could never afford it." He sat back on his heels and resumed their task. "These days, I must be practical. I must—how do you say it?—make the economies."

"Yes, I suppose many people do."

"But I am most fortunate. An income from my estates affords me rooms in Paris, and my mother and I live most comfortably. We travel, we enjoy fine hotels, good food and wine . . ." He paused to toss a pincushion into the basket. "What more does one need?"

"You live in Paris?" That surprised her. "But I thought you had estates in Spain?"

"I do, but I have leased the house. A rich American family lives in my villa. They pay much money to enjoy the beauty of my vineyards, but without the headaches, you comprehend?"

"That must be difficult, having someone else living in your ancestral home."

He made an expressive gesture with his hands. "It is tragic, but what else can one do? Between the rents and the wine, I make enough for my needs, and living in Paris is not expensive."

"Is that how you know Baroness Vasiliev? From Paris?"

"That is where we met, yes, but I would not say we know each other very well. She spends much time in England. In the winter, we sometimes encounter each other in the South of France—Juan-les-Pins, Nice, Cannes . . . the usual watering places."

To Marjorie, there was nothing "usual" about such places. To her, the count's cosmopolitan lifestyle seemed downright exotic, much more like the high society she'd imagined than Lady Stansbury's sewing circle. "I'm afraid I've never been to the Riviera."

"Not even to Nice? But that is a tragedy. You would love it." He flashed her a smile. "You can spend your fortune at the gaming tables, no?"

"I've never been to a casino either." Even as she said those words, she felt a pang. There was so much to see, so much to experience, and yet, she was still watching from a distance.

"I'm not sure I would be a very good player," she confessed. "The only card game I know is picquet. But I should love to see Nice."

"If you go, you will be enchanted. The mimosa, the sun, the water—so beautiful."

He was looking at her as he said it, demonstrating he wasn't really talking about the Riviera. Right in front of her, it seemed, was the romance she craved, but as she looked into the count's handsome face, another countenance, not so sleek, not so urbane, flashed across her mind.

The image—hazel eyes shot with scorching lights of gold, lean planes of cheek and jaw, a hard mouth set in a tight line—filled her with such frustration, she wanted to kick herself.

Here she was, talking to one of the handsomest men she'd ever seen, a cosmopolitan man who admired her and made it clear he had a romantic interest in her, but was she thinking about him?

No, she was thinking about a man who hemmed her in and held her back, who thought to pacify her with promises of what she'd have someday.

She was so tired of somedays and the men who promised them.

The count spoke again, and Marjorie shoved her damned guardian out of her mind, forcing her attention back to the man in front of her.

"Once you have spent time on the Côte d'Azur," he was saying as he dropped a packet of embroidery flosses into the basket, "you will never want to live in England."

Making an expression of his distaste for that country, he tossed a tin box of buttons into the basket and presented the basket to her with a little bow, then stood up and held out his hand to her.

"You don't seem fond of England," she said as she hooked the basket over her arm, took his hand, and allowed him to assist her to her feet. "Yet you are going there now."

"Everyone goes to London for the season, do they not? But I confess, England does not impress me. So cold, so rainy. But," he added, retaining her hand as she moved to withdraw it, "now that you will be there, I shall have to change my opinion. You would make the sun shine anywhere, I think."

Somehow, his lavish compliment did not impress her quite as much this time, perhaps because the tight way he held her hand was beginning to make her a bit uncomfortable.

"You flatter me," she murmured and pulled her hand from his.

This time, he let it go, and once again, he glanced past her. "They are most luxurious, these parlor suites, are they not?"

He seemed terribly curious about her rooms, she noted in some amusement. This was the second time he had brought up the topic, and she couldn't imagine what he found so fascinating.

She had no chance to ask.

Suddenly, like an explosion out of the clear blue sky, the count was flying back from the doorway into the corridor, his collar and the back of his jacket in Jonathan's grip.

"What are you doing?" Marjorie cried, stepping out of her room and watching in stunned dismay as Jonathan hurled de la Rosa down the corridor.

"Get out," Jonathan told him, his voice like the snap of a whip through the air. "Get out of my sight before I beat you to a bloody pulp."

The count didn't need to be told twice. "Farewell, *cherie*," he called over his shoulder as he fled down the corridor. "I fear we will not meet in London after all." With a last glance of regret, he ducked around the corner and vanished.

Marjorie turned to face Jonathan as the count's hurried, descending footsteps sounded from the stairwell. "What on earth is wrong with you?"

"With me?" He stared at her, actually seeming surprised by the question. "Nothing. Too bad we can't say the same about him."

She shook her head, baffled by the fury in his face. "I think you've gone crazy."

"That's quite possible," he acknowledged, glaring at her with a resentment she in no way deserved.

"I suppose," she said, glaring right back at him, "your sudden arrival means you've decided to stop ignoring me?"

"My behavior isn't the issue. Damn it, Marjorie, I warned you to stay away from that man—"

"Oh, please," she cut him off. "For five straight days, I've hardly seen you, much less had a civil word. I've tried to talk with you and been snubbed for my trouble, and I've been tearing my hair out, wondering what I might have done to earn your animosity. But now, after that boorish display, I'm wondering why in blazes I even care."

"I'm not the one who deserves censure here."

She stiffened. "Are you referring to me? Not that it would be surprising, since I always seem to be doing the wrong thing in your eyes."

Something flickered in his face, something that softened the anger in his countenance, but he looked away before she could define it. "I wasn't talking about you," he muttered, taking a deep breath. "I am fully aware that de la Rosa is the only one at fault here."

"On the other hand," she went on, in no frame of mind to let him shift the blame for his own conduct onto the count, "it's not much of an improvement when you finally do decide to make an appearance. What did you think you were doing just now?"

"I was defending you."

She lifted her hands in total exasperation, then lowered them again, rattling the contents of the basket over her arm. "From what?"

"That cur was in your room." He jabbed a finger toward the open door behind them. "Your room, for God's sake."

"He was not in my room. He was in the doorway."

"He was *blocking* the doorway."

"He was helping me! Lady Stansbury had sent me to fetch this." She paused, holding up the basket. "As I was coming back out of our suite, the count happened to be passing. We collided accidently, everything spilled out, and he was kind enough to help me put it all back—"

"Forgive me if I'm doubtful it was an accident."

"Would you listen to yourself?" she said in disbelief. "You took an instant dislike to him, and now, you insist on attributing any number of horrible vices to his character."

"Given his actions thus far, I'd say my initial assessment of him was quite valid."

She made a scoffing sound. "Why? Because he had the baroness change a few place settings the other night and helped me pick up my things after an accidental collision?"

Jonathan's jaw tightened to that stubborn line she was coming to know so well. "It was no accident. I warned you he'd try to get you alone."

"He didn't 'get me alone,' as you put it. I *was* alone. But nothing happened. He made no advances upon me, if that's what you fear. He was a perfect gentleman, which is more than I can say for you. Tell me, is this sort of behavior what I can expect from you regarding all my suitors?"

"Suitors?" he scoffed, ignoring the accusation she'd just leveled at him. "De la Rosa's no suitor. Courtship is the last thing on his mind."

"He wants to win my hand. At least, that's what you told me you overheard him saying to the baroness the other night."

"I also said that he has no intention of winning it in honorable fashion, a fact made clear by his actions today."

"Oh, for the love of heaven, we were just talk—"

She stopped as a door opened farther down the corridor, and she realized it was unwise to have a full-throated argument about this in a place where anyone could hear them. Leaning forward, she grabbed Jonathan by his necktie with her free hand and stepped back through the doorway, hauling him with her before he could even think to stop her.

"What the hell?" he muttered as she let him go, ducked around him, and shut the door, flattening her back against it and trapping them both inside. "What are you doing?"

"That was my question, one you still haven't answered. Is eavesdropping, skulking in corridors, spying on me, assaulting my friends—is all this going to be a habit with you? If so, I will be ecstatic when you sail off for Africa."

"That man is not your friend. And I was not skulking, nor spying. I was having tea at the other end of the promenade, reading my paper and minding my own business, when I saw you go by. A moment later, the count passed me, following you, and I knew something was in the wind."

"You can't possibly be certain he was following me."

"Yes, I can. He has no business being in this corridor. His cabin's all the way at the other end of A-deck, on the port side."

"How do you know that?"

"I made inquiries."

She rolled her eyes, not the least bit surprised. "He was exploring the ship and got lost. He told me that himself."

"Lost, my eye. He was looking for a chance to get you alone. If I hadn't come along, what could have happened? What would you have done if he'd decided to push in?"

"Push in?" She was shocked. "Into my rooms?"

"Yes, into your rooms, my sweet innocent."

Such a notion had never even occurred to her, and it seemed hardly credible to her that a man like the Count de la Rosa, a handsome man of position and prestige who could clearly have any woman he wanted, would attempt something so despicable. He wasn't a common masher or thug, and except for perhaps holding her hand a little too long, his behavior toward her had been impeccable.

"Think about it, Marjorie," he said in the wake of her silence. "How simple for him to persuade or even force his way into your room, having arranged for the baroness to come in after him at just the right moment—"

"The baroness would never cooperate in such a despicable scheme. And anyway, isn't she on your side now?"

"That woman is on whatever side will pay her the most money, and the count may have upped the stakes enough to regain her loyalty. But if you don't believe her capable of colluding with him, there's his own mother to consider. She wouldn't be the first matchmaking mama to swoop in and demand honor be satisfied."

"The only one who's done any swooping is *you.*"

"Or if he delayed you long enough," Jonathan went on as if she hadn't spoken, "it's quite possible Lady Stansbury could have come in search of you and found him with you in her suite. Whichever scenario was in his devious mind, the result would be an enormous scandal, and you'd have to marry the blackguard."

"You're being ridiculous."

"As your guardian, it is my duty to ensure that you are safeguarded at all times. I swore to your father—"

"The way you're acting," she cut in, completely exasperated, "anyone would think you *were* my father!"

"What?" He stared at her for a moment, then he gave a laugh, and though she had no idea what he found amusing, she wasn't about to stop and ponder the question, for she had a lot more to say.

"When I was a little girl, I used to imagine how wonderful it would be to be reunited with my father." She stared at Jonathan, shaking her head, baffled at herself. "Now, I'm wondering what I could have been thinking to ever have wanted a father at all. If you're anything to go by, having a father is like being wrapped in cotton wool and smothered to death."

"I'm like a father to you?" he muttered, rubbing his hands over his face. As he let them fall and lifted his head, he laughed again. "My God."

"I've managed to make you laugh, I see," she said, that fact making her even more cross. "I suppose being laughed at is better than being ignored, or being given lectures on propriety and dire warnings about my virtue, or being told all the ways people are out to take advantage of me. And it's certainly better than watching you assault my suitors in corridors. I'm glad I'm so amusing to you."

"I'm not the least bit amused, believe me."

He took a step closer, and she felt a sudden quiver along her spine— apprehension and something more, the same tingling awareness she'd felt when he'd put those jewels around her throat and looked at her in the mirror.

He was standing quite close to her, so close that she could see things about him she'd never noticed before. His hazel eyes seemed to hold a multitude of colors—not only brown and gold, but also green, and blue, and even violet. His lashes were longer than they looked, for though dark at the base, they were blond at the tips. There was a small, Z-shaped scar at his right temple, and on his lean cheeks was the faint shadow of beard stubble.

She wanted to hold on to her anger, but even as she tried, she felt it slipping away under his open, unwavering scrutiny and the inex-plicable change in the air. He seemed to sense it, too, for he stirred, easing even closer, close enough that his starched shirtfront, puffed out where she'd pulled it along with his tie, brushed against her breast.

She jumped like a skittish horse, flattening her back against the door, and she forced herself to say something. "I don't understand you at all," she said, trying to sound vexed, mortified when her words came out in a breathless rush instead. "If you're not amused, then why were you laughing?"

"I'm not laughing at you, Marjorie, if that's what you think." His gaze lowered to her mouth, and her heart gave an instinctive leap of excitement in her chest. "I'm laughing at myself."

"For what?" Her throat was dry, her question a whisper.

"For my conceit. For assuming things that were far off the mark."

She frowned, bewildered, finding it hard to think straight. "About the count, you mean?"

"No." His hand lifted to cup her face, and she gave a startled gasp as his fingers curled at her nape and his thumb slid across her lips. No man had ever touched her so intimately before, and the contact was doing strange things to her insides. Heat pooled in her belly, and her bones suddenly felt like rubber. "I'm talking about you."

The heat evoked by his touch was spreading throughout her body. She could hardly breathe. Her heart was thudding in her chest as if she'd been running. "I don't understand," she managed, her words a rasp against his thumb. "What things?"

"It never occurred to me that you regard me as some kind of substitute father."

It did seem ludicrous just now, but she gathered her scattered wits and marshaled every scrap of her pride. "No?" she countered, forcing a coolness into her voice she didn't feel in the least. "Given the way you've been ignoring me and snubbing me, I think it's a fair and accurate comparison."

"It's not, actually." His thumb slid beneath her chin, lifting her face. "Because the thoughts I've been having about you since we met aren't the least bit fatherly."

"They're not?"

"God, no." With an abruptness that took her breath away, he wrapped his free arm around her waist and hauled her hard against him. Then, as the sewing basket dropped from her fingers and hit the floor, he bent his head and kissed her.

Chapter 11

Having never in her life been kissed before, Marjorie had only been able to imagine what it was like—vague notions of a sweet and gentle brush of lips, but Jonathan's kiss was nothing like the product of her girlhood imagination. It was not sweet, nor was it gentle. Instead, it was hard, hot, and completely overwhelming.

She brought her hands up between them, but it wasn't to push him away. Instead, she curled her fingers into his lapels, pulling him closer, holding on tight, for this was her first kiss, and there was nothing else in the world that could possibly matter more than this moment.

She closed her eyes, bringing all her other senses to the fore. His scent—of castile soap, bay rum, and something deeper. His taste—of tea and strawberry jam. His touch—the warmth of his palm cupping her face and his fingertips against the nape of her neck.

Beneath her knuckles, she could feel the hard muscles of his chest and his hammering heart, and the knowledge that he felt what she did went to her head like champagne. Just as when he'd put that necklace around her throat and looked at her in the mirror, she felt a glorious, exhilarating sense of power, and she suddenly knew what it meant. It was the power of being a woman.

His lips parted, seeming to want hers to part as well, but when she complied, his tongue entered her mouth, and it was too much. She jerked in shock, breaking the kiss, and at once, he stilled, his mouth a fraction from hers, his quick breaths mingling with hers.

He moved as if to withdraw, but she couldn't bear for these exciting sensations to stop, not yet. Letting go of his lapel, she wrapped one arm around his neck, rose on her toes, and kissed him.

He groaned against her mouth and, as if in capitulation to her command, his arm pulling her even closer as his free hand tangled in her hair and he deepened the kiss, his tongue tasting hers.

Dark waves of heat flooded through Marjorie's body as he tasted her with his tongue. When he pulled back, she followed, tasting him in return, and the pleasure rose even higher, flared even hotter.

Who could ever have thought a kiss could be like this? It was the most intimate, shocking thing that had ever happened to her. It was amazing and glorious, and she wanted more.

Guided by instinct rather than conscious thought, she pressed her body even closer to his, her fingers raking through the short, crisp strands of his hair as she brought her other arm up around his neck. He made a rough sound against her mouth, and his arms held her as if he never wanted to let her go. His body, so much larger than hers, was strong and lean, and so hard, particularly where his hips were pressed to hers.

Standing on the tips of her toes, she stirred, her body moving against his. Given how tightly he held her, it was an infinitesimal move, but the pleasure it wrought was so acute, so unexpected, that she cried out in surprise against his mouth.

Without any warning, he tore his lips from hers, his embrace slackened, and his hands reached up to clasp her wrists and pull her arms down from his neck, an abrupt withdrawal that forced her eyes open.

"There," he said, his voice a harsh rasp in the quiet room. "I hope I've cleared up any absurd notions that I'm like your damned father."

He didn't wait for an answer. Instead, he put his hands on her arms and eased her to one side, then he opened the door, and walked out, leaving Marjorie in a stunned, breathless tumult as he shut the door behind him.

HIS BODY AFIRE, his mind in chaos, Jonathan strode down the ship's corridor, desperate to reach the deck—not the sheltered first-class promenade with its opened windows and strolling passengers, but the outer deck, where the bracing air of the open sea could cool the desire blazing inside him, put his priorities back in order, and help him regain his sanity, though he feared he might be fighting a losing battle.

His first look into Marjorie's velvety brown eyes and his first glance over that goddess body had been enough to spark his desire, but taking her into his bedroom and putting those jewels around her neck had flared that spark into flame. In the five days since, he'd been trying desperately to snuff it out, but after that blazing kiss, it was clear he'd failed, and if he kept on this way, he'd be burned to a crisp long before he got anywhere near Africa.

Anyone would think you were *my father.*

An appropriate way for a ward to regard her guardian, and quite understandable from her point of view. He ought to have been glad and relieved she viewed him in that light.

Glad? Relieved? What a crock.

He'd been appalled by the comparison and frustrated as hell. When a man was burning for a woman, the last thing he wanted to be told by the object of his desire was that he was like a father to her. Hearing that, any red-blooded man would have hauled off and kissed her.

But he wasn't any man. He was her guardian. That put what he'd done utterly beyond the pale, and now, he didn't know whether to laugh at himself for being a humbug or flog himself for violating the trust Billy had placed in him.

Jonathan paused and leaned against the ship's railing, breathing deep as he worked to bring his body back under his control.

All his guardianlike protections, all his lectures to her on proper behavior, and all his reminders to himself of his duty, and yet he'd just become the very thing he was trying to protect her from.

When he'd seen de la Rosa halfway through her door, it had ignited within him an unmistakably protective rage, but not one borne of any paternal feeling, as his subsequent actions had so ignobly proved.

When she'd pulled him into her room, he hadn't even thought to stop her. When she'd railed at him for acting as if he was her father, it had insulted his masculine pride and provoked him beyond bearing.

And when he'd pulled her into his arms, he'd tossed his promises to his best friend straight out the window.

Jonathan stared out to sea, pushing thoughts of Marjorie aside, making his mind go back six weeks, to his final visit to the sanitorium in Denver.

I never told you before, but I've got a daughter.

The smell of the ocean faded away, replaced by the dry mountain air of Colorado. The rush of the sea breeze was lost in the sound of hacking coughs. The view before him of endless blue water gave way to one of the lungers, their emaciated bodies lying on cots in the doorways of their huts—his friend among them, his face drawn and pale, a blood-spattered towel in his hand.

The doctors had already told him Billy's death was imminent; what he had not expected was his friend's deathbed revelations.

Her mother's family was society, top of the tree in Johannesburg. Prettiest woman you ever saw. She had subalterns and the sons of English lords swirling around her like flies around honey. But she chose me. They cast her off for it, you know. Her family.

Billy had known about Jonathan's mother—how she had been similarly ostracized and how well Jonathan understood that sort of injustice.

Marjorie's been at a finishing school back East, learning to be a lady, but it won't do her much good without connections. You've got those. I want my girl to have the best of everything, all the things I can't give her, all the things her mother gave up when she married me. Balls, pretty dresses, parties. Society, you know. Marjorie's like any girl. She wants those things. Promise me she gets 'em.

Jonathan's eyes stung. His chest hurt. The memory of pine-scented air made him feel slightly sick. He didn't want to think of this; he'd spent weeks pushing it away. But now, he made himself remember it, forcing it back to the forefront of his mind, where it needed to be if he was going to keep his word.

I want her to marry the right sort of man, her mother's sort, a real gentleman and nothing less. Not some fortune hunter out for the money. And not some dream chaser like me and you. You know what I mean?

He knew. Propping his forearms on the rail, he bent his head, cradling it in his hands as the last, labored words he'd ever heard his friend say rang in his ears.

I've got no kin. Her mother's folk won't take her—my fault. She's got no one else, so I made you her guardian. Jessop drew it all up. When I'm gone, you've got to look after my little girl, take care of her money like you did for me, keep the fortune-hunters away, and see she's settled proper when the time comes. Promise.

He'd promised. He'd never considered doing anything else.

And then, just minutes ago, after knowing the girl less than a week, he'd broken that promise. For lust.

Slowly, Jonathan lifted his head and straightened away from the rail. He'd let people down in the past, he couldn't do it again. He'd given Billy his word, and by God, he was going to keep it.

Even if it killed him.

IF MARJORIE HAD truly been a cursed princess in a fairy tale, her first kiss ought to have freed her, transformed her, changed . . . something. But she soon discovered that in real life, things were a bit different. That kiss, like the necklace, may have brought her an exhilarating sense of feminine power, but in practical terms, it didn't really amount to much.

During the evening that followed, Jonathan resumed avoiding her like she had the plague, Lady Stansbury continued to be awful, Baroness Vasiliev remained "seasick" in her cabin, and Marjorie's first ocean voyage once again became mind-numbingly dull. The following day, no one aboard ship could possibly have been more delighted than she when the misty Irish coastline came into sight.

Her first view of England, however, proved to be not much of a view at all, for as the *Neptune* entered the English Channel, it sailed straight into the teeth of a raging, late-spring storm. The rain was coming down in sheets as the steamship moved along the Solent, that part of the Channel between the Isle of Wight and the mainland. It had lightened to a drizzle by the time the *Neptune* slid into a dock at Southampton Port, only to be replaced by fog so thick the hired carriages transporting passengers from the docks to the railway station crawled along the streets of Southampton at a snail's pace.

The dismal weather rather tempered Marjorie's excitement about arriving for the first time in another country, but at the train station, as Jonathan purchased their passage to London, sent telegrams of their safe arrival to his sister, Mr. Jessop, and Mrs. Forsyte, and secured a porter to transfer their luggage, Lady Stansbury chose to lighten Marjorie's spirits.

"This is where I leave you," the countess said as she paused with Marjorie by the ticket counters while Baroness Vasiliev joined Jonathan in the queue to purchase her own London railway fare.

"You do not go on to London?" Marjorie asked, trying to look regretful instead of relieved.

"Bah," the countess replied, shaking her head. "I'm far too old for all that hustle and bustle. No, I'm going home to Chalton. It's less than twenty miles from here, very close to Torquil's ducal seat, you know. Too bad the duke and duchess aren't in residence. If they were at Ravenwood, you and Mr. Deverill could accompany me."

"Yes," Marjorie murmured. "That is too bad."

"When the duchess brings you back to Hampshire, Miss McGann, call on me at Chalton, and we shall have tea."

Marjorie, thinking of the travesties that had been committed upon her underclothing and the autocratic orders that had been barked at her during the past six days, decided she'd rather have teeth pulled. "You're very kind, ma'am," she said gravely. "Thank you."

"Not at all. You're a sweet child, for an American. Ah, there's Bates with our tickets, and the porter with our luggage. Not that way, young man," she barked to the uniformed porter, jabbing her cane in the air to send him and his cart of trunks and suitcases toward the proper platform. "I'm east, not northeast."

As the countess, her maid, and the unfortunate porter trundled off, Marjorie heard a chuckle behind her and turned to find Jonathan standing there, *billets* of fare in his hand and a porter beside him with a cart of luggage. "What's so funny?" she asked.

"Lady Stansbury calling you sweet."

Making a face at him, she took the ticket he held out to her and put it in her handbag. "I've never been so glad to be rid of anyone in my life. That woman sucks every scrap of joy out of life."

"Yes, well, you've got your baroness back now, from here to London, at least."

"You needn't sound so unhappy about it. Believe me, if you ever got to know her, you'd enjoy her company as much as I do."

He gave her a skeptical look, but he had no chance to reply, for the baroness joined them at that moment and suggested they board their train, which was due to depart in half an hour.

The train was crowded, and because they were late to the platform, their choice of seats was limited, despite being in first class. They did manage to find three seats together, but the other three seats in the compartment were also occupied—one by a crusty old colonel who glared at the baroness from behind his newspaper and gave a pointed harrumph every time her garrulous voice rose above a murmur.

Jonathan also opened a newspaper, and the baroness soon gave up any attempts at conversation, pulled a book from her traveling case, and offered another one to Marjorie.

She accepted it with gratitude, glad Lady Stansbury wasn't there to remind her that women in mourning weren't supposed to read novels. Sadly, however, even a novel wasn't sufficient to hold her attention, not with Jonathan sitting right across from her and that kiss still vivid in her mind.

Every time she looked up, the sight of him only a few feet away brought back those heated moments in her cabin. Even the fact that they were in a crowded train compartment could not stop her from remembering the feel of his strong arms around her and his mouth on hers, and the memory never failed to make her blush, forcing her to retreat once again behind a book she wasn't reading.

Thankfully, the weather decided to change as they journeyed away from the coast, and as the mist and rain dissipated, Marjorie was given her first real glimpse of England. Hoping the view outside would prove a better distraction from the man opposite than the baroness's book, she stared out at the lush green countryside and tried to imagine the wonderful new life ahead of her, a life she'd been dreaming of for three years now.

She'd been fourteen when her father had struck it rich, but she hadn't really thought of herself as an heiress, for her plan had been to go west to be with her parent. She'd listened with interest as her friends had talked of their future in this country, of how they would do the season and marry titled peers, but back then, it had all seemed like a romantic story to her and nothing more, for she'd never seen herself as joining them.

But upon her graduation, her father's betrayal had transformed her friends' talk of life in the British aristocracy from a story into a plan. Their descriptions of English country life, with its stately homes, enduring traditions, and deep family loyalties, had appealed strongly to the girl who hadn't had a real home since she was seven and whose only family member had never been loyal.

Her friends' accounts of the London season, with its lavish balls and parties and potential suitors, had sparked excitement in the girl who'd never experienced so much as a speck of romance.

Marjorie slid another glance at Jonathan, and she was startled to find him watching her above the edge of his newspaper. She could read nothing in his face, but as his gaze lowered to her mouth, she caught her breath and wondered if he was thinking of that kiss. But then, he returned his attention to his newspaper, and Marjorie looked again at the view outside, reminding herself that there was no point to romantic contemplations about Jonathan. The life she wanted, the one to which this very train was carrying her, was in the society he abhorred, and in only two weeks, he was returning to a life she had no desire to share.

She'd soon be meeting plenty of other handsome men, some of whom would kiss her—at least, she *hoped* so. She'd find one to love, one who'd want to settle down with her, who'd enjoy the house parties they'd throw and the estate they'd manage and all the London seasons that lay ahead.

Jonathan might hate that sort of life, but for her, it shimmered ahead like a dazzling paradise, and now that it was three thousand miles closer, she wanted it more than ever. And yet, when she stole another glance at Jonathan across the compartment and thought of his arms around her and his mouth on hers, she had the sinking feeling that none of the men she ever met in the future would ever kiss her like he had.

BARONESS VASILIEV WAS staying at Thomas's Hotel, which seemed to be along their route to the duchess's house, and she accepted Jonathan's offer to share their taxi from Victoria Station. Upon arriving at the hotel, Jonathan directed bellmen in unloading the baroness's luggage while she and Marjorie said their farewells.

"I am sorry I was not a better companion to you during our voyage," the baroness said. "But the mal de mer had me in its grip . . ."

Pausing, she pressed a hand to her stomach and gave a shudder as if recalling her weeklong bout of seasickness, and Marjorie had to suppress a smile. No wonder Jonathan thought the woman a fraud, for she wasn't really that good an actress.

"It's all right, Baroness," Marjorie said gravely. "Seasickness must be awful. And I'm sure we shall see each other here in town. After all," she went on, watching the other woman closely, "you do know the duchess."

"But of course we shall see each other," the baroness exclaimed, showing no sign of deception. "You do the season, no?"

"It doesn't look like it." Marjorie gave a wistful sigh. "I am supposed to be in mourning."

"Bah. You hardly knew your father. The duchess will not be such a . . . what is the word I want? Stickler?"

"Perhaps the duchess won't," Marjorie conceded, sliding a meaningful sideways glance at Jonathan. "But she isn't the only consideration."

The baroness laughed. "Your guardian is a man. I doubt he will gainsay his sister in a matter such as this. And even if he does . . ." She paused to give Marjorie a wink. "He will be gone before long, no? And the duchess lives a very short distance from here. No, no, we will see each other again soon, my young friend." She turned as Jonathan came up to them. "You shall call upon me tomorrow, Mr. Deverill, yes?"

"I am happy to do so. Shall we say three o'clock?"

Marjorie grasped the meaning behind that exchange at once, and after they had returned to their waiting taxi, she couldn't resist teasing him about it. "Paying her to feign seasickness was a cruel thing to do to me," she accused, shaking her head.

"You survived."

"So did Lady Stansbury. Lucky for her."

That made him grin, but once the taxi merged into traffic, he looked at her, his grin faded, and suddenly, the memory of that kiss was between them in the confined space of the carriage like a tangible thing. As they stared at each other, Marjorie could almost feel his arms around her and his mouth on hers. With no chaperones and no prying eyes and his tawny eyes looking into hers, all the wild, overwhelming sensations he had evoked came over her in a flood, as vivid now as the moment the kiss had happened.

Heat flooded her body, making her blush, and she looked out the window, forcing herself to say something. "The streets are so crowded here, aren't they?" Even as she spoke, she grimaced at the inanity of her own remark and the nervous pitch of her voice, but desperate, she persevered. "It's worse than Manhattan. We're scarcely moving."

"London traffic's always beastly. Believe me, I know. I grew up here."

She drew a breath and looked at him again, glad to have a neutral topic more interesting than the traffic. "How does it feel to be home again?"

With that question, the tension in the air seemed to dissipate, and he eased into the opposite corner of the taxi, stretching out his long legs as best he could in the confined space. "Odd," he admitted.

"It must be, after ten years away."

"It's all very familiar, naturally. Comfortable, too, in a way—rather like putting on one's favorite pair of old shoes. And yet . . ." He paused and glanced outside, then looked back at her. "It also feels crowded, a bit stifling. Alien, too, like I've stepped into the pages of a Jules Verne novel."

"And I feel like I've stepped into a romantic fairy tale."

"Perhaps you have." The gold lights in his eyes seemed to glint with sudden fire, and Marjorie's stomach gave a nervous lurch.

"Tell me about your sisters," she said, seizing on another topic. "Since I'm about to meet at least one of them in very short order, I suppose I ought to learn a bit more about them. What are they like?"

He hesitated, and she couldn't help a laugh. "Is it such a hard question?"

"It is, rather. As you know, I haven't seen my sisters for ten years, and even before then, I was away at school much of the time when we were growing up." He considered. "I'm sure they've changed a great deal since I went away. They're both married now, and they both have children. Didn't Lady Stansbury tell you anything about my sisters?"

"Not much." She made a rueful face. "I asked about the duchess, and the entire sewing circle went silent, all of them looking at each other as if they didn't know what to say. Finally, Mrs. Anstruthur said something about Her Grace being very political and modern in her views, whereupon I saw Mrs. Fulton-Smythe kick her—yes, actually kick her. Mrs. Anstruthur, poor woman, stopped talking and looked embarrassed. Lady Stansbury frowned at me, said she hoped I was not in any way political, and changed the subject."

Jonathan laughed, much to her bewilderment. "Irene has always had an independent streak," he explained, "and it seems to have gotten under the skin of Lady Stansbury and her friends. Irene is a staunch suffragist."

"I see." Marjorie grinned. "I think I like her already."

Jonathan's amusement faded at once. "Don't follow in her footsteps, please."

"Oh?" She straightened in her seat, a bit nettled. "Why not? Because you don't think women should have the vote?"

"Women in Idaho got the vote for their state elections ages ago, as have several other Western American states, and despite the dire predictions of most of the men, the world didn't come crashing down around our ears. No, I only meant that I don't want you getting arrested."

She blinked in surprise. "The duchess got arrested?"

"It was before she was a duchess, and no, she didn't actually get arrested, but it was a near shave. She'd been on some march for the vote, and she and some of her friends got hauled in by a constable. No fear of that happening nowadays, of course."

"No, I don't suppose a constable would dare to drag a duchess off to jail. And there's no need for her to march anyway, is there? Surely a duchess has more effective, less overt ways of swaying public opinion."

"Quite so. If her letters to me are any indication, she's been working on Jamie and his lot mercilessly."

"Jamie?"

"Torquil's brother-in-law, his late sister Patricia's husband. He's in Parliament. He was in the Commons, but he lost his seat after one term—if I'm remembering Irene's letters correctly. A few years later when his father died, he took his father's seat in the Lords, so Irene still works on him about the vote every chance she gets."

"He lost his seat in the House of Commons because of the duchess's suffragist work?"

"No, I believe it was because he married someone notorious. Not the duke's sister. I'm referring to his second wife, Amanda, who had some scandal attached to her name."

"Don't talk to me of scandals," she said, holding up her hand with a groan. "I've heard enough of those during the last six days to last a lifetime. Tell me about your other sister instead. What's she like?"

"Clara?" His grin vanished, his countenance becoming thoughtful. "Clara's a bit of a dark horse. She's quiet, shy, with a sphinxlike ability to hide what she's thinking. God only knows what she thinks of me nowadays."

"What do you mean?"

He was silent a long moment. "Do you remember that first night aboard ship, when I told you about my father?" he asked at last.

"That he disinherited you? Yes, of course."

"That wasn't the whole story. When my father booted me out, he told me I'd never amount to anything, and when your father and I struck silver, I knew I had the chance to prove my old man wrong. I couldn't give up that chance."

Marjorie frowned, puzzled. "Why should you have had to?"

"Because I'd already told my sisters I'd come home. Irene was getting married, and she didn't want to run the paper once she became a duchess, so she asked me to take it over. Clara didn't want to have anything to do with the newspaper business in those days. Like you, she wanted to have a London season, find a husband, get married—all that. So, for her sake, I agreed to come home and run Deverill Publishing. But the truth is . . . I didn't want to do it."

"But why not? It was your dream. Weren't you jumping at the chance to have it back?"

He gave a short laugh and looked away. "You'd think I would have been, wouldn't you? But once you've had a dream snatched from you, it's damned hard to give it a second chance."

Marjorie understood at once. "Yes, one doesn't want to get one's hopes up only to be disappointed again."

"Exactly."

"But why would you have reason to think that would happen?"

"Because even though Irene ran the paper, our father still owned it, and I knew he'd fight me tooth and nail. Oh, Irene said she'd make sure that didn't happen, that when she got back from her honeymoon, we'd stand against my father together—all three of us. But if that failed—which was quite a likely thing, in my opinion—our father would have booted me out of the company again, and none of us would have been able to stop it. And besides—"

He broke off, still staring out the window.

"And besides . . . ?" she prompted.

"Oh, let's be honest." He looked at her, and in his eyes, there was a glint of the same defiance she'd seen the first time he'd talked about his father. "After nearly four years in America, I didn't have much to show for it. My pride just couldn't stomach coming home to be under my father's thumb, to watch him smirk and hear him crow. When Billy and I struck silver, it was like the answer to a prayer."

"Except that you left your sisters in the lurch."

He sighed, his defiance vanishing. "Yes," he admitted. "Clara, in particular. She got stuck running things on her own. As I said, she's always been shy, and the idea of being in charge must have been terrifying to her."

"Do you think she's holding a grudge about that?"

"I don't know," he confessed. "She writes to me, says what happened is all water under the bridge. She still runs the company and seems to enjoy it, she married Viscount Galbraith, and loves him madly, so . . ."

"So, all's well that ends well," Marjorie finished for him, watching him closely. "Right?"

"I'm not sure," he confessed. "I let her down. I made her a promise, and I broke it. I don't like breaking promises." He took a deep breath and looked at her again. "Which brings me to you."

"Me?"

"Yes. There's something I must say to you, and since we're almost to Torquil House, I'd best say it now, while we're still alone. I may not have another chance." Abruptly, he moved to sit directly opposite her. "Yesterday, you said I'm like a father to you."

"Oh, don't!" she cried, hating to be reminded of that remark. It seemed ludicrous now, after their extraordinary kiss. "Forget I said that, please."

"I can't. It was a fair comparison, given my responsibilities. And yet . . ." He paused, and his expression changed, softened, something coming into it that was hot and tender and sent her heart slamming into her ribs. "I didn't see it that way at the time."

She stared into his eyes and the passion in their tawny depths made those torrid moments in her stateroom more vivid than ever. "You didn't?"

"No. In fact, I was quite insulted." He leaned back, putting distance between them. "And the result was unforgivable."

Marjorie stirred. "I wouldn't quite say that," she said faintly.

"I would. I must. I gave my word to your father that I would look after you, and what I did was the exact opposite of that. For my intemperate actions, you have my deepest apologies. I realize," he rushed on before she could speak, "that you resent your father, and you have good cause, but we both know I'm not much different."

"I don't know that." The words were barely out of her mouth before she remembered how she'd been telling herself all these same things aboard the train a short time ago. She did know. She'd known all along.

His next words reinforced that bitter fact. "Yes, you do. We both know the sort of man I am. I've never pretended to be anything else."

"But don't you ever want a home?" she cried, frustrated and baffled. "Don't you want to settle down, marry, have children?"

His expression hardened. "I did once," he said, reminding her of the dreams he'd had and lost. "But now? No." He paused, considering. "Someday, perhaps."

Someday. God, how she loathed that word.

"I don't understand," she said, feeling wretched. "You really intend to spend the rest of your days roaming the globe? Is that what you want from life?"

He smiled a little. "You asked me that same question the first night aboard ship."

"And you never answered it."

"Then let me do so now." He leaned forward, his knees brushing hers in the confined space. "I don't know what I want, Marjorie, and that's the truth. Growing up, I always had a clear picture of what my life would be. At eighteen, I was in love and engaged to be married. Like you, I was sure just where I fit into the world, and what I wanted. I had no doubts, no fears. And then, it all fell apart. In a single afternoon, I lost everything that mattered to me. And I don't think . . . I don't think there's anything that can replace it."

"Why does anything need to replace it? You're wealthy. You could be a man of leisure—"

"Be part of the idle rich, you mean?" He shook his head. "Being idle isn't in my nature, and as I already told you, money itself doesn't matter much to me. Oh, I relished the fact that my father could no longer say I was worthless, and I'm glad I was able to help my sisters save Deverill Publishing. And I do enjoy playing the markets, but that's just for fun. The truth is, I can't imagine what would impel me to settle down, but it would have to be bigger and more exciting than anything I've come across yet. I thrive on challenge—"

"Well, that means you're not like my father at all!" she cried, sounding as cross as she felt. "Because he never met a challenge he didn't run away from. And, whatever you say, I think you're a far better man than he ever was."

"Now you're just being romantic," he said, his voice so tender it hurt.

She looked away, knowing he was right. Despite everything she knew, despite everything she'd been telling herself, she had started having romantic notions about him without even realizing it. He may have given her her first kiss, but she suspected that sort of thing didn't mean much. Jonathan had probably kissed plenty of girls already, and God help any of them if they'd ever pinned any romantic hopes on him because of it.

People didn't change, she knew that well enough from her father's example. If a man was born to roam, he wasn't about to give it up, not even for love. She knew that from watching her mother's pain.

In the wake of her silence, he leaned closer, tapping the window that gave a view of the elegant street outside. "That's the life you want, but I left that life a long time ago, and I haven't missed it."

She didn't reply. Instead, she stared out at the opulent houses that lined Park Lane as the passion of her first kiss turned to dust and ashes.

"You say you resent your father for not settling down? Then resent me, too, for the same reason."

"But I can't," she cried, making that galling admission as the carriage rolled to a stop. "Not after . . . after . . ." She paused, the memory of that kiss making her blush even now. "I can't resent you," she whispered.

"I wish you would," he muttered. "Because if you don't—" He broke off and turned away to yank open the carriage door. "God help us both."

Giving her no chance to reply, he exited the vehicle without even waiting for the driver to roll out the steps.

Chapter 12

$\mathcal{H}$aving once stood in the foyer of Cornelius Vanderbilt's Fifth Avenue mansion, Marjorie was not completely unfamiliar with the opulent splendor in which the wealthy lived, but she hadn't seen enough of that sort of thing to be blasé about it, and as she stepped inside Torquil House, the grandeur of the four-story entrance hall took her breath away.

Creamy white Corinthian columns and Gothic arches supported the floors that ringed the open foyer and enormous potted date palms flanked the walnut entrance doors behind her. In front of her was the grand staircase, sweeping upward in a graceful curve to the floors above. Various niches along the walls displayed sculptures and pottery that had probably been acquired on some previous duke's grand tour, and oil paintings—priceless ones, no doubt—hung on every scrap of the remaining wall space.

"Bit grand, what?" Jonathan murmured beside her.

"A bit," she agreed in a whisper as they watched the butler who'd shown them in depart up that stunning staircase to inform the duchess of their arrival. "We're staying here?"

"Well, you are."

Surprised by the clarification, she looked at him. "Aren't you?"

"Well, I was supposed to." He paused, stepping closer to Marjorie as a pair of footmen moved past him, carrying luggage from their taxi. "But now that I'm about to toss you into Irene's lap with almost no warning, I'm wondering if I ought to reserve a room at a hotel."

"Nonsense," she scoffed, but then, she looked at him and noticed his thumbs tapping against his thighs. "Nervous?"

"After ten years, wouldn't you be?"

"What happened to the man who worked as a bounty hunter and bravely fought off claim jumpers and mining magnates with my father?"

There was no time for him to respond.

"You must be Uncle Jonathan."

Marjorie and Jonathan turned to find a pair of dark-haired, gray-eyed boys behind them, one perhaps five years of age, the other about three.

"I am," Jonathan answered. "You must be my nephews."

"Lord Mountmorres." The older boy bowed in rather formal fashion. "At your service."

"How do you do," Jonathan said gravely, giving a proper bow. "Lord Mountmorres."

"Mama says you may call me Henry." He gestured to his brother, who was staring at Jonathan in wide-eyed silence. "This is Lord Christopher. But we call him Kit."

"Pleased to meet you both." Jonathan gestured to Marjorie. "May I present Miss McGann?"

"Miss McGann," they said in unison. They bowed together, too, and Marjorie had to press her lips tight to hide a smile as she gave an answering curtsy.

"Master Henry?" a voice called from above. "Where are you?"

Henry heaved an aggrieved sigh. "Nanny," he informed them without enthusiasm.

"Master Henry? Is Kit with you?"

A stout woman, clad in a black dress and white lace apron and cap, paused on the crescent-shaped landing. "There you are!" she cried, her wide face creasing with relief as she waddled down the remaining stairs. "I've been looking everywhere. You're not supposed to go off without me. What have you been doing?"

"Meeting Uncle Jonathan," Henry told her, pointing at him as the nanny came toward them.

"Mr. Deverill," she said, dipping her knees in a quick curtsy as she came between the two boys and took each one by the hand. "Nanny Eliot. I hope the boys haven't been making themselves a nuisance?"

"Not at all."

"I'm glad of that, sir. Come along, you two."

"But I wanted to show Uncle Jonathan the train set I got for my birthday," protested Henry as they were led toward a door at the back of the entrance hall.

"Plenty of time for that later. Right now, we're going to the kitchens to see what Mrs. Mason's made you for high tea."

They had just vanished through the green baize door when another voice came echoing down the stairs.

"Jonathan?"

At the sound of his name, they both turned to watch a slender blonde in a teal-blue tea gown come tearing down the stairs, the butler and two female servants following at a slower pace.

One glance was enough to tell Marjorie this was one of Jonathan's sisters. She had the same golden good looks, hazel eyes, and brilliant smile as her brother—a smile that showed clearly how she felt about his return and should have reassured him at once.

"Oh, Jonathan!" She halted before them, but instead of making the restrained and elegant greeting a lady of the _ton_ would be expected to offer, she threw herself into her brother's arms with wholehearted abandon. "You're home, you're home at last."

He wrapped his arms around his sister, his body seeming to lose some of its tension as she planted smacking kisses on both his cheeks, and when she hugged him again, Marjorie saw his eyes close and his lips tighten as if in relief and profound affection. "Irenie," he murmured, pressing his lips to her hair.

She laughed again. "It really _is_ you. Only you ever call me Irenie."

She pulled back, glancing over him. "Oh, my," she breathed, pressing a hand to her chest as if overcome. "Look at you."

"Look at you," he countered. Smiling a little, he doffed his hat, stepped back, and bowed. "Your Grace."

"Oh, stop." She tossed her head, making a sound of laughing derision at the address. She glanced at the servants who had halted a discreet distance behind her, then she leaned closer to her brother and whispered, "Even I'm not used to that title, not even after six years. Every time I hear it, I look around, expecting to see the duke's mother standing nearby. And besides, you're my brother. You're not supposed to call me 'Your Grace.'"

"I've been away a long time. Forgive me for forgetting the proper protocol for titles." He grinned. "Duchess."

She groaned and turned to Marjorie. "He's such a tease. You must be Miss McGann. How do you do? Forgive me for not greeting you properly just now."

"Not at all." She curtsied. "Your Grace."

The duchess gave her a smile, reminding Marjorie again of her brother. "Didn't I just say I'm not used to that address? And your father was like a brother to Jonathan, so you're practically part of the family. No, you must call me Irene."

"If you wish. I hope you will call me Marjorie?"

"I'd be delighted to do so. Now that we've dispensed with the formalities, let us come to practical matters. Jonathan's telegram earlier today informed me that you've no maid? Well," she added, when Marjorie shook her head in reply, "we can remedy that easily enough."

She turned, gesturing to the servants hovering in the background. "You've already met Boothby, our butler? He'll look after you, Jonathan, since you've no valet with you."

"That's not necessary, Irene," Jonathan said at once. "I've never had a valet in my life, so I'm quite accustomed to dressing myself. And I'm sure Boothby has plenty to do without the added inconvenience of looking after me."

"Very well." She gave a nod to the butler, who gave a bow and stepped back, then she gestured to the older of the two female servants. "This is our housekeeper, Mrs. Jaspar, who will see that the footmen have put your luggage in the proper rooms."

At once, the housekeeper departed to carry out that instruction, and Irene beckoned the third servant forward. "And this is Eileen, our second housemaid. She'll attend you, Marjorie, until we can find you a proper lady's maid. Now then," she added as the servant gave Marjorie a curtsy and a tentative smile, "would you care for some refreshment, or would you prefer to go to your room to freshen up and change before dinner?"

Marjorie hesitated. She was famished after their long journey, for no formal breakfast had been served this morning, and the train from Southampton had not possessed a dining car. She also couldn't help a profound curiosity about the other sister, but she knew curiosity could not allow her to intrude on the first moments of a family's reunion.

"I think I would prefer to go up and change," Marjorie answered. "If you don't mind."

"Not at all. Eileen will show you to your room, and I will see you this evening. We dine at eight, but the family usually begins gathering in the drawing room about half past seven for cordials. Do join us there, if you wish."

Marjorie gave the duchess and Jonathan a nod of farewell and turned away, but before she could follow Eileen up the stairs, the front doors opened behind her, and a tall, willow-slim woman in a tailored beige walking suit came into the entrance hall. "I don't understand why editors always have to make such a fuss," she said, speaking over her shoulder to the tall, blond-haired man following her through the wide doorway. "You'd think I'd told him to get stuffed."

The man laughed. "You did worse than that, Clara. You told him he was being difficult."

"That's not what I said. But he is so aggravatingly old-fashioned. We must keep up with the times, and that includes printing photographs in our publications. Besides—" She broke off as she turned and spied Jonathan and Marjorie. Her steps faltered, and her body went still. She offered no ebullient greeting as her sister had done. She did not even smile.

Marjorie felt Jonathan tense beside her. She heard his sharp, in-drawn breath and his slow, resigned exhale.

"So, the prodigal returns at last," the woman murmured as she pulled out her hat pin and removed her wide-brimmed hat of leghorn straw. Her absurdly tiny nose gave a sniff as she wove the pin through the hat brim. "Better six years late than not at all, I suppose."

"Hullo, Clara," he said.

She made no reply, but her hands stilled.

Oh, no, Marjorie thought, feeling the tension in the air.

Irene gave a cough. "Clara, this is Miss Marjorie McGann. Marjorie, my sister, Lady Galbraith."

"Miss McGann." The woman's features relaxed into friendlier lines as she crossed the entrance hall. By the time she reached Marjorie, she was smiling, but she did not even glance at Jonathan. "Irene tele-phoned me at the newspaper office earlier and told me you were coming with our brother after all. Welcome to England."

"Thank you, Lady Galbraith."

"Clara, please," she said and gestured to the man who had come in with her. "This is my husband, Rex."

"Miss McGann." Lord Galbraith bowed to her, then he looked at Jonathan and held out his hand, hinting that he at least was of the same mind as the duchess about Jonathan's return. "Welcome home."

"Thank you," Jonathan replied as the two men shook hands.

There was another silence, shorter this time, then the duchess spoke again. "I was just about to have Boothby send tea up to the library," she said with a nod to the butler, who at once glided away in obedi-ence to this command. "It's a bit late, but one can always do with a cup of tea."

Her voice was smooth and cheerful, as if nothing at all was amiss, as if the tension brought with Clara's arrival wasn't as thick as an English pea soup fog. "Miss McGann is going up to change, but Jonathan . . ." She paused, and this time, her gaze paused meaning-fully on her brother. "Jonathan is joining me."

"How lovely," the viscountess said, her bright voice somehow managing to imply that it might not be lovely at all. The English,

Marjorie appreciated, thinking of Lady Stansbury and her circle, had an astonishing talent for civil insincerity.

"No tea for me," Lord Galbraith said. "I'm going up to change. It's almost six o'clock. And," he added, giving Jonathan a wink over his wife's head, "after Clara has finished shredding her poor brother into spills for being away so long, I suspect I'll be needed to offer him something stronger than tea."

"I've no intention of shr . . . shredding Jonathan into spills," Lady Galbraith protested, her voice faltering on the admission. "Even though he deserves it."

"It's good to see you, Clara," Jonathan said gently, but he didn't move closer. Instead, he waited.

"Is it?" Her round face twisted, her coolness seemed to shatter into pieces, and she gave a sob. "Oh, Jonathan!"

He closed the distance in an instant, and Marjorie gave a sigh of relief as the viscountess's straw hat and hat pin fell to the floor and she wrapped her arms around her brother's neck with another sob.

Marjorie watched them a moment longer, then she turned tactfully away and followed the housekeeper up the stairs.

THE DRAWING ROOM of Torquil House, with draperies of ivory and pale green and glittering crystal chandeliers, was every bit as grand as the entrance hall. But at the far end of the room, a pair of immense double doors had been flung back to reveal a much cozier room, with murky green walls, overstuffed bookshelves, and chintz-covered sofas. Electric lamps had been lit, and a fire burned in the grate, warding off the evening chill in the spring air.

Irene seated herself on one of the two sofas facing each other in the center of the room, Clara sat beside her, and Jonathan sank down opposite them.

"Now, Jonathan, you must tell us everything," Irene said, wasting no time on preliminaries. "Your letter last month said Miss McGann was a schoolgirl."

"That's what I'd been led to expect myself. I didn't learn otherwise until I met her."

"You couldn't have written again and clarified that she was a grown woman?"

"I did. In my telegram."

"Which was hardly edifying." Irene pulled a slip of paper out of the pocket of her tea gown and read, "'Miss McGann older than thought. Will need maid and room prepared for her. Explain all soon. Arriving about teatime. Jonathan.'"

Shoving the telegram back in her pocket, she looked at him again. "You might have warned us what to expect in greater detail than that."

"I would have done," he replied wryly, "if I'd had the opportunity."

He launched into explanations, but he'd barely conveyed Marjorie's unexpected arrival aboard ship before he was interrupted by a round of merry laughter from the two women opposite.

He watched them, not nearly as amused as they seemed to be. "I fail to see what you two are laughing about," he said, trying to assume an air of dignity.

"Serves you right," Irene said, still laughing. "After you just left her there."

"Well, I didn't know what else to do with her," he mumbled, shifting in his seat, reminded that nothing could make a man feel more of a fool than his sisters enjoying a joke at his expense. "It didn't seem right to—"

"Bully for Marjorie," Clara interrupted him. "Forcing you to live up to your responsibilities for a change."

"That's not fair," he countered, but as he watched her chin go up, he was reminded that he didn't have a leg to stand on there, not with Clara, and he sighed, his defenses collapsing.

"Clara, I am sorry I let you down six years ago."

"So you said in your letter on the subject. No need to apologize again."

"I think maybe there is," he said gently, "if your face is anything to go by. But the truth is . . ." He paused and leaned forward to take her hand in his. "As long as Papa owned the company, having me come home and take over the paper would never have worked."

"You don't know that."

"Yes, I do. And so do you. Papa would never have allowed me the autonomy and control he allowed you, and Irene before you. He'd have fought me every step of the way. Sooner or later, we'd have had another row, and he'd have tossed me out again."

"Oh, I suppose you're right," she cried, her hand squeezing his hard. "But we missed you, damn it! It hurt when you didn't come home. It really hurt."

"I know."

He paused, his thumb caressing the back of her hand. "What if I vow not to stay away so long next time? Would that satisfy you, petal?"

Her lips curved up a little at the use of her childhood nickname. "It might do," she conceded. "Jack."

At the sound of his own nickname—one his sisters had given him when he was about five because as a boy he couldn't sit still and was forever jumping up and down like a jack-in-the-box—Jonathan laughed, and Irene gave a gratified sigh.

"Thank goodness you two are through squabbling," she said. "Now perhaps we can return to the topic of Miss McGann?"

"Gladly," Jonathan answered, relieved. Letting go of Clara's hand, he leaned back again and turned to his elder sister. "As I was saying, Marjorie circumvented my plan to leave her where she was until she's out of mourning, so here we are. The question is, what's to be done with her now? She wants to make a life here in England—have a debut, do the season, find a husband, all that sort of thing. I don't want to impose on you, but—"

He broke off as the butler entered with a laden tray. "Tea, Your Grace."

"Thank you, Boothby," Irene said as the butler placed the tray on a small table beside her seat. "That will be all."

"Very good, ma'am." The butler set the kettle back down, bowed and moved to depart, but he halted by the door when Irene called after him.

"And Boothby?"

"Your Grace?"

"Would you please have Mrs. Mason send some sandwiches and tea up to Miss McGann? The afternoon train from Southampton has no dining car, and the poor girl must be famished."

The butler departed, and Irene returned her attention to the subject at hand. "First of all," she said as she poured a bit of steaming water from the kettle into the teapot, "let's dispense with any notion of imposition. We're family, which means Jonathan's obligations are ours as well. As to Marjorie, there's only one thing to be done."

She paused, swirling the teapot to let the hot water warm it, then she dumped the water into a bowl on the tray reserved for that purpose. "We'll introduce her into society and make a place for her, of course."

Clara nodded in agreement, and Jonathan squeezed his eyes shut in relief. "Thank you," he said, opening his eyes again. "I'm glad I can rely on you to look after her properly while I'm in Africa."

"Africa?" his sisters echoed in simultaneous surprise.

Jonathan tensed, his relief dissolving as he watched the two women exchange glances.

Irene spoke first. "You don't think you'll be going now, do you?" She shook her head, laughing a little, and he had the sinking feeling his plans were about to be tossed aside. "Jonathan, Clara and I are complete strangers to the girl."

"So was I, until a week ago."

"Which is a week longer than we've known her." She paused long enough to spoon tea into the pot and add water from the kettle, then she went on, "More importantly, however, neither of us is Marjorie's legal guardian."

"That distinction hardly matters much at this point—"

"On the contrary," she cut in as she put the lid on the teapot and turned to him again. "It matters to *me*."

"I'll be back by January." He stirred again, appreciating that he was skating on very thin ice. "Maybe by Christmas," he amended. "In the meantime, you two are far more capable of watching over the girl than I am."

"Perhaps, but we are not the ones who promised to do so," Irene said incisively. "You did."

A promise he knew might be in great danger if he stayed. He thought of Marjorie in the carriage a short time ago, with all the same desire he felt reflected in her eyes. But he knew, as she did not, where such desires could lead, and if he lingered here, he risked breaking the promises he'd made to her father. God help him, he did not think he'd have honor enough or strength enough to stop himself.

It was galling to admit how vulnerable he was where she was concerned. He'd known her little more than a week, and yet, she aroused in him a passion he was finding hard to master. If he gave in to it, he would prove himself to be the very thing he was supposed to be protecting her from.

"I will do all I can for her, Irene," he said after a moment, "but I'm of little use to her here. The best thing I can do is leave her to your excellent chaperonage while I see to her business interests."

"I care nothing about her business interests," Irene said with uncompromising bluntness. "I have no intention of allowing you to leave that poor girl with people who are virtual strangers to her and take off for the wilds. She is not a suitcase, and I am not a locker at King's Cross."

"I know that, but damn it, Irene, there's nothing I can do for her here. The girl needs to be introduced, brought out into society, and in that regard, I'm about as useful as a chocolate teapot."

"You'll be far more useful than you realize. A good-looking, single man with money and titled connections is akin to the Holy Grail, dear brother. You will be an irresistible attraction to the young ladies. A fact that," she added as he groaned, "will enable Marjorie to more easily meet young women her own age and make friends."

"Poor friends, indeed, if their sole reason for being so is to get close to a single man with money."

Irene, sadly, ignored that very valid point. "A man like you is an excellent asset to any hostess, especially during the season. You will be of great use at social events, balancing the numbers at dinner parties and entertaining our guests, that sort of thing."

He stiffened in dismay. "You cannot be serious."

Clara decided this was the perfect moment to offer an opinion. "Irene, I'm sure our friends will adore hearing tales of his life in the

American West," she said, making Jonathan realize in chagrin that they'd planned this, together, probably on the telephone right after Irene had received his telegram. "He can partner the wallflowers when we have dancing, perhaps introduce some of his old school-fellows to Marjorie."

"Absolutely not," he said, appalled by that thought. "If my friends from Winchester and Oxford are anywhere near as wild now as they were in our schooldays, I wouldn't let any of them within fifty yards of the girl—and neither would you, if you knew even a fraction of the things we did. As for the rest, I can't imagine she'll be doing much dancing. She's in mourning, you know."

"She won't be attending any balls, that's true," Irene conceded as she added milk to the teacups and began to strain the tea. "But it's quite all right if she dances here, in our home. Many of our friends play the piano, so we often roll back the carpets and have a bit of dancing after dinner. And if we do, I've no intention of telling Marjorie to go sit in the corner. As for you, Clara's right that you'll be an excellent dance partner for any of our female guests, including her."

Jonathan thought of Marjorie with flashing pink sapphires around her throat and a dawning sensual awareness in her eyes. He thought of her in his arms, her mouth beneath his, her body yielding to his advance without restraint. He thought of how it would be, continuing to have her so close, and yet forbidden, and he felt as if he'd just entered Dante's seventh circle of hell. "And how long am I expected to be the useful single man at dinner parties, dancing with wallflowers and introducing suitable bachelors to my ward?"

Irene considered as she dropped sugar into the teacups. "If I thought I could get away with it," she said, reaching for a spoon, "I'd say until she's married, but knowing you—"

"Irene, be reasonable!"

"You think I'm not being reasonable?" She paused, staring at him, one blond eyebrow lifted. It was a look he remembered quite well even though he hadn't seen it for ten years, and wisely, he decided to change tactics.

"But her trust fund has shares in South African companies. If war with the Boers breaks out, she could lose 10 to 15 percent of her inheritance. What sort of guardian would I be if I let that happen?"

"And yet, I remain unmoved."

"This is ridiculous," he muttered, ignoring Clara's smothered laugh. "Can't we fashion some sort of compromise?"

"As I recall," Irene said, "half the problems you had with Papa came from your inability—and his—to compromise."

"That's not fair, and you know it."

"Maybe not, but I'm thinking of the girl, not of what's fair."

Deservedly rebuked, he fell silent.

"How long," Irene asked as she stirred the tea, "until Marjorie is of legal age?"

"She turns twenty-one August thirteenth."

"Very well." Irene tapped the spoon against the rim of the last cup and set it aside. "Here is my offer: I will introduce the girl about, assist her in making friends and such. Clara will do the same. You, meanwhile, will postpone your trip until her birthday, and during that two months, you will put yourself at my disposal and hers, just as I described."

"And what am I to do between dinner parties? Lounge about, twiddling my thumbs?"

And torturing myself.

"Given your restless nature, I would suggest you find something useful and productive to do. As for the girl, you can assist me in preparing her for life as an heiress in British society. Ensuring that she is happily settled here is as much a part of being her guardian as watching over her finances, in my opinion. And no, this is not optional."

He exhaled a sigh, falling back in his seat. "And when she turns twenty-one, what then?"

"She'll be ready to begin making her own decisions about what she wishes to do, and you will see that whatever arrangements she desires are made. If she feels comfortable remaining with us while you go to Africa, then so be it, and off you go. If not, you will remain here until she is comfortable with us and with her new life. Either way, if doing the season and making a debut are what she wants, I will be happy to launch her, and I expect you to be here for her entire debut season. Are we agreed?"

She didn't wait for an answer. "Good," she said and held out his cup and saucer. "Tea?"

"No, thank you," he muttered, knowing he was as trapped as a fly in treacle. "After wrangling with the two of you, I'm now very much in need of that drink Galbraith offered me."

"My husband," Clara said with obvious glee, "is such a perceptive man."

Chapter 13

After wolfing down the sandwiches Irene had sent up, Marjorie felt much better. Her hunger sated, she bathed in a luxurious, surprisingly modern bathroom, and then, with Eileen's assistance, she changed into an evening dress.

Fearing the baroness's smashing black gown would not be appropriate, Marjorie was forced to make do with her only other evening dress, a dull garment of mauve velvet purchased when she was sixteen for the occasions when Mr. Jessop and his wife had brought her to Manhattan for the theater or an opera. It had a modest neckline and enormous leg o'mutton sleeves, and though hopelessly out of fashion, it would have to do. And since Lady Stansbury's maid had replaced all the ecru trimmings on the dress with black ones, she didn't see how anyone could fault her for choosing it.

She was proven wrong there, however, the moment she met Lady David.

The introduction had scarcely been performed before the duke's sister-in-law, an elegant woman in fashionable green silk, was looking at her askance, delicate auburn brows lifted.

"I see you've chosen to go into half-mourning, Miss McGann," she said, and though her comment seemed innocuous enough, something in the tone of her voice caused Marjorie to stiffen. "Rather a daring choice, so soon."

She thinks this is daring? If she only knew. Marjorie wondered what

Lady David's reaction would have been had she come down wearing the baroness's black gown. "Is it daring?" she asked, looking down, then back up, feigning surprise at the question.

"Not at all," Irene said, coming to her defense. "If I understand the situation, Marjorie, you hardly knew your father?"

"I hadn't seen him since I was seven."

"There you are, then. Ah, here's our husbands at last, Carlotta," she exclaimed, looking past Lady David to a pair of men in white tie approaching their corner of the drawing room. "You two are usually the first ones down. We were beginning to wonder if you were ever coming. Do let me introduce you."

Lady David was obliged to postpone the topic of Marjorie's dress as the duke and his brother stepped forward. "Henry, David," Irene continued, "this is Jonathan's ward, Miss Marjorie McGann. Marjorie, my husband, Henry, the Duke of Torquil."

Irene paused as the duke, a tall man with black hair and piercing gray eyes, bowed to Marjorie, then she gestured to a smaller man with lighter hair and the same gray eyes. "And this is the duke's brother, Lord David."

She presented her brother to them, and after the men had shaken hands, the duke offered sherry to the ladies. The offer was accepted, and as Torquil moved to the liquor cabinet, Lord David and Jonathan followed to assist him, leaving Lady David to return to the topic of clothes.

"It's a personal decision, I suppose, how long to wear full mourning," she said, earning a forbearing little sigh from the duchess. "But is it wise to flout convention and forgo it altogether?"

"In Marjorie's case," Irene said with decision, "full mourning ought to be optional. If she wishes to adhere strictly to custom and wear solid black for the full year—"

She broke off, biting back a smile as Marjorie gave her a frantic, pleading look. "As her chaperone," she resumed, "I think it would be perfectly all right for her to go straight into half-mourning. What do you think, Clara?" she asked as her sister joined them.

"Oh, I agree," she said, much to Marjorie's relief. "And come

August, when we go to the country, she could abandon mourning completely, in my opinion."

"You might have work convincing your brother about that," Marjorie said dryly. "He expected me to hide in seclusion for a year, wearing black crape and lashings of jet."

"What?" Irene laughed, glancing at her brother. "Oh, Jonathan, you didn't? For a father she didn't even know?"

Subjected to his sisters' teasing censure, he displayed all the embarrassment typical of men caught in such situations. "What do I know about these things?" he muttered, taking the pair of filled glasses the duke handed him and bringing them to the ladies. "Irene, if you wish to shorten Marjorie's mourning period, it's up to you," he said as he handed Marjorie and the duchess their glasses, "but for my part, I deemed it better to err on the side of caution."

"Caution?" Clara repeated, laughing as he turned away. "That's one way of putting it."

"Oh, but ladies, he's been even worse than you imagine," Marjorie assured, happy to join in the teasing and wreak some vengeance upon Jonathan for her week of needlework. "During our voyage, he put me in the care of Lady Stansbury."

Everyone groaned at the mention of that name, everyone but Jonathan.

"I stand by that decision as well," he said firmly as he returned again with sherry for Clara and Lady David. "Better to have Countess Stansbury chaperoning Marjorie than that Vasiliev woman."

"Baroness Vasiliev?" echoed Irene in lively surprise. "Was she on board?"

Jonathan made a sound of derision. "Baroness, my eye."

"Oh, but she is," Irene assured, giving Marjorie no end of satisfaction. "Henry and I were introduced to her in Paris while on honeymoon, and Henry insisted to me that she couldn't possibly be a real baroness—"

"That's what I said!" Jonathan turned to Torquil. "I'm glad someone shares my view."

"Except that I was wrong, it seems," the duke informed him as he poured sherry for the men. "I looked her up in the *Almanach de Gotha*, and there she was."

"Ha!" Marjorie put in, giving Jonathan a triumphant look. "And you thought she was a *poseur*."

"I can hardly be blamed for that opinion," he countered at once. "To my mind, the woman is far too theatrical. The title may be in the *Almanach de Gotha*, but how do we know she's the genuine article?"

"Oh, for heaven's sake," Marjorie muttered, rolling her eyes. "You see?" she added, appealing to his sisters. "You see what I've had to put up with?"

They nodded in commiseration, and, outnumbered, Jonathan held up his hands, palms toward her in a gesture of surrender. "All right, all right, I may have been wrong about that woman," he conceded, "but I was right about the Count de la Rosa, wasn't I?"

"De la Rosa?" David made a sound of disgust as he accepted a filled glass from his brother. "That blackguard? Was he on the voyage, too?"

"He was," Jonathan said. "And if he's in the *Almanach de Gotha*, I'll eat my hat."

"He's not," David assured him. "Our hall boy has more aristocratic lineage in his ancestry than that blackguard."

"But he is handsome," Lady David said with a wistful little sigh. "And so charming. Not quite top drawer, of course, but he gives fabulous parties. We went to one at his villa near Cannes seven or eight years ago, remember, David?"

"I doubt he gives parties like that nowadays," her husband responded. "He's got enormous debts, I heard."

"That's not surprising," Rex put in and took a sip of sherry. "And there's no arguing his character. He's rotten all through, even if the ladies never seem to see it."

Marjorie's mind went back to the episode in her cabin doorway with the count, seeing it with the benefit of hindsight. She thought of his hand, holding hers so tightly, of the way he'd leaned so close—signs of desperation, she appreciated now. Deceived by his charming manner, she hadn't sensed it at the time, or the danger it might present to her. Jonathan might very well have saved her from social disaster, or something worse.

She looked at him, startled to find him watching her, but she could read nothing in his face. "On the contrary, Rex," he said, his voice light. "Some ladies aren't the least bit charmed by him. Lady Stansbury certainly wasn't."

"Ah," Irene said, smiling, "now we see why you asked her to be poor Marjorie's chaperone aboard ship."

"Just so," he said. "Tease me for it all you like, but—"

"And we shall!" Clara declared and turned to Marjorie. "My brother was very cruel to leave you in the care of that odious woman. I suppose she made you knit something?"

Marjorie shook her head. "Embroidery," she said solemnly, earning herself commiseration from all the women, even Lady David.

"I knew it had to be something like that," Clara continued. "She's forever after all of us to make things for the church Bring and Buy Sales when we're down at Ravenwood. She's Irene and Torquil's neighbor, you know."

"Much to her dismay," Irene said with cheer. "Oh, she adores Torquil, but she quite disapproves of me, as I'm sure Marjorie was made aware."

"I did gather you weren't one of her favorites," Marjorie admitted. "It seems Lady Stansbury does not approve of women having political opinions."

"Oh, it's worse than that." Irene's hazel eyes danced with mischief above the rim of her sherry glass as she took a sip. "She feels that women oughtn't to have opinions at all, at least not until we marry, at which point we need our husbands to tell us what our opinions should be. I earned her disapproval by having dared to form my own opinions long before I met my husband, and I saw no need to alter them after the wedding."

"Much to my chagrin," the duke put in. "My wife, Miss McGann, is happy to contradict my opinions whenever the opportunity presents. Sometimes, I think she does it merely for sport."

"Someone has to stand up to you," the duchess replied at once. "You'd be impossibly tyrannical otherwise. Your sisters would agree with me, if they were here."

"I'm rather glad they're not," David put in. "It's much less of a madhouse around here during the season now that Sarah and Angela have their own establishments, and Jamie's boys are back at Harrow for summer term."

"We'll call on Sarah and Angela tomorrow, shall we?" Clara suggested. "They'd love to meet Marjorie. And I know they're dying to meet Jonathan," she added and looked at her brother over her shoulder. "You should come with us, brother. We'll be paying calls all afternoon."

"Can't, thanks," he answered at once. "I'll be far too busy to gad about London paying calls."

"Busy with what?" Clara asked curiously.

"I'll think of something," he muttered.

Everyone laughed at that, particularly the men.

"I'd love to rescue you," Torquil told him, "but I have to be in the Lords. Important vote tomorrow."

"Is there a vote tomorrow?" asked Lady David. "Then Jamie's sure to be in town." Her face puckered, as if she'd just eaten a lemon. "I do hope he didn't bring that woman with him."

"Her name is Amanda," Irene said, her voice suddenly hard. "After over five years of having her in the family, one would think you'd know it by now."

"I know it." Lady David gave a sniff. "Doesn't mean I have to use it."

The tension between the two women was thick enough to cut with a knife, and in Irene's hazel eyes, so like Jonathan's, Marjorie recognized the same golden sparks of battle. Thankfully, however, Clara spoke again, breaking the tension.

"So, Irene, what can we do that won't violate Marjorie's mourning period? No balls, naturally, and no large parties. The theater or opera would be all right, I suppose, but we have to think of more amusements than that."

"What about a water party?" Torquil suggested. "We could take the *Mary Louisa* up the Thames, have a picnic at Kew."

"The *Mary Louisa* is a ship, I take it?" Jonathan asked.

"My second yacht."

"You have more than one?"

"The *Mary Louisa* is a smaller craft, for use on the river. The *Endeavor* is a larger vessel, for sailing the Solent and jaunts across the Channel."

"Two yachts?" Marjorie murmured sweetly, giving Jonathan a wide-eyed stare of amazement. "Imagine people spending their money on things like that," she continued, ignoring his wry answering glance. "Tell me, Your Grace, do you have racehorses and motorcars, too?"

"I'm afraid not. Irene and I have discussed buying a motor, but until we have better roads and petrol is more widely available, I can't see the point. As to racehorses, no, I'm not a racing man. Why do you ask?"

"That," Jonathan put in before she could answer, "is Marjorie's little joke. Do you host many water parties, Duke?"

"We've had two already this season."

"We'd have one every week," Irene assured, laughing, "if Henry had his way. My husband, you see, will seize any opportunity to be on the water. Which means, I should start planning one for Marjorie. Late June or early July, perhaps. That will give us time to introduce Marjorie to other members of the family and our friends. In the meantime, there's the theater and the opera, as Clara said, and we'll pay calls, have a few Afternoons-At-Home, that sort of thing."

"It all sounds lovely," Marjorie said with heartfelt appreciation. "I also have several friends from schooldays who are living here in England, and if any of them are in town, I'd love to call on them, if that's all right? But first . . ." She paused, giving the ladies an apologetic look. "Would you mind if I visit a modiste and obtain a proper wardrobe? I have no clothes but my teacher's uniforms, two Sunday frocks, and two evening gowns."

"That's all?" Lady David asked, looking appalled on her behalf, her scandalous sister-in-law forgotten. "Oh, my dear, you *are* in desperate need. Irene, we must take her to Jay's first thing."

"Of course," Irene said. "Sarah and Angela will have to wait. We'll go to Jay's tomorrow, and order you a few things in gray, mauve, and white—enough to carry you through to August. Then, before we leave for the country, we'll have our modiste fit you with an entire autumn wardrobe. You can come out of mourning at that time and have your clothes made up in any colors you like."

"Thank you," Marjorie said, relieved. "I'm grateful you're willing to bend the rules, Irene. I hope . . ." She paused, biting her lip. "I hope people won't think I'm unfeeling because of it."

"Not unfeeling," Lady David said, her voice light, but the disapproval beneath it was clear. "Though perhaps somewhat cavalier."

She wandered away to join the men, and Irene leaned closer to Marjorie. "You mustn't mind Carlotta. She's terrified of anything that might taint the family name. And she's a bit of a snob. The first time she ever met me, she gave the dress I was wearing the same once-over she gave yours tonight."

Marjorie glanced at the duchess's stunning gown of sapphire blue silk, a mark of the other woman's good taste. "I can't imagine your clothes could ever give cause for disapproval."

"Can't you?" Irene smiled. "When I first met Henry's family, I had no taste for fashion. I was running our newspaper business, Clara was my secretary, and we both dressed to suit our occupation—plain skirts, white blouses, and neckties. When we first came to stay in this house, it was an unexpected event, we had no proper clothes, and we had to make a mad dash to a department store on our way. Carlotta was horrified by our unpressed Debenham and Freebody dresses, wasn't she, Clara?"

"Well, yes, but that's because she's so concerned about what people think. She's nicer than she seems. Truly," Clara added, laughing as Marjorie politely didn't reply. "When Irene was on honeymoon, she chaperoned me, and I was able to appreciate that she just wants to show our family in the best light. And when it comes to clothes, she does have excellent taste. She taught me a great deal."

"And me," Irene said, gesturing to her dress. "I would never have picked something like this six years ago, but Carlotta was a great help to me, and you'll find her advice about clothes is impeccable. We should also begin our search for a maid for you as soon as possible. Eileen's a sweet girl, very willing, but though you won't be doing the season properly until next year, you must have a true lady's maid. Heavens," she added, as if surprised by her own words, "who'd ever have thought six years ago I'd say something like that?"

"Not me," Clara assured, taking a sip of sherry. "The reason we stopped at Debenham and Freebody on our way here that day so long ago was because I insisted. Had it been left to my sister, we'd have arrived on a duke's doorstep looking like a pair of typists, ink stains on our cuffs and pencils behind our ears."

Marjorie smiled, imagining these two standing in the duke's elegant entrance hall dressed as Clara described. "Your family has been in newspapers for many years, I understand?"

"Our great-grandfather started things, but it was his son who built Deverill Publishing into an empire," Irene said. "To no avail."

"Poor Papa," Clara said with a sigh. "He wanted to be a good businessman, but he wasn't. It must have been terrible for him, knowing his father and his son were both better at business than he was."

"And his daughters, too," Irene said stoutly. "I like to think Clara and I have both handled things rather well. And after Papa died, Jonathan was able to invest in the company, which enabled us to expand for the first time since my grandfather's day."

"I run Deverill Publishing now," Clara said with pride. "It's been a lot of work, and without Rex's help, I don't think I could manage, but I do love it so."

"You didn't always," Irene reminded her.

"No," Clara agreed. "I was like you, Marjorie. I wanted to do the season, find a husband, have a family. But when Jonathan decided to stay in America while Irene was away on honeymoon, I had no choice but to take over."

"Were you very angry with your brother?" Marjorie asked.

"Angry? What an inadequate word! If Idaho wasn't on the other side of the world," she added, raising her voice so that Jonathan could hear, "I'd have gone there and shot him."

"Don't I know it?" he said as he came to join them. "Why do you think I stayed away? I'm not an idiot."

"That's a debatable point, dear brother."

Watching them, Marjorie was glad to note the ease with which Jonathan and his sisters had so quickly slipped into a mode of teasing and laughing and chaffing each other. That, she realized, was what families were—or at least, what they were supposed to be. They quarreled and made up, teased and squabbled, and circumstances might send them to different ends of the earth, but underneath it all, there was a bedrock of love and support, acceptance and forgiveness. There was loyalty. She'd missed all that.

Suddenly, her heart twisted with a bittersweet pang. Never had she felt the pain of her lack of a family as acutely as she did now.

"Penny," a low voice murmured in her ear, and she turned to find Jonathan right beside her. "For your thoughts," he prompted as she gave him an uncomprehending look.

She forced herself to smile. "They're not worth that much," she said and turned quickly to Clara. "So, you run the company? An impressive accomplishment."

"Terrifying is more like it. But once I accepted the situation, I began to enjoy it. It's amazing how not getting what you want can lead to amazing discoveries."

"Such as?" Marjorie asked, curious.

"How strong I could be, how to trust my own judgement—"

"How to be bossy," Rex cut in as he joined their circle.

"Well, yes, that, too," she agreed as Marjorie and Irene laughed. "But most important, I learned that sometimes the things we fight the most turn out to be the best things."

Her smile faded to a grave expression, and she bit her lip, looking at her brother. "That's why I could never truly be angry with you, you know. Your decision changed my dream into something so much bigger and so much more wonderful than anything I'd imagined. I wouldn't change a thing, Jonathan. And I mean that."

"I'm glad, petal." He leaned toward her and planted a kiss on her cheek. "So glad."

"Relieved, too, I'll wager," Rex said. "Had you come home you'd have been saddled with Lady Truelove instead of me."

"What?" Jonathan and Marjorie said together, making the others laugh.

"You're Lady Truelove?" Jonathan asked, staring at him. "You are?"

Rex grinned. "Need any advice?" he asked and bowed. "I am at your service. It's supposed to be a secret, though, so don't tell anyone. Clara hired me to do the column while Irene was gallivanting across Europe, and I still do it to this day."

"Well, I'll be damned," Jonathan muttered. "That makes my decision to stay away even more sensible."

Clara jabbed him in the ribs.

"What?" he asked, giving his sister an innocent look. "I'd have made a terrible advice columnist."

"Come to the offices tomorrow," Rex suggested. "I'll be there in the afternoon. I can give you a tour, and we can discuss the financial condition. You own a third of the company and you ought to see how it's doing."

Jonathan shook his head. "Another day, perhaps," he said. "I must visit a tailor. My tweeds are in tatters."

"I hate to be the one to break it to you, old chap," Rex replied, looking him over, "but your evening suit's not much better."

Jonathan grimaced, acknowledging the truth of that. "All the more reason, then. And I have various other business matters to attend to in the next few days. Another time?"

"Of course."

"Do you need tweeds?" Torquil asked as he joined them. "Surely not, if you're headed to Africa?"

"I'm staying a bit longer than I'd first thought."

He was staying? Marjorie stilled, her sherry glass halfway to her lips, feeling a rush of unreasoning hope and happy surprise.

"Marjorie's birthday is August thirteenth," he went on, glancing at his eldest sister. "I can't miss that."

As he and Irene exchanged glances, Marjorie realized the decision to stay longer had not really been his. Happiness faded and hope fizzled, but somehow, she managed to don a bright smile.

"How delightful," she said, pride making her voice light. "But you needn't delay important business on my account. I shall have many more birthdays."

"Still," Irene said, "we must do something to mark this one. Turning twenty-one is a rite of passage."

"In Marjorie's case, it's more than that," Jonathan said, looking at her. "It's the start of a whole new life."

A life he did not want. He'd reminded her of that in the carriage this afternoon, seeing her romantic hopes about him even before she had, crushing them before she'd ever realized they were there. She supposed he was trying to keep her from being hurt, but he hadn't succeeded, because right now, hurt was like a fist squeezing her heart, and it took everything she had not to show it.

"What about a big house party?" Clara suggested in a voice that sounded strangely far away to Marjorie's ears. "It'll be the right time of year for it."

"A house party sounds like great fun," Marjorie replied, still holding Jonathan's gaze. "As long as those invited truly want to be there."

Jonathan pressed his lips together, showing that she could wound him, too, but for Marjorie, it was no victory, and she was relieved when Boothby came in to announce that dinner was served.

The duke offered her his arm and as he escorted her to the dining room, she forced away any absurd sense of disappointment. She knew what she wanted from life, and if Jonathan didn't want that, well, it was his loss, and none of her business. She could not resent him, but she could take the words he'd told her in the carriage this afternoon to heart, and she intended to do so. Life was too short to expect a man to change or to wish for what could not be. Her father had taught her that lesson. Best if she never forgot it again.

Chapter 14

Jonathan had never had a high opinion of aristocratic society, but as he glanced around the Duke of Torquil's dining table, he realized he would have to revise his opinion, at least as far as his own relations were concerned.

From all that he could see, Irene and Clara were every bit as settled as their letters had indicated, and their husbands seemed good and honorable gentlemen. On their behalf, he was both glad and relieved.

As the others conversed with Marjorie, asking her about her life in America and making suggestions about what she might enjoy doing here in England, he said little, content to observe and enjoy the sight of his sisters' smiling faces in the candlelight.

It was good, he thought, to be home.

He straightened a little in his seat, startled by the notion. This wasn't his house. This certainly wasn't his life. And England wasn't his home anymore. After ten years away, he was a fish out of water here, and yet, it wasn't as strange to be back as he'd feared. Perhaps one could never completely leave behind the place one had been born and raised, no matter how far one traveled or how long one stayed away.

"I think I'm the one who needs to give you a penny," Marjorie murmured, breaking into his contemplations. "You're very quiet."

"Am I? I was just letting it all sink in—being in England again, seeing my sisters."

"But are you glad you're back?"

"I am, yes, and it surprises me. In fact—" He broke off and gave a laugh, a little embarrassed. "I don't know what I was so worried about."

That made her smile. "I'm glad you've made peace with your sisters."

"So am I. It was easier than I thought it would be." He paused, thinking of Irene's definition of his duties as a guardian. "I hope you'll be happy here. If there's anything I can do to make your transition easier, I will."

"There is, actually," she said. "I've been thinking, and I've got an idea."

"Uh-oh," he murmured. "That's trouble."

She made a face at him. "I'm serious."

"So am I. Your ideas always seem to wreak havoc in my life."

"This one won't," she assured him. "In fact, I think what I have in mind just might make everything easier for both of us."

That sparked his curiosity, but before he could inquire further, Irene's voice intervened.

"Ladies," she said, standing up and bringing everyone else to their feet, "shall we go through?"

She started out of the dining room to leave the men to their port, the other ladies following her, but Marjorie lingered long enough to lean down and whisper in his ear, "We'll talk about it after dinner."

With that, she departed, forcing him to put his curiosity aside, but afterward, when the men joined the ladies in the drawing room, neither he nor Marjorie was given a chance to bring up the topic, for David suggested bridge.

"There are eight of us," he said. "No one would be left out."

"We can't," Clara said, setting aside her coffee cup and standing up. "It's nearly ten, so Rex and I must be going home. If my daughters keep to the routine they've developed of late, Daisy will be waking up any minute, crying like a banshee, which will wake Marianne, and between them, they'll soon have the nursery in chaos."

"How old are your daughters?" Marjorie asked.

"Marianne's nearly four, and Daisy's eighteen months, so they're rather a handful. I must go stand by Nanny."

"She just wants an excuse to tuck them back into bed," Rex explained and turned to his wife. "I ordered the carriage brought around already."

She nodded and turned to Jonathan. "Welcome home," she said, underscoring his earlier thoughts about what home actually meant, and when she opened her arms, he walked into them gladly. "Don't you dare stay away so long next time," she whispered as she hugged him tight.

He couldn't reply. Instead, he held her close, tightness squeezing his chest, the pain of love and regret. "I won't," he managed at last. "Besides," he added, impelled to lighten the moment as they drew apart, "now that I know you won't shoot me the minute I walk through the door, it's an easy promise to keep."

"You're never safe on that score, little brother," she countered at once, her voice severe, but she was smiling as she turned away.

After she and Rex had departed, David again suggested cards, but Jonathan glanced at Marjorie and negated that idea. "Why don't the four of you play?" he said. "Don't worry about us. Marjorie and I have some business matters to discuss."

"My idea isn't about business," Marjorie whispered to him as the others moved toward the card table at the other end of the drawing room.

"Perhaps not, but there are some things involving your father's estate we do need to go over. I'll be back in a minute."

He left the drawing room, and by the time he returned with his dispatch case, the others were immersed in their first rubber of auction bridge, and Marjorie was seated at a table on the other side of the room. Joining her, he set the black leather case on the table and sat down opposite her.

"As your guardian, I feel it's important for you to know where you stand," he began, but at the wry look she gave him, he stopped.

"It seems to me," she said, "you already made where I stand pretty clear this afternoon. But don't worry," she added as he grimaced. "I'm not about to develop any romantic notions about you."

Put like that, his assumption that she was in danger of such a thing seemed the height of conceit, and yet, her next words told him he hadn't been too far off the mark.

"I have to admit," she murmured, her expression softening, her cheeks tinting a faint pink, "I was feeling a little bit dreamy-eyed about you for a while. You were . . . I mean . . ." She glanced across the room to the couples playing bridge, then she leaned closer to him, and added in a whisper, "You were my first kiss, after all."

In an instant, the memory of that kiss came flooding back, reminding him that she wasn't the only one in danger of developing romantic notions—or at least, in his case, erotic ones.

"But," she went on, "you're the last man on earth a girl with sense would ever pin her hopes on."

A point he'd attempted to underscore that very afternoon. "Quite so," he said with an emphatic nod he feared was as much for his own benefit as hers. "Absolutely."

"All that aside, we do seem to spend a great deal of time rubbing each other the wrong way."

Or the right way, his baser masculine nature whispered to him. *Depends on how you look at it.*

Telling his baser masculine nature to shut up, he strove to give her a more appropriate reply. "It's understandable you'd chafe a bit under my guardianship. Though my ward, you are a grown woman." Even as he said those last few words, his body began to burn, and he felt like the worst of hypocrites.

"Exactly," she agreed with disconcerting enthusiasm. "So, I was wondering if we might just dispense with titles?"

He frowned, puzzled. "I'm not sure what you mean."

"Guardian . . . ward . . . can't we get past all that? Redefine our roles?"

"But I am your guardian. You are my ward. Those are facts."

"Yes, but in such cases, the ward is usually a child. I'm not, as you just said."

With that kiss still so vivid in his mind, he was beginning to find having his own words tossed back at him in this fashion rather aggravating. "I think we've already established that I don't think of you as a child," he said, and though he strove to keep his expression and his voice neutral, he couldn't resist adding, "I demonstrated that point quite strongly aboard the *Neptune*, as I recall."

The color in her face deepened at the reminder. "Yes," she whispered, "but hauling off and kissing me isn't really a feasible way to resolve our disputes, is it?"

There were worse ways, but he didn't point that out.

"If we don't find a new way forward," she continued in the wake of his silence, "one that puts us on a more equal footing, I fear we will just continue to . . . to . . ." She paused, licking her lips, drawing his gaze to her mouth, but he jerked it back up again at once.

"Rub each other the wrong way?" he supplied, straight-faced.

"Yes. Can't we start over, try to see each other in a different light?"

"Or you could just accept the situation as it is and cede to my authority. But," he added with a sigh, "if you did that, the earth would stop turning and tides would stop ebbing, and I'd die of shock. Just what are you suggesting?"

"What if we just try to . . . to be friends?"

"Friends?" He froze, staring at her in dismay, fearing that being friends with Marjorie would prove an even greater hell than the one he was already in.

Something of what he felt must have shown on his face. "Goodness," she said with a laugh that sounded forced. "Is my idea so difficult to imagine?"

It was more than difficult. It was impossible. And yet, trapped between obligation and desire, what other choice did he have?

"Not at all," he lied. "It's just that it isn't the usual thing, is it? Men and women being friends."

"But do you think we might try?"

He pasted on a smile. "Of course. It's an excellent idea. Perfect. The best thing to do."

"I'm so relieved you said that," she breathed, pressing a hand to her chest, laughing again. "I thought you'd object."

He didn't even blink. "Nonsense."

"Is it?" she asked ruefully, making a face at him. "You're a bit closed-minded when it comes to my ideas, Jonathan."

"That's not true," he began, but then he stopped, appreciating as she grinned that he'd just made her point. "Touché," he conceded instead. "As to the rest . . ." He paused and took a deep breath. "Friends it is."

He was rewarded with a radiant smile that reminded him of just what torture being her friend was going to be, and he knew he had to get off this topic.

"Now that we've settled that," he said and gestured to the documents on the table, "I'm still your guardian, and there are some things I need to discuss with you. If we're to be friends," he added as she groaned, "we shall both have to make compromises."

"Oh, very well. But," she added, giving him a frown of mock severity, "any compromises I make better not involve wearing black crape or hiding in my room."

"No fear. Irene's already come down on your side there, remember? And she's a far better judge of such things than I am. No, what I want to discuss involves your finances."

He opened his dispatch case and pulled out a rosewood box and a thick sheaf of papers tied with string. "This," he said, shoving the documents across the table to her, "is a copy of your father's will, an inventory of all your property, and the most recent financial reports of all your investments. I know you've already read some of this, but I feel it's important that you read the rest."

"Oh, so now I'm allowed to read these?" she teased. "They're not just your private papers anymore?"

"Don't be cheeky. Some of my private papers were on that desk, and I think you know that."

"Perhaps. But I didn't read them," she added at once. "I wouldn't. Friends don't do things like that."

"I'm glad to hear it. You can go through these at your leisure, but reading legal documents is sometimes like wading through hip-deep mud, so if there is anything you don't understand, you can ask me, or your solicitor."

She frowned. "Mr. Jessop?"

"No. Jessop's the executor of your father's will, and one of your trustees, but now that you are living here, you'll also need a British solicitor. I'll ask Torquil to recommend one for you."

"If you can answer my questions, do I need a solicitor?"

"I want you to have a lawyer of your own choosing. As an heiress, it's not wise for you to trust anyone completely, Marjorie. Not even your own trustees. You've inherited an enormous fortune, and that's a great responsibility. It can also be a burden."

"How enormous?"

"It's hard to give an exact amount, for it's all invested, but at current rates of exchange, it amounts to around twenty million dollars."

"Twenty *million?*"

Her amazed voice must have carried to the couples across the room, for Irene gave a cough and bid, "Seven diamonds," in an unnecessarily loud voice to keep the others' attention on their game.

"Good heavens," Marjorie said, staring at him, clearly staggered by the amount. "I thought one or two, maybe. But twenty?" She sat back, considering. "You say it's invested," she said at last. "In what?"

"Property, funds, stocks, bonds. American, mostly, and some British."

"And South African," she reminded, looking down at the sheaf of papers, idly flipping one corner of the stack in her fingers. "Which is why you're going there."

"Yes."

"But it's not the only reason you're going, is it?" Her hands stilled, and she looked up. "You want to go."

"I do," he admitted frankly. "Your father's descriptions and stories fascinated me. He said Africa has some of the most beautiful country in the world. I'd like to see it."

She nodded, and her acceptance of his answer ought to have relieved his mind, but it didn't. Quite the opposite, for he suddenly felt off-balance, uncertain, and he didn't know why.

What does matter to you? What do you want from life?

Marjorie's question was one he'd been asking himself ever since he'd left these shores, but he'd never been able to answer it with any degree of success. He thought he'd made peace with his own ambivalence, but as he looked at the woman across from him, he realized he'd made peace with nothing.

Taking a deep breath, he forced himself back to the matter at hand. "I want you to read these," he said, gesturing to the sheaf of documents. "Study them, learn all you can about your inheritance, Marjorie. You have the right to know, and besides, it's crucial that you begin thinking like an heiress and learn to guard yourself, for there are many people who will try to take advantage of you."

She bit her lip, staring down at the documents between them. "People like Count de la Rosa, you mean," she said after a moment.

"Yes. I'll help you avoid that as best I can, but Irene and Clara and their husbands will be of greater assistance to you than I, for they know far more about the people you'll meet here than I do."

"Jonathan?" She looked up, her brown eyes wide and dark. "What would have happened, if the count had . . ." She paused as if finding it hard to ask the question. "What if he had taken advantage of me and I'd had to marry him?"

Violence erupted inside Jonathan, sudden and hot, and he had to curl his hands into fists beneath the table. But when he spoke, his answer was one that did not involve ripping the count's throat out. "Mr. Jessop and I would have done our best to restrict his income in a prenuptial agreement, but your reputation would have been in the balance—he'd have seen to that. That's why it's so important that you not only rely on your chaperones, but also exercise discernment yourself."

"Trust no one, in other words," she said with a sigh, plunking an elbow on the table and her chin in her hand. "I don't really like that aspect of my new life."

"There are compensations. We'll open a bank account for you, with an allowance. It'll be a generous one, but don't overspend and expect me to give you more. I won't. Heiress or no, I expect you to be responsible with your money."

"No racehorses?" She grinned, the impudent minx. "No yachts? No motorcars?"

"No."

"You're such a tyrant."

"Am I?" He put his hand on the rosewood box on the table, and the temptation to tease her was suddenly irresistible. "Then I suppose I'll just put your jewels in a bank vault until August."

She straightened in her chair, glancing at the box then back at him. "The necklace is in there?"

"More than just that."

"I have other jewels? Can I see them?"

"Hmm . . ." His fingers drummed on the box. "I'm not sure I should. I am a tyrant, after all."

"You're impossible, that's what you are," she cried, jumping up to circle the table, heedless of the four people across the room who had now stopped their card game and were staring at her in surprise. "Oh, do let me see them, do."

He couldn't help but laugh. Relenting, he slid his hand away and let her open the box.

"Why, they look like pebbles," she said in surprise, peering at the stones nestled in the various velvet-lined partitions. "And bits of colored glass."

"These are uncut gems. Those," he added, pointing to one pile of stones, "are diamonds."

"Diamonds," cried Carlotta, setting down her cards and rising to her feet. "I have to see those."

Irene and her husband stood up as well. Ignoring David's protest that they were in the middle of a bridge hand, the other three crossed the room to examine the gems.

"An impressive collection," the duke commented, leaning over his wife's shoulder. "Amethysts, opals, star garnets—" He broke off and looked at Jonathan. "I can store them in the ducal vault downstairs, if you like. I keep Irene's jewels there."

"That's just what I was hoping. Thank you."

"We'll put them there tonight, once the ladies have had a good look at them. But, really, what you ought to do is take them to a jeweler and have them cut. I recommend Fossin and Morel in New Bond Street."

"Jonathan?" Marjorie's voice drew his attention. "Where's the Rose of Shoshone?"

He lifted the top tray of the box, revealing the Tiffany box nestled in the compartment beneath. Setting aside the tray, he pulled out the box, removed the lid, and held up the necklace for their inspection.

Carlotta and Irene both gasped, but it was Marjorie who held his attention. Her pink lips were curved in that mysterious smile, and in her dark eyes was a hint of the sensual fire he'd awakened when he'd put this necklace around her throat, the fire that had scorched him yesterday afternoon and was still threatening to flare up again. He tamped it down, however, reminding himself that Marjorie was right.

Being friends was the only choice he had, and yet, as he thought of that kiss and all the passion it had awakened, Jonathan feared being her friend was going to be like walking a tightrope over a thousand-foot drop. Very tricky, indeed.

Chapter 15

Marjorie's first fortnight in England went by in a frenzy of activity. As planned, she was taken to the famous Jay's, and despite the limited choice of colors and the necessity of trimming every garment in black, she was able to order a surprising number of day frocks, walking suits, and evening gowns she liked.

Even Carlotta was sympathetic upon learning of the travesties Lady Stansbury's maid had committed upon Marjorie's underclothes, and a full day was spent with various corsetieres and other modistes of lingerie.

She was also taken to a dizzying array of milliners, glovers, and cobblers. She bought fans, handkerchiefs, and handbags. She ordered calling cards and stationery. She visited Harrods, treating herself with the best French-milled soaps and lotions her money could buy. As Irene had promised, they hired her a true lady's maid, and though Miss Gladys Semphill was surprisingly dour in her own appearance, she proved an excellent lady's maid with such a talent for hair that she was able to transform Marjorie's rebellious red mop into a mass of soft, perfect curls every time she dressed it.

Irene and Carlotta took her to call upon the duke's sisters, Angela and Sarah, as well as many other acquaintances. They also called upon Baroness Vasiliev, who expressed great delight at meeting the duchess again after so many years and endured Carlotta's somewhat disapproving scrutiny with cheerful indifference, for which Marjorie was grateful.

She wrote to her friends from schooldays, and found, much to her delight, that two of them were in London for the season. Dulci was now a peeress, having married Baron Outram in April, and Jenna had just become engaged to a certain Colonel Westcott, the second son of the Earl of Balvoir. Plans were made for tea at Claridge's, so Marjorie could be told all the romantic details.

She saw Jonathan at breakfast and dinner, but seldom in between, for all she'd done so far was shop and pay calls, and despite Clara's teasing suggestion that he go along, he had emphatically negated the possibility.

So, no one was more surprised than Marjorie when, on her fifteenth day in London, she and her shopping companions spied him in Bond Street.

Clara, who had taken a day away from the paper to accompany them, was the first to see him. "Why, ladies, would you look at that!" she cried, stopping on the sidewalk and bringing her companions to a halt. "Irene, I do believe I saw our brother going into Fossin and Morel's across the street. I think we all know what he's doing there," she went on, turning to give Marjorie a wink. "Shall we go and see?"

This suggestion met with eager assent, and after several minutes of navigating their way across the crowded street, the four ladies entered the elegant premises of one of London's finest jewelers.

Jonathan was nowhere to be seen, but a dark, well-dressed gentleman hastened forward. "Your Grace," he greeted Irene, hands spread in a gesture of welcome. "And Viscountess Galbraith and Lady David, too. How delightful."

"Good day, Mr. Prescott," said Irene. "I believe my brother is here?"

"Mr. Deverill? Yes, indeed. An affable gentleman, Your Grace, with a most remarkable collection of stones." The urbane Mr. Prescott's dark face lit up with the interest of his profession. "Diamonds, peridot . . . some exceptional star garnets and black opals. Yes, most remarkable."

"This is my brother's ward, Miss Marjorie McGann. The stones belonged to her late father."

"Indeed." Mr. Prescott turned to her. "I do hope you will decide to have the stones set, Miss McGann. Some of them promise to be exquisite when cut."

"I don't doubt it," she answered. "My father was a mining engineer, and gemstones were his passion."

Mr. Prescott blinked as if nonplussed, and beside her, she heard Carlotta's sharp indrawn breath—two clues she'd committed some sort of faux pas, but she couldn't imagine what.

In the awkward pause, Mr. Prescott turned to Irene. "Mr. Deverill is with Mr. Fossin in his office, composing an inventory of the gems. Would you like me to inform them you are here?"

"No, there's no need. We can wait a few minutes." She glanced past him to one of the glass display cases. "Have you any emeralds to show me?"

"Of course." He turned, stretching out his arm to allow her to precede him, and as they departed for the other side of the shop, Marjorie turned to Clara. "What did I say?" she whispered.

Carlotta answered before Clara had the chance. "It's hardly necessary to inform people of your late father's profession, my dear. I should advise discretion on that score."

"But why?" she asked in surprise. "What's it matter?"

"It doesn't," Clara put in. "Oh, look," she added, hooking one arm through that of her sister-in-law and steering her toward a nearby case. "Pearls, Carlotta. Your favorite."

Marjorie followed, hoping to press Clara for further information, but she had no opportunity, for only a few minutes later Jonathan emerged from the back rooms, a sheet of paper in his hands. "Thank you, Mr. Fossin," he was saying to a small man with an enormous mustache who walked beside him. "You will inform me when you've given the stones a full evaluation?"

Assured on this point, he turned, immediately spying Marjorie standing with Carlotta and Clara. "What the devil?" he said, laughing in surprise.

"We saw you from across the street," Irene said as she joined them. "We couldn't resist coming in."

"Naturally," he agreed, folding the sheet in his hands and tucking it in a pocket of his morning coat. "Women around jewels are like moths around flame."

"We're on our way to Claridge's for tea with two of Marjorie's friends from Forsyte Academy," Clara put in. "Do join us. You won't be the only man. Rex will be there, and Paul—one of Rex's cousins."

"For a moment, I thought I'd have six ladies all to myself," he said. Shaking his head in mock disappointment, he stepped around them and opened the door. "Ah, well."

They emerged onto the sidewalk, but as the other women began walking toward Claridge's, Marjorie lingered, waiting for Jonathan. "May I walk with you?"

"Certainly." He pulled the door shut behind him and moved to stand between her and the street, then they fell in step to follow the others. "I presume you want to know what Mr. Fossin had to say about the stones?"

"I'd love to hear, but that's not it. I had a question to ask you." She related the conversation inside the jeweler's and the reactions of both Mr. Prescott and Carlotta. "What did I say?" she asked as he laughed.

"I don't know why you have to ask. After spending a fortnight in her company, you must know Carlotta's a snob."

"I knew that after an hour. But Mr. Prescott's hardly in a position to be snobbish."

"I'd wager Prescott wasn't disapproving so much as taken aback. Fossin and Morel deal with a very exclusive clientele. He's probably unaccustomed to young ladies who announce their fathers' professions."

"No, but it's not as if my father was a ditchdigger or a longshoreman. I could see how a snob might disapprove of that. But my father, for all his faults, was an educated man, and he had a worthy profession."

"That's just it. In Britain, a profession for a gentleman is looked down upon. So is a useful education, if you want the truth. England—the upper crust, anyway—prefers to send its young men to university to study poetry and learn dead languages."

"But Clara has a profession," Marjorie said, still bewildered.

"Even worse, since Clara's a woman. I daresay she doesn't talk much about it outside the family."

"So, society knows about her involvement in Deverill Publishing, but as long as she doesn't talk about it, people let it pass?"

"More or less. If you want society's good opinion, it might be best to avoid mentioning your father was a mining engineer."

"Carlotta said the same." She sighed, shaking her head. "Sometimes, British life doesn't make much sense to me."

"If it's any consolation to you, it doesn't make much sense to me either, and I was raised in it. Not the aristocracy, of course, but close enough. My mother was a viscount's daughter, though she was disowned when she married my father. We Deverills do like turning the aristocracy on its ear."

"A fact you seem to take great delight in," she commented, laughing as he grinned. "Lilies of the field, I think you said?"

"And was I not right?"

She sniffed. "Only about some of them. You couldn't describe Galbraith or Torquil in such a way."

"I notice you don't mention David. He's a lily of the field if ever I saw one. Takes great pride in the fact, too, I daresay."

"Well, you've got me there," she conceded. "But I don't see why it's anything to be proud of. In the States, gentlemen are encouraged, even expected, to take up a career."

"While gentlemen on this side of the pond are expected to work as little as possible. As an American, it's a cultural difference you might find difficult to accept, especially if your goal is to marry a titled peer."

Somehow, marrying a duke or an earl didn't seem quite so appealing now. The reason, of course, was the man walking beside her, a fact she found both frustrating and depressing. Still, there was no point in dwelling on it, so she looked away, hoping for a diversion, and found it almost immediately when they passed the next shop. "Would you look at that?" she cried, stopping in genuine relief and happy surprise. "It's a Trotter!"

"It doesn't look like a horse," he said doubtfully, making her laugh. "But I shall take your word for it."

"A Trotter is a camera, silly." She leaned as close to the window as her hat brim would allow and immediately gave a cry of delight. "It has a Lancaster lens, too. Look!"

"That, if the tone of your voice and the smile on your face are anything to go by, is a good thing." He also leaned closer to the window. "It seems to have a carrying case as well."

"Well, of course it does. It is a field camera." Laughing, she turned her head to look at him, and at the sight of his face so close to her own, the fabulous camera in the window was forgotten.

He was smiling, watching her in a way that made her catch her breath, and suddenly, the memory of their kiss aboard the *Neptune* went through her mind, and she had to fight to remember what she'd been about to say. "That's why it has a case," she blurted out in a rush. "A field camera is designed to be portable, so one can . . . can . . . take pictures outdoors. Landscapes, you know. In . . . in . . . ."

"Fields?" he teased, his smiling widening. But then, his lashes lowered, he eased a fraction closer, and his smile vanished, causing her heart to give a lurch of excitement.

Was he going to kiss her? she wondered wildly. Surely not, not right here on the street. And yet, even as she negated the possibility, she leaned closer, too, pulled toward him like a magnet, her heart hammering in her chest.

But then, he looked up, his eyes grave as they met hers. "Perhaps I should get one," he murmured.

Dazed, she blinked, unable to remember what they'd been talking about. "One what?"

"Field camera." He nodded toward the window. "It might be a handy thing to have on my travels."

The reminder that he was leaving shifted everything back into place, and the spell was broken. Perhaps that had been his intent. "We should go on," she said flatly and pulled back from the window. "If not, I'll be late."

Seeming surprised, he nodded to the Trotter. "Don't you want to buy it?"

She hesitated, biting her lip, tempted, but then she shook her head.

"No," she said and turned away to resume walking. "There's no point. Not anymore."

As she spoke, she was startled by the tinge of bitterness in her voice, the bitterness of a long-ago, almost forgotten disappointment. As he fell in step beside her, she could feel his eyes watching her, and it goaded her into speech.

"Do you remember you told me that once a dream is dead, you don't want to give it a second chance?"

"I do, yes. Photography was a dream of yours, was it?"

She nodded. "When I was about twelve, I got this crazy idea I'd follow my father out West and be a photographer. That I'd go with him, take pictures of what we saw, be the first woman to photograph the Wild West . . ." She paused a moment, thinking of the girl she'd been then, a girl who'd thought her father still wanted her, a girl who'd made every excuse in the world for him. "It was stupid."

"It doesn't sound that way to me," he said gently. "Why would you think it so?"

"You have to ask?" She turned her head to look at him, laughing, trying to make light of it. "My father letting me tag along with the two of you?"

"I suppose not," he muttered. "Did you learn photography at school?"

"Oh, no. Forsyte Academy is a prestigious finishing school. Girls are taught the classical arts—sketching, watercolors, painting in oils."

"But those didn't appeal to you?"

She glanced at him, making a face. "I can't draw."

He chuckled. "I see. But if you didn't learn photography at school, how did you learn?"

"A local photographer in White Plains offered a course on the subject when I was fifteen. I thought it was my chance, and I begged Mrs. Forsyte to let me sign up. She agreed, on the condition that I persuade at least one other girl to participate, so I roped in my friend Jenna, who you'll meet today. She was always up for anything fun."

"And did the course live up to your expectations?"

"I loved it. And I was good, too," she added proudly. "The instructor said I had a true talent. But—" She broke off and swallowed hard. "I gave it up."

"Why? Not because of anything to do with your father, I hope?"

She shook her head. "The photographer offered to apprentice me—outside my studies, of course—but Mrs. Forsyte refused to allow it. She didn't think it appropriate."

"I can't think why. Women have been taking up photography for decades. It's not considered unwomanly."

"Perhaps not, but you'd probably have agreed with her reasons. The photographer was an unmarried man. It was absurd," she added at once. "The poor man had no designs on me. He was sixty if he was a day, and I was only fifteen."

"Still," he began.

"Oh, I know," she agreed at once. "One must observe the proprieties or tongues will wag." She shot a meaningful glance in his direction. "At least, that's what people keep telling me."

He smiled. "As your guardian, I am duty-bound to agree with Mrs. Forsyte that it would not have been proper to be that man's apprentice. But as your friend . . ." He paused, his smile fading. "I'm sorry you had to abandon something you loved for the sake of propriety."

She shrugged, forcing aside past disappointments. "It's all right. I have a different dream for my life now, so it doesn't matter."

"On the contrary," he said. "It does matter. It matters to you."

The quiet certainty in his voice startled her, and she stopped walking, but she couldn't quite look at him. "What makes you say that?"

He stopped beside her, bending a bit to look under her hat brim and into her eyes. "Because when you said you had to give it up, you looked like a dying duck in a thunderstorm."

Marjorie couldn't help laughing at his way of putting it. "A dying duck? You British have the strangest expressions."

"Given the look on your face a few minutes ago, the metaphor was appropriate. And if you want to take up photography again, you needn't worry about any objections from me, and I'm sure Irene would approve. And you certainly wouldn't have to worry about what Mrs. Forsyte would think of it."

"Thank goodness for that," she said wryly.

"Was it very bad?" he asked, grimacing. "At Forsyte Academy?"

"Awful," she said at once, striving not to smile at his abashed expression. "Like a workhouse in a Dickens novel." She shook her head with a sigh of long suffering. "And you expected me to stay there."

His lips twitched. His shoulders relaxed. "Only for eight more months."

"During which I'd have died of boredom. It's true," she insisted as he made a skeptical sound. "Everyone was very kind, and everything was very proper and staid and so damnably boring. When I was a student, it wasn't so bad, for I had my friends, and we'd get up to a bit of mischief now and again."

"You?" He grinned. "I'm shocked."

"I never got into any serious trouble," she assured him. "Just silly stuff—sneaking out sometimes, pranks, smoking cigarettes, that sort of thing. But once I became a teacher, there was no more fun of that kind. A teacher at Forsyte Academy," she intoned in an excellent imitation of the school's headmistress, "must set a proper example for her students and be impeccable in her conduct at all times." She sighed. "It was very dull."

Jonathan chuckled. "I can see how you might find it so."

"Exactly. Which is why I came up with a more exciting plan for my life."

He gave her a dubious look. "You think being married to a British peer and living on a country estate will be exciting?"

"More exciting than teaching girls to curtsy and speak French," she countered at once.

"I'll grant you that, especially since you intend to spend all your money on furs and jewels and extravagant house parties."

"I was teasing you about that part," she admitted. "But the main reason for my choice was that I knew I wanted to be married and have children of my own, and there was no way that would ever happen if I stayed teaching at Forsyte."

"Because schoolteachers can't be married?"

"And because I'd never meet any men there. So, I had to do something." She paused, swallowing hard. "You see, I'd figured out by then that my father was never going to let me join him. And don't you dare make excuses for him," she added as he opened his mouth to reply.

"I won't," he said quietly. "I've come to accept the fact that my friend wasn't much of a father. Though I do think his illness played a part in his decisions, Marjorie. I honestly do."

She tried to look at it that way, and after a moment, she gave a reluctant nod. "Perhaps. But he should have told me he was sick. I had the right to know."

"I won't argue that point. What's remarkable is that you both had the same future in mind for you. He wanted you to have all this—the sort of life your mother had in South Africa. He felt he'd taken that away from her, and he wanted you to have it."

"That must be why he chose you to be my guardian."

"I think so, yes. Did he get the idea from you? Did you tell him what you had in mind—to come here, join your friends?"

"No, never. I didn't want to give him the chance to refuse."

He grinned at that. "Better to ask for forgiveness afterward than permission before?"

"Something like that."

"I shall keep this tactic of yours in mind for future reference. I think I'll warn Irene, too."

"Oh, dear," she said, laughing. "I've given myself away now, haven't I? Either way," she added as they turned toward the entrance to Claridge's Hotel, "I hope you see now why I wasn't about to let you go off and leave me behind."

She started up the wide front steps, where a liveried doorman was holding the door open for them, but Jonathan's voice stopped her. "Marjorie?"

"Hmm?" She turned to look at him and was startled by the sudden, strange intensity in his face. "What is it?"

His lips parted as if he intended to reply, but then he pressed them tight. Slowly, he shook his head. "Nothing."

I WOULD HAVE come back for you.

The words hung in the air, unsaid, as Jonathan watched Marjorie walk away, her shapely hips swaying in her close-fitting dress of white silk, jet buttons, and black lace as she walked up the wide steps of the hotel entrance. He still wanted to say them; even now, they hovered on his tongue. But what would be the point?

Everything he'd told her in the carriage two weeks ago was true. He'd used truth to push her away, to protect her, and he'd succeeded. They were friends now, a nice, safe middle ground, if he could keep his head. He ought to be relieved. So why the hell would he want to tip the scales and undo that delicate balance by trying to pull her close again?

Even as he asked himself that question, he was beginning to fear he already knew the answer. Hadn't he always known, from the moment he'd first set eyes on her?

Marjorie stopped at the top of the steps and turned, the flaring trumpet hem of her dress swirling in a froth of black and white to settle around her ankles. Beneath her white straw hat, an outrageous affair of stuffed gray doves, white ostrich plumes, and black silk ribbons, her brows drew together in a puzzled frown. "Aren't you coming?"

Left with no choice, he mounted the steps and followed as she turned and went through the doors. Once inside the hotel, they walked together across the foyer and through the lobby to the entrance of the tearoom, where his sisters and Carlotta were waiting with a dark-haired man— Rex's cousin Paul, no doubt. Beside him was a girl so similar to him in looks that she had to be a sister, and though Jonathan was reasonably sure he'd never met the woman before, the man seemed oddly familiar.

"You two took your time," Irene chided good-naturedly as he and Marjorie came abreast.

"Are we late?" Marjorie asked.

"No, no," Irene assured her at once. "Your friends have not yet arrived, so the maître d'hôtel informs me, and Rex isn't here yet, either. But his cousins are," she added, gesturing to the couple beside her, "so I'd best go ahead and make the introductions—"

"Some introductions won't be necessary, Irene," the man called Paul put in as he grinned at Jonathan. "Hullo, Jack."

Startled, Jonathan blinked, then he began to laugh, realizing his initial impression of familiarity had been right. "Good lord, Paul Chapman? I'll be damned. You're Galbraith's cousin? I had no idea."

The two men shook hands, and as they drew back, Jonathan realized everyone was looking at them in surprise. "Schooldays," he explained. "Winchester."

"And Oxford," Paul added.

"That hardly counts," Jonathan demurred. "I was only there half a term."

"Half a term, but still a legend," Paul said. "Or have you forgotten carving naughty limericks into the ancient oak trees?"

The girl beside Paul spoke up before Jonathan could answer. "Since Paul's ruined any hope of formal introductions," she said, giving her brother a jab in the ribs, "we shall have to make informal ones. I'm his sister, Henrietta, but if anyone calls me that, I tend to ignore them—"

"It works like a charm," Paul interrupted, earning himself another jab.

"Call me Hetty," she said without batting an eyelash and turned to Marjorie, holding out her hand. "You must be Miss McGann. What a smashing dress."

"Thank you."

Hetty returned her attention to Jonathan and grinned, an impish grin in a pretty, rakish face. "Back from the wilds, Mr. Deverill, so I hear. We shall expect stories over tea."

He was given no time to respond.

"Marjorie?"

All of them turned, watching as a dark-haired young woman in green silk approached their party, a pale blonde in blue following her.

"Dulci! Jenna!" Marjorie cried, rushing to meet them. "Oh, it is so good to see you."

She wrapped an arm around each of her friends in an uninhibited embrace, too delighted to notice their uncomfortable glances around the lobby, but Jonathan noticed. He also saw the way some of the hotel patrons were staring at her askance, and he wondered how long it would be before her American joie de vivre was snuffed out by his own nation's staid sensibilities. That would be for the best if she was going to adapt to life here, a fact he'd been trying to make her see all along, but as he looked at her face, so radiant and happy, he was rather glad he hadn't succeeded.

Paul leaned closer to him. "You devil," he murmured. "How in hell did you manage to become guardian to that stunning lovely?"

Jonathan drew a deep breath. "Just lucky, I suppose."

"And she's not engaged, or attached, or mooning over some chap back in America?"

Jonathan set his jaw and did the honorable thing. "No."

"So, once she's out of mourning, I've got a chance?"

"You?" Jonathan turned, smiling, and honor went to the wall. "Not a chance in hell."

Chapter 16

Marjorie's reunion with her friends seemed a smashing success. But then, why shouldn't it be? Jonathan thought, watching her with her friends across the tearoom's large round table. This was the life she wanted.

I am going to laugh and dance and enjoy myself and wear whatever colors I please. I'm going to do the season, meet young men, fall in love, and get married.

What a blessing, he thought, to know what you wanted. To be so certain of your course and your future. He envied her that. He hadn't felt that way about his own life for over a decade.

This was the world she would move in, marry in, live in. She found some things about British life incomprehensible, but that wouldn't last. With Irene's help, she would soon find her place here, like a piece fitting into place in a jigsaw puzzle.

He, on the other hand, was more like a stray puzzle piece accidently tossed in the wrong box. Or maybe he didn't have a box. Maybe he didn't fit in anywhere, and no matter where he went, he never would.

What do I want? he thought, glancing around the tearoom, exasperated by his own discontent. *For God's sake, what do I want?*

Even as he asked himself that question, his gaze swerved to Marjorie again, pulled to her by the same magnetic forces that had pulled him through the doors of Claridge's a short time ago—impossible forces of desire and need, the same forces that had caused him to take her into his bedroom aboard ship and wrap jewels around her throat, that had impelled him to haul her into his arms and kiss her. The same need he desperately wanted to deny because he knew it could lead nowhere.

Nonetheless, as he remembered those passionate moments aboard the *Neptune*, arousal began thrumming through his body as impossible fantasies ran through his mind—of taking down her hair and running his fingers through the fiery strands. Of undoing all the black jet buttons down her back and pulling that frothy gown down her hips. Of finding and kissing every inch of her creamy skin, from the tip of her nose to the soles of her feet.

Here, in the elegant ambiance of Claridge's tearoom, he let his imagination run wild. He touched that magnificent body, shaping the exquisite fullness of her breasts and the lush curves of her hips. He caressed her, the cries of her pleasure echoing through his head and drowning out all the civilized sounds of crystal and china and polite conversation around him.

As if sensing his scrutiny, she turned her head in his direction, and as their gazes met, he strove to keep his face impassive and his torrid thoughts hidden, but when her eyes widened, her lips parted, and her cheeks flushed a delicate pink, he knew he'd failed, and he felt every bit as naked as he'd been in his imagination.

Desperate, he tore his gaze away. Reminding himself of the safe middle ground that was supposed to be between them now, he strove to regain his control, but even after he'd accomplished that feat, he still felt as transparent as glass, and he knew he had to get out of here.

Thankfully, fate decided to take pity on him. Rex chose that moment to say something about having business matters to attend to, and when he excused himself from the group and stood up, Jonathan did the same.

"Going to Deverill Publishing?" Jonathan asked, hoping he didn't sound as desperate as he felt. "Mind if I come along," he went on as the other man nodded, "and have a look at the new premises?"

"Not at all. I did offer you a tour, after all."

Relieved, Jonathan bowed to the ladies, agreed with Paul that they needed to meet for a drink soon, and followed Rex out of the tearoom.

"Thank you," he said as the doorman hailed them a hansom cab.

"Too much high society?"

He was happy to seize on that excuse. "I'm not used to it these days, so again, thanks for the chance to escape."

Rex chuckled. "I think Paul should thank us both," he said as the hansom pulled up to the curb and rolled to a stop. "You've done him quite the favor, leaving him a clear field to your lovely ward."

Jealousy, powerful and raw, smote Jonathan with such force that he paused by the cab, paralyzed. His blood, barely cooled after his imaginings in the tearoom, heated again—not with desire, however, but with the same primal sense of possession that had nearly led him to toss the Count de la Rosa over the side of the *Neptune*, a feeling he had no right to claim.

"Don't worry about Paul," Rex said at once, seeing his reaction before he could try to mask it, but also, thankfully, misinterpreting it. "He's not the wild chap he was at school. No title, obviously, but plenty of money and a post in the diplomatic. He'd be a very good match for the girl, in fact."

Reassurances like that were no help at all, but they should have been. They damn well should have been.

Jonathan set his jaw, stepped into the hansom, and slid over on the leather seat to make room as Rex gave instructions to the driver and climbed in beside him.

"Still, the girl can take her time," Rex said as the driver pushed the lever that folded the cab's padded wooden doors over the knees of his passengers. "At twenty," Rex added as the hansom jerked into motion, "there's no rush for her to marry anyone."

"Unfortunately," Jonathan muttered. He glanced sideways, noting Rex's inquiring gaze on him, and he rushed again into speech. "Dear Lady Truelove, my ward is driving me crazy," he said, forcing a laugh that even to his own ears seemed filled with self-mockery. "I have to marry her off and get her out of my life. Do you have any advice to offer? Signed, Going Mad in Mayfair."

Rex smiled. "I doubt she'll be your problem for too long. Once she's out, the men will be flocking to her like bees to honey, and Paul will have plenty of competition."

Jonathan began to think escaping with Rex hadn't been much of an improvement over his previous torment. "Of course," he agreed at once, and decided to change the subject.

During the remainder of their journey across town, the two men discussed possible winners at Ascot, the chance of the fine weather holding for Irene's upcoming water party, and the possibility of playing some tennis when they went down to Hampshire, and by the time they reached Fleet Street, Jonathan felt as if he'd regained his equilibrium.

Deverill Publishing had moved its offices five years ago, so to Jonathan, there was nothing familiar about the exterior of the place, but when they walked inside, he was struck at once by something very familiar: the smell in the air, a combination of scents he'd grown up with and knew well—the pungent, vinegary scent of ink mixed with the dusty one of paper.

The sounds, too, struck a chord in his memory—typists busy at their machines, tapping keys, shoving carriage levers and causing the bells to ring, the distant but rhythmic whir and thud of printing presses in the production rooms at the back, the hurried tap of footsteps as clerks and journalists rushed in and out the doors and up and down the stairs. It was a cacophony of sound as familiar to Jonathan as his own heartbeat, and yet, it stirred in him no emotion but simple recognition.

Rex led him to an electric lift operated by an attendant. They were taken to the first floor, where he followed Rex into a quieter, more elegant suite. A secretary, her auburn hair touched with a few threads of gray, looked up from one of two enormous desks piled with stacks of newspapers, magazines, and letters to give them a smile. "My lord," she greeted Rex as she stood up, then she cast a curious glance at Jonathan.

"This is Mr. Deverill, Miss Huish. Jonathan, this is Miss Evelyn Huish, Clara's secretary. Stephen's gone for the day, I assume?" he asked, nodding to the empty desk beside hers.

"Yes, sir," Miss Huish replied. "I'd be happy to step in, if there is something you need."

"No, no, Evie, thank you. Go on home. Jonathan, let's go into my office."

He followed his brother-in-law around the empty desk and through the door behind it into a spacious office suite with modern morris chairs and masculine teak furnishings.

"Nice view," he commented, nodding to the pair of large windows behind Rex's desk that gave a view of Fleet Street and the Strand. To his right, an open door led to a much more feminine room, of pale pink, white, and ebony. "Clara's office?" he guessed with a grin. "Pink always was her favorite color."

Rex grinned back at him as he closed his own door. "That's why we each have our own office. We couldn't agree on a color scheme." He spread his arms wide. "Well, here's where part of your investment went. What do you think of the place?"

"I'd have chosen a bigger building," he admitted. "Two floors doesn't give you much room to expand."

"True, but then, we haven't thought much about expansion. Five papers are about all we can handle at present." He gestured to a nearby table with glasses, whiskey, and a siphon. "Care for a drink? Or would you prefer a tour first?"

"A tour, definitely. Then the drink."

Rex complied, taking him around the offices first, where he met the various accountants, clerks, and secretaries who were preparing to depart for home, then Rex took him through the newsrooms, where journalists were still hard at work.

By the time they returned to the ground floor, all the clerks and typists had departed for the day, and the place was quiet as they moved toward the production rooms in the back. There, the printing presses had stopped, and the sheets of an evening daily were now being run through large, hot iron plates to dry the ink before being folded, bundled, and stacked at the back door by production workers for the delivery boys to take out to the streets.

He was introduced to various production workers, he asked a

variety of questions, and he gave opinions when Rex asked for them, but despite all that, he felt disconnected from his surroundings. He'd lived and breathed this business for the first eighteen years of his life, he owned nearly a third of the company, and his surname was still on a brass plate above the front door, but his tour had stirred within him no passion for what had once been the primary purpose of his life. He might just as well have been touring a factory or a brewery—or any of the many other companies in which he had a vested interest. It didn't seem at all like the family business that had been his dream since before he could walk.

Their tour completed, the two men returned upstairs, where Rex poured them each a whiskey. "We're having a board meeting next week," he said as they settled themselves in two of the morris chairs. "Since you're here, you might as well come, hear what's going on, give us your thoughts and ideas."

Jonathan considered, then shook his head. "I lost the right to any say in Deverill Publishing ten years ago."

"Nonsense. You're on the board. You bought 30 percent of the shares from Irene and Clara when your father died. It was your cash that enabled us to move the premises out of your father's house. Of course you have a say."

"Perhaps, but to be honest, I doubt I have any ideas to contribute. Clara, you, Irene—you've been here, you're involved in the daily operations, you know what the competition is doing, you've got your fingers on the pulse of it all the time. In the newspaper business, that's vital. I'm just a silent investor who's been thousands of miles away."

As he spoke, he felt again that familiar restlessness of spirit that had haunted him for so long, and the frustration that always came with it.

What do I want from life? he wondered. A question Marjorie had asked him, one he'd been hard put to find an answer for. If heaps of money and total freedom weren't enough to satisfy him, what would be?

"You're far more than an investor," Rex said, bringing his attention back to the conversation at hand. "Deverill Publishing was supposed to be yours by right."

"Right of primogeniture, you mean?" Jonathan grinned. "That's your aristocratic lineage talking, Lord Galbraith. The Deverills are much too middle-class for such things."

Rex chuckled. "Nonetheless, Clara, Irene, and I all agree that you have the right to be involved." He paused and took a swallow of whiskey. "If you want to be."

The comment was offhand, casual, and yet, Jonathan sensed it was nothing of the kind. "Why do I have the feeling you're not just inviting me to sit in on a board meeting while I'm passing through town?"

Rex hesitated. "Clara, Irene, and I discussed your return in depth before you arrived," he said at last, "and we all agreed that if you wanted back in, you'd be welcome."

Jonathan blinked, taken aback. "Come back into Deverill Publishing in an active role?"

"Yes. You mustn't think I'm jumping the gun by telling you this. Clara felt you might be more open to the possibility of returning if she was not the one presenting it."

"And she's all right with this idea?"

"She was the one who suggested it," Rex told him, much to his amazement. "But she said she didn't want you to feel obligated to accept out of any misplaced sense of guilt. Nonetheless, she and Irene want you to know that there's always a place for you here."

"But I'm going to South Africa."

"This is an open offer, naturally. You could take it up on your return. I'm presenting it now as food for thought, something to consider while you're away."

"But what would be my duties?"

"Editorial director is one possibility. Or perhaps you could start a magazine division. Or books. Whatever you wanted would be on the table."

"Whatever I wanted," he repeated thoughtfully, staring down into his glass. "There's the rub, as they say."

Rex didn't comment, and the silence allowed Jonathan to consider the offer without interruption. He was tempted, he had to admit. A big part of what he'd once hoped so desperately to regain handed to him on a silver platter, just like that. Such a simple solution, so easy, so safe. The past all wiped out, like wiping a slate clean.

Uncertain what to say, he laughed a little. "You've caught me by surprise. I didn't think Clara would let me anywhere near the company, after I bailed on her last time."

"Your sisters want you involved."

"You mean they want me home," he corrected, smiling a little.

"That, too. But they feel it's only right, since the whole thing was supposed to come to you anyway. Your grandfather wanted it that way."

"Then the old boy should have made a will." Oddly, he felt none of the old bitterness as he spoke. His words were a mere statement of fact.

"That's a mistake we can rectify, at least to some extent. We can make a place for you."

"Ah, but that's just it," he said, realizing that although he might not know what he wanted, he knew what he didn't. "I don't want a place made for me."

"I've phrased it badly—"

"No, no. It wouldn't matter how you phrased it, or who presented it, or what the responsibilities would be. The truth is—" He broke off, considering what he was about to do, then he did it, tossing the last shred of all his old dreams out the window because they were dead and gone and could not be made to live again.

"Deverill Publishing isn't mine anymore," he said. "Yes, I know, I own 30 percent, and so does Irene, but the person the company really belongs to now is Clara. She's the true captain of this ship. She's earned it, by her guts and her years of hard work. And perhaps it's terribly plebeian of me, but I think the one who's done the work and taken the risks, not the one who walked away, should be the one to reap the rewards."

"I see." Rex was silent a minute, then he said, "So, it's off to Africa, then?"

"Yes."

"What will you do there?"

"I have to deal with Marjorie's trust investments first, and some of my own as well. After that, I'm not sure. I'll roam a bit, see what piques my interest. I am aware of dozens of ventures seeking capital, but they need to be investigated."

As he spoke, he was surprised by his own lack of enthusiasm for the trip. Perhaps because the reality was sinking in that the friend who'd planned it with him wouldn't be along, or perhaps because deep down he knew that whatever he was looking for wasn't to be found there—a much more disturbing possibility. Or perhaps, he thought in chagrin, his desire for Marjorie was the reason for his reluctance to go. An irony, that, given all his efforts to keep away from her.

But if he stayed, those efforts would be in vain, and someone's heart—probably his, and possibly hers, too—would end up in pieces. He'd had his heart broken once already; he really didn't want to do that again.

And besides, he had no purpose here, not now. He had no desire for Deverill Publishing, and there was no doubt in his mind that turning it down was the right decision, but if he stayed here, what would he do with himself? What did he want?

"Are you limiting yourself to African investments these days?" Rex asked, breaking into his thoughts. "Or would you consider some British ones?"

With an effort, he forced aside the pesky, unanswerable question that seemed to be endlessly rattling around in his brain these days. "I'm always open to a potentially profitable venture, regardless of where it's based. Why do you ask?"

"I have connections you may be interested in. Men who want to form joint ventures and need men like you."

That made Jonathan grin. "You mean they need men with money?"

"Well, finding capital always does seem to be the stumbling block in the way of big ideas, doesn't it? But if you really are looking for investment opportunities, I have a suggestion for you. Join a club."

He groaned. "First the club, then the old school tie. What's next? Standing for Parliament and buying a country house I can dash down to at weekends where I shall host parties of great political importance?"

"I'm serious, Jonathan," Rex said even as he smiled. "Being a member of a club would be a tremendous asset to you. And many of the members will have connections in Africa that might be of use to you."

As much as he loved to poke fun at his country's more pompous institutions and traditions, he also appreciated the wisdom of his friend's advice. "I suppose you're right, though why any club with sense would have a reverse snob like me as a member, I can't imagine."

"I'd recommend Travellers. Given your ten years in America and your upcoming trip, you'd be an asset to the membership. And it's a club that would suit you. Also, Henry is a man of great influence and he has a membership there, as do I. With us to recommend you, there's no question you'd be admitted. And until then, you could come as my guest, or Henry's."

"Oh, very well," he said with a sigh of mock forbearance. "You've convinced me. After all, I've got heaps of time to kill before I leave for Johannesburg. Might as well put it to good use."

"Do you still intend to return in January?"

"I'm not certain. Since Marjorie seems settled here now . . ." He paused, words suddenly stuck in his throat, and took a moment before he could go on. "I may stay in Africa a bit longer. We'll have to see."

"Just don't stay away ten years next time." Rex glanced at the ticking clock on the wall and then at the darkened windows outside. "God, it's half past seven. We'd best be on our way."

The two men stood up, swallowed the last of their whiskey, and returned downstairs. "There's a mews just around the corner," Rex told him as they left the building. "My driver usually waits there, and I'm sure he's wondering what's become of me. The family likely is, too."

"Are you and Clara joining us this evening?" Jonathan asked as the two men started down the sidewalk.

"We are, and the duke's cook will make no end of a fuss if we're late. He's such a temperamental fellow."

With those words, Jonathan's thoughts returned to what had happened earlier in the tearoom at Claridge's, and suddenly, the idea of sitting across from Marjorie at dinner seemed unbearable. Deciding two hours of erotic fantasies about her was enough self-torture for one day, he stopped on the sidewalk.

"You go on," he said, and as Rex stopped beside him, looking surprised, he hastily invented an excuse. "I've just remembered I'm supposed to meet an old friend for dinner."

"What restaurant? I can drop you."

"No, no, it's the opposite direction. I'll take a hansom." He started walking backward toward the taxi stand. "Make my excuses to everyone, would you?"

"Of course. Good night."

Rex resumed walking toward the mews, and Jonathan continued toward the taxi stand, where a hansom cab was already waiting, its doors flung back. The driver straightened up on the box as he approached. "Where to, guv'nor?"

An excellent question, Jonathan thought. *In more ways than one.* "Number Twelve Belford Row," he said on impulse. "Holborn."

Ten minutes later, the cab pulled up in front of a large terrace house and came to a stop, then the hatch in the roof above Jonathan's head opened.

He pulled a handful of change from his pocket, selected the required sixpence fare, and held it up through the opening. The driver took the coin from his fingers, shoved the lever to open the doors, and Jonathan emerged onto the sidewalk, replacing his remaining change back in his pocket.

"Wait here," he ordered, then turned around to face the house where he'd grown up, moving forward to stand on the very same square of pavement where he'd stood with a suitcase a decade ago.

He felt suddenly as if he'd spent the past ten years wandering in a desert, walking and walking, and yet only going in circles. How fitting, then, that he should be back in the place he'd started.

The house had been sold upon his father's death five years before, but despite the change in ownership, it looked the same now as it had when he was eighteen.

Well, he amended at once, not precisely the same. It was night this time around, and lit lamps shone in some of the windows. Rain wasn't dripping off the eaves, Clara and Irene were not standing in the bay window of the dining room watching him go with shocked, disbelieving faces, and his father was not scowling down at him from between the curtains in the window above. Most important, he wasn't looking at it from the point of view of a rebellious eighteen-year-old youth, but as a man nearing thirty. It was an entirely different perspective.

He'd left here filled to the brim with anger, pain, and resentment toward his father, his grandfather, and the girl who'd broken his heart, but all of that was gone now, disappearing into the ether during his years in America, fading away so gradually that he hadn't even noticed the departure.

When he'd stood here ten years ago, he'd had a fire in his belly and things to prove. He'd succeeded. He was wealthy, and by most people's definition, he was successful, but to him, it was a shallow success. He no longer had the fire of anger to fuel his ambition, and he should have felt at peace, but he didn't. Instead, he felt empty. His dreams were gone, his best friend was dead, and even though a big piece of what he'd lost all those years ago had just been offered to him on a plate, he'd turned it down.

What do you want from life?

It haunted him, that question—had been haunting him ever since Marjorie had first asked it of him aboard the *Neptune*. Or perhaps it had been haunting him ever since he'd last stood here, and he'd spent the past ten years running from it.

He moved, he wandered, but it wasn't out of some zest for adventure, and it wasn't even in a search to replace what he'd lost, not really. The truth was much less romantic. His restlessness came from fear: if he stood still, he feared he'd stop moving altogether, sink into the life of apathy, privilege, and ennui so common in the British upper classes, a life where things like which fork to use and which invitations to accept took on crucial significance and one had nothing more important on one's calendar than visits to the tailor, whist at the club, and chasing down hapless foxes at the country house.

He had the money for that life, certainly, but unlike Marjorie, he didn't want it. He wanted something else—something more, and though it seemed as elusive as a rainbow's end or a mirage on a desert horizon, he knew he wouldn't find it standing here.

Turning around, he walked back to the cab. "Where can a man obtain an underdone porterhouse, a plate of chips, and a pint of good ale in London these days?" he asked the driver.

"Black Swan's just up around the corner, guv'nor. On the High Street. Best beefsteak in Holborn."

Jonathan pulled another sixpence out of his pocket, handed it up, and ignoring the driver's profuse thanks, he started toward High Holborn. Behind him, he heard the snap of reins, the clatter of wheels, and a moment later, the hansom rolled past him up the street.

As he followed in its wake, Jonathan had the curious, nagging sensation that he'd left something undone. He stopped, realizing what it was, and why he'd really come here.

Slowly, he turned to look back over his shoulder to the lace-curtained upstairs window.

"Good-bye, Papa," he said. "Godspeed."

With that, he once again turned his back on his father's house, his grandfather's unfulfilled ambitions, and his own lost dreams. He did it not with rancor or resentment, but with relief, and he knew at last that the past was truly behind him.

The question he had to face now was what to do with his future, and he suspected finding an answer to that was going to be much harder than letting go of the past.

Chapter 17

Marjorie's reunion with Dulci and Jenna had been delightful, reliving days at Forsyte and laughing about their escapades there, but in the days that followed tea at Claridge's, she rarely saw either of her old friends. Their social calendars for the remainder of the season were already filled, and their circle of acquaintances was an entirely different one from Irene and Clara.

In addition, Marjorie's mourning period prevented her from attending any significant social events, so as the days of June went by, her path crossed very little with that of her friends, but both of them promised to attend the house party for her birthday in August.

She was able to participate in some of the season's activities, however, thanks to Irene, Clara, and Rex's cousin, Hetty. Due to their efforts, Marjorie attended teas, paid calls, shopped, and went to picnics, Afternoons-At-Home, several small dinner parties, the theater, and the opera. Marjorie enjoyed her new life, although after a lifetime of no society at all, she found the pace a bit overwhelming. Had she fully participated in the social whirl as the debutantes did, she'd have been exhausted by it.

As for Jonathan, she saw him every day. They made small talk across the breakfast table every morning and over sherry nearly every evening. She listened with the members of his family to his stories of life on the American frontier. He was cordial and attentive and scrupulously polite, and yet, she felt as if there was a wall between them. They never sparred, they never disagreed. When she asked his opinion, he gave it, but he never tried to tell her what to do, what to wear, or who to see. Their conversations were amiable, as those between friends should be, and yet, they always had the curious result of leaving Marjorie unaccountably depressed.

Not once did she see in his face what she'd seen at Claridge's. Not once did she catch him watching her in the way that made her lips tingle and her heart race, and as the days passed, she began to wonder if what she'd seen at Claridge's had been nothing but her imagination. Even their passionate kiss aboard the *Neptune* seemed now like nothing more than a wild, fevered dream.

By the day of Irene's water party, Marjorie was tempted to do something wildly outrageous just to see if she could get a rise out of him, but she refrained, for she didn't wish to embarrass her hosts or hurt her newfound social position. And what would be the point? It wouldn't change anything.

To prepare for the water party, the duke and his brother left before breakfast, wanting to look over the *Mary Louisa* and make certain the crew had the vessel ready for the day's excursion, and Jonathan chose to accompany them. Irene did the same, having preparations of her own to make as hostess, so when it was time for Marjorie and Carlotta to depart for Queen's Wharf, it was Rex and Clara's landau that rolled up in front of the house to fetch them.

The landau's top was rolled back to the fine July morning, but one glance at the couple in it told Marjorie not everyone was in a sunny mood.

"I still think you should talk to him again," Clara was saying to Rex in an insistent tone as Marjorie and Carlotta approached the vehicle. "We both know—"

She broke off to give Marjorie and her sister-in-law a nod of greeting as Torquil's footman assisted them into the carriage, then she returned her attention to her husband and their conversation. "We both know how persuasive you can be when you choose. If you presented the offer another way—"

"Clara, he doesn't want it," Rex said and looked up at his driver as Torquil's footman closed the carriage door. "Walk on, Kettridge. Good morning, ladies," he added as the footman stepped back and the vehicle pulled away from the curb.

"He doesn't know what he wants," Clara muttered with a toss of her head. "That's obvious."

"It's equally obvious he knows what he doesn't want, as I've already told you multiple times now."

"But Deverill Publishing is his company, too," Clara said, making Marjorie realize they were talking about Jonathan. "And since we don't even know yet what his duties might encompass, I don't believe he can be as decided about it as he seems. And," she added, over-riding her husband as he tried to speak, "I don't see why you're so adamant about not talking to him further."

"Well, now, what's this?" Carlotta asked as she opened her parasol over her head. "I hope you two aren't having a quarrel on such a lovely day?"

It was a clear attempt to change the subject to something less personal, but Clara seemed in no frame of mind to take the hint. "A disagreement isn't a quarrel," she said, giving her sister-in-law a somewhat impatient glance before returning her attention to her husband. "Maybe I should talk with him. Ask him to reconsider."

"Guilt him into staying?" Rex countered. "Yes, that sounds like the perfect plan. It worked so well last time."

"That's not fair," Clara replied. "I never used guilt to try to make Jonathan come home. Never. And I wouldn't now."

"You never used guilt deliberately, I'll grant you that. Either way," he rushed on before she could dispute the point, "I advise against it. You might make things worse."

"I don't see how."

"Don't you, my darling?" Rex laughed. "I know what it's like when you open up those big round eyes of yours and ask for something. Saying no to you then is like trying to hold back the tide. But partici-pating in Deverill Publishing isn't what he wants, and if he gave in, I think he'd regret it."

"You offered Jonathan a place in Deverill Publishing?" Marjorie asked, jumping into the conversation before she could resist, remembering too late that her guardian's life had nothing to do with her. "Sorry," she added at once. "It's not my business."

"There's no need to apologize," Clara assured her. "If we wanted to keep it a secret, we wouldn't be talking about it. We asked Jonathan to take an active role in the company, yes."

"And he refused," Marjorie said, the words bitter on her tongue.

"He did," Rex confirmed, giving his wife a meaningful glance. "And Clara," he added, "if you love your brother and want to maintain the peace you two have achieved, I'd advise you to accept his decision with grace, and support him in whatever he does decide to do. You can't force him to stay where he doesn't want to be."

Marjorie had known that all along, of course, but hearing someone else say it out loud hurt more than she'd thought possible, and she was relieved when the other woman dropped the subject.

Carlotta stepped tactfully into the silence with a comment about how outrageous the hats at Ascot had been this year, and for the remainder of the ride to Queen's Wharf, she was able to keep the conversation on inconsequential topics like fashion, the delicate state of the elderly Queen's health, and the weather.

"It looks to be a gorgeous day on the water," she told Marjorie as Rex's carriage halted by the pier where Torquil's yacht was moored. "And the wind seems just right, too, thank heaven," she added as she and Marjorie followed Rex and Clara along the quay toward the duke's waiting yacht. "If the breeze is too light, we usually have to cancel."

"Not always," Clara said over her shoulder with a laugh, indicating that her good mood had been restored. "Remember last year, Carlotta, when we decided to chance it and we found ourselves becalmed at Kew? We had to be towed back by a steamer."

"I'd rather have that than the other," Carlotta said as they started up the gangplank. "If the breeze is too strong, all the ladies go home with headaches because of our hat pins."

"As a man, I take a different view," Rex said as he stepped aboard and turned to assist his wife. "With a strong breeze, the ladies' skirts

blow up, giving gentlemen the opportunity to admire the pretty ankles of our wives."

"Which does you no good at all, darling," Clara replied as she
grasped his hand and stepped on deck, "if your wife has a headache."

They all laughed at that valid point as Rex guided Marjorie onto
the ship, where Irene was waiting to greet them, a footman beside her
with a tray of filled champagne flutes.

"Welcome aboard the *Mary Louisa*," the duchess said as she handed
Marjorie a glass.

"Irene, your husband is shameless," Clara put in as she also accepted a glass of champagne. "He's roped our brother in to help,
I see."

Marjorie turned and saw Jonathan seated over the point of the bow,
his long legs dangling on either side. His jacket off, his shirtsleeves
rolled back, and a cap shading his eyes, he looked completely at ease
as he knotted rope, securing the sail.

"You know how it is with Henry," Irene said. "Any man aboard can
be pressed into service."

"True," Clara agreed, "but Henry doesn't usually let anyone handle
the sails who isn't experienced."

"Well, Jonathan has some experience," Marjorie commented. "He
was a fishing boat captain once."

"He was?" Clara and Irene said simultaneously, and when Marjorie
looked at them, she found both his sisters staring at her in surprise.

"It was when he first went to America."

"Well, that's one story we've missed hearing over the dinner table,
haven't we?" Irene said, then glanced past Marjorie's shoulder. "Ah, I
see more guests coming up the gangplank, if you'll pardon me?"

Marjorie and the others moved out of the way, leaving Irene to greet
the next group of arrivals. Rex went in search of David to see how he
could help, Carlotta ensconced herself in a deck chair, and Clara and
Marjorie walked toward Jonathan in the bow.

"Look at you, sailor," Clara greeted him as they approached, causing him to look up from his task. "Decided to do an honest day's work
for a change, have you?"

He straightened, grinning at his sister. "Says the woman who's sipping champagne and doing anything but working." He paused and pulled off his cap to wipe sweat from his brow with his wrist. "Still," he added as he settled his cap back on his head, "the two of you look so pretty, I can't complain."

It was a compliment, but a glib and impersonal one, the sort he might have given any female acquaintance, and to Marjorie, the invisible wall between them seemed more impossible to breach than ever.

"That's why," he went on, still smiling at his sister, "I haven't the heart to point out how lazy you're being."

"Lazy?" Clara cried, giving a huff of mock aggravation. "Well, I like that. I don't think we need to listen to any more of my brother's backhanded compliments. C'mon, Marjorie. I shall give you a tour of the ship."

Marjorie turned and started to follow, but then, she glanced back at Jonathan, thought of Rex and Clara's conversation about him in the carriage, and changed her mind. "You go ahead," she told the other woman. "I'll be along in a minute."

Clara gave a nod and continued back toward midship, and Marjorie turned to Jonathan again. Occupied with his task, he seemed oblivious to her presence, but she spoke anyway. "I understand Clara and Irene offered to bring you back into the company."

He didn't even look up. "Yes."

"But you turned down their offer?"

"I did." He tied off the knot, grabbed a bit of rigging, and hauled himself upright. Balancing on the point of the bow, he swung around the sail he'd just secured and slid back down to secure another.

"But why?" she cried, spurred on rather than deterred by these taciturn responses. "Your father's gone, so you wouldn't have to worry about his interference. And coming back into Deverill Publishing would give you back what you lost."

His hands stilled. "Nothing can do that," he said and glanced past her. "You'd best go," he advised and returned his attention to his task. "Clara's waiting for you."

It was a clear dismissal, and it stung, making her suck in a sharp breath. So much for smashing down walls, she thought and turned away, wondering why she'd even bothered to try, but she'd taken only two steps before his voice stopped her. "Marjorie?"

She forced herself to look at him, pride keeping hurt at bay. "Yes?"

"You should keep your parasol up," he said.

She blinked, startled by such an unexpected remark. "What?"

"Your parasol." He nodded to the ebony-handled concoction of white linen, black ribbon, and mauve lace in her hand. "The sun's brutal on the water, and that little boater you've got on won't do a thing to protect you. Your skin is so—"

He broke off, swallowed hard, and looked down, forming a knot with the rope in his hands. "Your skin is fair, and you'll burn if you're not careful."

It was the first truly personal thing he'd said to her in days, and she was so astonished and relieved, it took her a moment to think of a response. "This is a bit like old times," she said, laughing as she opened her parasol over her head. "You advising me about my wardrobe. It reminds me of our days on the *Neptune*. Do you remember?"

"Yes."

One word, and yet, the intensity of it was like a shot, reverberating through the air between them. He looked up, and when he did, she almost dropped her parasol, for in his face was everything she'd seen at Claridge's.

Her body responded at once. Warmth pooled in her midsection and spread outward, her lips tingled, and her heart gave a leap of pure, unreasoning joy in her chest.

But then, as suddenly as it appeared, it was gone, and he continued his work as if nothing had happened, making it clear the wall between them was still very much in place.

She waited a moment, but when he made no effort to continue the conversation, she gave up and walked away, vowing not to waste a single moment of what promised to be a glorious day worrying about him.

As the day went on, however, she found it a hard vow to keep, for with each hour that passed, it became more painfully obvious that no matter where she was, he wanted to be someplace else, and it left her feeling both baffled and hurt.

One would think that on a hundred-foot yacht, avoiding a particular person for an entire day would be impossible, but somehow, Jonathan managed to avoid her. If he wasn't up at the helm with Henry, or helping David and Rex, he was playing checkers with Paul, or laughing with Hetty, or talking with any number of the other forty guests aboard.

Marjorie's considerable pride enabled her to hide the sting of being so obviously and inexplicably snubbed, but it wasn't until midafternoon, when the *Mary Louisa* was starting back to Queen's Wharf, that she was able to finally quell the hurt. She stopped scanning the deck looking for him among the crowd, she gave up wondering what had gone wrong with their newfound friendship, and she decided that if he wanted a wall between them, that was just fine with her. It was at that point that she finally began to enjoy herself.

When some of the other ladies set up shuffleboard on the port side, she joined in, glad there was no Lady Stansbury to frown in disapproval. When Henry explained navigation to her, she listened eagerly, and when he offered to let her take the helm, she happily steered the ship all the way from Chiswick to Battersea Park before Henry made her give it back.

"You are proving an excellent sailor, Marjorie," Clara said as Marjorie joined her and several other ladies who were sitting in deck chairs under the shade of a tarp. "You might have been born to it. The first time I tried to steer the ship, I almost ran us aground, and it was the next summer before Henry let me take the helm again. I—"

She broke off, frowning, leaning forward to study Marjorie's face. "Your lips are chapped and a little red."

"Are they?" She pressed her finger to her mouth, wincing as she felt the sting of windburn.

"You ought to put some zinc oxide paste on it. I've got some below, if you want it. It's in the little desk at the bottom of the stairs."

Marjorie touched her mouth again and decided the zinc oxide was a good idea. "Pour me some tea, would you, Clara?" she asked over her shoulder as she walked to the cabin. Shoving the door open, she went inside and went below deck, but though she found the desk Clara had mentioned at once, the lip salve proved elusive. She searched all three drawers of the desk, but she was finally forced to concede defeat.

She shut the bottom drawer, but as she straightened, she realized she wasn't alone down here. Behind her, the door to one of the bedrooms suddenly opened, and as she turned around, the man who had been avoiding her all day came out, his hair damp and his dark blue reefer jacket in his hand.

He stopped in his tracks at the sight of her, and the dismayed expression on his face made her want to sink into the teak floor beneath her feet.

"I came down for zinc oxide, but I can't seem to find it," she said, then stopped, realizing she didn't owe him any explanations.

"I have some." He slid on his jacket, then reached into one of its pockets and pulled out a small glass jar. Stepping forward, he held it out to her.

"Thank you." Taking it from his outstretched hand, she unscrewed the lid and turned toward the mirror bolted to the wall above the desk. But before she could apply some of the thick white paste to her lips, she saw his face in the mirror, and once again, she caught a glimpse of what she'd seen at Claridge's three weeks earlier.

She froze, the jar and the lid in her fingers. "What are you thinking when you look at me like that?" she whispered.

At once, he looked away. "I'd better get on," he said, and moved as if to leave.

"Wait," she said, turning around, desperate for some excuse to make him stay. She wanted to ask him what was different, what had changed between them, what was wrong, but as she looked into his face again, the fire in his tawny eyes was gone, and his countenance was so wooden, so stiff, that her question stuck in her throat, and she lost her nerve. "You forgot this."

She moved to dip her finger in the jar to take a little of the salve before giving it back, but his voice stopped her.

"Keep it," he said and once again started to step around her.

The curtness of his voice proved one snub too many for Marjorie. "I don't want it!" she cried, too stung for even pride to come to her rescue. She screwed the lid back on, then grabbed his hand and slapped the tiny jar into his palm. "What I want to know is why you are treating me like a stranger. What have I done to deserve it?"

He stiffened, his fingers tightening into a fist around the jar. Slowly, with deliberate care, he pulled his hand from her grasp. "I don't know what you mean."

"Yes, you do," she said, confirmed in that opinion when he shifted his weight, looking uneasy. "That afternoon when we walked to Claridge's for tea, it was so lovely. We were talking and laughing—like friends, you know, but then . . ."

Something flickered in the stiff lines of his face, a trace of emotion. "That's when everything changed," she went on, pushing. "Ever since tea that day, it's as if there's this wall between us, and I don't know how it got there. And today, you're avoiding me altogether, ducking away every time I come within ten feet of you. Did I offend you by asking about the paper?"

"Not at all."

"Then maybe you just find the conversation of every single other person on board more appealing than mine? Whatever the reason," she said before he could answer, "it's clear something's gone wrong between us, and it—"

She stopped, for her pride just couldn't allow her to make the humiliating admission that she was hurt. "I thought we were friends," she said instead.

"So we are. Now, I must—"

"You make that assurance with such conviction," she interrupted as he turned his back, "and yet, somehow . . ." She paused again, then whispered, "I don't believe you."

He stopped, one foot on the stairs, his back stiff, his shoulders rigid. "God have mercy," he muttered, and then, suddenly, he turned, his arm catching her around the waist.

He pulled her hard against him, and the jar of lip salve dropped from his fingers as his other arm wrapped around her shoulders. He tilted his head, ducking beneath her hat brim, and then, his mouth was on hers, hot and fierce, but so tender that her lips parted at once in willing accord.

He groaned, and his tongue entered her mouth, tasting deeply of her. Overwhelmed, Marjorie closed her eyes, but at once, everything began to spin. Thinking to steady herself in the maelstrom, she moved to slide her arms up around his neck, but then, his hands came up between them, closing over her wrists. With another groan, he pulled her hands down and broke the kiss. He pulled back, his breathing hot and quick against her cheek, and when she opened her eyes, she found his blazing with all their color and light.

"Being friends with you is killing me," he muttered. "For God's sake, don't you understand? It's killing me by inches."

Abruptly, he grabbed her arms, shoved her back, and let her go. He turned away, and this time, he did leave, going up the stairs without another word or a backward glance, leaving Marjorie staring after him. Men, she thought, shaking her head, were completely inexplicable.

HAD THE *MARY Louisa* still been on a more remote part of the Thames, Jonathan might very well have dived overboard and swam for shore.

After weeks of fighting and suppressing desire, he'd finally given in. He'd allowed himself one hour of wild sexual fantasy about his ward, and he'd been paying for it ever since. Instead of being a relief, that afternoon in Claridge's tearoom had made his agony even more acute, and during the weeks that had followed, being in her company had become an almost unbearable torture.

Now, after an entire day of evading her—a task that had required considerable ingenuity on his part—he'd been forced to take refuge below deck, where he'd swallowed two fingers of whiskey, dunked his head in a basin of cold water, and reminded himself at least twenty-seven times of things like duty and responsibility and gentlemanly conduct.

He'd barely returned to a sane state of mind, however, before she'd come below and he'd ruined all his own good work by hauling off and kissing her. After that scorching hot disaster, getting away by swimming for shore began to seem his only alternative.

Unfortunately for Jonathan, the yacht was well past Battersea Park when he emerged on deck, so even if he'd wanted to employ such desperate means of escape, there were far too many ships on the river to attempt it.

As it was, Jonathan had no choice but to do what he'd been doing for the past several weeks. He endured. He suppressed any naughty thoughts about her the moment they entered his head. He reminisced about schooldays at Winchester with Paul and kept Hetty entertained with tales of her brother's boyhood misdeeds. He mingled, he mixed, he told stories of his life in America, and he smiled so much that by the time they reached Queen's Wharf, his jaw ached.

In the days that followed the water party, he took steps to ensure that what happened on the *Mary Louisa* could not happen again. Sending Irene's plans for his social calendar to perdition, he stayed away from the house on Upper Brook Street and its voluptuous, ginger-haired guest as much as possible.

Most men in his situation, he supposed, would have turned to another woman to relieve the agony, but to Jonathan, such a course held no appeal. He'd never been one for the brothels. Even on the American frontier, where prostitutes were an unmarried man's only viable choice, he'd never had much taste for them, and he'd seldom sought their company. Besides, he knew any relief he might find in the arms of another woman would be purely physical and also temporary, for Marjorie was the only woman he wanted. He joined a gymnasium instead and discovered that a punching bag and fencing foil were decent, if not fully effective, physical outlets for his frustration.

He also sought other distractions. He looked up old friends from schooldays. He handled the various business matters his stop in London had required. He took cold baths and went for long walks.

Following Rex's advice, he applied to be a member of the Travellers Club, and with Torquil's influence, Rex's endorsement, and the recommendations of various schoolfellows with whom he'd become reacquainted, he was shuffled to the top of the waiting list. In the meantime, he was able to attend as a guest, and in order to avoid Upper Brook Street, he took advantage of both his brothers-in-law in that regard as often as possible.

"You realize your sisters are becoming aggravated with us," the duke told him as they met Rex there for drinks one night in late July. "They know you're ducking society, and the fact that we're helping you do so is not sitting well with them."

"It's just a few more weeks," Jonathan said, and took a sip of whiskey. "Thank God."

Henry chuckled. "Dear Lady Truelove," he said, looking at Rex, "the women in our lives are insisting we mingle in society, but after all these weeks of doing the season, we are exhausted, and we just want some peace. How can we make our wives understand that nights at the club are vital to our masculine health and well-being? Signed, Bored with Balls in Belgravia."

Jonathan and Rex both laughed, not only at the duke's double entendre, but also at the fact that he was usually far too proper a chap to make a naughty joke like that.

"Lady Truelove," Rex said after a moment, giving his brother-in-law a look of mock reproof, "would never advise a man to go to his club instead of his home. Unless," he added with a grin, "he's got a very good reason."

"Which is what?" Henry asked. "Best if we get that story straight, gentlemen, before we leave here."

"I've already arranged for that." Rex glanced past the duke's shoulder and his grin widened. "In fact, our reason for being here tonight just walked through the door. The Marquess of Kayne has arrived."

Jonathan, who didn't know the Marquess of Kayne or anything about him whatsoever, did not understand the significance of the man's arrival, but Henry seemed to do so.

"Aha," the duke said with a nod and a discreet glance over his shoulder. "I see where your mind is heading, Rex. You are a clever devil."

"Why, thank you," Rex murmured, brushing a speck of dust from his lapel, donning a show of modesty. "I do my best." Leaning closer to Jonathan, he went on, "Kayne is someone you need to meet, which is why I've asked him to join us this evening. And, given what I've told him about you, he very much wants to make your acquaintance."

Jonathan had no opportunity to reply before a tall, dark-haired man paused by their table, bringing all three of them to their feet.

"Torquil," the marquess greeted. "Galbraith. Good to see you both. It's been a while."

"We haven't seen much of you this season, Phillip," Henry commented. "Not since your annual May Day charity ball."

"I've been busy down in Hampshire, so my wife and I have done very little this year. I've only been coming up for the Lords."

"Would you allow me to introduce my brother-in-law, Jonathan Deverill?" Henry asked. "Jonathan, the Marquess of Kayne."

If this man truly was eager to meet Jonathan, he didn't show it. A pair of cool blue eyes flicked over him in polite, impersonal fashion, and his handshake, though firm, was brief. "Mr. Deverill."

Henry inquired if the other man had yet dined, and upon learning he had not, an invitation to join them was given, an invitation the marquess accepted.

"How's the shipping business these days, Phillip?" Rex asked after they had ordered joints of beef and bottles of claret and settled back in their chairs. "Lord Kayne is a very forward-thinking peer," he explained to Jonathan. "He got into industry early on."

"Hawthorne Shipping was my father's doing, not mine," the marquess said. "Though I admit, I'd have done something if he had not. Any peer that still depends on land rents for his income isn't just a snob, he's a fool."

That piqued Jonathan's interest at once. "What does Hawthorne Shipping do?" he asked. "Import and export?"

The marquess shook his head. "We build transatlantic steamships, both in Liverpool and in Southampton."

"Indeed? Cargo or passenger?"

"Cargo. I had—" He broke off, shooting an inquiring glance at Rex that did not escape Jonathan's notice. Rex must have nodded, for Kayne continued, "I should like to expand into building passenger liners as well."

Hence the purpose of this meeting. The man needed capital. "You wish to manufacture and sell passenger liners to Cunard, White Star, and—" He broke off in surprise as Kayne shook his head.

"That's an option, certainly, but it's not the plan I'd like to implement." Those cool blue eyes met Jonathan's, a hard, shrewd glint in their depths. "I prefer to think bigger."

Jonathan was intrigued. "You don't want to build for them," he said, feeling his interest rise as he appreciated the other man's true vision. "You want to compete with them. A bold strategy," he added as the other man nodded.

"Yes," the marquess said simply. "It is."

He paused for a swallow of whiskey, then went on, "My partner was to be my brother's American father-in-law, Colonel Dutton, and my brother was to assist me with the venture. Unfortunately, Dutton lost a packet in the last Wall Street crash, so we had to scrap the plan, and my brother took up a diplomatic post with the British embassy in Washington."

"But you still want to do it?"

"Yes. Having already spent several years on this project and invested a small fortune, I do not want to abandon it altogether."

"So, you need investors to take Dutton's place. Have you arranged for any as yet?"

"Not yet," Kayne admitted. "I've scarcely begun to look."

"That," Rex interjected, "is where you come in, dear fellow."

Jonathan considered. "I like the idea," he said after a moment, "but to compete head-on with the existing companies, you'll have to establish ports and routes and gain the moorings."

"My brother had already begun that process, making arrangements with both Ostend and New York before he left for Washington. And I am due to meet with moorings officials in Gibraltar next month to continue what he started. But if I can't find capital, it will all be for naught."

"You've piqued my interest, Lord Kayne," Jonathan said and meant it. "It always interests me to meet men of vision. Most men think too small. Send your prospectus to me at Upper Brook Street. I will look it over, and if I like what I see, we can talk further."

At that moment, their meal arrived, and talk of business was abandoned. Afterward, Kayne suggested bridge, and though Henry and Rex were obligated to refuse, having social engagements to attend that evening, Jonathan was happy to accept the marquess's invitation, and if the money the two men earned as bridge partners that evening was any indication, a joint venture between them would prove highly profitable.

By the time Jonathan returned to the house on Upper Brook Street, it was well past midnight, and the door had already been latched, but since Irene had given him a key, he was able to let himself in.

The house was dark and silent, indicating that everyone, including the servants, had gone to bed. He started up the stairs, thinking to do the same, but on the first-floor landing, he paused, noticing light spilling into the corridor from the drawing room.

A lamp or gas jet left unattended could be dangerous. Rather surprised that one of Torquil's servants could be so careless, he went down the corridor, thinking to put the light out before going to bed, but when he entered the drawing room, he found that Torquil's servants had not been careless at all.

Through the opened double doors that led into the library, he could see Marjorie sitting on the floor, an opened trunk in front of her, a trunk he recognized, for he'd been the one to fill it with her father's things and send it to White Plains. Following the instructions in his telegram, Mrs. Forsyte had shipped it here.

Marjorie didn't seem to notice him in the doorway. Her head was bent, the long, loose braid of her hair falling across one shoulder and over her breast, the soft white fabric of her nightdress billowing around, making it seem as if she was sitting on a cloud.

He started toward her, but she didn't even look up, and as he approached the library, he could see over the top of the open trunk that she was reading a letter, a letter on paper of an unmistakable robin's egg blue.

He stopped, staring at it, his own mind realizing for the first time the deeper implications of the information it contained. And when she spoke, he knew she had realized those implications, too.

"He was in New York," she said, letting the letter fall into her lap. She looked up, and in her big brown eyes, he could see shock and pain. "Three years after he left me at Mrs. Forsyte's, he came back to New York, but it wasn't to see me."

Her face twisted, went awry, and his chest tightened in response, her pain squeezing him like a vise. When a tear slid down her cheek, he felt it burn him like acid.

"He came all the way from Idaho. He was an hour away from me by train. One hour. And he did not come to see me."

Jonathan couldn't stand it. He started forward again, but he'd only taken a few steps before remembering what had happened the last time he'd found himself alone with her.

He stopped again, fully aware of her vulnerable state and his own. He reminded himself of the reasons why he ought to turn around right now and walk out, but it did no good. He could not leave her, not like this.

Taking a deep breath, praying for fortitude, Jonathan walked into the library.

Chapter 18

$\mathcal{H}$er eyes, wide and dark, were like those of a wounded animal, and he approached her that way, moving slowly into the room and closing the doors behind him as softly as possible. He circled the trunk, then he pushed the billowy folds of her nightgown out of his way to avoid sitting on them and eased down cross-legged on the floor beside her.

"Marjorie," he began, but she gave him no chance to say more.

"This is an appraisal of the Rose of Shoshone necklace," she said. "It's dated July 21, 1888, three years after he left me. Did you see it? Of course you did. You packed his things, you had charge of his affairs."

He glanced at the letter, then back at her. "Yes, I saw it."

"So, you knew." Her eyes narrowed in accusation, and he felt it like an arrow through his chest. "You knew my father had come to New York while I was there, and you didn't tell me."

"No. I mean, not exactly," he amended as he saw the disbelief in her face. "Yes, I knew he'd gone to New York to have the sapphires cut and set, but that trip was five years before we met, and I didn't learn about you until two months ago. You know that. And yes, I saw the appraisal when I packed his things after he died, but because I had thought you were a child, I took it for granted that his trip to New York was before you were born. After I met you, I didn't connect your age with the date of Tiffany's appraisal."

He stared at her, unhappily aware he'd had other things on his mind since they met. "Call me thick, but I didn't put the pieces together until this very moment. If I had, I'd have told you. I'm sorry, Marjorie."

"Why?" she asked, all her earlier bewilderment back in her voice. "Why didn't he come see me? You knew him. Tell me why."

He wished he could. "I don't know," he admitted. "If I were to guess, I'd say he meant to, and then . . . well . . . he funked it at the last minute."

"He was a coward. That's what you mean."

"It's hard for me to think of him that way." Jonathan considered, trying to be objective about the man who'd been like a brother to him, but it was impossible. "We braved many things together, and he never shirked. He had plenty of physical courage, but . . ."

"But he was afraid of a little girl?" She made a sound of contempt, one he was forced to admit her father richly deserved.

"I'm only guessing," he said.

"And you called him a friend?" She shook her head. "A poor friend, who abandons his own daughter, makes promises to her that he doesn't keep, and strings her along with hope for something that he knows won't ever happen."

He couldn't argue that, and he realized that ever since meeting Marjorie, his opinion of his friend had been steadily eroding, though his own grief and sense of loyalty had prevented him from seeing it. "Yes," he agreed simply. "I'm sorry."

Her face twisted, and it took everything he had not to move. She needed a shoulder to cry on, a comforting embrace, but he could not provide that sort of solace. He didn't dare. God help him, he wasn't strong enough.

Instead, he did the safe thing, the proper thing. He pulled out his handkerchief.

"I hate him," she choked, her words a seething rush of pain and anger as she snatched the handkerchief. "I hate him," she repeated, but with less venom. Her head lowered, her shoulders sagged. "Hate him," she whispered, crumpling Jonathan's handkerchief into a ball.

"No," he said gently. "You don't."

She looked up, the tears making her brown eyes glisten in the lamp-light, and he felt as if he were sliding precariously close to the edge of a cliff. "I should hate him."

"Undoubtedly. But you don't."

She gave a sob, acknowledging the truth of that, and more than ever, he wanted to wrap his arms around her, comfort her—no, he corrected at once, shredding any pretenses of that sort. Chivalry would just be an excuse.

Desperate for a distraction from the dangerous direction his thoughts were taking, he turned to the trunk, rising on his knees. "If it's any comfort," he said as he began rummaging through the trunk, "I know how it feels to have a rotten father. And what it's like to want to hate him. But you can say one thing about your parent that I cannot say about mine."

"What's that?"

Instead of answering, he pulled out what he'd been looking for—a good-sized wooden box that looked rather like a pirate's treasure chest and a ring of keys. He moved back a bit to set the chest on the floor, unlocked it with one of the keys, and lifted the lid, revealing folds of yellowed silk that he pulled back so that she could see the fat bundles of letters beneath, each one tied with a ribbon.

Tossing the keys back in the trunk, he pulled the top bundle of letters out of the chest and held them out to her. "Yours, I think?"

"Yes," she whispered in astonishment, dropping his handkerchief and rising on her knees to take the bundle from his hand. "But . . ." She paused and looked up, frowning in perplexity. "Did you read them?"

"Certainly not," he answered, affronted. "A gentleman does not read another man's letters, even if the man's dead."

"Sorry," she apologized at once. "But how did you know they're mine?"

He turned one bundle over so that she could read the address written on the back of the bottom envelope. "I don't think he knew two girls at Forsyte Academy, do you?"

"He kept my letters." She looked at the chest, then back at the bundle in her hands. "It looks like he kept them all."

"Not only that. He stored them in a treasure chest, wrapped in silk."

"But—" She broke off and looked at Jonathan again, clearly confounded. "Why would he do that?"

"Perhaps because, in his inadequate way, he loved you. Treasured you."

She stared at him, shaking her head as if refusing to believe it. Suddenly, her hands fell to her sides, and the letters slid out of her fingers, hitting the carpet by her hip with a thud, and then she was crying, silently, tears sliding down her cheeks, and he couldn't bear it.

"Don't." His voice was fierce to his own ears as he lifted his hand to cup her cheek. "Don't cry."

"I don't know why I am," she whispered.

He thought of his own lost dreams. "I do," he murmured, his thumb brushing tears away. *"Hiraeth."*

"What?" She frowned, puzzled by a word unfamiliar to her. "What's that?"

"It means grief for that which is past and gone, or for things that never were, or homesickness for places that exist only in our imaginations." He paused, aware of her warm skin beneath his fingertips and her silky, loosened braid against the back of his hand, dangerous fuel for the fire inside him.

"It's a Welsh word," he went on, feeling desperate, and yet unable to do the sensible thing and pull back. "I learned Welsh at school, along with Latin, Greek, and several other languages I'll never use. That's what preparatory school's for, you know. Teaching well-bred men things of no practical value."

She laughed, her smile like sunshine peeking between rain clouds. "Finishing school's the same. We learned to waltz, write in perfect copperplate, and speak proper French."

"French is at least useful if one goes abroad. Many speak it. Try talking to a Continental maître d'hôtel or waiter in Welsh and see how far you get."

She laughed again, and so did he, but as their laughter faded, he felt the change between them—in the rising tension within his own body and the quickening of her pulse beneath his fingertips. He heard it—in the sudden silence between them and the hard thud of his own heartbeat. He saw it—in the parting of her lips and the lowering of her lashes.

Jonathan felt his resistance slipping. Desperate, he tried to remind himself she was in a vulnerable condition, and what he was thinking right now was the conduct of a cad, not a gentleman. He stared at the tears still damp on her cheeks and reminded himself of his promises and her innocence.

But then, she leaned closer, her quickened breathing soft and warm on his face, and he felt a crack in his resolve.

Don't, he thought, desperate, uncertain if his unspoken warning was for her or for himself. *Leave. Now.*

Even as he gave that order, his fingers slid to the back of her neck, honor fading away, arousal flooding his body, longing for her tearing him apart. This time, he was the one who leaned closer, his thumb moving beneath her jaw to tilt her head back.

Slowly, he bent his head. His lips grazed hers, the barest touch, and yet, after weeks of torturing himself with memories of their previous kisses, the pleasure of this one was so exquisite, he groaned against her mouth.

The first time he kissed her, he'd known he was playing with fire. The second time, he'd lit the match and blown it out. But now, as her arms came around his neck, and her lips parted beneath his, the fire flared so high, he simply could not contain it.

He deepened the kiss instead, sliding his tongue into her mouth. She moaned in response, fanning the flame, her fingers raking through his hair, her mouth opening wider, her tongue meeting his.

He slid his arms around her and pulled her closer. She came with all the naïve willingness of her innocence, a reminder and a warning—one last chance to protect her virtue, but her mouth was so sweet, her body so warm and her kiss so lush, he couldn't stop, not yet.

Keeping one arm tight around her waist, he slid his free hand up her spine, making a sound of pure masculine appreciation at the knowledge that a scant two layers of muslin stood between him and her naked skin. Still tasting deeply of her mouth, he slid his hand under her arm and between their bodies to cup her breast.

She broke the kiss with a gasp even as her body arched instinctively closer. "It's all right," he murmured, uttering that lie as his arm tightened around her waist and his other hand embraced the full, round shape of her breast.

She stirred, making a sound of agitation, and he stilled, his heart thudding in his chest, his body in chaos. But when she didn't pull back, he began again, cupping and shaping her breast against his palm as he murmured words to coax and soothe, and his mouth trailed kisses along her cheek, over her jaw, and down the side of her neck, where the tendons of her throat were taut as harp strings.

Under his palm, he could feel the shape of her nipple, and he shifted his hand to roll the hard bud in a gentle tease between his fingers.

She moaned, her arms tightening around his neck, her hips stirring against him, reminding him he'd have to stop soon, but not just yet. Keeping one arm around her waist, he let go of her breast and pulled apart the edges of her wrapper.

"Jonathan?" she whispered.

A question or a plea or maybe both. "It'll be all right," he said, praying he had enough strength to keep that from being a lie, and bent his head. He opened his mouth over her nipple, dampening the fabric of her nightgown as he suckled her breast.

She gasped, arching her back, her hips brushing his groin. He was fully aroused, and the contact was an exquisite torture that sent shards of pleasure through his body, flaring his arousal into lust and reminding him that he didn't have much time before he'd have to stop.

He reached down, working his free hand beneath the hem of her nightgown. Just as he'd imagined, she was naked beneath, and her skin was scorching hot. He slid his palm up her thigh, across her hip, and down her buttock over and over, burning the contours of her shape more deeply than ever into his memory, as his mouth suckled her breast, his tongue using the damp fabric to arouse her further.

She said his name, a soft, muffled moan, her body stirring against his, telling him what she wanted.

Glad to comply, he eased her onto her back, following her down, capturing her mouth again. Slowly, gently, he slid his hand between her thighs and cupped her mound.

She broke the kiss with a sound of shock, her hips jerking sharply as he slid his finger into the crease of her sex. She was slick, ready, and the knowledge of what was so close threatened to overwhelm him. But he knew this moment was not about him, and he strove to banish any thought of his own need. He caressed her, relishing her agitation, and her soft, panting sounds.

"That's right, darling," he murmured, watching her face as she approached orgasm. Her eyes were closed, her cheeks flushed with rosy color, and he knew that no matter where he went from here, or what he did, or how long he lived, he would never see anything more beautiful than Marjorie was at this moment. "You're nearly there."

Even as he said it, she hit the peak, and as she came, the sight of her face as she climaxed was the most beautiful thing he'd ever seen.

She collapsed, panting, against the carpet, but he continued to stroke her, building sensation and bringing her to orgasm again, and then again.

At last, he eased back, and as he slid his hand from under her nightgown, he once again became aware of his own need. He knew he had to leave her now, while he still had a scrap of resistance left in him.

He kissed her once more, then he sat up, agony ripping through his body at the withdrawal. Taking a deep breath, he pulled her nightclothes back down. He didn't add to his torture by peeking down at her ripping legs and lush hips, but instead, he looked into her face.

The sight of it was like an arrow straight to the chest.

She was radiant, smiling, so lovely in the afterglow of what had just happened, and never had he wanted a woman more. His groin ached, his heart hurt, even his soul burned with longing, but he'd sworn to see that she was cared for, looked after, protected. Taking her virtue on a library floor wouldn't just break that promise, it would annihilate it, and him, and any sense of honor he'd ever had.

He hauled himself to his feet. He held out his hand to help her up, but he did not meet her eyes, and the moment she was on her feet, he let her go. "We'd best go to bed," he advised, staring determinedly at the wall beyond her shoulder. "Before I forget—"

He stopped, because he'd forgotten he was a gentleman over half an hour ago. "Before anyone finds us here like this," he amended and turned away, relieved to discover he'd had the wits to at least close the door before coming in here.

"Goodnight, Marjorie," he said and turned away. "Sleep well."

"You, too," she called as he left the room, and he couldn't help a caustic chuckle, for he knew he wouldn't sleep a wink. In fact, as he went up the stairs and across the house to his own room, he feared the memory of what had happened tonight would haunt him for the rest of his life.

UNLIKE JONATHAN, MARJORIE didn't go straight upstairs, for to her, sleep seemed impossible. Never had she felt more awake, more alive, than she did at this moment. Or more confounded.

For weeks, he'd been polite and distant, driving her to distraction. Then, with a suddenness that had taken her breath away, he'd kissed her on the *Mary Louisa* and made that amazing admission.

Being friends with you is killing me.

His words and actions had conveyed a passionate regard for her. At least, she'd *thought* so at the time, and she'd been left in a dizzy state of glorious anticipation as a result, dying to see him again, living on tenterhooks, only to spend the next two weeks being ignored once again. In fact, she'd hardly seen him at all, a development that had left her chagrined, insulted, and more confused than ever. In light of all that, what was she to make of tonight's events?

Marjorie had no past romantic experience to go by. And in any case, to deem what had happened tonight romantic seemed such an inadequate description. His caresses, so hot and tender, had ignited a passion within her she'd never known she was even capable of. And the pleasure, wave after wave of it, so unexpected and so intense, she felt shattered to bits in consequence. It had all been terribly wicked, even carnal. But what did it all mean?

There was no way to answer that question, but Marjorie spent most of the night trying, and as she went over everything that had happened between them since the moment they'd met, her emotions bounced from joy to perplexity to desire to anger and back to joy again, over and over, round and round.

By dawn, exhausted and cross and more confused than ever, she gave it up. There was only one way to make sense of all this and that was to ask him.

This, however, proved to be no easy task. As had become his habit of late, he was not in for breakfast, and a discreet inquiry of Boothby informed her that he had breakfasted before everyone else and gone out, though where, the butler could not say.

He remained equally elusive for the reminder of the day, but Marjorie had no intention of spending another two weeks in this state of agonizing uncertainty. The family was going to a ball that evening, and she decided she'd find a way to corner him before he departed with the others and demand explanations. Jonathan, however, managed to thwart her plans, sending a note to Irene late that afternoon that he would dine at his club and see them at the ball afterward.

Marjorie, unable to attend because she was still in half-mourning, knew full well what Jonathan's note actually meant. He was back to avoiding her like a disease, and she was not going to stand for it. Once the rest of the family had departed for the ball, she ensconced herself in the library to wait up until they returned, determined that before the night was out, she'd find a way to speak with him alone.

As she waited, she tried to occupy her mind with the estate papers Jonathan had given to her to study, but dry-as-dust legal and financial documents were no distraction at all from the stunning events of the night before.

The trunk was gone now, taken to the attic by a footman this morning, but Marjorie's eyes had no trouble homing in on the exact spot where Jonathan had kissed and caressed her. She bit her lip, staring at the patch of carpet where they had lain, and even twenty-four hours later, the memories made her blush. She wasn't ashamed, exactly, but she was a bit shocked, for she'd never known herself to possess such primitive, corporeal feelings, or even that such feelings existed.

Forsyte Academy was a proper girls' school, and during her time there, no one had seen fit to give her any facts regarding the intimate relations between men and women. Mothers were expected to provide that very necessary information, and though Mrs. Forsyte had been the closest thing she'd had to a mother since her own had died, the headmistress had not seen fit to take on that particular aspect of a mother's duty.

In addition, though Marjorie's career as a teacher had given her access to certain books on human biology, the information provided by the volumes of the academy's library had been vague, euphemistic, and profoundly unsatisfactory.

But then, could any book really explain the reality? The rising tension, the exquisite sensations, the shattering conclusion?

"Your coffee, Miss McGann."

Boothby's voice, so matter-of-fact, tore her out of these carnal speculations, and as the butler entered the room with a laden tray, she returned her attention to the papers spread out on the table before her. As he poured her coffee and brought it to her, she bent her head as if fully occupied with the current financial status of her investments.

"Set it on the table, Boothby," she said, picking up a pencil to scribble a nonsensical note in the margin of one sheet.

The cup and saucer rattled as he did as she had instructed. "Will there be anything else?"

"No, thank you, Boothby. You may go."

He bowed and departed, and Marjorie leaned forward, pressing her hot cheek against the cool sheets of paper on the table with a groan. If she was going to dissolve into blushes every time she contemplated last night's events, how was she ever going to face Jonathan and ask him to explain what it all meant?

That question had barely crossed her mind, however, before more footsteps sounded in the corridor. She sat up and grabbed her pencil, pretending vast interest in the papers before her, but the moment the object of all her tortured contemplations walked into the room, she felt her face heating all over again.

He stopped just inside the doorway, and though she longed to take refuge in the legal documents before her, she reminded herself of her purpose, told herself not to be a ninny, and looked up.

"Hello," she said, ignoring her hot face and working to keep her voice cool. "I thought you'd be at the ball." As she spoke, she noted in puzzlement that he was not in white tie, but an ordinary morning suit of charcoal gray. "Aren't you going?"

"No." He came in, shutting the library door behind him, and this exact repetition of his first action last night jerked Marjorie to her feet. Surely he wasn't intending to repeat the rest of those events, was he?

Her blush deepened with her thoughts, heat spreading through her body. He perceived her reaction, his lips tightening, and her determination to confront him began to falter. When he started toward her, she looked past him, feeling a sudden, craven desire to run for the door.

She shoved aside such cowardice, seized her courage, and shored up her pride, and as he circled the table, she turned to face him, gripping her pencil tight in her fingers as she readied herself to demand what he was doing, batting her about as if she were a tennis ball.

He paused in front of her. "I wanted to speak with you, and this seemed the best opportunity."

"Indeed?" she asked, absurdly proud of the incisive tone of her voice. "That's a change from the usual."

His gaze moved to the empty space of carpet on the floor, then back to her face. "I meant I wanted to speak with you alone."

Despite everything, she felt a stirring of excitement, but she quashed it. "Again, a change from the usual," she muttered.

He reached out, his fingers closing over her pencil as if to take it from her, and she felt a strange, almost irresistible temptation to grip it harder, but she forced herself to relax and let him pull it from her fingers.

He tossed it onto the table beside them, then he faced her again, and to her complete amazement, he took her hands in his and said the last thing in the world she'd ever have expected.

"I think we should get married."

Chapter 19

$\mathcal{H}$e was proposing? Marjorie blinked, utterly stupefied. "You want to marry me?"

"Yes." Despite this confirmation, she still couldn't quite believe it. It was just too incredible. "Yes. After what happened last night, I think it would be best."

Watching him, comprehension struck her like lightning.

"Oh, my God." She snatched her hands from his, horrified as gossiping voices of her colleagues at Forsyte Academy came back to her, whispered words about a fellow teacher that she'd paid little heed to at the time.

It was that man she walks out with. She laid with him, the little strumpet, and he wouldn't marry her . . . that's why she had to leave, you know, to have the baby.

"I laid with you," she whispered in horror, and she cursed her aversion to gossip. If she'd paid more attention to such talk back then, she might have known enough to prevent disaster now. "There, on the floor, in this very room. I'm ruined."

"No, you're not." His voice was low and hard, and not the least bit reassuring. "Not yet, anyway."

She shook her head, trying to think, but she was too overwhelmed for that, any happiness she might have taken in her first marriage proposal obliterated by raw panic.

"Marjorie," he said gently, seeming to sense her feelings, "nothing happened."

"Nothing?" she echoed, her voice rising a notch. "Is that what you call it?"

"I only meant that what we did—what I did," he corrected at once, "won't ruin you. It might have, of course, had anyone caught us. But no one did."

She made a sound, a hitching hiccough of fear, and swayed on her feet.

His hands gripped her by the arms to steady her. "The doors were closed. Everyone was in bed and asleep. No one saw us."

"But . . . but . . ." She paused, thinking hard, but there was just no delicate way to bring up the crucial point. "But what about a baby?" she burst out.

He blinked, and then, to her complete consternation, he gave a shout of laughter.

"This isn't funny!" she cried.

"No," he agreed, assuming his former grave expression, but in his eyes, there was a lurking hint of wry humor that made her scowl.

"Sorry," he said. "I know this isn't amusing. But Marjorie, you do have a way of forever knocking me off my trolley. I had thought myself thoroughly prepared for this moment and anything you might say, but knowing you, I should have known better."

"What you're prepared for isn't of much concern to me just now, Jonathan," she said crossly.

"No, but I took it for granted that someone would have explained all that sort of thing to you ages ago. Mrs. Forsyte, or one of your married friends . . . someone . . ." His voice trailed off, implying a question, but when she shook her head, he resumed, "What happened last night isn't how babies are made. That's not how it works. At least, not precisely. I mean," he added as she sucked in another panicky breath, "things between us didn't go far enough for that."

"Oh," she gasped, relieved that her apprehensions were groundless, but curious, too, for she couldn't imagine what "going far enough" would have entailed. To her mind, the intimacies of last night had gone pretty far.

"But they could have done," he said before she could ask, the humor vanishing from his eyes. "And that would have put you beyond the pale. I fear they will go that far at some point."

"I see," she said, an inadequate reply, for she didn't see at all, but she had no idea what else to say. She couldn't seem to think straight.

Jonathan was proposing. Marriage. To her. She still couldn't take it in.

"So, I'm not ruined?" she asked. "And," she continued when he shook his head, "there's no possibility of a baby after . . . after . . ." She paused, giving him a dubious look. "Are you sure?"

He smiled, a tender smile that sent her heart slamming into her ribs. "I'm sure."

"But then, why on earth would you want to marry me? Are you—" She broke off, staring at him in renewed shock as a new reason occurred to her, one she'd never even thought of as a possibility before, but she had no chance to voice it, for he spoke again, and it was almost as if he'd read her mind.

"You want to know my feelings, of course." He let her go and took a step back. "I shall confess them, though it means confessing things that are never easy for a man to admit. First, let me say quite bluntly that I want you."

Heat hit her in the belly, spreading outward, overtaking her entire body, and she could manage only one word. "Oh."

"I feel for you a deep and passionate desire."

Romantic thrills began shooting up inside her like fireworks, but given his infuriating disregard of late, it seemed incumbent upon her to appear as unmoved by this exciting confession as possible. "Yes," she said, but her matter-of-fact reply came out in a strangled whisper and shredded any pretense of sophisticated indifference. She gave a little cough and tried again. "Yes, I . . . umm . . . ahem . . . I did gather that much."

"I'm sure, but what you may not know is that I have wanted you almost from the very first moment we met."

"What?" Marjorie was beginning to feel like Alice in Wonderland, except that the six impossible things she was supposed to believe were happening at midnight, not before breakfast.

"Given my position as your guardian, I have known all along such desires are inappropriate, but even I was not aware of how ungovernable my desire for you would become. I instinctively tried to shield you from it—first, by leaving you behind in New York, then by putting Lady Stansbury between us, and then by attempting to leave you with my sisters and escape to Africa."

He gave another laugh, a caustic sound of self-deprecation. "I told myself and you that all these actions were motivated by my duty, and that I was protecting you from the unsavory attentions of other men. But after last night, I can no longer even attempt such hypocrisy. I am compelled to be honest with both of us." He met her eyes, his gaze resolute and steady. "What I have really been trying to protect you from all this time is me."

Marjorie's heart was thudding so hard in her chest, it was as if she'd been running, and her head was still in a whirl.

"To be blunt, the past two months have been hell for me. Being mere friends with you is impossible, for the more I am near you, the more I want you. Despite my attempts to resist, I feel that resistance fading, making you more vulnerable to attentions of this sort from me with each day that passes. As I seem to repeatedly demonstrate," he continued with obvious self-disdain, "I cannot be trusted to behave honorably where you are concerned."

Marjorie, who'd never been the subject of masculine attentions, dishonorable or otherwise, could not share his low opinion of his conduct. Perhaps she had a wild streak in her nature, but what Jonathan had done to her last night was the most thrilling, glorious thing that had ever happened to her. She might have said so, but words were beyond her at this point.

"In such circumstances," he continued, "the right thing to do would have been to remove myself from your society altogether, but my sisters gainsaid me there, insisting that I stay through your birthday. Having broken my word to them once before, I knew I could not do so a second time."

"Wait," she implored, spurred out of her speechless state. "Go back to the part about your ungovernable desires, for I'd like to hear that part again. I'm not sure I understand what you mean."

"Don't you?" A smile touched his mouth. "After last night, I think you do."

She bit her lip, unable to deny it, too embarrassed to admit it, though she supposed her own wanton behavior last night made any admission unnecessary.

"Because of that," he continued in the wake of her silence, "there can be only one result, and I would prefer that result to be an honorable one, made by choice and not by circumstance."

She frowned, trying to understand. "So, you think we'll lose our heads and do . . . something stupid and be forced to marry."

"I'd prefer it didn't come to that. In marrying me, you wouldn't need to worry you were marrying a man who had designs on your money. And no one could argue that it wouldn't be a suitable match. It's quite fitting, really—you and I."

"But—" Marjorie broke off, uneasiness seeping into her consciousness, nudging aside delirious, romantic thrills about her first proposal. "Are you—"

She stopped again, though she didn't know why it was so hard to ask the obvious question. But she had to know. "Jonathan, are you falling in love with me?"

Even as she said it, she laughed a little, for it seemed so absurd, despite his confession of passion.

"No," he said. "I'm already there."

Any inclination to laugh vanished. She stared at him, feeling as if the floor was sliding out from beneath her. She didn't believe him. How could she? It was just too ridiculous. All he'd done lately was snub her. And besides, men like him didn't fall in love and settle down, not for real, not for life. And that was what marriage was—at least for her. A life, together, forever.

"And after last night," he went on as she didn't speak, "I thought perhaps you might have similar feelings."

She inhaled sharply, fearing he was right.

"That's ridiculous." She jerked her hands free. "Two months is far too short an acquaintance for feelings like that."

"Is it?" He made a rueful face. "I think I started falling for you the moment I found you in my cabin aboard the *Neptune*. It was only after last night that I finally stopped fighting it and admitted it to myself."

Inside, she began to shake. "Well, even if that's true for you, it isn't for me!" she burst out. "I refuse to fall in love with a man just because he's the first one who's ever kissed me! It's the principle of the thing," she added, scowling as he pressed a smile from his lips.

"I hope that doesn't mean you intend to sample other men's kisses before you decide? Because if so, I fear I shall have to jump off a cliff."

She made a stifled sound halfway between a panicked sob and a wild laugh, and, desperate, she changed tactics. "So, let me see if I have this right," she said, her voice hardening as she forced herself to cast aside romance and consider the cold, hard facts. "We marry, we have a few weeks together, satisfying our . . . our . . ."

"Mutual passion?" he supplied when she couldn't find the words.

"Infatuation," she corrected. "And then you go off to explore Africa while I wait by the fireside like a dutiful wife. Is that the plan?"

"Well, I hadn't got as far as making definite plans, but as for South Africa, you can't come with me. If war with the Boers breaks out, things could get dicey. I won't put you in that sort of danger. But—"

"But you'd put yourself in it," she interrupted. "God, Jonathan, if anything happened to you—" She stopped, the horrific possibility of his death choking her, indicating that his guess about her feelings had some validity, and she worked to regain her composure and prove him wrong. "If you died out there, I'd be a widow," she said at last, managing to inject a prim disinterest into her voice she didn't feel in the least. "No, thank you."

"I could just as easily die hit by an omnibus while crossing a London street," he pointed out.

"It's not the same thing!"

"It would be to me," he said dryly.

"Stop joking!"

"Sorry," he said at once. "But I'm a bit nervous, Marjorie, I admit. Most men are, I suppose, when they come to propose marriage. As for my death, I don't intend to die in South Africa. I have too much waiting for me here."

"Only if you decide to come back."

"Ah," he murmured, "now we're getting to it."

She didn't reply, and when he cupped her cheek, she stiffened, his touch threatening to shatter her resolve.

"I will come back," he said.

"When?" she asked, trying to harden herself against him, for she wasn't about to let the abandonment and loneliness of her past become her future. "In eight months? Ten years? Someday?"

"All right, then. Let's make this simple." He let her go, his hands falling to his sides. "I won't go. I'll find an envoy to go in my stead, and I'll stay here."

Oddly enough, instead of assuaging her apprehensions, that suggestion intensified them. "Even if you did stay, what then? If we marry, how would it be? How long before society starts to bore you, and you're tired of it all, and you want to move on? What then? I'll be stuck, waiting, wondering when you'll come back from wherever you've gone off to. I watched my father do that to my mother plenty of times. I heard him make the same promises to her that he later made to me."

"But I am not him," he said, his voice so tender, it almost dissolved her composure. "And it wouldn't have to be like that for us. If I do want to go off and roam a little, there's nothing that says you'd have to stay behind. You could come with me."

"And do what?" she cried. "Hole up for a year or two or three in a mining cabin in Idaho or a beach hut in Florida or a shack beside a South Africa shale field?"

"I think we could afford better accommodations than that."

"That's not the point, and you know it. You told me that you live the way you do because you're searching for something to replace what you lost. But I have no intention of wandering across the globe with you while you keep looking for it. And what if you never do? I don't want the sort of aimless life you live, and I certainly don't want it for my children."

"Marjorie," he began, but she shook her head, refusing to listen to some description of how exciting it would be to go off with him to parts unknown and explore the world.

"No, Jonathan. I told you what I want the very first day we met. I've been sheltered and secluded most of my life, I know, but I have a new life now, a life of company and society, and I've only just begun to enjoy it. I haven't come out, or had suitors, or even been to a ball. I'm not ready to marry anyone and, as you said yourself two months ago, I have plenty of time. I shall take that time to find the right man for me."

Her voice was shaking as she spoke, from fear and doubt and the frustration of feeling forced to a choice that she knew would be unbearable to live with. "The right man will be able to court me honorably, demonstrating that he can be not only my lover, but also my friend, my companion, and my partner forever. That man will have a firm grasp on what he wants from life and a clear vision for the future and be glad to put down roots and make a home. We both know that man is not you."

Her voice wobbled on the last word, the last vestiges of her self-control dissolving, and she knew she had to finish this before she started to cry. She'd cried in front of him last night, precipitating this whole mess. She had no intention of doing that again.

She swallowed hard, marshaling all her self-control. "I'm sorry, Jonathan, but my answer is no."

She started to move around him, but he stepped in front of her, blocking her path. "There must be some sort of middle ground here. God, Marjorie," he choked when she didn't respond, "is there no place for us? Is there no way to carve out a life that would suit us both?"

She felt an irrational burst of longing and hope, but she snuffed them out. "I don't think so."

He still didn't move. "I do."

She began to shake inside, feeling desperate. "I've given you my answer. Now, please let me go."

"All right," he said quietly, moving aside to let her pass.

She did so, practically running for the door, but as she opened it, his voice called back to her.

"I'm not giving up. I want you too much to give up."

She ignored that and walked out, head high, but if she thought she was achieving any sort of escape, she was mistaken, for as she raced down the corridor and up the stairs to her room, his words came back to her.

I want you. I feel for you a deep and passionate desire.

She shut her bedroom door behind her, trying to shut him out, but it was useless.

I'm not giving up. I want you too much to give up.

With his words still ringing in her ears, she couldn't help thinking back to that day in White Plains, and what her most important goal back then had been. She'd wanted, more than anything, to be wanted.

It seemed she'd gotten her wish.

Marjorie sank down on the edge of her bed and burst into tears.

HAD JONATHAN BEEN inclined to ask his sisters for their opinion regarding his proposal to Marjorie, he knew what they would have said. They'd have pointed out that his request for her hand had not been a request at all, that it had been intemperate, ill-considered, and cavalier, and they would have deemed her refusal just what he deserved.

And they'd have been right.

He'd had a much more eloquent proposal in mind—down on one knee and all that—but Marjorie, in characteristic fashion, had managed to veer him right off his intended course, and as a result, he'd blundered through the entire business like a moth blundering in the lamplight. Still, though his proposal had not been particularly eloquent, it had been honest and heartfelt.

Last night, when he'd looked into her face, so radiant and lovely, his mind had accepted what his heart and soul had known all along.

Marjorie was his woman, and that to love her and make her happy and keep her from harm had become far, far more than a promise to a dying friend. They were the foundation on which he could build a new life, the very thing he'd been seeking for over a decade.

Marjorie, however, didn't see things that way. Her objections had been valid, no doubt about it, but he was reasonably certain they stemmed from fear, not from a lack of feeling for him.

Still, she had good cause to be afraid, and he knew if he was going to change her mind, he had to find a way to overcome that fear. Despite her uncompromising answer, he knew there was a middle ground for them, and he was going to find it, even if he had to carve it out of rock with his bare hands.

Upon her refusal of his proposal, Jonathan had declared he was not giving up, but during the week that followed, he made no attempts to reopen the subject, offer counterarguments to her refusal, or persuade her to change her mind. In fact, in the days that followed, he acted as if the entire conversation had never taken place.

That was the right and proper thing to do, and she ought to have been relieved. But she wasn't, because now she knew the true reasons why he had been keeping his distance, reasons that insisted on going through her mind and testing her resolve at every possible opportunity.

The past two months have been hell for me. Being mere friends with you is impossible, for the more I am near you, the more I want you.

That explained some things, she supposed, but it was hardly satisfactory. Didn't the man understand that a girl wanted and deserved to be courted properly?

Despite my attempts to resist, I feel that resistance fading, making you more vulnerable to attentions of this sort from me with each day that passes.

The attentions to which he referred were the intimacies they had shared that night in the library, kisses and caresses that could only be honorably shared by husband and wife. But when memories of them came back to torment her late at night, she could not imagine ever sharing such intimacies with any other man, a fact that did nothing to reassure her that she'd done the right thing.

Making things worse, it wasn't long before those erotic memories began to shadow her days, too. In tearooms and drawing rooms, during ladies' luncheons and carriage rides in the park, they would come flooding back, no matter how she tried to suppress them.

That's right, darling. You're nearly there.

Even a fortnight later, as she sat in the wholly feminine enclave of a dressmaker, the memory of his sensuous words, hot caresses, and her own passionate responses had the power to flood her body with desire.

Certain she was the same rose-pink color as the plush velvet sofa on which she sat, Marjorie cast a frantic glance around the opulent showroom of Vivienne, but she found that no one in the modiste's showroom was paying the least attention to her. Irene was in another room being fitted for a gown, and the ladies with Marjorie in the main showroom were far too preoccupied with observing the mannequins snaking before them in the latest fashions to pay any mind to her.

Marjorie, who had already ordered all the pieces of her post-mourning wardrobe, glanced around again, desperate for something to occupy her attention besides erotic memories of Jonathan. She could order a few more frocks, she supposed, but she already had more than she could possibly wear. A couple of months ago, being in the showroom of a fashionable dressmaker, choosing designs, fabrics, and trims, had been so much fun, but after so many weeks of shopping, she was beginning to find it rather monotonous. And the endless routine of calls, teas, and Afternoons-At-Home, though exciting at first, was becoming more of a tedium than a pleasure. In fact, her new life was becoming a bore.

Marjorie straightened on the sofa, startled and dismayed by the realization. This life was just what she'd imagined, everything she wanted. How could she possibly be bored?

But even as she asked that question, Jonathan's words from the day they'd met came echoing back to her.

The time will pass more quickly for you here at Forsyte Academy, where you have a vocation.

Marjorie fell back against the sofa, suppressing a groan. That man really needed to get out of her head. She did *not* miss being stuck out in the middle of nowhere, teaching dance, piano, and French. She did miss her pupils, true, and the challenge of teaching, but that would surely dissipate when she was married, and had children of her own.

I think we should get married.

Desperate, Marjorie straightened on the sofa and picked up one of the ladies' magazines that lay on the table before her and began flipping through the pages, but advertisements for wrinkle creams, bust improvers, and French letters—whatever those were—proved to be no distraction at all from the impossible man dominating her thoughts.

I want you . . . I have wanted you almost from the very first moment we met.

That was so unbelievable, she almost wanted to laugh. He'd done nothing but push her away from the very start, but now, she was just supposed to accept this abrupt and complete reversal? Now she was supposed to believe that he was sincere and that his affections would last? How on earth could he have thought she'd accept such a proposal?

No one could argue that it wouldn't be a suitable match. It's quite fitting, really.

Fitting? She sniffed. The man was delusional. He had no plans for the future, no consideration for what she wanted, and despite his declared feelings, he clearly had no intention of settling down.

Sadly, all these reminders of why she'd been right to refuse him did nothing to reassure her. In fact, the more she told herself how sensible she'd been to refuse him, the more muddled and miserable she became. How could she marry him? But how could she marry any other man, let any other man touch her and caress her in that extraordinary way? Both seemed equally unthinkable.

"Ach, Marjorie, you wicked girl," murmured a familiar voice beside her ear, and she turned her head to find Baroness Vasiliev standing behind the sofa, leaning over her shoulder.

"Baroness!" she cried, relieved and glad of a worthy distraction at last. "How wonderful to see you."

The other woman straightened, laughing as she came around the sofa to sit beside Marjorie. "It is good to see you, too, my young friend. And do not worry," she added, her blue eyes dancing with mischief. "I will not tell anyone."

Marjorie wondered wildly if her naughty thoughts had been loud enough to be audible to the woman beside her, but she tried to muster her dignity. "I don't know what you mean."

"No?" The baroness leaned closer to tap her finger on the opened magazine in Marjorie's lap. "French letters," she said in a teasing whisper. "You should not be reading about such naughty things."

Marjorie frowned, bewildered. "I don't understand. What could be naughty about letters? Although they are French," she added, "so I suppose that explains it. Though why anyone would want to buy someone's letters, French or otherwise, I don't quite see—"

The baroness's merry laughter cut her off. "Oh, darling Marjorie, I have missed you. You are such a delightful innocent."

Marjorie was growing tired of being called an innocent. It was irritating that everyone around her seemed to know far more about life than she did. Worse, no one ever seemed willing to explain anything. Obviously, a French letter was something she wasn't supposed to know about. Still, if anyone would be able to enlighten her, it would be the baroness. "But what is naughty about these letters?" she asked in a whisper. "You must tell me."

"They're not letters at all."

"But what are they, then?"

"They do not concern you yet," she said, frowning and trying to look severe. "For you are not married. For me, however," she continued with a wink that ruined any attempt at severity, "a French letter is a very convenient thing."

"But you're not married," Marjorie said, still confused. "You're a widow."

"I may be a widow, darling, but I'm not dead!"

"I see." She didn't, quite, but she was beginning to get an inkling—a vague one—of what they were really talking about, and it had something to do with men.

The baroness's next words confirmed this theory. "Men ought to be the ones who take care of such details, but they can never seem to be relied upon. So, I keep a few French letters myself, because after all, one never knows. And a baby . . . ach, that would not do. It would be most inconvenient at my time of life."

"Oh." Marjorie colored up, thinking of Jonathan's words about babies, and about what had and had not happened between them in the library. Wanting specifics about babies, French letters, and all other such forbidden subjects, she leaned closer, but she was given no chance to ask further questions.

"Oh, I'm so glad that's over," Irene's relieved voice interrupted as she came around the sofa, and Marjorie suppressed a groan of frustration at the interruption and slapped the magazine shut. "I do hate first fittings. A muslin makes it so hard to tell what the gown will look like, and one's always afraid it'll be a disappointment. Baroness," she greeted the other woman with a smile. "How lovely to see you."

"Duchess." The baroness stood up. "Please let me say how happy I was to receive your kind invitation to your house party at Ravenwood. I am so looking forward to it. I only regret that I will not be able to arrive until Saturday."

"But you will arrive in time for the ball?" Marjorie asked.

The baroness gave her an affectionate smile. "I would not miss that for the world." She turned to Irene. "My train arrives at 4:15."

"I shall send a carriage to the station for you," Irene told her. "We are looking forward to having you."

"Baroness Vasiliev?" another voice inquired, and one of the showroom's sylphlike mannequins came into view. "Vivienne is ready for you, if you will come this way?"

The baroness stood up. "Forgive me, ladies. It seems I must leave you." She turned and bent down to give Marjorie an affectionate kiss on each cheek. "I will see you soon. And once you have made the come-out, you will be meeting many young men and looking to marry, so remember our conversation today, for it will serve you well in years to come." She gave Marjorie another wink and turned to follow the showroom model toward the fitting rooms, adding over her shoulder, "And remember, never rely on a man more than you rely on yourself."

In the wake of her departure, Irene gave a little laugh. "What on earth was that about?"

"Nothing," Marjorie said, donning a neutral expression as she tossed the magazine onto the table. "Nothing at all."

Chapter 20

Refusing to give up was all very well, but during the fortnight that followed Marjorie's rejection of his proposal, as Jonathan considered what he might do to change her mind, he found himself rather at a loss.

Pressing his suit at once would likely harden her further against him, so he was forced to resume a respectful distance. And since courtship was going to be required of him, a task that would demand all the strength he possessed, he knew he could do with a bit of distance, too.

Because of that, when the family made the journey down to Ravenwood a week before the house party, he did not accompany them, but chose instead to arrive the same afternoon as the other guests.

Being a man of action, playing a waiting game did not suit him, but he tried to keep busy. He bought Marjorie a birthday present, he picked up her cut gemstones from Fossin and Morel, and though it might prove an unjustified optimism on his part, he bought an engagement ring.

As he'd promised her, he canceled his trip to South Africa and hired one of Torquil's solicitors to make the journey in his stead. To further demonstrate his sincerity and his willingness to become at least somewhat domesticated, he hired a valet and tried to accustom himself to letting someone else tie his ties and fasten his shirt studs.

On his new valet's recommendation, he paid another visit to his tailor. He ordered an entire wardrobe suited to autumn in the country, and as he was fitted for tweeds and riding boots, he tried to envision himself hunting grouse and riding to hounds.

He looked at various London houses for sale or lease, but as he walked through stately rooms of Victorian elegance, he knew that whatever else he might have to do to accommodate Marjorie's vision of married life, decorating their home in the stuffy, ornate style of the British upper crust couldn't be part of it. Flocked velvet wallpaper was just a bridge too far for any man.

As he worked to fashion a life that Marjorie could be persuaded to share, her words echoed through his mind again and again.

You live the way you do because you're searching for something to replace what you lost. But I have no intention of wandering across the globe with you while you keep looking for it.

And who could blame her? Jonathan knew to have her, he would have to answer the question he'd spent years avoiding.

What do I want?

He wanted Marjorie, but the answer to his question was deeper even than love. Love, marriage, children, domestic life—these things would never be enough if he didn't have a purpose, an ambition of his own. He might be able to put on tweeds and ride to hounds during weekends at the country estate, but he knew being the country gentleman could never be his entire way of life. He needed something more.

His goal was to find it before the house party, and to that end, he spent many hours at his club, seeking out the company of other members who were also men of business, but though many of them wanted his investment capital, he was in search of a greater challenge than contributing money to someone else's company. He wanted to create something of his own, build something his children could expand and carry into the next century, but it also had to be something that excited him, and nothing he came across seemed to meet his criteria. Like his country tweeds, none seemed to fit, and by the time he boarded the train for Hampshire to join the others at Ravenwood, he was forced to accept that what he was attempting wasn't going to be achieved as quickly as he'd hoped.

Nonetheless, during the train journey, he went through the stack of prospectuses he'd been gathering, and to his surprise, he found one that did appeal, one he'd received weeks ago. Given his preoccupation with Marjorie, he'd almost forgotten it, but as he read through it on the train, he realized it might be just what he was looking for. It was not, sadly, a perfect solution, particularly where Marjorie's vision of the future was concerned, but it could be the middle ground he'd been seeking, and it had exciting possibilities.

Still, even if he'd just found his future, convincing Marjorie to share it might take months, or even years, and as the carriage Irene had sent to fetch him from the station arrived at Ravenwood, Jonathan was forcibly reminded that time was not on his side.

As the landau swept around a wide expanse of lawn where guests were having tea, playing tennis, and enjoying the fine summer afternoon, Marjorie's bright hair caught his eye. Dressed in a white tennis dress, a racquet in her hands, she was on the court, standing behind the baseline chalked on the grass, talking with some chap in cream-colored dittos and a natty tie.

As his carriage rolled past, Jonathan saw the other man lean intimately close to Marjorie, and he felt a jolt of jealousy so strong, he nearly came out of the carriage.

The thing that restrained him was the knowledge that Marjorie probably wouldn't appreciate the gesture. She hadn't been impressed when he'd tossed the Count de la Rosa down a corridor, and if he acted like a jealous boor during her birthday weekend, he would do himself no favors.

Jonathan forced himself to relax his hold on the door handle, knowing Marjorie would be meeting dozens of other men in the weeks and months to come, and there was nothing he could do but accept the fact with as good a grace as he could muster and hope he was the one she chose.

The carriage rolled to a stop, bringing him out of his reverie, and when he looked up, he saw Irene running across the gravel drive to greet him, a most welcome distraction.

"Nice little cottage you've got here, Irenie," he said, nodding to the four-story Italianate structure behind her that sprawled in every direction.

"Terribly grand, isn't it?" she agreed, glancing over her shoulder as he exited the vehicle. "I sometimes call it The Mausoleum just to tease Henry." She glanced past his shoulder. "You didn't tell me you were bringing a friend," she murmured.

"Friend?" Glancing back, he gave a chuckle. "Not a friend, Irene. That's Warrick, my valet."

"You hired a valet? Now?" She laughed merrily. "Whatever for? Do you need your suits pressed in Africa?"

"I'm not going. I canceled my trip."

Her laughter died at once. "You did?"

"Yes. You see, I—"

A cry of surprised delight interrupted him, and Irene hurled herself at him, wrapping her arms around his neck. "You're staying longer? What wonderful news!" She gave him a smacking kiss on one cheek, then the other. "How much longer? Never mind," she added at once. "I won't press you. But you know you can stay with us as long as you like, don't you?"

"Careful," he warned. "I may become one of those tiresome guests who never leaves."

"If that happened, no one would be happier than I," she said, turning to hook her arm through his. "Now, do you want to go up to your room first? Or would you rather walk down to the south lawn and join the others for tea?"

"Tea," he said at once, for he wasn't about to leave Marjorie to some young dandy in dittos.

As he and Irene crossed the lawn, he noticed that the tennis seemed to be over. Marjorie was now sitting with Clara and Rex on the lawn by the tea table, but he could take no comfort in that, for her tennis partner was right beside her.

Henry, David, and Carlotta were there as well, and Jonathan greeted them first. Then, after he'd accepted Carlotta's offer to pour his tea,

Irene took him around, introducing him to any of the guests he hadn't
already met, beginning with those at the table, and ending with the
lithe blond dandy sitting beside Marjorie on the blanket.

"Jonathan," Irene said, "this is Mr. Cecil Ponsonby. Cecil, Mr. Jonathan Deverill, my brother."

Ponsonby stretched out his hand without bothering to stand up.
"The duchess's brother, eh?"

"I am." Jonathan leaned over the fellow, his most genial smile on his
face, warning in his eyes, as he gripped Ponsonby's hand hard enough
to make the other man wince. "I also happen to be Miss McGann's
guardian."

He thought he heard Rex make a choked sound, but his attention
was fixed on Ponsonby, who wilted under the scrutiny. The moment
Jonathan let go, then poor lad jumped up, mumbled something about
needing to find his sister, and sped away across the grass, shaking
his sore hand. Jonathan watched him go, feeling far more satisfaction
than he probably ought.

"Your tea, Jonathan."

He took the cup Carlotta held out to him with a murmur of thanks,
plucked a cucumber sandwich off the nearest tray, and still grinning,
sank down on the blanket in Cecil's vacated spot, but his grin faded as
he caught Marjorie watching him through narrowed eyes.

"Really, Jonathan," Clara said with a sigh. "I'm proud of you for
taking your guardianship duties so seriously, but did you have to send
the poor fellow scurrying off in terror the moment you arrived? He
may never come to stay at Ravenwood again."

He saw the rebuke in Marjorie's gaze, but he just couldn't find it in
him to be repentant. "If I've driven him away with a simple statement
of fact and a handshake, would it be such a loss?"

"It would," Clara replied, easing back on the blanket, resting her
weight on her elbows. "He's unmarried, handsome, and quite agreeable. He's also an excellent tennis player—though I don't know why
I'm praising him for that, since he and Marjorie are so good they
trounced Rex and me in straight sets a while ago."

Rex leaned back beside his wife with a sigh. "I'm not as young as I used to be."

"Oh, stop," Clara said, nudging his leg with her foot. "I'm the weak link, and I know it."

"Put a croquet mallet in her hands, though," Rex told Jonathan, "and watch out."

Jonathan laughed, remembering childhood days. "Don't I know it."

He glanced at the empty tennis court, appreciating there might be a way to soften Marjorie's resentment. He gulped down his tea, popped his last bite of sandwich into his mouth, and stood up, looking at her. "C'mon," he said, nodding toward the court as he pulled off his hat and jacket and dropped them onto the grass. "Let's have a go so that I can see how good you really are."

"But I just played three sets."

"Then you're nicely warmed up." He removed his cuff links, tossed them into his hat, then removed his tie, undid his collar, and began rolling up his sleeves. "While I haven't held a racquet in a decade. One set. Unless," he added as she continued to hesitate, "you're afraid?"

"Be warned, my friend," Clara interjected. "Jonathan was a cracking good player at Winchester. Helped them win the doubles three years running."

"Doubles?" Marjorie made a scoffing sound, and when Jonathan held out his hand, she allowed him to pull her to her feet. "Had he won the singles for his school *four* years running, I might be impressed." With the warning that he might have a fight on his hands, she bent down, grabbed her racquet and a ball from the lawn and started toward the baseline of the left-hand court as if to serve.

His words stopped her before she got there. "No coin toss?"

She turned, one eyebrow going up. "A gentleman usually allows a lady the first serve. But if you'd prefer not to be a gentleman . . ."

"No, no. I'm happy to allow you the courtesy." He smiled in deliberate provocation. "Everyone knows you are the weaker sex. I'll even spot you a point," he offered as she made a sound of outrage, "just to make it sporting."

She ignored that. "Rex?" she called, looking past him. "Get a coin. I call tails."

She won the toss, but before Jonathan let her serve, he beckoned her to the net. "Care to place a wager on this?"

"Love to," she said with unnerving swiftness. "If I win, you stop intimidating my friends."

He tried to look innocent. "I don't know what you mean. I wasn't the least bit intimidating."

"No?" She gave a cough, then continued in a noticeably deeper voice, "'I also happen to be Miss McGann's guardian,'" and made a sound of derision. "Is this how you think you're going to win me over? By running roughshod over every male that comes within shouting distance of me?"

An appealing idea, but he wasn't about to admit it. "I can't help it if your friend's got the nerves of a rabbit. As to my chances of winning you over, your words imply that I do at least have a chance."

"You are delusional," she said, so quickly that he felt a spark of hope.

"You've already refused me, so why should you care?"

Her face hardened. "I don't. Now, if I win this game, you agree to stop bullying the men who pay attention to me. Is it a bet?"

"We haven't decided what happens if I win."

"What do you want?"

His gaze lowered to her soft, pink mouth. "That's an interesting question."

"Stop it, Jonathan." Her face twisted a little. "Why are you doing this?"

He met her gaze. "I told you I wasn't giving up."

He thought he saw a hint of alarm spring up in her eyes, another good sign, but he couldn't be certain, and he had no chance to decide.

"Are you two going to play or not?" Clara called, and Jonathan decided what he wanted.

"If I win," he said, "I want to hold you in my arms."

"What . . ." She paused, the alarm in her eyes obvious now, and his spirits soared. "What do you mean?" she asked in a whisper.

"I want three waltzes tomorrow night."

She made a scoffing sound. "Not a chance."

"One then," he amended. "But make it the last one."

"One waltz?" The tension in her relaxed. "Done," she said and turned away, stalking back to the baseline.

He turned away as well, taking position to await her serve. When playing tennis, women were hampered by their corsets and skirts, which usually gave a man all the advantage, but any hope of that went straight to hell on Marjorie's first serve, when she sent the ball right past him in an unreturnable shot to the corner. And when she continued to pound that corner, winning their first game in a walkover, he began to fear he'd be spending the weekend pining for her from afar like a lovesick adolescent.

"Having trouble, old chap?" Rex called, laughing as Jonathan moved to serve.

"No," he lied, hefted the ball into the air, and sent it over the net in a cracking shot that she had to scramble to return. She managed it somehow, but much to his relief, it was out. It also told him she might be a bit weak on her backhand, and though he exploited that for all he was worth, his tennis was rusty as hell. Despite his best efforts, he barely won the second game. The third game went seven-all before he pulled ahead and won by a mere two points, only doing so because she stumbled over her skirt.

When they came to the net to shake hands, she looked ruefully at her torn hem and said, "If we play tennis again this weekend, I'm wearing bicycle trousers, and I don't care if it shocks everyone at the house party."

"You want another go?" He shook his head, giving her a pitying look. "You are a glutton for punishment."

She scowled. "I didn't mean I'd be playing you."

"Oh." He grinned, too relieved by his victory to be chastened. "My mistake."

"I suppose now I have to dance with you tomorrow night," she said with an aggravated sigh. "You'll have the last waltz, but I don't see how you think it'll help you change my mind, since you're leaving the very next day."

"But I'm not."

The aggravation in her face faded a bit, faltering into uncertainty. "What do you mean?"

"I told you I would cancel my trip, and I did."

She recovered at once. "Stay or go," she said with a shrug, "it doesn't matter to me. We both know you will leave eventually anyway. It's as predictable as the tides."

She turned and started back toward the house. He didn't try to stop her, and as she walked away, he was the one who felt the pain of being left behind, but instead of putting him off, it made him more determined than ever to change her mind.

"Did you truly cancel your trip?"

He inhaled sharply, turning to find his sister beside him, a little smile on her lips. "You heard all that, I suppose?"

Her smile widened. "Most of it."

He groaned, reminded of the universal truth that sisters always managed to find out a man's business. "How mortifying."

"Don't worry. I don't think anyone else did." Her smile faded, revealing the grave, shy girl he'd known in their childhood. "It's serious, then?"

He didn't even try to dissimulate. "It is for me. It remains to be seen if it's serious for her."

"Oh, Jack," Clara murmured and smiled again, shaking her head. "You never cease to surprise me, little brother."

Chapter 21

If Marjorie was worried that Jonathan would push her to reconsider his proposal, she soon discovered her worries were unfounded. After their battle over the tennis net, Marjorie didn't speak with him again that evening. She did see him, however, seated at the far end of the duke's long dining table, and she couldn't help noticing that the dinner companions on either side of him were both young, pretty women who seemed thoroughly entertained by his company.

Not that it was any of her business, a fact she had to repeat to herself several times before the end of the meal. Later, after the port, he paired up with one of those pretty dinner companions for bridge, along with Irene and Henry, and though Marjorie ought to have been grateful and relieved, she was neither, and she didn't understand herself at all.

The following morning, Jonathan was already gone by the time she came down to breakfast, and later, when she went out with Clara to follow the shooting, the other woman confirmed that he would indeed be away for the entire day.

By the time the shoot was over and they came back to the house, he still hadn't returned, nor was he back by dinner, and as she went up to get ready for the ball, she wondered indignantly how the blasted man expected to change her mind about marrying him when he didn't seem inclined to spend any time in her vicinity. Standing before the cheval mirror as her maid slipped her orchid-pink ballgown of silk chiffon over her head, the first ballgown she'd ever worn in her life, Marjorie felt none of the excitement she'd experienced when she'd first chosen the fabrics and the trimmings and discussed the design with Vivienne.

"Oh, my," breathed Semphill, her usually dour face breaking into a pleased smile. "You look like a princess."

Did she? How fitting. After all, she was living a fairy tale, wasn't she? And yet, as Marjorie looked in the mirror, all she could see were her own troubled eyes staring back at her. This was her night, her ball, her beginning, but she could not rid herself of a terrible, agonizing uncertainty—a feeling that had begun the night she'd refused Jonathan's proposal and which had been growing stronger every day since.

Over and over, she questioned if she'd done the right thing in refusing him, but when she contemplated how she'd feel if she had said yes, Marjorie's uncertainty and confusion only grew. She'd given up the notion that people could change for love when she'd given up on her father, and she just couldn't see that Jonathan would be any different. He wouldn't change for her, and why should he? Why should she expect him to be anything but the man that he was?

She felt trapped, caught between two impossible choices. On one side was the dream life she'd spent the past three years envisioning, and though it wasn't quite the exciting life she'd imagined, it was safe and predictable. On the other side was the life Jonathan offered, one that filled her with fear because every time she imagined it, all she could see was herself in her mother's shoes, crying over a man who was always leaving.

What is wrong with me? she wanted to shout at the mirror. *What is wrong?*

A knock on the door interrupted these agonizing contemplations, and then, the door opened, and Irene came in, smiling and excited, a rectangular box of robin's egg blue in her hand. "I have something for you."

Marjorie stared at the box, reminded of what had happened that afternoon aboard the *Neptune*, and the uncertainty she felt deepened even more. "Thank you, Irene," she said and turned back to the mirror. "Put it on the dressing table, would you?"

If Irene was surprised by her lukewarm reaction, Marjorie didn't know it, for she was occupied with pretending a sudden vast interest in the state of her hair.

"I will see you downstairs," Irene said, walking back toward the door. "Henry is waiting outside. He will escort you down when you are ready."

When the door closed, Marjorie walked to her dressing table and sat down. She stared at the box for a moment, then opened it, earning another astonished gasp from her maid.

She lifted the necklace from the box, but as she held it to her throat, she felt none of its former magic, and when Semphill moved to fasten the clasp, Marjorie stopped her. "I don't think I want to wear it," she said, pulling the necklace from her maid's fingers and setting it back in the box.

"Not wear it?" Her maid stared at her in the mirror as if she'd just grown a second head. "But it's so lovely. And it looks ever so fine with your dress."

Fortunately, she was saved from replying by another knock on the door, and when it opened, Marjorie gave a sob of happy relief. "Baroness," she cried, turning from the mirror, "you've arrived."

"I come at last," the other woman said, sailing in on a cloud of emerald silk charmeuse and expensive French perfume. Closing the door behind her, she started forward, hands outstretched.

"Better late than never, is it not so?" she asked, clasping Marjorie's hands in hers. "I would have been here this afternoon, but I missed my train at Victoria, and had to take the—what do they call it?—the circle train to Waterloo Station, and once I arrived there, I—"

She stopped suddenly, frowning in concern. "But what is this?" she cried and let go of one of Marjorie's hands to cup her chin. "What is this sad face I see, little *kiska*? And on your birthday?"

"It's not my birthday yet. Not until midnight."

"Bah." The Russian woman waved a hand dismissively in the air. "A few hours, that is all. The celebrations have already begun downstairs. What is the cause of all this unhappiness? Come," she urged when Marjorie didn't answer, guiding her into the chair before her dressing table and shooing the maid toward the door. "You shall tell me your trouble, and I will see what can be done."

She pulled another chair forward, sat down, and patted Marjorie's hand. "Now," she said as the door closed behind the maid, "tell me all about it."

"Talking about it isn't going to help, I'm afraid."

"Then I shall have to guess." She tilted her head, studying Marjorie's face. "I think perhaps," she said after a moment, "you are in love?"

Marjorie's heart gave a violent lurch of alarm. "What makes you say that?"

"Well, it is not money that worries you, that I know. And it cannot be your living arrangements. Or your friends. Or the life you live. These are things you have wanted, and they seem to suit you."

With those words, Marjorie had an unaccountable desire to burst into tears.

"You are young and beautiful," the baroness continued, "and all of life is before you. So, it must be love, for what else could trouble you? And . . ." she paused, slanting Marjorie a mischievous look. "I do not forget our conversation at Vivienne a fortnight ago, and your curiosity about a certain subject. So, who is the man?"

"I don't see why I should tell you," Marjorie countered at once. "Since you are so good at guessing."

The baroness did not seem the least put out by this rebuke. "If you ask for a guess, then I say it is that long-legged English guardian of yours."

Something in her face must have given her away, for the baroness gave an exclamation of triumph. "Ah, I am right, then! But what is the trouble? Is it that he does not love you? If so, then—"

"That's not it!" she burst out. "He says he is in love with me. He wants to marry me."

"Then what is the problem? No one can say he is not suitable. He is rich, he is handsome—it would be an excellent match."

"Even if I am not in love with him?"

"Is that it, *kiska*? You do not love him?"

"I don't know!" Marjorie cried, heartsick as she made the wretched confession. "How can that be? How can it be true love, real love, if I am so uncertain?"

"And you think sitting here, hiding in your room, brooding and crying about it, will enable you to answer that question?"

"You said you wanted to help. This is not helping!"

"But what is it you want me to say? You are not a child any longer, sheltered away at school. You are a woman, living in the world. You know, or ought to know by now, that life is not always how we think it should be. Love is not some clear-cut path that leads straight to blissful happiness forever. Does not Shakespeare say the course is not so smooth as that? Love is troublesome and terrifying, and yet, so wonderful that life would be a wasteland without it. Life is full of pain and loss, danger and heartbreak, as well as happiness and joy. You will experience every one of these things in the years ahead, my young friend. That is," she added, smiling, "if you are lucky."

"Loss and fear and pain are lucky?" Marjorie stared at the other woman in disbelief. "Heartbreak is lucky?"

"Yes! For without the bitter, how could we have the sweet? Without risk, how could life ever be anything but a bore?"

"But marriage is forever. What if I make the wrong choice?" she cried. "What if I marry him and he leaves me? What then?"

"If you want certainty, I can tell you that there is one clear choice before you." The baroness stood up, lifted the necklace from the box, and moved to stand behind Marjorie's chair. "You can live behind safe walls and wait to be sure and take no risks and feel no pain. Or . . ."

She paused, slipping the necklace around Marjorie's throat. "Or you can live, my dear. You can experience each moment of your life as it comes. The pain and the joy, the bitter and the sweet."

She paused again to meet Marjorie's eyes in the mirror. "If you want the former, then why did you ever leave your school? And if the latter, then what are you doing up here?"

Marjorie stared at her reflection as the baroness fastened the clasp at the back of her neck, and suddenly the shadow of uncertainty and fear that had been haunting her dissipated and floated away, and she felt the girl aboard the *Neptune* coming back, the one who did not want to live behind walls, who wanted romance and love and a life worth living.

The baroness was right. She didn't know what her destiny would be, but whatever it was, she was not going to find it by sitting here and playing safe.

When the baroness straightened and stepped back, Marjorie rose from her chair and took a deep breath. "Let's go down. I've got some dancing to do."

INSISTING ON HIS waltz being the final one of the night, on being the last man to hold Marjorie and speak with her and dance with her, had seemed a brilliant strategy to Jonathan yesterday. By coming last, he would be the final memory of her first ball, and hopefully, he would be the man she dreamed about tonight when the ball was over. Coming last also enabled him to slip out to the cardroom or the terrace once the ball was underway, sparing himself the torment of watching her dance with a dozen other men before his turn came.

That had been his plan anyway. But then, she came downstairs.

On Torquil's arm, in a frothy, deep pink confection of a gown, she seemed to float down from above like some goddess at sunrise descending to earth. Her hair, shining like incandescent fire beneath the chandeliers, was piled in a mass of curls behind her head that looked ready to tumble down at any moment. Her father's jewels sparkled at her throat, but he knew it was her smile, wide and full of joy, that made everyone gasp. She was as radiant and beautiful as the sun, and it hurt his eyes to look at her. But he could not look away.

When she reached the landing, she saw him, standing in the crowd below, and her dazzling smile vanished. For a moment, his heart stopped, cold with fear. But then she smiled at him—the mysterious, tipped-up curve of lips he'd first seen that afternoon aboard the *Neptune*, the smile of Eve, the smile with which countless women through the ages had beguiled countless men. In her dark eyes, he saw a sensual gleam that could touch all the erotic places inside a man and drive him mad. In the proud lift of her chin and the confident poise of her head, he saw the kind of beauty that did not fade with time.

Ever since he'd first seen that smile, he'd been trying to run from it, because he'd sensed even then that a moment like this would come and that it would bring him to his knees.

He didn't slip out for cards. He didn't go to the terrace for fresh air. He didn't dance with anyone else. Instead, he moved to an obscure corner of the room and waited for his turn.

Sometimes, a footman would happen by, enabling him to snatch a flute of champagne, or an acquaintance would approach him for a few minutes of conversation, but otherwise, he remained apart, in the shadows of potted ferns and palms, and as he waited, he watched her and thought of the plans for the future he'd made today.

His call on Lord Kayne this morning had been beyond anything he could have hoped for. The marquess had been eager not just for his capital, but also for his ideas, and the two men had spent much of the day hammering those ideas into a workable partnership. Then he'd gone into Southampton on a very specific shopping expedition, and to his astonishment and relief, he found what he'd been hoping for within only a few hours. By the time he'd arrived back at Ravenwood to dress for the ball, he'd known he had the right plan for his future.

What he didn't know was if it would be enough to convince Marjorie. For one thing, she had an unnerving ability to toss his plans and intentions into a cocked hat. And for another, it would involve some compromises she might find hard to make. But it was all he had, everything he wanted, and he could only hope she could let her fears go and trust him and help him make it work. If not, he feared he'd be wandering in the desert of the heart for a long time to come.

At last, about half past one, his moment came, and he stepped out of his darkened corner to claim it. He bowed, offered her his arm, and led her to the floor, and when the lilting strains of Strauss began, he held her in his arms and danced with her.

They didn't talk much, for waltzing wasn't the sort of activity that allowed for prolonged conversation. He asked if she was enjoying her first ball, though the sparkle in her eyes and the radiance of her smile told him she was even before she confirmed it. After several turns across the ballroom floor, she commented that he hadn't danced much, a very encouraging remark to his way of thinking, for it meant that despite having champions to the left and right, she'd paid some attention to his whereabouts this evening.

"No," he agreed. "I haven't danced at all, until now."

"Why not?"

"Isn't it obvious?" He met her eyes. "There's only one woman here I want to dance with, and because she so cruelly denied me the three waltzes I asked for, I'm forced to be content with one."

He was rewarded with a smile, though she looked away at once, and it was several more turns around the ballroom before she replied. "Three waltzes with the same man implies an engagement," she said at last. "And, if you remember, I turned you down."

"That's not the sort of thing a man forgets, believe me. But—" He broke off, wondering if a ballroom floor was the right moment to take the next step, but hell, what did he have to lose?

"But," he resumed, "I told you I wasn't giving up, and I meant it. I've done a lot of thinking since you refused me," he rushed on as she opened her mouth to speak. "About the reasons you gave and what I could do to overcome your objections, and how I might change your mind and gain another chance with you."

"Jonathan—"

"I think I may have found a way to give us both what we want. It's my vision of the future—mine, and hopefully, yours, too, and I want to show it to you. Tomorrow morning. Ten o'clock. Clara can bring you in the pony trap."

"But where are we going?" she asked.

"To my home."

She stumbled, and he had to wrap an arm around her to steady her. "Careful," he cautioned, easing back, letting her go when all he wanted was to pull her closer, for many eyes were watching them.

"What do you mean, your home?" she asked as they resumed dancing. "You don't have a home."

"I do now. I bought a house. That's part of what I was doing today. If you don't like it," he added, getting nervous as she stared at him, "I'm willing to sell it and look for something else. But to me, it felt like the perfect house, especially given what I'll be doing with my life now."

The waltz ended before she could reply, a good thing, since the bewilderment in her face told him he'd said enough already. "It'll all make more sense tomorrow, believe me," he said as he offered his arm to escort her back to her place. "I'm hoping it will cause you to reconsider your decision, but if not, I'll wait. If you want to have a season, meet other men . . ."

He paused, the words to set her free sticking in his throat, but they were nearly across the ballroom, so he forced them out, speaking in a rush. "I won't like it, but I'll endure it. I'll wait. I'll court you in honorable fashion. I know you don't think I'm the right man for you, but I intend to change your mind because I know you are the only woman for me. I love you, and I want to spend my life with you. All I ask is that you give me a chance. Give us a chance."

There was no time for more, for they had reached Irene's side. He gave his sister a nod, then reached for Marjorie's hand.

"Ten o'clock tomorrow," he said. "I hope you'll come."

With that, he bowed over her hand and turned away, departing the ballroom without a backward glance.

Chapter 22

*T*he ball was over. All the guests who lived in the county had climbed into their carriages and departed for home, and all the guests staying at Ravenwood had gone to bed. Even the servants had called it a night, and now, the house was dead quiet, indicating that everyone was asleep.

Everyone, that is, but Jonathan.

After he'd left Marjorie in the ballroom, he hadn't stayed with the family for goodnights and farewells to the guests. Instead, he'd gone to his room. He'd undressed and gotten into bed, but he didn't sleep.

Instead, he stared at the ceiling and thought of her—of how she'd come down those stairs looking so beautiful it made him ache, of her in his arms as they danced, of her mysterious smile that could drive him to the brink.

He thought of the plans he'd set in motion today, of the future he'd begun and all the exciting possibilities that lay ahead. He knew it was the right future for him, if he could only convince Marjorie to share it with him.

Jonathan reached up and lifted his pocket watch off the hook on the wall, turned the face toward the window, and read by the shaft of moonlight between the curtains that it was just after three. Still wide-awake, he decided to go for a walk. It was a fine night, and there was plenty of moonlight for a stroll.

He shoved back the counterpane and got out of bed, then lit a lamp and walked to the armoire, but he'd barely pulled on a pair of trousers and a smoking jacket when the door of his room suddenly opened.

Startled, he whirled around, and was astonished to find Marjorie standing in the doorway, a lit candle in her hand. "What the devil?" he muttered, as she slipped inside his room.

"You're still awake," she whispered, closing the door behind her and blowing out the candle. "I'm so glad. I thought I'd have to wake you."

"What's wrong?" he asked in alarm, also keeping his voice low. "What are you doing at this end of the house? And how do you even know which room I'm in?"

"The baroness found out for me. But," she added as he expelled an exasperated sigh, "it took me forever to find my way over here. It's hard to navigate this house with just a candle."

"I daresay. But . . ." He paused as the reality of the situation began to sink in, a reality that was so much like his erotic imaginings that his throat went dry. Marjorie was in his room, wearing nothing but a nightgown and wrapper, her hair loose and tumbling in long waves around her shoulders. "But why are you here?"

"I needed to see you."

"Now? It's three o'clock in the morning."

"Yes, which means we don't have much time."

"Time for what?"

"Well, not for a conversation." She laughed softly, an exhilarated little sound he didn't understand. "I'm here to seduce you."

"What?" Not, sad to say, a worthy response to such delicious news, but he supposed eloquence didn't matter, since he was obviously dreaming. Though how that could happen when he was wide-awake and hadn't slept a wink, he wasn't quite sure.

"Shameless of me, I know. But life is too short to worry about proprieties, don't you think?"

"No," he said at once. "I don't."

Even as he spoke, arousal was already rising in him, an ache far too familiar to him these days. "What I think is that you've had a bit too much champagne this evening." He leaned around her and reached for the doorknob, but when he tried to nudge her out of the way to open the door, she didn't move.

"No, no, it's not the champagne. I think it's the necklace." She lifted one hand, slipping pearl buttons free at her throat to reveal the Rose of Shoshone still around her neck. "I have to say," she whispered, leaning closer as if she was imparting a secret, "whenever I have it on, it's amazing how it makes me feel."

"How does it make you feel?" he asked and wanted to kick himself in the head.

"Wicked," she confessed, and his control slipped a bit. "A bit wild."

A wicked, wild Marjorie was just too much for a man to bear, and he knew he could not hear any more. Not another word. Force might not be noble, but in this case, it was required.

He reached out to grab her arm, thinking to haul her out of the way so he could get the door open and boot her shapely bum into the corridor, but she ducked around him, then turned, her beautiful, laughing face pushing him to the brink of his endurance.

"Marjorie, you've got to get out of here. Now."

She shook her head, moving closer, close enough that he could smell the scent of her, the fresh, pristine scent of lavender soap and talcum powder. She'd bathed before bed. The knowledge made him dizzy, his resolve teetered, and he wondered if there would ever come a time when this woman did not manage to make him feel as if he was sliding off the edge of the earth.

Desperate, he tried again. "You don't even know what seduction is, but if you stay here much longer, you'll know its result."

"Gosh, I hope so. Otherwise, I'll have worked up my nerve, stumbled my way through this enormous house, and risked humiliating myself and ruining my reputation by plunging into the wrong room, all for nothing."

Far more was at stake for her than embarrassment. He had to make her understand that. "If you don't go, I'll take your innocence, and then you'll have to marry me. You won't have a choice. I'll have ruined you, and as tempting as it is to know that I could win your hand by such delightfully nefarious means, I'd prefer to do it the honorable way."

"So, you are tempted? That's encouraging."

"Of course I'm tempted. What do you think I'm made of? Stone?"

"I'm not sure. Shall we find out?" She moved closer, lifting her arms as if to touch him, and he shied away as if he was the virgin here.

"For God's sake, Marjorie," he whispered, growing desperate as his desire deepened and spread. "Don't you remember what I said earlier? I want to persuade you to marry me. I don't want you to marry me because a baby is on the way. And please don't make me explain why that would be a possibility if you stay. My nerves can't take it."

She made a sound of derision, as if he was talking nonsense. "There's not going to be a baby."

"When it comes to this subject, you don't know what you're talking about, a fact we established weeks ago. But unlike you, I do know, and I can assure you that if you stay, I will give you everything you are so lusciously asking for, making odds of a baby quite high."

"I don't think so." Reaching into the pocket of her robe, she pulled out a red velvet envelope that his checkered past enabled him to recognize at once.

"I'm told," she said as he stared at her in disbelief, "that the device inside this packet prevents babies."

"God," he choked, stepping back again, at the absolute end of his tether. "Oh, my God."

"It's called a French letter."

"I know what it is," he shot back, his voice a rasp. "How do you know what it is?"

She shrugged, so nonchalant, she might have known about condoms all her life. "I saw something about them in a magazine. I didn't know what they were, not then, but—"

"Where did you get it? You can't buy them since you're not married."

"The baroness, of course. I went to her after the ball, and she gave it to me."

He groaned. "The baroness. Of course. I should have known."

"She explained everything. How babies are made, what happens, and . . . and . . . all of that." Her cheeks flushed rosy pink. "It was quite a revelation, I must say."

He could not talk about this with her. Not now, not when she was standing in front of him—*again*—in nothing but a nightgown. "I'm so glad you've been made aware of the facts of life," he said tightly, pulling the envelope from her fingers and tossing it aside.

She seemed not to notice the sarcasm. "That night in the library makes so much more sense now. I'm so glad I understand what to expect."

"I had a plan, damn it," he muttered, appreciating—not for the first time in the past two months—that when a man was in love with a madcap ginger, chaos was the order of the day. "Why is it that every time I have a plan, you manage to wreck it?"

"Sorry." She bit her lip, trying to look contrite, but to his eyes, she just looked deliciously naughty. "But when you realize how you truly feel about someone, waiting even a few hours to tell them seems intolerable. That's why I'm here."

He stared, hope and disbelief warring for control, his jaded side telling him not to go making assumptions.

"I seem to have rendered you speechless," she murmured.

"Let's get this clear." He grabbed her arms, held her fast, not certain he could ever let her go again. "I'm in love with you. Are you saying you're in love with me?"

"Yes." She smiled, so radiant and beautiful, he couldn't breathe. "Yes, I'm in love with you. I realized it when we were dancing, because when you were talking about standing by and letting other men have a chance, I couldn't imagine it. In fact, I can't imagine letting any other man ever touch me the way you did."

He was too thunderstruck to reply. What could a man say when he was handed heaven on a plate?

"So," she said in the wake of his silence, "are you going to let me have my way with you? Or do I have to be even more shameless," she continued as she freed another button of her robe, "and take off all my clothes before you capitulate?"

He tried to hold back, his instincts, his reason, and all his superior experience telling him that despite her declaration of love and all her newfound worldly wisdom about the physical side of things, she didn't truly understand what she was doing.

And what about their future? Yes, he'd bought a house, he would be giving her the home she wanted, but the plans he'd made would mean other compromises, big ones, ones he knew she wouldn't want to make. He ought to resist, wait, at least until after tomorrow.

But then, she slipped another button free, his throat went dry, his resistance crumbled, and any notions of waiting or resisting went straight out of his head.

"Only if you're sure," he said. "Because once it's done, there's no undoing it."

"I understand, and I'm sure." She tugged at her sash, her robe came apart, and he could take no more. He grabbed her, hauled her into his arms, and kissed her.

When his lips parted, hers did, too, and he took her mouth in a long, slow kiss as he slid his hands between them. As he unbuttoned her nightgown, his knuckles brushed her breasts, threatening to flare his lust out of control. But he strove to keep it in check, knowing he had a long way to go tonight if he was to win more than her body.

To slow things down, he slid his hands away from her breasts and took a step back, earning a cry of dismay from her that caused him to press a finger to his lips.

"If we're going to do this," he said softly, "we have to be quiet about it. There's chaps on both sides of me, and if we make any noise, they'll wake up and know I've got a woman in my room. And since you're the only one I've danced with, they'll guess that it's you. We can't have that, so mum's the word. All right?"

She nodded. "As long as you're not stopping," she whispered.

"No. I don't think I could resist you now if my life depended on it."

But he didn't move to touch her, and when she stirred as if to move even closer, he held up one hand to stop her. "I want this to be right for you, and despite your recently acquired knowledge, I know a bit more about this than you do. So, we go at my pace, not yours. I'm in charge. Agreed?"

"Agreed." She smiled back at him, then bit her lip, slanting him a wicked look from beneath her lashes. "For now."

Jonathan drew back, raking a hand through his hair and working to get his bearings. Virtually all his sexual knowledge had been gained with women who were anything but innocent. It had been a decade since he'd been at risk of deflowering a virgin, and during that episode, he'd been a fumbling eighteen-year-old of woefully limited experience, a formal engagement had already been announced to both families, and he and the girl in question had been fully dressed and standing in a coat cupboard under a staircase—hardly the place for slow and tender lovemaking. Nonetheless, he knew that was precisely what would be required of him tonight, and having already spent weeks in a very precarious condition, he paused a moment to draw a profound, shaky breath.

"All right, then," he said at last and reached up to slide her robe off her shoulders. As it fell to the floor, he could see the faint circle of her nipples beneath the thin batiste nightgown, a sight that threatened to snap the tight leash on his control before they'd even begun, but he paused for another slow, deep breath, then lifted his hands and cupped her breasts through the fabric.

Her arms came up around his neck. Her breathing quickened, warm against his throat, as he shaped her breasts in his hands. They were every bit as full and lush as he remembered—not surprising, since that night in the library at Upper Brook Street had been haunting him for days.

Her nipples were hard and round as pebbles, and he toyed with them, rolling them in his fingers. She gasped, her arms tightening around his neck, and when her hips stirred against his own, he groaned low in his throat.

Jonathan pulled back, but he could gain no reprieve. Her arms slid down and her fingers began pulling apart the edges of his smoking jacket.

He groaned again, knowing what she wanted, uncertain he could endure giving it to her. He grasped her wrists. "I'm supposed to be in charge, remember?"

"But I want to see," she whispered, blushing as she kissed him.

He relented, releasing her wrists and letting her slide the garment from his shoulders. When she touched him, fanning her palms across his bare chest, he inhaled sharply, tilting back his head, enduring the sweet agony as her hands glided over his shoulders and chest, but as they lowered to his abdomen, he couldn't take any more.

He once again grasped her wrists. "If you keep teasing me this way," he said as he pulled her hands down, "this is going to be over far too soon."

She slanted him a wicked look, that necklace sparkling at her throat. "Would that be so bad?"

"Yes, it would. I told you, I'm in charge. And it's my turn for a peek." He gathered the folds of her nightgown in his fists. "Lift your arms."

She complied, and as she stretched her arms toward the ceiling, he pulled the gown upward and over her head, baring her body completely.

He didn't touch her, but just the sight of her was enough to threaten what little control he had left, for the reality of her was even more exquisite than any of the images conjured by his fevered imagination. If raw sexual heat could kill a man, he'd have burned to ashes on the spot.

She was blushing all over, her skin a soft, delicate pink. Her face was turned away, loosened tendrils of her gorgeous hair falling across her cheek. Gently, he pushed back the loosened strands, tucking them behind her ear, then he ducked his head, pressing kisses to her hot cheeks, her nose, her forehead, her lips.

"Now that I know you love me," he murmured as he tossed her nightgown aside and cupped her breasts again, "there's something else I've got to know."

"What's that?" she asked, a soft gasp as he caressed her.

"Will you marry me?"

She nuzzled his neck, pressing a kiss to the base of his throat. "You said earlier I had plenty of time to decide about that."

"That was before you came to my room in the dark of night, hurled yourself at me in this shameless fashion, and admitted you're in love with me. I think I'm entitled to a definite answer on the subject of matrimony, because if you think I'm going to let any other man near you after tonight, you've got another think coming."

"Trying to play the heavy-handed guardian again, I see."

At those words, he felt a twinge of alarm, suspecting that she was equivocating, but when he pulled back, he saw that she was smiling—that mysterious, knowing smile—and he laughed low in his throat.

"Oh, so you want to tease, do you?" he murmured. "Two can play this game."

He captured her mouth, kissing her deep and slow as he slid his hands down her breasts, over her stomach, and around her hips. "Marry me," he said against her mouth as he shaped her buttocks in his hands.

She stirred and brought her hands to the waistband of his trousers as if to unfasten them. But he knew he couldn't let her. He was rock hard, and if she started making explorations of that sort, he'd never be able to hold out, and he wasn't about to spoil her first time by going too fast. Besides, his other objective was just as important.

Hands on her hips, he gently pushed her backward, maneuvering her toward the foot of the bed, then he eased one hand between her thighs. "Still can't decide?"

"Jonathan," she moaned, her arms coming up around his neck, her hips stirring against his hand, her legs tightening instinctively, but he did not relent.

"I can see I shall have to be more persuasive," he murmured and turned his hand, cupping her mound. She made a shocked sound, her knees buckling, her arms tightening around his neck. He caressed her, relishing the silken wetness of her core, but then he pulled back again. If she wanted to tease, so could he.

He grasped her wrists, then he pulled her hands down to her sides. "Hold on," he ordered, and wrapped her fingers around the brass of the footboard behind her.

He kissed her again, sliding his hand back between her thighs. She eased back against the footboard with another soft moan as he continued to caress her, and the sight of her this way, with her head tilted back and her lips parted with desire and her body fully bared to him for lovemaking, she was more beautiful than anything he could have imagined. Her breasts rose and fell with her rapid breathing, round and full, their nipples a rich brownish-pink in the lamplight.

He bent his head to suckle her breast as he caressed the silken folds of her sex, relishing how slick and wet she was. Her breathing was coming in pants, her hips working against his hand.

"You are naked in my arms," he said. "I think you should do the honorable thing and marry me."

She didn't answer, and he decided it was time for more ruthless tactics. He pulled his hand from between her thighs and sank to his knees, kissing his way down her stomach as he wrapped his arm around her hips and pulled her close.

"Jonathan," she whispered. "Oh, oh."

He pressed his mouth to the triangle of curls between her thighs. She shivered, her hips bucking, but he tightened his arm to hold her still and heighten the tension further as he began to caress her with his tongue, stroking the crease of her sex over and over, lightly, relent-lessly, until, with a final, shuddering gasp, she came, collapsing in his hold.

He held her this way a moment longer, kissing and nuzzling her sex as the shudders of orgasm rocked her body. Then, at last, he rose, lifting her into his arms. He carried her around to the side of the bed and laid her down. His gaze locked with hers, he began to undo his trousers. "I think you should marry me and make an honest man of me."

Wordless, she stared at him, not knowing what to say, not wanting to spoil the moment. He was demanding something she wasn't ready to give. Her body, yes—she'd come tonight willing to give him that, including her heart. But he wanted more than that. He wanted the rest of her life. He'd said he was building a future they could share, but what if he was wrong?

He began unbuttoning his trousers, and Marjorie thought of what the baroness had said about choices, about how one could play safe or enjoy every moment, and as Jonathan slid his trousers down his hips, she tossed worries about the future aside. This moment was what mattered.

His linen followed his trousers, and when he stood naked beside her, the sight of him so flagrantly aroused made her suck in a sharp, startled breath. Even the baroness's detailed explanations had not prepared her enough, she realized, but at least, she finally understood just what the French letter was supposed to do.

Jonathan waited, letting her have a good, long look, then he retrieved the velvet pouch from where he'd tossed it earlier and removed the long, lambskin sheath. She stared in amazement as he slid it along the length of his shaft, and then, she heard a choked, panicky sound from her own throat. She reached up to touch the jewels around her throat, as if the necklace were a lucky talisman— and perhaps it was, for her apprehensions slipped away, and she felt only the surging power that came from knowing how much he wanted her and how much she wanted him.

He seemed to sense the change in her, for he leaned over to tenderly kiss her mouth. Then, he eased his body down onto hers, pressing her back into the sheets before her courage could fail again. She opened her arms, sure she knew now what to expect, but then, he stopped, resting his weight on one arm, suspended above her as his hand eased that hard, sheathed part of his body between her thighs.

"Marjorie, listen to me." His voice sounded hoarse, his breathing labored. "I can't hold back any longer. I love you, and I wanted to hold out until you agree to marry me, but I can't. I'll have to trust you on that." He smiled, but she could tell it was forced. "Do you trust me?"

"Yes." She touched his face, kissed him. "Don't hold out," she whispered, moving her hips. "Don't wait, Jonathan. Do it, now."

"Can't, yet." When she moved again, sliding her thighs against his shaft, he gritted his teeth. "Don't, for the love of God. Don't move. Listen."

He took a deep breath, as if striving for control. "I've got to warn you about this. You've never been with a man before, so it's likely to hurt."

As he spoke, his hips began rocking against hers, and as the hard part of him rubbed where he had kissed her and stroked her before, that delicious pleasure washed over her again, growing stronger, hotter. She arched into him again with a soft moan.

"Christ," he muttered, and shifted his body to rest his weight on his forearms, burying his face against her neck, and flexed his hips against her. That hard part of him pressed deeper onto her and then into her.

Caught up in a sensuous haze, she was sure she knew what was coming, but when he thrust hard, shoving deeply into her, the sudden, burning pain seemed to sear her like a fire inside, and she cried out.

He smothered the sound with his mouth, catching her shock and pain in his kiss. Holding himself rigid above her, he kissed her everywhere he could—her hair, her throat, her cheek, her mouth. "It'll be all right. I promise. I love you, Marjorie. I love you."

As he spoke to her and kissed her, the pain began to recede. "I'm all right, Jonathan," she whispered, wriggling her hips, trying to accustom herself to the strange fullness of him inside of her.

At that unspoken urging, he began to move, slowly at first, then more quickly, his thrusts against her becoming stronger and deeper. His eyes were closed, his lips parted, and it was almost as if he'd forgotten about her, but he was stroking her hair and saying her name, and she realized the truth. He was caught up in the pleasure of her body and this moment.

As for herself, that first searing pain had faded. Now, her own desire was building, desire he'd evoked before with his hands and his mouth. She pushed upward to meet his next thrust, and he groaned, his arms sliding beneath her as if to pull her closer when he already seemed as close to her as he could possibly be, and she thrust up again, striving to move with him, urging him to a faster pace, and faster still, until they were both frantic, breathing hard, moving as one.

The pain was now gone, obliterated by rising desire, and with each thrust, her need rose, hotter and deeper. And then, without any warning, it reached its peak, roaring up within her in a violent, beautiful explosion that sent waves of that sweet pleasure through her entire body. "I love you," she panted against his ear, her legs tight around him, her body clenching his as the pleasure kept coming. "I love you."

With those words, he seemed to follow her over the peak. Shudders rocked him, and he cried out, a smothered cry into the pillow. He thrust against her several more times, and then collapsed, burying his face against her neck.

She raked her fingers through his hair, she stroked the hard, strong muscles of his back and shoulders, reveling in the moment, and when he kissed her hair and murmured her name, happiness rose within her like a fierce, surging tide.

Yes, she thought, this was why she'd come tonight. Because she wanted to enjoy this, and every other moment of her life, and she vowed that no matter what the future brought, the memory and beauty of this moment would stay with her forever.

Chapter 23

After the extraordinary events of the night, the last thing Marjorie wanted was to go to bed. As she slipped back through the house to her own room, she didn't feel the least bit sleepy. The agonizing uncertainty that had been tearing her apart was gone, and she felt exhilarated and joyously happy. Feeling like that, who could sleep?

The first hint of dawn was peeking around the curtains as she slipped back inside her room, reminding her that in less than five hours, she would see him again. He would take her through the house he'd bought, the one he wanted to be their home. They'd tour the rooms, walk the grounds, plan the future, begin building their life together. With such delights in store, sleep seemed impossible.

Marjorie removed her robe and tossed it aside, then pulled back the counterpane, slid into bed with a dreamy sigh, and was asleep in three seconds. The next thing she knew, Miss Semphill was shaking her shoulder. "Miss Marjorie?"

"Hmm?" She rolled over and promptly fell back to sleep.

Her maid shook her awake again. "I'm sorry, Miss Marjorie, but Lady Galbraith is waiting downstairs. She says you two have an outing this morning."

Marjorie's heart gave a joyous leap, making her fully awake in an instant. "That's right," she agreed, laughing as she opened her eyes and tossed back the bed linens. "We do. At ten o'clock. What time is it now?"

"Nearly nine. Lady Galbraith waited as long as she could to wake you," Semphill added as she walked to the armoire. "But she said that if you don't hurry, you might be late."

"Then I'd better dress myself," she said. "You go down and tell Lady Galbraith I'll be ready in a few minutes, so she can have the gig brought around."

"Her ladyship already did that. It's waiting in the drive." Semphill pulled out two walking suits. "Do you want to wear the green wool or the tweed?"

Ten minutes later, dressed in her green walking suit of summer-weight wool, Marjorie, breathless and excited, was stepping up beside Clara in the gig. "Where are we going?"

"I'm not supposed to tell you anything," Clara replied as she snapped the reins and the gig jerked into motion. "Jonathan said it's a birthday surprise. Happy birthday, by the way."

Marjorie laughed. "Well, this isn't such a surprise. I don't know where we're going, but I do know what he wants to show me."

"Do you, indeed?" Clara's smile widened knowingly, making her blush. "We're going to Beaulieu, if that enlightens you at all."

It didn't, and since Clara refused to say any more, she could only wait in delicious suspense as the carriage rolled through the country-side. Like yesterday, the day was fine and warm, the air was sweet and fresh with a hint of the nearby ocean.

Marjorie tilted her head back and closed her eyes, savoring the sun on her face and the sweetness of anticipation and the exhilarating joy of being loved and in love. She couldn't imagine ever being happier than she was at this moment.

Beaulieu proved to be a charming little village a few miles from Southampton, and after traveling along its high street of shops, pubs, and thatched roof cottages, Clara steered the gig onto a wooded lane. They went another mile or so, crossed over a charming stone bridge, and turned to pass through a pair of wrought-iron gates.

Marjorie caught her breath. Ahead of her, a tree-lined lane led straight to a classical Georgian home, rectangular in shape, with a

Corinthian portico in front and a rotunda above it. Behind one corner of the house, she could see a splendid view of lawns and gardens that led down to sprawling green fields and hedgerows. Far in the distance, she could see the Port of Southampton, and beyond it, the glittering water of the Solent and the faint outline of the Isle of Wight.

I'm home, she thought with sudden, joyful certainty. *I am home at last.*

In the circular drive, another gig was parked, showing that Jonathan was already here, and Marjorie could hardly contain her excitement. Clara hadn't even pulled the brake before Marjorie jumped down and raced toward the house, opened one of the two entrance doors, and walked into a rectangular entrance hall.

"Jonathan?" she called, her steps and her voice echoing through the empty, unfurnished house. She paused in the center of the hall, her gaze lifting from the wide staircase ahead of her to a mezzanine with a brass grillwork railing and a stunning domed ceiling of glass panels overhead. "Jonathan?"

"Here," he called, and she turned, her gaze lowering again to the mezzanine, where she saw him leaning on the rail, watching her. "It's called Ainsley Park," he said with a nod to their surroundings. "The house was designed by Wyatt. Not up-to-date at all, I'm afraid, but that's easily done." He spread his arms. "What do you think?"

She laughed. "I don't know yet. I just walked in."

"Wait there. I'm coming down."

He moved along the mezzanine and vanished from view as Clara's footsteps sounded on the travertine floor behind her.

"It has beautiful lines, doesn't it?" Clara remarked, glancing around as she paused beside Marjorie. "One can really see the architecture when there's no furnishings to get in the way."

She had no chance to respond as more footsteps sounded, and she turned, watching Jonathan descend the staircase. As he came toward her, he glanced at Clara, who immediately gave a cough.

"The grounds seem quite lovely," she said. "I believe I'll take a stroll."

"I'd suggest the front gardens," Jonathan replied, his eyes meeting his sister's in a meaningful glance Marjorie didn't understand.

Clara seemed to understand it, however, for she gave a nod and turned, heading back the way she and Marjorie had come in.

The front door had barely closed behind her before Jonathan was pulling Marjorie into his arms. "How do you feel this morning?" he asked, smiling a little.

"All right. A bit sore." She blushed, feeling shy and flustered. "But happy."

"Me, too." He bent his head and kissed her mouth, then drew back and took her hand. "Come on. There's so much I want to show you, and we don't have much time."

"No, I suppose we don't," she agreed as he pulled her toward the stairs. "Irene has a birthday lunch planned for me with the ladies before everyone starts leaving for the station. Did Torquil have something for the gentlemen?"

"It's not that. But I'll explain later."

He showed her the upstairs floors first, and as they walked through the two adjoining suites that would form their apartments as husband and wife, Marjorie felt more certain than ever that she'd come home. They agreed that the nursery needed to be moved closer to their own rooms, and at least four of the twenty-six bedrooms would have to be converted to baths, then they headed back down to the ground floor.

"All the reception rooms flank the terrace," he told her as they paused at the back of the main hall where a wide corridor stretched in opposite directions toward the wings. "Drawing room, library, and music room to the right, and billiard room and ballroom to the left. This," he added, pulling her into a spacious room of teak floors and white millwork, "is the drawing room."

Marjorie's attention was caught at once by the French doors that stretched along the back, showing off the magnificent view beyond. She crossed the room, unlatched one of the doors, and walked out onto the flagstone terrace, Jonathan behind her.

"That's the way we came when we arrived in England," she said, pointing toward the sea as she crossed to the stone balustrade. "The *Neptune* sailed right past here, didn't it? We couldn't see anything that day," she added, smiling as she stared out over the water. "All that rain and fog."

"Look down there," he said, pausing beside her, pointing to a snake-like trail of murky green leading in from the sea. "That's the Beaulieu River. We've got a quay and a boathouse, so whenever Henry and Irene take the *Mary Louisa* or the *Endeavor* out on the Solent, they can come up the river, dock at the quay, and—"

"And visit us," she finished in delight as she turned toward him.

"Or fetch us, if we want to go along. We can even have a yacht of our own, if we wish."

That made her laugh. "I thought things like yachts were a waste of money," she said, wrapping her arms around his waist as she reminded him of his words aboard the *Neptune*. "You said I couldn't spend my money on frivolities like yachts."

He grinned. "Yes, well, I think I might be changing my mind about that." He paused, nodding to their surroundings. "Do you like the house? If not, we can look for something else."

"No, no, it's—" She broke off, happiness clogging her throat, making it hard to form words. She swallowed hard, glanced around, then looked at him. "It's perfect," she whispered. "Absolutely perfect."

That pleased him, for his smile widened, creasing the edges of his mouth and the corners of his eyes. "I'm glad."

"Shall we look at the rest?" she asked. "We haven't looked at the kitchens, or the servants' hall, or any of that."

He hesitated, then shook his head. "We can't, not today. There's something else we need to discuss, something important, and we don't have much time."

That was his second mention of time, and as he drew back from her, his arms sliding down so that he could take her hands in his, Marjorie felt an odd shiver of apprehension, but she shoved it aside, telling herself not to be silly. "Why are you so concerned about time today? Is your day so very full?"

"It is, actually." He cleared his throat, looking down at their clasped hands. "Do you remember what I told you at the ball? Why I wanted to bring you here?"

"Yes. You said you wanted to show me the house you bought for us. And you have. And I love it."

"I also said I wanted to tell you what I'll be doing with my life." He looked up, meeting her gaze. "You know Clara wanted to make a place for me in Deverill Publishing, and I turned it down because it wasn't my dream anymore. I knew I had to find a new dream, and—" He broke off and took a deep breath. "I have."

"That's wonderful!" she cried. "What is it?"

"A month or so ago, I met the Marquess of Kayne. Rex introduced us. Lord Kayne owns a company called Hawthorne Shipping. They build cargo ships—big, steam-driven transatlantic cargo ships, right here in Southampton. Kayne wants to build passenger liners, too, but can't do it alone. I met with him yesterday, and we agreed to form a joint venture for the project."

"You're going to build ships like the *Neptune*?"

"Yes. We'll be based right beside Hawthorne Shipping." He let go of her hands, put his hands on her shoulders, and turned her around so that she was facing northeast, toward Southampton, then he stretched an arm over her shoulder, pointing. "Right there, at Hythe, across the port from where Cunard docks its ships."

"So, you'll sell the ships you build to Cunard, and White Star, and such?"

"Not exactly."

There was an odd inflection in his voice, and for no reason she could identify, Marjorie felt another pang of apprehension, and when he turned her around to face him, it deepened into fear, for his countenance was graver than she'd ever seen it before.

"We're going to build our own ships," he said, once again taking her hands in his. "We'll be competing with Cunard and White Star, not selling to them. To do it, we'll have to arrange routes, get the moorings, study the competition . . ." He stopped and took a breath. "That's my part."

"What are you saying?" she asked, but even before he replied, the sick feeling in her stomach gave her an inkling of what he was going to say.

"I'll have to travel, Marjorie. A great deal, especially in the beginning."

Her worst fears confirmed, she felt suddenly cold, and she jerked her hands from his. "Why am I not surprised?"

"Marjorie, listen to me, please. This is the first thing I've found since Deverill Publishing that excites me, the first thing in a decade that makes me truly want to settle down."

"But you won't be settled, will you? No wonder this excites you. It's the perfect way for you to go where you want and do what you want. Meanwhile," she went on, overriding him as he opened his mouth to reply, "I'll be alone, in this lovely house you bought for me, waiting for you to come back, the same way my mother waited for my father? Is that it?"

"No!" he cried, grasping her arms as she tried to turn away. "I won't be gone all the time, and when I do have to go, you'll come with me."

"And do what?"

"See the world, of course. For God's sake, Marjorie, you spent most of your life cooped up inside a school. There is a huge, beautiful world out there, and you've never seen any of it. Don't you want to? Don't you want to see Venice, or Gibraltar, or the Greek isles? Don't you want to walk with me through a copper bazaar in Tangier, or stand under the cedars of Lebanon, or take a tour up the Nile?"

That all sounded grand, but Marjorie feared the reality wouldn't be quite so romantic. "What you're saying is that we'll be living like rich wanderers instead of poor ones. What about children? What are we to do with them? Stick them in a school somewhere and leave them there?"

He actually had the nerve to smile. "I think we can afford a nanny to come with us, don't you?"

"Don't laugh at me!" she cried, jerking her shoulders, wrenching free of his hold. "Don't you dare laugh at me."

His smile vanished at once, and his expression became tender, tearing at her heart. "I'm not. But I do wish you'd get this idea that we'll be homeless vagrants out of your head, because that's not how it would be at all."

"Why? Because you bought a house? I can't think why you bothered if your plan is for us to live in hotels?"

"Because that's not my plan. We'll travel, yes, but . . ." He paused and spread his arms. "We'll always come home."

"And when," she choked, "would all this world traveling begin?"

"Well, for you, I thought we could start with a honeymoon. For me, however . . ." He paused a fraction of a second. "I have to leave this evening."

"Tonight?" She stared at him, unable to believe what she was hearing.

"I have to go to Gibraltar. Kayne set up a meeting about moorings there," he added, speaking quickly, as if sensing her shock and hoping to diffuse it. "He was supposed to go, but since I'm involved now and handling the moorings shall be one of my primary responsibilities, we agreed I should go. My ship sails at five o'clock."

"You're leaving." Even as she said it again, she still couldn't quite believe it. She couldn't believe that he could present her with such a perfect, beautiful life and then immediately abandon it. "You canceled your trip to South Africa, only to replace it with one to Gibraltar."

"This won't be for long. Just one month."

As if the amount of time mattered. "You knew yesterday you were leaving. You knew this new venture would take you all over the world. You knew, and you didn't tell me."

"I intended to tell you today," he muttered. "I had it all planned. That's what I was talking about when I told you at the ball that I knew you'd need time to decide if I was the man for you. Remember? I told you I'd wait for you to be sure, and that while I waited, I'd be building a life for us. I thought while I'm away, you'd consider what I'm doing, and that when I got back, we'd talk it over, perhaps find a way to make it all work. But then, you came to my room—"

"So, why didn't you tell me then?" she demanded, stepping back from him, feeling misled and manipulated. "Before I told you I loved you, before I shamelessly threw myself at you and gave myself to you, you could have told me all this, but you didn't."

His gaze slid away, the glimmer of a guilty conscience. "I was going to tell you, but then you started taking your clothes off, and I . . ." He paused, met her eyes again, and sighed. "I lost my head."

She stared back at him, aghast. "Last night, you persuaded me to marry you, knowing this. You pushed me to agree, never saying a word—"

"You came to me last night. I didn't come to you. Hell, I've been doing my damnedest to avoid what happened last night. Forgive me if I just couldn't fight it anymore. Would you have preferred that I lie with you without wanting or expecting marriage? Would that make me more honorable in your eyes, or less?"

He stepped closer, closing the distance she'd put between them, gold glints sparking in his hazel eyes, glints not of desire, but of frustration and anger. "Did it ever occur to you that my heart was on the table last night? Did you consider what it would have done to me if I bedded you only to find out afterward you didn't love me or that you wouldn't agree to marry me and share my life? I'll tell you what it would have done. It would have broken my heart."

Still reeling from shock, still feeling deceived, Marjorie couldn't find it within herself to worry much about his heart just now. "So, better to avoid telling me the truth until afterward, and risk that my heart will be the one broken?"

"Your heart isn't broken, and by God, you're working damned hard to make sure it never will be. That's what this is about. You're afraid of the day when I go off without you, as if that's fated and inevitable."

"Given everything I know about you, it's a likely possibility."

"No, it's not. You know why? Because I am not like your damned father. I will not leave you." He gripped her arms again, ducking his head to look into her eyes when she tried to look away. "I will never leave you."

"You are leaving me! You're leaving me tonight."

"But I will be back in a month."

"How long before it's two months, or six, or a year?"

"Or never, like your father, you mean? You will just have to trust me. What I want to know," he continued, ignoring her derisive snort, "is how long before you stop thinking you're like your mother?"

"What is that supposed to mean?"

"Your mother may have sat home and cried, but you don't have to, because you're not her. You are the girl who was going to follow her father and take photographs of the Wild West. The girl who, when her first dream was scrapped, made another and decided to move to another country, one she'd never been to in her life. The girl who hopped aboard a ship and followed me across the ocean without a second thought. The girl who was jumping up and down with excitement when she saw a field camera in a shop window."

She shook her head, clamping her hands over her ears. "I don't want to hear this," she cried with a sob, fear clawing at her.

"I think that girl has a sense of adventure," he went on relentlessly. "I think that girl would love the life I'm offering her, if she could just stop clinging to some dream of how things should be, a dream she got from her friends."

Marjorie sucked in her breath. "That's not true."

"I think it is."

She didn't answer, for what was there to say? Instead, she stared at him, and he stared back, their mutual anger and differing views like a chasm between them, one that widened with each silent second that passed, tearing her heart apart.

"Go," she cried at last, unable to bear it any longer. "Go to Gibraltar. Just don't expect me to be waiting until you decide to come back."

"I am going," he said, holding her gaze. "But I'll be back in a month, and we will have this conversation again. And again, and again, because I am not giving up. I am going to keep hoping that the unpredictable girl I fell in love with is still as much in love with me now as she said she was last night. And that one day, if I keep trying, she'll love me enough to give her heart to me and trust me and come with me to the ends of the earth and back again to this house that we both love."

"Stop," she cried, "Just stop."

"That's my plan, and I'm sticking with it, because, contrary to certain assumptions made about me by the woman I love, I am a man who can stick. And by God, I'm going to prove that to her if it takes me the rest of our lives."

With that, he turned and walked away, and as she watched him go, Marjorie's heart broke at last, shattering into a thousand pieces.

Chapter 24

*T*he ladies were already gathered under a tent in the rose garden for her birthday luncheon when Marjorie and Clara arrived back at Ravenwood. With no time to change, both women hurriedly thrust their hats, jackets, and gloves into the arms of a footman, straightened their skirts, and turned toward a pair of mirrors hanging in the entrance hall to smooth their hair.

But when Marjorie looked at her reflection, her puffy face and tear-reddened eyes reminded her that her hair was the least of her problems, and she had the sudden, craven desire to plead a headache and run to her room.

Last night, she'd thought herself ready to experience everything life had to offer—the bitter and the sweet, the love and the pain. But now, the wild, fearless, seductive woman of last night was gone, and she was not only uncertain and afraid, she was also a heartbroken mess.

I think that girl has a sense of adventure.

Adventure? Whoever said she wanted adventure? She wanted a home.

We'll travel, yes, but we'll always come home.

At once, a picture of Ainsley Park came into her mind—not the classical façade or the interiors, but the beautiful terrace, and its view of the port and the ocean and the horizon that stretched endlessly beyond.

I do wish you'd get this idea that we'll be homeless vagrants out of your head, because that's not how it would be at all.

Marjorie was by no means certain of that. And he'd never addressed her concern about children either. She set her jaw, brushed a few wayward, sea-frizzed curls off her forehead, and reminded herself that her father had been right about one thing. A life roaming the globe was no life for children.

I think we can afford a nanny to come with us, don't you?

"Marjorie?"

Clara's voice broke in to her thoughts, and she stiffened, shoring up her resolve, then she donned a smile and turned her head, but when she looked into the eyes of the woman beside her, she knew Clara wasn't fooled.

But then, how could she be, after she'd found Marjorie sobbing on that beautiful terrace in the wake of Jonathan's departure? To her credit, she'd asked no questions, and their carriage ride back had been blessedly silent, but Clara's sympathy and compassion were obvious in her eyes.

"You go ahead," Marjorie said, keeping her artificial smile in place. "I'll be along in a minute."

Clara hesitated, then gave a nod and departed, and Marjorie returned her attention to the mirror. She worked a bit longer to smooth her hair, but at last, she gave it up, and turned away.

She walked through the house, out to the terrace and down to the rose garden, and with each step, she told herself it didn't matter where he went or what he did and that she didn't care anyway—all the same lies used by a little girl who'd been left behind.

As the rose garden came into sight, as she saw the table set with white linen, silver, and Spode and the footmen darting around with plates of dressed salmon and chilled asparagus, she was reminded that this was her life now, the life she'd wanted and chosen. A life of luncheons and balls and working for charity, of doing the season and marrying a peer and running a country estate.

I think that girl would love the life I'm offering her, if she could just

*stop clinging to some dream of how things should be, a dream she got
from her friends.*

Marjorie held her head high and walked a little faster.

By the time she reached the open tent where the ladies were
seated, she had gathered her pride and anger around her like a
defensive wall. And though her friends must have seen the pain in
her still-puffy face, no one asked her any questions.

"Sorry I'm late," she murmured.

"You mustn't apologize," Irene said smoothly. "Not on your birthday.
Clara already told us about the horse going lame."

Marjorie shot Clara a grateful glance as she slipped into her seat.

"At least it's a lovely day," Dulci said brightly. "Nothing is more
beautiful than an English summer day."

Marjorie felt a sudden, inexplicable irritation. Did the weather
always have to be the topic seized upon in an awkward moment?

"Miss Thornton," Hetty said, turning to Jenna, "I understand your
wedding is in three weeks. Have you learned yet where Colonel
Westcott will be posted afterward?"

The other woman heaved a sigh. "Bombay," she said with gloom,
earning a groan of commiseration from several women at the table.
"We are leaving the day after the wedding."

"Bombay?" Dulci cried. "Oh, no! It'll be so hot there. What about
your complexion?"

"I expect your maid can help you deal with anything of that sort,"
Irene put in, but Jenna only sighed.

"My maid is refusing to come. She's given notice. With everything
else to be done before the wedding, how am I to find a decent lady's
maid?" Jenna added, eliciting more murmurs of sympathy. "One who
is willing to go halfway around the world to some foreign country?"

Despite her own current difficulties, Marjorie couldn't help thinking
her friend's words a bit incongruous, since—being American—Jenna
was already living in a foreign country. She said nothing, however,
but continued to stare at her untouched luncheon plate.

"The Colonel says I can find a maid there," Jenna went on gloomily,
"but men never understand these things."

"No maid in Bombay will have any knowledge of current fashion," Dulci said gloomily. "How will you ever manage?"

"I was so hoping we'd be staying here," Jenna said, words that struck a depressingly familiar chord with Marjorie. "I want to live in London. I have no interest in Bombay. It's so far away. I can't imagine anything of interest ever happens there."

There is a huge, beautiful world out there, and you've never seen any of it. Don't you want to?

Marjorie stirred in her seat as Jonathan's words echoed through her mind.

"Speaking of happenings," Carlotta said, "did anyone hear about Lady Mary Pomeroy? She's engaged at last." She leaned forward, clearly willing to impart juicy details to the other ladies. "To a curate."

"No!" Dulci cried as if dismayed, but Marjorie didn't miss how she leaned closer to Carlotta, equally eager to engage in gossip at another woman's expense. "A curate, really?"

"Is it so surprising?" Jenna said, her own troubles seemingly forgotten in light of this bit of news. "I mean, after the scandal, a curate was probably the best she could do."

Shades of Lady Stansbury, Marjorie thought, remembering the talk about Lady Mary Pomeroy in the countess's sewing circle, and as she glanced at her friends, she was suddenly struck by how different Dulci and Jenna seemed now from the schoolfriends who had dreamed with her of romance and adventure and living across the sea. Perhaps her memory was at fault.

Or perhaps there was another explanation.

If you want to move in society, you must play by society's rules. It's that simple.

She glanced from her friends to Carlotta and back again, appreciating just how well Dulci and Jenna had learned those rules. Too well, perhaps. How long before she was the same?

"Well, a girl has to marry someone," Dulci said. "Better a curate than no one, I suppose."

"I don't see what's wrong with a curate," Marjorie put in, goaded into speaking up.

"No need to get touchy, Marjorie," Jenna said with a sniff. "You've been dreaming about marrying a man with a title just as much as any of us ever did."

"I was an idiot," Marjorie blurted out without thinking, a remark that earned her a frown from Dulci.

"I married a man with a title," she said acidly. "Am I an idiot?"

"That's not what I meant," Marjorie mumbled, rubbing four fingers over her forehead, feeling suddenly weary of it all. "I'm sorry if I offended you. Let's not quarrel."

"Perhaps it's time," Irene murmured tactfully, "that Marjorie opened her presents."

This suggestion was greeted with everyone's approval and relief. Boothby was tasked with bringing the presents, and as she opened them, Marjorie was obligated to put her artificial smile back on.

From Irene, she received a silver inkstand, and from Clara, a set of fountain pens inlaid with mother-of-pearl. Baroness Vasiliev had already departed for London, but she'd left behind a present that reflected her own flamboyant character—an enormous ostrich-feather quill that was clearly decorative rather than functional.

As Marjorie set these gifts aside, she wondered what letters she would write to the other teachers back in White Plains. They were eager, no doubt, to hear all about her wonderful new life and how happy she was.

Her smile faltered at that thought, and she had to clench her jaw to keep it in place as she reached for Dulci's gift and opened it.

"Handkerchiefs," she said. "How lovely."

"They're made by a firm in Paris," Dulci offered. "Very fashionable. Happy birthday."

She wasn't quite certain why handkerchiefs had to be fashionable, but she didn't inquire. "Thank you, Dulci."

She moved on, opening more gifts—books of verse, sketches, pressed flowers, all perfectly suited to a young, unmarried woman of society. Even Lady Stansbury had sent her a present, a face towel embroidered with roses.

"What pretty needlework," Jenna said, leaning closer. "Mine isn't nearly as good, as hard as I try."

Marjorie turned, puzzled. "When did you take up needlework? When we were at Forsyte, you hated sewing. Your passion was fencing."

Jenna smiled, but it was an awkward smile, with a curious hint of apology in it. "Fencing isn't really something many British ladies do, so I gave it up."

That sort of conformity did not sound at all like Jenna. Granted, Marjorie hadn't been able to spend much time with her friend, but the Jenna she remembered from schooldays had been athletic and adventurous and up for anything. That Jenna had never cared what other people thought.

That girl has a sense of adventure. That girl would love the life I'm offering her.

With an effort, Marjorie shoved the memory of Jonathan's words aside. "When did you start caring so much about what other people think?" she asked Jenna.

Her friend bit her lip, looking uncomfortable. "The colonel's mother doesn't approve of fencing."

Marjorie gave an unamused laugh. "She sounds a lot like Lady Stansbury."

Jenna drew herself up. "Lady Stansbury and the colonel's mother happen to be very good friends," she said with dignity.

Marjorie was tempted to ask if Jenna would be able to find a nice boiled pudding in Bombay. She refrained, but as she studied her friend's abashed face, she couldn't help wondering if, in a year or two, she'd be taking up needlework and giving up things that she enjoyed to suit the sensibilities of others. Given the things she'd said to Jonathan this morning, it seemed depressingly possible, and she was relieved when Boothby diverted her with another package.

"Goodness," she said as the butler placed a box about eighteen inches square in front of her. "Another one?"

"This is the last one, Miss McGann," the butler murmured. "From Mr. Deverill."

A chorus of teasing oohs and aahs rose around her, much to her irritation, and her friends at once began speculating about what the box contained.

"Maybe it's more jewels," Dulci said. "Didn't you say he'd taken some of your father's gems to Fossin and Morel? Maybe he had some of them set for you?"

Marjorie hoped not. One necklace had already gotten her into enough trouble.

"Goodness," Hetty said in her well-bred drawl, peering across the table. "Given the size of that box, if it is jewels, the man's certainly generous."

"But in that case," Jenna put in, sounding doubtful, "wouldn't Marjorie have to give them back? Jewels aren't appropriate. He's Marjorie's guardian, not her husband."

"He is the former, but maybe he wants to be the latter," Dulci said, making most of the ladies laugh.

Marjorie bit her lip, staring at the package, in no mood to laugh with them.

"I think," Irene said, her voice so gentle Marjorie wanted to burst into a fresh fit of weeping, "we should stop any pointless speculation and let Marjorie open it."

Aware that everyone's eyes were on her, Marjorie reached for the scissors, cut the string, and pulled away the paper, revealing a plain, unimpressive wooden crate.

"Heavens, what is it?" someone asked with a tittering laugh as Marjorie lifted the lid. "Eggs from the farm?"

But it wasn't eggs. And it wasn't jewels. It wasn't even a predictable and appropriate gift, like books or pens. No, it was something else entirely, something that obliterated Marjorie's shored-up resolutions, crumbled her defenses of pride, anger, and hurt, and turned to dust and ashes all the illusions she'd been carrying about how her life was going to be.

Inside the box was a field camera.

"ARE YOU CERTAIN you want to do this?"

Jonathan looked up from the plans spread across the desk, giving the Marquess of Kayne a surprised glance. "I thought we'd agreed. The engineers must add more lifeboats to the design."

"That's not what I mean. Just after you decide to cancel your departure for South Africa, I'm the one responsible for sending you off again. The duchess can't be pleased with me."

The duchess wasn't the only one. Jonathan looked down again, pain squeezing his chest as he thought of how he'd left Marjorie on the terrace at Ainsley Park a few hours ago. "The duchess isn't the problem," he muttered as he pretended to resume his study of the ship's design plans Kayne had presented for his perusal. "Believe me."

"Still, I was supposed to go, and though I'm grateful you're taking my place, I feel I've dumped an enormous task on you with no warning. I was surprised you agreed."

"Were you?" Jonathan stared down at the plans, an ironic smile curving his lips. Yesterday, when he and Kayne had discussed this venture, he'd known almost at once that it was what he'd been searching for, not only because it suited him and excited him, but also because he'd seen how it could bridge the gap between what he wanted and what Marjorie wanted. And after last night, when she had come to his room, when she'd given herself to him and admitted she loved him, he'd been sure she would at least be willing to listen to his plans. But now, thinking of her appalled face and the hurt in her eyes, he realized he'd been a bit too optimistic there. Still, he was only in the first stage of what he'd known would be a long campaign.

"One of us has to go," he said as he straightened and began rolling up the plans. "And it ought to be me, since arranging the moorings is now my responsibility." He held up the plans. "I may take these to show the men in Gibraltar, I assume?"

When Kayne nodded, he secured the roll of plans with an elastic band and bent to retrieve his dispatch case from the floor. "Then, since my ship sails in less than an hour, I'd best be on my way. If I delay much longer, my valet will begin to wonder if he's bound for Gibraltar without me."

"I'll walk down with you."

The two men departed the marquess's dockside offices together. Ten minutes later, they had said their farewells, and a ferry was carrying Jonathan across the port from Hythe to the opposite marina where a Cunard ship waited to take him to Gibraltar.

As he passed through the crowd of people who were gathered on the dock to say good-bye to their loved ones, he searched for Marjorie's face, though he knew it was futile. After this morning, he doubted she was in any frame of mind to come to the wharf and say good-bye. And even if she did, what would be the result? Leaving her at Ainsley Park had been one of the hardest things he'd ever done. If he saw her now, would he be able to tear himself away a second time?

On the other hand, could he toss all his newly made plans aside and give up what he knew he wanted to do, and try to settle down to the insular, self-contained world of a British country gentleman?

Even as he asked himself that question, he knew it wasn't possible, not for him. Even if that was what Marjorie wanted, even as much as he loved her, he could not do it. He needed a wider world than one tiny corner of England.

No, he decided as he paused at the gangplank for one last look around, if he saw her now standing here on the dock, the thing he'd be most inclined to do was heave her over one shoulder, scandalizing anyone who might be watching, and haul her aboard. He almost smiled at the notion, appreciating just how far he'd come from the overprotective guardian who'd thought he could make her stay in her room for propriety's sake.

It made him laugh at himself now to think of that, for he knew Marjorie would never be controlled by his expectations, or anyone else's. He knew she had an adventurous streak; it had been his greatest frustration two months ago. He could only hope that with time, it would prove to be his ally. If not—

The ship's horn blew, a welcome distraction from the gloomy direction his thoughts had almost taken, but also a warning that he could not delay any longer. He turned and crossed the gangplank, where Warrick was waiting for him.

"I've seen to the luggage, sir," the valet said, handing him his passkey. "Your stateroom is A-18. Shall I show you?"

Jonathan hesitated, glancing again over his shoulder. "No," he said, holding out the plans and his dispatch case. "Here, take these, and order me some tea. I'll be along."

"Very good, sir." Warrick departed, and Jonathan moved to stand with the other passengers at the rail as the ship pulled away and started out to sea. He kept his gaze fixed on the dock until the ship made the turn at Calshot and merged into the Solent, then he turned away and went to his stateroom, but to his surprise, he found it empty. Warrick had placed his dispatch case on the floor beside the writing desk and unrolled the plans on the desk's surface, but the valet himself wasn't anywhere in sight.

"Warrick?" he called, but there was no answer. Jonathan tossed his hat and passkey on the table by the door, then crossed to the bedroom, but it was empty as well, and he could only conclude that his valet had gone on some necessary errand.

Deciding the best way to take his mind off Marjorie was by doing some work, Jonathan proceeded to get comfortable for the task, removing his jacket, necktie, and collar. He was just starting on his cuff links when the outer door to his suite opened.

"Warrick?" he called.

"Yes, sir," the valet called back. "I've brought your tea."

Jonathan frowned, a bit puzzled. "Why didn't you have a waiter do it?" he asked as he tossed his cuff links and tiepin onto the dressing table and began rolling back his shirt cuffs.

There was a pause. "It would have taken too long," the valet said at last. Another pause, and then, Warrick resumed, "They didn't put any milk on the tray. I'll fetch it."

"I don't need milk," he called back, but the door closed before he'd finished speaking. With a shrug, he finished rolling back his shirt cuffs, then walked into the bath and splashed a bit of cold water on his face. Grabbing a towel, he dried off as he returned to the sitting room, but he'd barely stepped through the doorway before he came to an abrupt, astonished halt.

Standing by the tea tray, disheveled, hat askew, breathtakingly lovely, was Marjorie.

"What the devil?" he muttered, staring, too stunned to move.

She laughed. "Well, at least you're dressed this time. Mostly, anyway."

He was moving before she'd even finished speaking, tossing aside the towel and taking the few quick steps to bridge the distance between them. "My God," he muttered, sliding his hands up and down her arms to be sure she was real. "My God. What are you doing here?"

She bit her lip, giving him a look of pity. "Don't you know by now how much I hate being left behind?"

He began to laugh, joy welling up inside his chest. Incredulous, still stunned, he hauled her into his arms. "Marjorie, my darling. My mad, wild, crazy ginger."

He kissed her with each word, her mouth, her nose, her cheeks, her hair, and then her mouth again. "How did you get here? Do you have luggage? Are you real?"

"Very real," she assured him and proved it by wrapping her arms around his neck and kissing him. "As for how I got here, you'll be happy to know my chaperones brought me."

"Poor chaperones, indeed," he replied, slipping his arms around her waist, "if they let you do something like this."

"Well, I did promise them that we would get married. In fact, Clara said if we're off to Gibraltar together, you'd better marry me, or she'd come find you and shoot you."

Given that Clara had been making that threat ever since he'd been old enough to annoy her, he might have been amused, but Marjorie's mention of marriage shredded any notions of humor, and he drew back a little, looking into her eyes. "You want to marry me? You're sure?"

"Yes, Jonathan. I've never been more sure of anything in my life."

She sounded sure, but he wasn't ready to dance a jig about it. "You weren't last night. As I recall, you never did give me an answer. And this morning, when I told you my plans, you were dead set against ever marrying me."

"I wouldn't quite say that. I admit," she went on as he raised a skeptical eyebrow, "I wasn't sure last night, but before the night was over, you managed to change my mind."

"And change it back. Or have you forgotten our quarrel this morning?"

"No, but your news was like a lightning bolt. One minute, you were showing me that lovely house you'd bought for us, and the next minute, you were telling me you were leaving. I felt as if everything I'd ever wanted had just been dangled in front of me and then snatched away. It all happened so fast, and I had no time to think."

"Believe me, manipulating you or rushing you were not at all what I'd intended. Quite the opposite, in fact. Before you came to my room last night, I was readying myself for a long courtship. I thought you might need months or even a year or two to make up your mind about me. I thought you'd want to do the season, meet other men before you decide, and if that was going to be the case, I knew I'd have to have an occupation, or I'd go mad. When I met with Kayne, and we discussed making the deal, I knew at once it was the right thing for me, but I knew to persuade you would take time. When Kayne suggested I be the one to go to Gibraltar, I agreed, thinking it a good move on my part."

"A good move to leave me? I like that!"

He smiled a little. "Call it a strategic withdrawal. I thought it would give you the opportunity to consider my plan. And I hoped," he added, pulling her closer, "it might make you miss me a little. Realize you couldn't live without me."

"Oh, how conceited men are!" she cried.

"I was far too unsure of your feelings to be conceited. When you came to my room last night, I should have booted you out straightaway, because in the back of my mind, I knew it wasn't fair play otherwise, but I just couldn't do it. I'm weak as water where you're concerned. What can I say? And then, later, when I had all your clothes off and you still wouldn't agree to marry me . . . well, by then, I knew you loved me, so there was no way I was letting you go."

"I didn't want to let you go either, obviously," she whispered, blushing a little, her arms tightening around his neck as she rose on her toes and kissed him.

"I'm glad, but this morning, it made telling you my plans so much harder. When I showed you the house, I knew I had to tell you what I'd agreed to take on, but it kept getting more difficult to say, and finally, I just blurted it out. And then, well, everything rather went to hell."

He bent his head and kissed her. "This morning, I accused you of being afraid, but the truth is, I was afraid, too, Marjorie. I was afraid I'd ruined everything. I thought about not going, about backing out of the deal, but Kayne and I had already made an agreement, and if I failed to honor that, how could I ever expect you to count on me?"

She nodded. "I see that now, but this morning, I was just so shocked. But after I had time to think it over, I realized you were right, that I was clinging to old fears and other people's ideas. And I didn't want to do that anymore, not after what the baroness had said to me."

He groaned. "That woman."

"Well, you should thank her because what she said was what sent me to your room last night, and what made me realize I was in love with you, and what changed my mind this afternoon. She said life isn't perfect, and things don't always go according to plan—"

"Tell me about it," he murmured, earning himself a punch in the arm. "Ouch."

"She also said that life would be very dull if we never took any risks. And today, after I got over the initial shock of your news, I remembered her words, and I realized that if I refused you out of fear and the need to feel safe, I'd regret it forever. After all, my dull, risk-free life was the reason I jumped on a ship and followed you in the first place."

"And despite all my efforts to see you properly looked after, here you are again."

"Well, yes. You see . . ." She paused, smiling. "I got this smashing field camera as a birthday present. And I decided," she added as he laughed, "the best way to put it to good use was by coming with you. Which reminds me . . . you've told me your career plans, but you haven't heard mine."

He blinked, taken aback. "You want a career?"

She nodded. "I've decided I want more for my life than balls and parties and being one of the idle rich. Are you surprised?"

"Since I met you, darling, surprise is my perpetual state. So, what is this career you're embarking on? I hope it's something you can do while you come along with me?"

"As a matter of fact, it is. I'm going to work for Deverill Publishing as a photographer and writer. I'm going to take pictures of our travels and write essays about them, and Clara's going to publish them."

"What a smashing idea." He planted a kiss on her nose. "I love it."

"I'm glad." Her smile faded, her expression becoming serious. "Because I love you, Jonathan, and wherever you are is where I want to be, too." The words were scarcely out of her mouth before she was laughing. "You look almost as stunned now as when you first walked out and saw me here."

"I'm not just stunned, Marjorie. I'm awed." He cupped her face and kissed her mouth. "An hour ago, I was wondering if I'd ruined everything, and now, here you are, making all my dreams come true." He slid his hands down to take hers. "I love you with all my heart and soul, and I promise on my life that I will never abandon you or leave you behind. And no matter how much we travel, we will always have a home, for ourselves and for our children."

"At Ainsley Park?"

"If that's the home you want."

"It is. I loved that house the moment I saw it, and I'm very much looking forward to making a home for us there. But first . . ." She paused to slide her arms back up around his neck. "I want a honeymoon. A long honeymoon, so I hope Lord Kayne doesn't mind if you lengthen your trip a little?"

"I'm sure he'll be delighted as long as I also secure some additional moorings. But as to getting married, darling, we're in a bit of a pickle. I don't think ship captains can legally marry people."

"They can't," she answered at once. "Irene told me so. But she also said that we can get married at Gibraltar, and if we do that, the scandal of our elopement will die down after a while."

"It seems my efforts to be a responsible guardian have gone completely awry." He paused, giving a sigh. "To mitigate the scandal, I don't suppose I could persuade you to remain in your room during this voyage?"

"Not a chance," she said and kissed him.